Moot

Rob McInroy

RINGWOOD

Ringwood Publishing
Glasgow

First published in Great Britain in 2024 by
Ringwood Publishing

0/1 314 Meadowside Quay Walk, Glasgow G11 6AY

www.ringwoodpublishing.com
mail@ringwoodpublishing.com

ISBN 978-1-917011-00-6

British Library Cataloguing-in Publication Data
A catalogue record for this book is available from the
British Library

Printed and bound in the UK
by Lonsdale Direct Solutions

For Margaret McInroy, my number one fan
Sorry you didn't get to read this one, mum

And for Jackie Pitcher
For everything, forever

Publisher's Notes

The terms "tink" and "tinker" are now considered pejorative and the word "Traveller" is preferred. This is the term used in the novel, except in dialogue, which reflects the usage of the time.

Monzie, the site of the Rover Scout Moot, is pronounced Mon-ee, stress on the second syllable.

Praise for Rob McInroy

Moot

'We need truth to survive. Truth is important. We depend on it and we trust the systems of governance to truthfully protect our lives. But do they? Or do we? For every truth there is a falsity.

'For every revelation there is a reckoning. In Moot, truth is woven beautifully yet uncomfortably with falsity but you'll have to trust me when I say read the book, unpick the lies, learn the truth, find the reckoning.'
Jim C. Mackintosh, Poet and Makar, Federation of Scottish Writers 2021

'As evocative as it is thrilling. Bob Kelty is a hero fit for the time period.'
Nick Quantrill, novelist

Barossa Street

'Set in the 1930s, Barossa Street is a powerful and resonant novel that explores the prejudices and injustices of the time and their impact on policing. Dark, thrilling and sinister, it will keep you guessing until you reach the last page.'
CL Taylor, novelist

'Rarely has a book transported me so completely to a place in the past than Barossa Street. Part murder mystery, part gritty crime, part immersive historical fiction – 100% excellent.'
Dan Malakin, novelist

'Enjoyed this mystery immensely. It kept me guessing right until the end. Meticulously researched, it paints a vivid image of life in the 1930s. Most of all it highlights the unfairness and prejudice in society and the justice system which is as true today as it was then.'
Rhonda Ferguson, reader

'Rob seems to so skilfully intertwine the response of the British public towards the shortcomings of the government in the 1930's. Like always, Rob seems to brilliantly bring historical events and figures into the fictional narrative, which leaves you frantically researching it all after!'
Rosie Watts, reader

Cuddies Strip

'It is very much a contemporary novel. It deals with misogyny, it deals with institutional corruption, it deals with the problem of policing. I highly recommend it.'
Val McDermid, novelist

'I read this wonderful novel with a tear in my eye. I could hardly bear to read the ending but it was beautiful.'
Cathi Unsworth, novelist

'This is a gripping story, made all the more moving because real people were involved. Totally immersive and absolutely recommended. A brilliant well written book.'
Daisy Hollands, novelist

'What a sensational book. After a few pages I became completely immersed until I reached the haunting ending.'
WA Burt, reader

Thursday 13th July

A Day of Death

Miško Čurović walked beside the blond-headed man in silence. He looked behind, at the campsite and the neat rows of white tents dotting the hillside. The men crested a gentle slope and the path they were following, bounded on either side by wet sedge, led into light woodland. A field lay to their right, beyond a teetering stone wall. Miško's breathing was shallow. His heart was pounding.

'I'm sure you did not expect to see me again,' the blond-haired man said. His accent was European, his tone friendly.

'No.'

'It make things difficult for you, I think?'

'Not really.'

There were starlings in the canopy, flitting energetically, the rush of their wingbeats overlaid on the rustling of the trees, sudden and thrilling. Grass shivered. A recent shower brought smells of the soil to the surface. The air was heavy. There would be rain.

Miško Čurović fell behind and picked a heavy stone from the side of the path. It fitted neatly into his palm. He walked on, listening to the sounds of existence, watching the blond-haired man's final movements.

He swung his right arm wide and shallow and caught the man on the side of the head with the stone. The crack of crushed bone alarmed the birds aloft and they swooped away

1

from a predator who cared nothing for them. Miško Čurović cared nothing about anybody or anything, other than Miško Čurović and the instructions he had been given.

The blond-haired man fell to the ground and did not move.

Miško left him where he lay. He placed the stone, blood side down, by the edge of the path and turned and walked back towards the campsite. On the way, he lit a cigarette.

As he turned into a bend, approaching him was a man with a horse pulling a creaking and aged wooden cart. Miško greeted the man with a wave.

*

After waiting for a few minutes to be sure the path was clear, István Kedály emerged from behind a monkey puzzle tree and stooped to inspect the dead man. He shook his head in irritation and looked around the lightly wooded slope, deliberating on what to do next. When he saw Miško Čurović returning, he retreated into cover once more.

'That man is a fool,' he said. 'He'll ruin everything.'

Friday 14th July

A Day of Encounters

Mist curled in the wind above the trees. The sky was grey and sodden. For three days, rain had fallen on the volunteers erecting tents in the Maitland and Makgill camps, on high ground beneath the tree line of the northern slopes of the Knock Hill. On lower ground, surrounding a natural amphitheatre in the middle of the Monzie estate, final preparations were being made at the headquarters of the third international Rover Scout Moot, a quadrennial gathering of mostly eighteen to twenty-four-year-old Rover Scouts. Both Maitland and Makgill camps were capable of housing two thousand young men. Each camp was subdivided into smaller groupings of five hundred and then into units of fifty. Down in the main concourse, a neat circle of variously sized white canvas tents, flags billowing beside them in the wind, housed the information centre, the bank, cafés, first-aid point, post office and a barber's shop, the full panoply of services required over the next ten days for three-and-a-half thousand Rover Scouts from across the world. Rudimentary wooden markers on the pathways between the tents described what service each one offered. At the entrance to the catering tent, resting his foot on a wheelbarrow and smoking a pipe, Bob Kelty was preparing himself for what he hoped would be the busiest week of his life. Next to him was his wife, Annie. They studied the campsites above them.

'The place is hoachin already,' said Bob.

The Moot wasn't due to open until the next afternoon, but already there were some six hundred Rovers on site, arrived from Britain, Scandinavia and mainland Europe and from as far away as Egypt, Rhodesia and India. Although three-and-a-half thousand were expected, initial estimates had been for over six thousand, and a third campsite, Crichton, had been planned. In May 1939, however, the Military Training Act had been passed in Great Britain, compelling men of twenty and twenty-one to undertake six months' military training, the first civilian conscription during peacetime in British history. Unsurprisingly, many of those young men were Rovers who would otherwise have attended the Moot. By grim coincidence, the first day of the Militiamen's call-up was tomorrow, the opening day of the Moot. Meanwhile, Rovers from other countries – notably Japan and Italy, but also many from America – stayed away because of the international situation. In Germany, the Scouting movement had been banned, its place taken by the increasingly militaristic Hitler Youth.

Annie watched a group of lads erecting a tent on the hillside. 'The information office isnae even meant to be open yet,' she said, 'but it's been richt busy. I was only supposed to be doin my trainin this mornin. I ended up helping a Swedish laddie work out how much money he had.'

'How much *did* he hae?'

'Fifteen pounds, fourteen and six.'

'I hope you telt him to keep it oot of sicht.'

'I telt him to put half of it in the bank.'

They were approached by two men, a tall and angular African of about twenty in a colourful uniform and red fez, and a shorter, squatter white man wearing a circular, martial-looking cap and a beautiful, woven tie instead of the usual Rover neckerchief. A brown cloak fixed around his neck trailed almost to the ground, making him appear even

4

shorter than he was. The African, smiling broadly, held out his hand and Bob shook it.

'*Merhaba efendim*,' the man said. 'I am Abdalla Ben Salah.' He gestured around him at Monzie and the Knock. 'Beautiful,' he said. 'So green.'

'Aye, a wee bit wet, though.'

'Indeed,' said the squat man. 'Jozef Kawala. From Danzig.' He shook Bob's hand and smiled at Annie. 'My new friend and I were just going to hunt for some dry wood. Everything on the site – all wet.'

'It will be,' said Bob, 'it's barely stopped rainin since Tuesday.'

'We go this way, I think,' said Jozef.

'No. There's just open moorland there. Nothin sheltered. You'd be better goin that wey.' He pointed towards the gentle rise of the foot of the Knock. 'There's plenty trees there. Conifers. Anythin lyin beneath them'll most likely be dry.'

Jozef smiled and turned. 'We go this way, then.'

'Why don't you go wi them, Bob?' said Annie. 'Show them the wey.'

'Aye, why no?' he replied. 'And I hae just the thing to help.' He gestured to the wheelbarrow he was resting against.

'Let us go,' said Abdalla.

'Let's go,' said Bob.

He led them over the shallows of the Shaggie Burn towards the Knock. 'Where are you from?' he asked Abdalla.

'Alexandria. Egypt.'

'My, I was fair interested in Tutankhamun when I was a laddie. Never thocht I'd meet a real Egyptian.'

'I think you will meet people from all over the world this week. I have already made friends with boys from India. Finland. Norway. Such white hair, Norwegian men.'

'Aye, it's a regular League of Nations.'

'But more use, I hope,' said Jozef.

Bob laughed. 'You're no wrong there.'

5

Midway up the hillside, they arrived at a curious construction, a wooden canopy built over a natural dip in the ground, held in place by two struts at the front and festooned with towels and shirts. Scratched onto a plank of wood nailed to a pole secured in the ground were the words "Meikle's Nook." A youngish man, mid-twenties, lean and lanky with a shock of brown hair, wearing only boots and khaki shorts, appeared to be making running repairs. He was whistling tunelessly.

'Mr Meikle,' said Abdalla, stretching out his hand.

'Abdalla. How's your throat, son? Hoarse fae last night's singin?'

'I gargled with salt water. Good as new.' He turned to Bob. 'Mr Meikle and his friends, they erected most of the tents on the site. Dug latrines. Without them we would never be ready in time.'

The man introduced himself to Bob as James Meikle. He had a Glaswegian accent and spoke very fast. He was harder to understand, Bob thought, than either of his new foreign acquaintances.

'We're fae Pollokshields,' he said. 'We could see they were naewhere near getting aw the tents up so we lent a hand.'

'Good of you,' said Bob.

'Come up any time.' He pointed to a vest hanging from a rustic-looking flagpole. 'Whenever you see that flyin, that means we've scran on the go. Buckshee.'

'Steady,' said Bob lightly, 'I'm runnin ane of the cafés in the main ring. Dinnae go offerin free food, you'll put me oot of business.'

'Ach, I'm sure your scran's much better than ours. Worth payin for.' He knocked a wooden post into the ground with a large, flat-edged stone. 'Don't suppose you huv any butter goin spare?' he said.

'Aye, back at the café. I'll bring you some the morn.'

'Any meat would be handy an aw.'

'That's mair difficult.'

'Even rabbit wid do. Or pigeon. Just somethin to bulk oot the stew, but.'

'I'll see what I can do.'

They walked on and emerged onto a rough track that headed uphill through a wood of conifers. The air darkened and grew cooler as a canopy spread over them. Sweet cicely was growing somewhere nearby, its aniseed scent filling the air. The ground was damp but not wet. They gathered fallen branches every few yards and left them by the side of the path.

'We'll put them on the barrow on the wey back,' Bob said. 'Otherwise we'll be cartin them all the wey up the hill just to bring them back doon again.'

'Good thinking,' said Jozef.

'The English, you see,' Abdalla said. 'So organised.'

'Well,' said Bob, 'I'm Scottish, no English, but thank you onywey.'

'I hope I have not offended you, sir.'

Bob waved cheerily. 'Takes mair than bein called English to offend me.' He paused. 'No much, richt enough.'

'You live here?'

'Aye, I run a café in Crieff. Cloudland. Bottom of James Square.'

'I will come and visit you.'

'I've no doubt you will. You seem to get all ower the place.' He spotted a large, broken branch a few feet away, nestled against a stone dyke, and waded through damp grass towards it. Close up, he could tell it was from a monkey puzzle tree. Scattered around were large cones from the same tree. He looked up and saw the monkey puzzle stretching high above them and wondered how such an exotic specimen could have ended up in this remote spot. He punched the bark of the tree hard with his bare fist.

'Does that not hurt?' said Jozef.

'Naw. The bark's soft as shite. Try it.'

Jozef and Abdalla took turns punching the tree, laughing at the pliability of its surface, marvelling at the lack of grazing on their knuckles. They turned as they heard a noise behind them.

'What you beatin up my tree for?'

A man in a tweed suit and deerstalker stood on the path, shotgun cocked over his arm. Although still young, mid-twenties perhaps, his face was already creased and weathered from a lifestyle spent permanently outdoors. Deep-set eyes stared out at them.

Abdalla clapped his hands. 'Sandy!' he said.

'You dinnae ken him as well?' said Bob.

'I met Sandy yesterday night. He showed me hunting rabbits.'

'Snarin,' said Sandy.

'Snaring. Yes.'

'You havenae got any rabbits goin spare, have you?' said Bob. 'A guy at the camp's lookin for some.'

'Aye, I've half a dozen up the wey there. You can hae a couple.'

'Three?'

'On account.'

'You're a hard man, Sandy Disdain.'

'Rabbits dinnae grow on trees.'

'Just as well for you. Imagine how hard the snarin would be, hingin fae a tree.'

Sandy took out a Capstan and lit it and threw the match to the ground. 'So what are you hittin my tree for?'

'Your tree?'

'My faither telt me, years ago, that the day he found oot my mither was pregnant wi me he came oot here and planted that monkey puzzle tree in my honour. It's like my ain twin brother.'

8

'Is that so?'

'Well, if it is it must hae taken him aa day to get here. They worked on a fairm in Panbride at that time. Other side of Carnoustie.' He inhaled heavily. 'Took me years to figure that oot.'

'Aye well.' Disappointment sounded in Bob's voice. 'It's a grand story, onywey.'

'I suppose so. If you like stories.' Sandy crinkled up his nose. 'What's that smell?'

'What smell?'

He strode through the undergrowth towards them. 'Smells like someone's been burnin their tea.'

'I cannae smell nothin.'

'Yes,' said Jozef, 'I smell something.'

Sandy leaped onto the dyke bounding the neighbouring field and settled himself, then jumped down on the other side. The others followed as he tracked along the edge of the field, avoiding puddles and slipping occasionally in the mud. The trees alongside rustled in the wind. Rabbit runs criss-crossed the grassy field. In the far corner, twenty yards or so distant, there was a dilapidated canvas tent. As they neared, it became apparent that the tent had been partially burned, the roof disintegrated. The smell of burning grew stronger, more acrid, and it was obviously the smell of burned flesh. Bob felt a pulse in his throat start to pound. Sandy strode forward and looked inside the tent.

'Christ,' he said.

Lying in a foetal position, badly charred, was a man's body. Half of his face was burned beyond recognition. His clothing had burned away and most of his body was black and red, raw and glistening. Sandy leaned into the tent and touched the body.

'Stone cold,' he said. 'He's been deid for hours. Yesterday, I'd guess.' He stared at the body and studied the ruined skull. He turned it upwards. Beneath, unaffected by fire, the skin

9

was broken and the skull fractured. There was a stone on the flysheet of the tent, the size of a fist. Sandy took it out and inspected it in the daylight. There was blood on it, and fragments of skin and blond hair. The men looked at one another.

'That's what killed him,' said Bob.

'Aye, looks like.'

'We need to get the polis.'

Sandy stood up and wiped his hands on his trousers. 'Aye, you do. I'll just be on my wey first, though.'

'How?'

He shrugged. 'No really a good idea for me to be fund here.'

'You're allowed to snare on Hydro land, are you no?'

'Aye, but this isnae Hydro land. This is Monzie estate. And they're buggers for dealin wi poachers. Ay prosecute them. The boundary's up yonder.' He pointed uphill. 'Whaur my rabbits are. You still want some?'

Bob looked at the dead body in the tent. The thought of food was not appealing. 'Maybe later,' he said.

'I'll bring them roond.' And he marched back towards the dyke.

*

Bob and Annie waited for the police beside Sandy Disdain's monkey puzzle tree. They had telephoned from the information centre at Moot headquarters, but all agreed it was best for the Rovers not to be further involved. Annie insisted on accompanying Bob. He tried to argue, but arguments were not Bob Kelty's strength, certainly not with Annie, who got her own way more often than not now they were married. They looked uphill, expecting the police to arrive from the Crieff end, and were taken by surprise by the approach of two officers from Gilmerton.

'You the ones reported a body?' said the taller of the two

policemen, Sergeant Rudd. Constable McAnuff, nineteen and petrified, remained silent.

'Aye. Ower there,' said Bob.

'Could it have been left onywhere mair inhospitable?' The sergeant was breathing heavily, his face red beneath his helmet.

'Well, I suppose the top of the Knock micht have been a bit mair of a trauchle for you.'

'Or Ben Chonzie,' said Annie.

Rudd glowered at her. 'That would be ootside my jurisdiction, hen.' He turned to Bob. 'Show me. You twa …' He gestured at Annie and McAnuff. 'Stay here.'

Bob clambered over the dyke and Rudd followed. A moment later, Annie followed too. PC McAnuff stayed put. Rudd turned and glared at Annie.

'I said stay there.'

'Aye. I heard you.' She took Bob's hand and they walked on, negotiating once more the muddy ground at the edge of the field towards the burned-out tent and its dreadful contents.

'Did you …'

'No.'

'No what?'

'No, I didnae touch anything. You ay ask that, you folk.'

'You're Kelty, aren't you?'

'Aye.'

'Used to be a bobby.'

'Aye.'

'Couldnae hack it.'

'No. I guess I just found the polis … inhospitable.'

Rudd sniffed and turned to the tent. 'Tink's tent, I'd say.'

'Aye, looks like it.'

'So presumably the body is the tink.'

'Cannae tell. The face is badly burnt.'

'Burned to death. Hellish wey to go.'

11

'No necessarily. Look.' Bob bent over and twisted the head, as Sandy Disdain had done, revealing the ugly wound on the side. 'Hit his heid on that,' he said, pointing to the stone on the flysheet.

'I thocht you didnae touch onythin?'

'I didnae.'

Sergeant Rudd was trying to position himself between the body and Annie, protecting her from the sight. He sighed heavily as she stepped to one side and peered in. 'Probably fell,' he said, 'banged his heid on the stane, knocked himself oot and fell into the fire. It engulfed him while he was unconscious. I expect he was drunk as a skunk. Bein a tink an aa.'

'Why would he hae a muckle stane in his tent?' said Annie. 'And mair to the point, why would he be lightin a fire inside it?'

'To cook his tea?'

'This is a bow tent.'

'So?'

'A bow tent doesnae hae an openin for smoke to escape. You wouldnae light a fire in a bow tent. You'd suffocate in five minutes. Any tinker would ken that. He'd mak a teepee alangside wi a hole in the roof and cook in there.'

'You ken a lot aboot it. Touch of the tink in you, is there?'

'No, there isnae. No that it would matter if there was.' She studied the body. The man seemed young, his face, or what was left of it, fresh and light-skinned. The remains of his clothing, however, looked older than he was, threadbare and much repaired, the trousers half an inch too short. He had nothing on his feet.

'Whaur's his boots?' Annie said. She peered inside the tent but there were no boots to be seen. She searched outside and again could find no sign of a pair of boots. She turned to Sergeant Rudd. 'Why's he no got any boots?'

Rudd shrugged. 'Maybe a fox ran aff wi them.'

12

'In case it gets blisters on its paws, aye?'

'How do I ken?'

'Doesnae mak sense. Nane of this.'

'Seems like a straightforward accident to me,' Rudd said, 'but the doctor's on his wey. He'll be the judge.' He frowned at Annie. 'Him bein the expert.'

Annie looked at the body again. 'You dinnae think this looks suspicious?' she said.

'Look, hen, there's goin to be four thoosand laddies descendin on Crieff by the morn's morn. The place is goin to be hoachin for the next ten days. We're all on overtime as it is. Leave cancelled. So, from where I'm standin it doesnae look in the least suspicious that a tink's deid in his tent. If that's alright wi you.'

'No,' said Annie. 'It isnae.' She turned and walked back towards Constable McAnuff.

'You've got your hands full there, son,' Rudd said. Bob shrugged and followed behind Annie.

*

The campfire that evening was initially subdued. Sandy Disdain had made good his promise of three rabbits, causing consternation by leaving them at the information centre, and in falling light Bob, Annie, Jozef and Abdalla sat watching James Meikle turn the first of them on a wooden spit over the campfire at Meikle's Nook.

'Must have been a hellish thing to see,' James said.

'It was,' said Bob.

'You don't expect to come across deid bodies at our age. No in peace time anyway.'

Annie took Bob's hand as she felt him flinch. Bob Kelty was not a stranger to death. It was Bob, aged twelve, who discovered the dead body of his father, alongside the shotgun with which he had killed himself. When he was a policeman in Perth City Police, as young and frightened as Constable

McAnuff had been today, he was first on the scene of the murder of his friend and fellow footballer Danny Kerrigan, shot dead on the Cuddies Strip on the outskirts of the city. Months later, helping out another friend, he had discovered the brutally murdered body of Hugh Smithson in Barossa Street in Perth. The sad tale of that murder led to the later discovery of another, long-dead body. These deaths were remembered now by Bob and Annie. What Annie didn't recall, but Bob did, was the night he lay beside his Gran, holding her tightly, waiting for the final breath of her seventy-one years' existence to be purged from her lungs. That was the most recent death and the worst, leaving Bob all alone in the world until he had married the woman who would be his rock forevermore. He squeezed her hand.

Jozef lit a cigarette and blew a smoke ring. 'Your police think it was accident?'

'They seem to, aye.'

'It wasnae an accident,' said Annie. 'That wouldnae mak sense.'

'No, it look strange to me. Something not right. Will they not investigate then, if they think it was accident?'

'It's no up to the local polis," said Bob. 'Doesnae matter what they think. The doctor will hae a look. They'll do a post-mortem. The Procurator Fiscal will attend. He'll decide whether or no to investigate.'

He tried to sound positive but the dead man was troubling him, that and Annie's certainty of foul play. She was seldom wrong and Bob didn't know what to do. He would have liked to talk to Victor Conoboy about it, but his old boss had had a heart attack a month before and his doctors had advised him to avoid all stressful situations. Talking about murder could probably be classed as stressful.

'If they do decide to investigate,' said Annie, 'I wouldnae like to be aboot when Sergeant Rudd finds oot. He'll no be happy.'

'Aye, he seems to share the sunny disposition of maist of the police sergeants I used to work wi.'

'You were in the polis?' said James.

'No for long. No my cup of tea.'

'How no?'

'I like to look for the good in folk, no the bad.'

'That is a good philosophy,' said Abdalla.

'But hard to follow,' said Jozef. 'Especially in these times.'

'In these times it's even mair important,' said Bob. 'That's what all this is aboot, isn't it?' He gestured around at the camp. 'Your Moot. Friendship. Understandin.'

Jozef flicked his cigarette into the flames. 'We are only the young men of the world,' he said. 'We don't make the rules. We don't make decisions.'

'But do we have to accept the decisions that *are* made?'

'In Germany, yes. In Italy, yes. Probably in Danzig, sooner or later. We will have no option. Even here in England, perhaps.'

'Scotland.'

Jozef pulled out a cigarette and lit it. 'Where I come from, the *Wolne Miasto Gdańsk*, it is part of Poland but the people in it, they are ninety-nine per cent German. Hitler wants to take it back. He has already said he will.' He drew heavily on his cigarette and waved it at the group. Bob had the sense he was becoming agitated. 'But we will protect ourselves. We will fight. Stand up. Poland has mobilised one million men already. I will join, too. We will never give power away. I would rather die.'

'Well,' said Abdalla, 'perhaps *you* would rather die. But your leaders? The world is never quite what we think it is. In Egypt, we asked the British to leave two years ago. They went. At least, the soldiers did. The influence? It is still there, I think.'

'So your people must fight against it!' said Jozef. 'They

must rise up. Revolution of the proletariat!'

Abdalla smiled and leaned his head to one side. 'Communism will never succeed in my country. Perhaps you are right, though, that we should fight against things. But it is difficult for ordinary people like me to do that when our leaders, they are still dealing with the British, behind everyone's back.'

Jozef shook his head. 'You are right, my friend. The City Senate in Gdańsk, our leaders, they are mostly Nazis now. They try to open the back door for Hitler. Try to let him in. But we will fight them, too. Kill them if we need to. We will not be defeated.'

For all his pacifism, Bob admired the passion of the Polish lad. His homeland was in danger. Its identity. Its very existence. Hitler had occupied the Rhineland, the Sudetenland, annexed Austria, marched into Czechoslovakia, most recently occupied the seaport of Memel in Lithuania. The Polish corridor – and Danzig with it – would surely follow.

'Aye well,' James said. He took the first rabbit from the spit and jointed it and distributed it onto tin plates which he handed around. He skewered the second rabbit on a fresh rowan branch and placed it on the spit. 'Bob's right,' he continued. 'Whatever's goin on in the world, we cannae dae anythin about it. We're just the poor bloody squaddies. Or we will be. But right here, right now, everythin is about friendship and solidarity. Wan world.'

'One world!' the group shouted, and they settled down to eat their roasted rabbit. In all honesty, Bob thought it a bit teuch, and the grim expression on Annie's face suggested she was finding it hard to swallow, too. Nothing was said, though, and they settled back as night descended on the Ochils, spreading a light chill, the air crisp, much fresher now the rain had stopped. Tomorrow would be a grand day. The fire crackled before them. All around, the campsite was

16

fading into darkness. Smell of grass. Rustle of animals in undergrowth. Sway of trees. Singing from nearby tents, Scottish lads in full voice, *Wild Mountain Thyme*. Lights from Gilmerton lit up the sky behind them, but all else was consigned to the seclusion of night. In such anonymity, the campfire, the people around it and their new foundation of friendship, grew in importance. This would be a moment to savour, in years to come, long after the rancour of ordinary living had subsided and only memories remained.

'How about a wee tune, Bob?' said Annie. 'I brought your whistle.' She dug in her handbag and pulled out a tin whistle and handed it to him. Bob took it reluctantly. Music was his one overriding talent, the thing he knew he was not only good at, but better at than most people, but playing in public was always a trial to him. Even so, he could see the enthusiasm of his friends, their keen expressions captured in the capricious light of the campfire. The discovery that afternoon had been something terrible. Perhaps music would lighten the mood, cheer the group, bring them back to the hope and anticipation with which they had begun the day. He willed himself into his private space and raised the whistle to his lips and started to play.

He began with the *Jig of Slurs*, a tune he knew as well as any other, and he played it more slowly than usual, aware that his hands were shaking. By the time he had completed two rounds, though, he was calmer and his eyes were focused on a spot in front of the campfire and he felt himself in control. He shifted into *The Jolly Beggarman*, a jaunty 2/4 hornpipe and, on the second round he picked up speed ready for the transition into the final tune, *The Royal Belfast*. Even thinking about that made him nervous. He could get it right most times when he played at home, but the tune was fast and elaborate, rushing up and down the scales with abandon. He finished *The Jolly Beggarman* and took a deep breath and launched into *The Royal Belfast*. Every note was perfect.

17

He could hear his friends clapping in time, one, *two*, three, *four*, one, *two*, three, *four*, and he started the second round, playing even faster, and again every note was perfect, then he played it a third time and finished with a flourish, taking the final note up an octave and holding it. He put down the whistle and looked around.

Everybody cheered. Abdalla clapped him on the back. Jozef shook his hand. Annie leaned over and kissed him.

'Braw,' she said.

Bob smiled, accepted the congratulations of his new friends, tried to look forwards. Looking forwards was not something he found easy at the best of times. Now, there was a dead man out there. Someone who, if Annie was right, had possibly been murdered. Evil had descended, left its mark once more on Bob Kelty's existence. There would be a reckoning, there would be trouble, that much he knew. But this evening, here, now, Annie by his side, his new friends chatting happily, smells of roast rabbit in the air, everything was, indeed, braw.

Saturday 15th July

A Day of Equivocation

At 6:00, as Bob was preparing to leave for the Moot, the
door to Cloudland jangled open and Leslie Comer walked
in. She hung her old-fashioned rain cape on the coat rack
creaking by the door and removed her hat. She was a small
and neat woman in her mid-fifties, lips permanently pursed,
philtrum creased by years of cigarette smoking. A once tight
perm was loosening and in need of attention.

'Early start, this,' she said as she tied her pinny around
her waist. She pulled open the kitchen dresser and took out
a bag of flour. She gathered butter and milk from the fridge
and tubs of baking powder and cream of tartar from a shelf
behind.

'Aye,' said Bob. 'I'm just aff to the Rovers' camp.' He
kissed Annie's cheek, affixed bicycle clips to his trousers
and gave a wave as he threaded his way through the dozen
or so wooden tables dotted around the cafe, a long wooden
box in his hand.

'He's keen,' Leslie said.

'He's aff to play the bagpipes at the camp,' Annie
explained.

'This time of mornin?'

'To wake aabody up.'

'Aye, well, he'll do that, richt enough. Maybe no mak
him that popular, though.' She lit the gas oven and measured

19

a couple of teaspoons of cream of tartar into the milk.

Annie placed a mixing bowl on the counter beside her. 'Ach, naebody can stay angry wi Bob for lang.'

'No, very true.'

Leslie Comer had cause to appreciate Bob's unpredictable ways more than most. Two years before, when Bob was investigating a murder of which a friend of his had been accused, it seemed Leslie might be implicated but he had said nothing to the police and their own investigations had proved fruitless. Offering her a new start, Bob suggested she move to Crieff from Edinburgh and since then she had been working with Bob and Annie, helping out when Cloudland was busy. This week, with Bob and Annie both at the Moot, she was in sole charge. The prospect frightened her more than she would admit, and she began to knead the butter into the flour with enough aggression to ensure the scones would probably not rise as much as normal.

'Will you be alright on your ain all day?' Annie asked. 'Shut doon for a whiley in the efternoon if you're needin your denner.'

'Dinnae fash yoursel, lassie. I'll be richt as rain here. You go and get yoursel ready to get up to the camp. I'm sure there's laddies there will be in sair need of your help.'

Annie studied the knowing expression on Leslie Comer's face. As usual, she was unable to say whether or not the older woman was somehow teasing her.

Probably, she thought.

*

Half an hour later, Bob stood at the high point of the Makgill campsite and blew air into his bagpipes. When they had planned this over the campfire the previous evening, the success of his tin whistle performance still fresh in his mind, it had seemed like a grand idea, a traditional Scottish wake-up call for the international visitors camped at the Moot. But

20

now, alone and watching the sun rising over the Campsies to the east, he felt self-conscious and foolish. He started to play *Banish Misfortune* and the din from the pipes startled him. Somehow, the outdoor air seemed to amplify their sound, make it crisper, cleaner. He marched up and down as he played and was rewarded by the sight of puzzled or amused or angry heads appearing one by one from the tents beneath him.

Abdalla approached and sat cross-legged beside him, the hem of his shorts rising up his thighs. '*Hayırlı sabahlar,*' he said, bowing his head. A couple of minutes later, Jozef sloped uphill towards them in his knitted tie and expansive cape.

'*Cześć,*' he said to Abdalla, and then again to Bob. Bob nodded but carried on playing.

'Shut that bloody row!' The shout came from over on the far corner of the camp, down in a hollow, backed by a run of ash and elm trees. A rustic wooden sign hoisted between two poles embedded in the ground beside a large cluster of tents had the word "London" burned into it. This was the temporary home of over one hundred and fifty Londoners attending the Moot, one of the biggest groupings outside of the major Scottish cities. In only half a day they had become well-known voices throughout the camp.

Abdalla jumped to his feet and clapped his hands. 'Come!' he said, laughing. 'We march.' And he started downhill, walking stiffly in imitation of a military gait, arms waving at his side in time with Bob's music, the tassel of his fez bouncing from side to side. Bob fell in behind him and Jozef brought up the rear as Abdalla led them through neat lines of tents towards the London enclave, waving to acknowledge the ripples of applause that accompanied their march. From a tent near the Shaggie Burn, in an area marked "Dundee", another piper dived out of his tent, ran towards them, and took up position beside Bob.

21

Bob started to play *The Black Bear* and his new partner joined him. Another flurry from the Dundee enclave saw a drummer running towards them and he, too, fell in line. By the time they reached "London" the band of three was in full flow. Abdalla stopped beneath the London sign, flourishing his hand above his head, and turned and began to conduct the pipes and drum, waving his arms in approximate time with the music. The pipers, sensibly, ignored him and carried on with their tune.

'More!' he shouted. Bob struck up *Scotland the Brave* and his new partners joined him. From the Dundee camp half a dozen lads began to sing:

'Hark when the night is fallin
Hear! Hear the pipes are callin,
Loudly and proudly callin
Down thro the glen.
Land of my high endeavour,
Land of the shinin river,
Land of my heart for ever,
Scotland the brave.'

The London boys, led by a lad wearing, rather incongruously, a glengarry, and leaning on a broom, watched on feigning indifference. Finally, Bob and the band came to a halt.

'You needn't think you're doing that every morning, Jock,' the lad said in a strong London accent.

'Well,' said Bob, grinning, 'I hadnae, but now you've gien me the idea ...'

'Don't even think about it.'

'I'm sure we can rustle up a few mair pipers an aa.'

'That would mean war, Scotchman.' But Bob saw the smile playing at the corner of the London lad's mouth. 'Mickey Peterfield,' the lad said. 'Cable Street Irregular.'

'Nice to meet you, Mickey Peterfield. I have to say, you

English arenae as bad in the flesh as folk make out.'

Mickey feigned gratitude. 'But you Scots are every bit as ugly as they say,' he replied.

'I'll no argue wi you on that, but I'd like to think my lady wife micht, on my behalf.'

'Her and her guide dog.'

*

Miško Čurović walked up the wooded path he had climbed two days before. Without breaking stride or in any way acknowledging the fact, he passed the monkey puzzle tree and the spot where he had committed murder. He clutched a hand-drawn map showing the route through the woods towards Ferntower and into Crieff. Quicker than the main road, the soldier in the information tent had assured him. He needed to make town as quickly as possible, and to find his way around this strange country. He had much ground to cover in the next week.

There was a man to be found and dealt with, for one thing. Orders from on high. He looked at the address he'd been given on a scrap of paper. "The Old Ploughman's Cottage, Laggan, Crieff". How on earth was he going to find that?

He lit a cigarette and inhaled deeply. In a field to his right, a rabbit sat hunched close to a wall, sheltering in longish grass. It appeared to be trembling. Miško shaped his arms and hands as though holding a shotgun and made to fire.

'Bang,' he shouted and the rabbit took fright and louped through a gap in the wall. 'You're dead.'

Miško Čurović walked on. He was untouchable. That was the truth of it.

*

Mid-morning, and Bob was sweltering in the heat of the canvas tent. A lengthy queue of Rovers waited patiently for tea and bacon rolls. James Meikle was helping, a favour in

23

return for the three pounds of butter Bob had brought that morning. It was as well because, even two-handed, the queue was almost out of the tent.

'I thocht Rovers were meant to be self-sufficient?' Bob said. 'Live aff the land.'

'Wi bacon rolls on the go?' James replied.

'Aye, fair point.'

'Well, you took some findin.'

Bob looked up and saw a policeman standing behind the queue, flushed in his serge uniform and helmet. 'Geordie Macrae,' he said.

'Sergeant Macrae to you.'

'They've never made you a sergeant?'

'Aye, they have. Just think, if you'd stuck around you could've made inspector by now.'

Bob shuddered. 'I think the world's close enough to catastrophe as it is.'

Geordie laughed. 'You took some findin,' he repeated. 'I went to your café – nice place – but there was only some old biddy there.'

Bob felt a tremor of apprehension. The old biddy, of course, was Leslie Comer, still officially wanted by Perth City Police – and, though he didn't realise, by Geordie Macrae in particular – for the affair in Barossa Street. Bob trusted that Geordie's innate lack of inquisitiveness would come to his, and Leslie's, rescue.

'Seemed a nice lady,' Geordie continued. Bob let out a steady breath. 'Telt me you were up here. Man, this is a big site, though …'

'Three-and-a-half thoosand laddies.'

'I ken. I've met maist of them. You took some findin.'

'You said.'

Geordie hitched his head towards the exit. 'Can we go for a wee talk?'

Bob gestured to the queue of men patiently watching this

24

small scene unfold. 'I'm a bit busy, ken?'

'Bob, I *am* the polis.'

'Come off it, Geordie, I never did what the polis said when I was *in* the polis.'

'When d'you get a break?'

'When I run out of Rovers or bacon, whichever comes first. Go and hae a walk aboot. I'll come and get you when I'm done.'

'How will you find me?'

'The polisman in uniform?'

'Aye, right.'

It was a half after midday before Bob felt he could leave James alone. He strolled to the information centre in the middle of the site and hunted for Annie. The queue for her services was longer than Bob's bacon line and she looked puggled. Her boss, Brigadier Ross from the Black Watch, told her to take a break and they walked outside into the sunshine.

'My,' Annie said, 'I thocht cleanin for the Conoboys was hard work.'

'Are you enjoyin yoursel, though?'

'Grand. We've been getting the queerest enquiries.'

'Oh aye?'

'Laddie first thing, fae France, I think, came and asked "are you planning a trip to America?" "That's a wee bit far for a day trip," I says to him. And then we had an English lad came in, richt studious lookin, and he asked "what's the altitude of Monzie Castle?"'

'And did you ken?'

'What do you think? But the army lads that are helpin me did. They had a map and they kent how to read it and aathin and they telt the lad the answer. What he wanted it for I couldnae say.'

'You never ken when stuff micht come in useful.' He took her hand as they walked past the barber's and the chemist, both with queues outside. 'Geordie Macrae's lookin for us.'

'The bobby fae Perth?'

'The same. Sergeant Macrae now, would you believe?'

Annie snorted. 'They must be gey hard up. Geordie's a lovely lad ...'

'I ken. I had to stop mysel sayin the same thing.'

They found Geordie admiring a fifteen-foot Loch Ness Monster carved out of a fallen tree and painted in greens and red. He was having a surreptitious cigarette and he threw it into the bushes when he saw them approaching.

'I was just sayin to Annie,' Bob said, 'you've been made sergeant.' He pointed to the three chevrons on Geordie's sleeve.

'Aye,' said Annie, 'I'm fair impressed.'

'No only that,' said Geordie. 'Sergeant in the CID.'

'CID?' said Bob. 'But that's in the County force.'

'Aye. I transferred from the City Police to the County.' He pointed to the badge on his chest. 'I'm the highest ranking CID officer in Perthshire.'

Bob opened his mouth but could think of nothing to say. The idea of Geordie Macrae being in charge of criminal investigations was remarkable. Troubling, in fact. 'I think I'll tak to crime,' he said finally.

'Very funny.'

'So what brings you here?' said Annie.

'Your discovery. Yesterday. The body.'

'Are you goin to lead the investigation?'

Geordie shifted uneasily. 'No exactly.'

'No exactly?'

'I had a look at the tent last night.'

'You were here last night?' said Bob.

'Aye.'

'You should hae said.'

'I tried. I couldnae find you. You tak ...'

'Some findin. Aye, you mentioned. So what aboot the

investigation?'

'The word I got from on high, like, was we dinnae really want an investigation unless it's absolutely necessary.'

'What, like if someone's been murdered, you mean?'

'Aye.' Geordie stopped, searching for the right words.

'Somebody has been,' said Annie.

'We dinnae ken that.'

'No,' said Bob, speaking slowly. 'That's why you undertake an investigation. You bein a CID officer and all. Criminal investigation bein your job …'

'They wanted …'

'Who wanted?'

'On high.'

Bob rolled his eyes. 'On high wanted what?'

'Unless I was sure there'd been a murder, and unless I was sure …' He paused again. Bob and Annie waited, not understanding what was making him so reticent. 'And unless I was sure it wasnae a tink, then on high dinnae want an investigation.'

Annie looked at him incredulously. 'So even if it was murder, if it was a tinker you were told no to investigate?'

'More or less.'

'"More or less"? Who on high? The Chief Constable?'

'Higher, I think.'

'The Procurator Fiscal?' said Bob.

'Higher.'

Bob stared at him. 'The government?'

'The Chief Constable was on the phone for half an hoor yesterday afternoon. Hellish mood when he came aff. It was the Home Office called him.'

'That doesnae mak sense,' said Annie. 'Why would the Home Office care?'

'Because,' said Bob, 'the Moot's a big international event. It's even on the wireless the morn. It'll be in all the papers. They winnae want a murder on the very edge of the

27

campsite. International peace and friendship and aa that. They winnae want anyone thinkin a murder's onythin to do with the Moot.'

'So they'd cover it up?'

'No cover it up. Just no investigate it.'

Annie turned to Geordie. 'So what do you think? Was it a murder?'

'I couldnae say.'

'But you could hazard an opinion.'

'It could be.'

'And you think it micht be a tinker?'

'Looks like it, does it no? It is a tink's tent, efter all.'

Bob whistled. 'So you're no goin to do anythin aboot it. D'you mind the last time the polis couldnae be arsed investigatin a crime? Barossa Street?'

'Exactly. That's why I'm here.'

'How?'

'Barossa Street, you did your ain investigation.'

'We did, aye.'

'Dinnae do it again. Please.'

'How no?'

'Cause if it is murder, and you find who did it, how would that look for me?'

Bob pulled his pipe from his jacket and tamped tobacco into the well. 'If I find onythin you'll be the first to ken.'

'That's what you said last time.'

'I never found onythin.'

'You and I both ken that isnae true.'

Bob stopped. He thought again about Leslie back at Cloudland. He couldn't do anything to threaten her safety.

'Right, Geordie,' he said. 'I'll no do onythin that micht embarrass you. Deal?'

'Deal.'

Bob looked at Annie, shook his head imperceptibly.

*

28

'Good afternoon, Miss.'

The man addressing Annie wore a peaked hat adorned with plumes of prairie grass. It looked ridiculous. Annie presumed he must be from a southern African country, Rhodesia perhaps. She had encountered several Rhodesians already and found them very friendly, even if they were a touch difficult to understand.

'I am István Kedály from Hungary. Pleased to make your acquaintance.'

'Welcome to Scotland. How may I help you?'

He was a short man with a nervous air and a smile that seemed to be trying too hard. He could have been aged anywhere from his twenties to his fifties. His voice was high and rapid. 'I am looking for a laundry in the local town, please.'

'There's a laundry on site,' said Annie. 'Just down the main path towards the loch ...'

'I have seen that, yes. I look for a different one in town, please.' Annie studied his earnest face. There was something about it. Crouse, maybe. He smiled again. 'I fear the one in camp is not good enough. I have some heavy staining.'

'Well, there's the steam laundry in Ramsay Street.'

'And will that be open today?'

'Until five o'clock, I should think.' Annie gave him directions. 'Just after the Crown Inn on the High Street, turn left, downhill.'

'Thank you so much.' He gave a brief salute and another insincere smile and departed. Annie watched him go, thinking his bouncy walk was most peculiar.

'He's only been here half a day,' she said aloud. 'What can he hae got so dirty?'

*

'Sandy said he micht drop by wi a couple of rabbits,' Bob said to Annie as they walked hand-in-hand along the avenue

29

from Bob's tent towards the amphitheatre. It was a little after five and they had both finished for the day. They were exhausted, but exhilarated.

'Well, dinnae let him bring them to the information tent this time.'

'I dinnae think Sandy's a man you tell what to do.'

'A good woman, that's what he needs.'

'Aye, but pity the woman, though.'

Pedalling towards them on a black post office-issue bicycle, wobbling precariously, was Patrick Kemp, known to all as Pat the postie. A short, barrel-shaped man with a drinker's nose and rheumy eyes, he had a large bag draped across his shoulder and another on the pannier on the front of his bicycle. He was sweating profusely beneath his peaked cap. Beside him was a young woman, still teenage, pretty, eyes permanently lowered to the ground as though in search of jeopardy.

'Mair post, Pat?' Bob said.

'I've never kent onythin like it. Third drap the day. I'll be mair knackered than a salmon in spawn by the end of the week. The lassie's had to gie me a hand.' He jerked his head to the young woman. 'Mary, my bairn.' Mary flashed a momentary smile at Bob and Annie before impassivity overtook her features once more. Bob was about to ask Pat a question when Annie gave a yell. She pointed at Sandy Disdain, heading for the Information Office, wielding a dead rabbit in each hand, and called out his name. Without acknowledging the call, Sandy turned towards them.

'As promised,' he said, holding one of the rabbits up directly in front of Mary Kemp. They had been gutted but not skinned, the brightness still in their eyes suggesting they had been freshly killed. Mary Kemp shrank backwards. Sandy noticed. 'They winnae bite,' he said. He studied her small face, oval, frightened. 'Probably.'

'Dinnae,' said Pat the postie. 'Frightened of her ain

shadow, that ane. Ay waitin for the death that winnae harm her.'

Sandy studied the young woman again. He could see the fear in her eyes. *What hell it must be to live like that.* He turned to Bob. 'Since I've brought you some rabbit, any chance of gettin a bittie tea? I havenae eaten since yesterday denner-time.'

'Aye,' Bob replied. 'Come awa up to Meikle's Nook. James'll sort you.' They made their farewells to Mary Kemp and her grumbling father and headed uphill through the camp.

'Bob!' shouted Abdalla as he saw them approach. 'Annie, Sandy!' The quartet sat cross-legged by the campfire that James Meikle was in the process of lighting. Jozef joined them.

'Now,' Abdalla continued, 'How is the investigation of our sad discovery going?'

'No great. The polis spoke to me earlier. They dinnae want to touch it. Think it was an accident. And that the deid man was a tinker.'

'A tinker?'

'Travellin people. They dinnae live in a hoose, but travel from place to place lookin for work.'

'Nomads.'

'Aye, I suppose.'

'And this makes a difference?'

'Seems like.'

'That does not seem fair. I thought English sense of justice …'

'Scottish.'

'My apologies once more.'

Bob waved away Abdalla's embarrassment with a smile. Jozef had been listening to the conversation and he snatched an ear of overgrown grass and raked his thumbnail down it, stripping it into two.

'It is not good to have an underclass,' he said. 'People who are different. Treated different. Very often they are treated not so well.'

'Aye,' said Bob. 'It's a worry. It's gettin harder and harder for tinkers here. Places they used to be welcome now have "No Tinks" signs up. They're no wanted in maist places noo. It's a damned shame.'

'And why is this?'

Bob thought for a moment. 'I really couldnae say. Just because they're different, I suppose. They get blamed for aathin that goes wrong.'

'We dinnae get many tinkers in Glesga,' said James, 'but it's the same thing. The Irish, or the Tallies, they get blamed whenever anythin goes wrong. Easier to find a bogeyman than admit there's somethin wrong wi your ain fowk.'

'This is what Hitler is doing with the Jews,' said Jozef. 'Turn them into demons. Make people hate them.'

Bob kicked the dead embers of last night's fire. Kristallnacht had happened eight months before, the moment it became impossible to ignore the savagery of the Nazis' treatment of Jews. In towns and cities throughout Germany and annexed Austria and the Sudetenland, Jewish men, women and children were chased through the streets by Hitler Youth and the SA and hoodlums wielding axes who were shouting "Germany awake!" and "Perish Judah!". Hundreds of synagogues were destroyed, thousands of Jewish businesses looted. Thirty thousand Jewish men were arrested and despatched to concentration camps. All of this, Bob knew, was of a different scale from the tribulations being experienced by the Scottish traveller folk, but then such violence would have been unimaginable in Germany only six or seven years ago, too. Who knew what could befall a society? The cancer of fascism has already been established in the body politic before it begins to reveal itself.

They sat for some moments in quiet reflection, watching

the flames crackle and grow as the fresh wood piled on the fire took light.

'Thon was never an accident,' Sandy said.

'That's what Annie thinks, an aa.'

'Nane of it maks sense. Thon man was killed. There's nae other wey aboot it.'

Bob looked away, at the line of trees above them, the hills around them, the tents below. Sandy was right. Annie was right. He put his pipe in his pocket. 'Come on,' he said.

'Whaur?'

'We left all oor sticks at the side of the track yesterday. Let's go and get them. And hae another keek at the scene.'

Quarter of an hour later, Bob wheeled his wheelbarrow up the same path he had the day before, with Sandy and Annie following. In the distance he could see the monkey puzzle tree. To his right was a clump of broken branches he had gathered for collection. He set down the wheelbarrow and reached for the branches. Beside them was a fist-sized stone and, through some instinct he didn't understand, he picked it up. The underneath was bloodied. Hair and skin adhered to it. Silently, he showed it to the others.

'Thon's blood,' he said.

'It is, aye,' said Sandy.

'Could be fae an animal.'

'On the side of a path? Face doon?'

'And barely a hundred yards fae another bloodied stane,' said Annie, 'which definitely was used on a man.'

'Aye, too much of a coincidence.'

'So we hae twa murder weapons,' said Sandy.

'This would hae been the first ane,' said Bob. 'And the ane in the tent was to mak it seem like that's whaur it happened.'

'When it actually happened here.'

'Aye.' They looked around the rough ground either side of the path in search of clues. A flattened area of grass could

33

have held a body, but there was nothing else to corroborate the fact. They searched for fifteen minutes and found nothing.

'Let's hae another keek at the tent,' said Bob, but when they climbed the dyke into the field where the tent had been there was nothing to be seen.

'Geordie must hae taken it doon last night,' he said.

Sandy crouched low to the ground and ran his palm over the grass. A rectangular area was lightly flattened. 'You can see whaur it was,' he said. 'But it wasnae there lang. Naebody had slept in it, bided in it ony length of time. The grass isnae flat enough.'

'Would it no have bounced back up again?'

'No yet. No this much, onywey.' He stood up again and looked around the field, peering into the trees and tracking the length of the stone wall. 'I'll tell you somethin else. That man wasnae a tink.'

'It was a tinker's tent.'

'Maybe so. But he wasnae a tink.'

'How no?'

'Tinks dinnae come roond here. Same as me. The Monzie estate, it's well known for bein strict about people on its land. Winnae hae onythin to do with tinks. Or onyone else much.'

'But it was definitely a tinker's tent. And it *was* on their land.'

'Aye. *If* it was a tink put it up, he'd hae needed a damned good reason. And he wouldnae hae gone lightin ony fires. That would have alerted the factor in minutes.'

'What d'you mean "if"?'

Sandy took out another cigarette. 'That tent wasnae put up by onyone wha kens aboot puttin up a tent.'

'How?'

'The tap of the tent was burnt oot. But you could see, at ane end, the inner and ooter skin were both ower the tap pole.' He stared at them. 'You cannae do that. If it rains, the tent'll be soaked in minutes. The twa skins cannae come into

34

contact. Nae tink would do that.'

'You could tell by his complexion he wasnae a tinker, onywey,' said Annie.

'Aye,' said Bob. 'Far too peely-wally.' He thought for a moment. 'There's twa things dinnae mak sense here. One, he wasnae a tinker, but he was wearin a tinker's clothin. And two, even if the body wasnae a tinker, it really was a tinker's tent.'

'So if the deid man isnae the tinker ...' said Annie.

'Whaur's the tinker gone?'

'And how?'

'And what's he wearin?' He turned to Sandy. 'How do we find a missin tinker?'

Sandy inclined his head. 'No easy,' he said. 'They keep themsels to themsels. I'll ask aboot, but if folk think I'm askin for a reason they'll no say a word. Especially if they think the polis micht get involved.'

'Well, we're probably safe on that score.'

'Meanwhile,' said Annie, 'there's the identity of the body to figure oot an aa.'

Bob took out his pipe and tobacco. 'If it was someone local, nae doot we'd hae heard by noo he was missin. So it's probably no a local.' He looked at Sandy and Annie. 'Noo tell me, where in Crieff have three-and-a-half thoosand non-locals just appeared?'

'The Moot,' said Annie.

'Right.'

'You think it's somebody fae the camp?'

'That's the maist logical answer.'

'So we need to find out if there's onyone missin in the camp.'

'We do, aye.'

Sunday 16th July

A Day of Openings

When Bob arrived at the top of the site at six-thirty, a scratch pipe band was already waiting, half a dozen pipers, including a couple of Irish lads in green kilts, three tenor drummers and even a bass drummer.

'We'll mak some din the day,' he said.

They swept through Makgill camp, picking up a couple more pipers on the way, then headed for Maitland camp and came to a halt outside the London enclosure to impart another blaring rendition of *Scotland the Brave*. The London lads stood by their tents, mostly in vests or bare-chested, eyes still sleepy. They jeered and hissed. Mickey Peterfield waited until the band finished.

'You ain't getting no better,' he said.

'I wouldnae expect your philistine ears to understand,' said Bob.

'You call me a philistine?' said Mickey, laughing. 'After making that hideous bloody row?'

'Says someone who sings *Down at the Old Bull and Bush.*'

'Not me, squire. That's from Hampstead Heath way. They're all soft up there. I'm Shadwell and proud.'

'It's all the same to me. Fancy London weys.' Bob blew into his mouthpiece to fill the bag and started up *Scotland the Brave* once more, and he and his band marched out of

36

the camp and up the hill.

'That was some racket,' said James Meikle, grinning and handing him a pewter mug of tea a few minutes later. 'You must be makin quite an impression wi those English boys.'

'I'm no sure they appreciate it ower much.'

'Barbarians.'

'Aye, somebody has to civilise them.'

They joined Jozef and Abdalla, already seated by the campfire and attempting to eat for the first time the Scottish delicacy of porridge. Bob filled them in on the discussions of the previous evening, their new twin aims of finding the traveller and determining whose the body was.

'A difficult task,' said Abdalla.

'Aye,' said Bob. 'In aa thae detective stories, the clues fall into the detective's lap. Every time he needs a break, somethin turns up. It's no like that, let me tell you. You're footerin in the dark the hale time.'

As they spoke, all four of them had become aware of an odd humming noise coming from below them in Makgill camp. The noise was growing louder, *needle-naddle, needle-naddle* and they saw, approaching them *en masse*, a phalanx of Rovers, at least a couple of hundred strong, marching in file and making a high-pitched nasal whine. Most had blankets wrapped round their waists in imitation of kilts, and sponge bags or rolled up towels in place of a sporran. They carried improvised bagpipes, lengths of wood strung together or rolled up newspaper slung over their shoulders, and some of them were banging sticks or cutlery on tin plates. By the time they halted in front of Meikle's Nook the sound was deafening. Bob held his hands over his ears.

'Greetings, Scotch people,' said Mickey Peterfield, brandishing his glengarry. 'I hope you like our tribute to your pipe music.'

'No awfae much, no,' said Bob.

'Exactly. And at least it's not half-six in the bloody

morning. We wish to protest against this primitive custom of yours.' Behind him, three hundred English Rovers cheered and waved their fists. Scots from all over the site joined the scene and Bob found himself in the middle of a stand-off, the auld enemies facing one another across the slopes of Monzie. A sudden gust of wind blew through the camp, whipping up the improvised kilts and stirring the canvas tents. The shirt hanging from James Meikle's flagpole billowed wildly.

'You English tried to ban the bagpipes and tartan once afore, in 1746,' Bob said. 'We just bided our time and brought them back first chance we got. You'll no keep us doon.'

'It's not you we want to keep down, Jock, it's your noise.'

Bob laughed. 'Tell you what, call off your warriors and we'll wait till eight the morn's morn before we start.'

'Deal! Nice doing business with you, my good man.'

Bob returned to the group at Meikle's Nook. James was staring at him. 'What?' he said.

'Ye're no really goin to wait till eight the morra, are ye?'

'What do you think?'

*

By nine o'clock, the skirmish between the English and the Scots was over and the Rovers were back in their enclaves preparing for the opening ceremony. The campsite had grown quiet. Rain that had threatened all morning finally began to fall, heavy and sustained, throbbing against the taut canvas of the tents, turning the maze of paths into mud tracks, gathering in pools in any low-lying land. Bob and Annie hurried towards the information centre, where around thirty Rovers stood, heads bowed in the rain, waiting for it to open.

'Man,' said Annie. 'Look at that queue. I'll no be able to do any investigatin until we've cleared that up.'

'No,' said Bob, trying to hide his disappointment. Their plan was to contact the lead Rover for each country and each

38

British area contingent, and check with them for any Rovers who hadn't turned up. They suspected there would probably be lots of lads who, for whatever reason, didn't make the Moot. The international situation virtually assured that. Even so, they couldn't think of an alternative plan. Annie pulled open the flap at the rear of the information tent and they stepped inside just as Brigadier Ross was opening the front entrance to allow the Rovers to flood in.

'Right,' said Bob. 'If you can gie me your list of lead Rovers, I'll start copyin it oot. Then I can get on wi speakin to them aa.'

Annie handed him the list. 'There's forty-eight countries here. And maybe seventy or eighty British groups. It'll tak ye maist of the mornin just to write them aa oot, never mind gettin to speak to ony o them.'

'We hae to start somewhere.'

'Miss, may I ask you something?' Annie hadn't even made it to her enquiry desk, but the throng of Rovers seeking assistance made anyone with an official badge fair game. A tall man stood before her, probably mid- to late-twenties, older than most of the Rovers. He had an affable smile and dark, deep-set eyes, slightly askew. 'May I ask, where could I get a horse?'

'A horse?'

'For riding. I am Miško Čurović. From Yugoslavia. I like riding horse. I would like to borrow one for the day, please.'

'I dinnae ken,' said Annie. 'Maist folks will be usin their cuddies. This is fairmin country. I dinnae ken whaur there'd be ony spare.'

'The Hydro estate,' said Bob. 'They hae plenty cuddies.'

'Cuddies?' said Miško.

'Horses. The Hydro might lend you one for the day.' He gave directions up the hill out of the Moot camp and past the monkey puzzle tree and the scene of the crime, along the lower slopes of the Knock to Ferntower House and left into the Hydro stables. Miško, recognising the way from his trip into town the previous day, tipped his hat and bade them good morning.

'Let me mak a start,' said Bob.

'Okay, go ben the back. If anyone asks wha you are and what you're doin just say you're writing up a spare copy. There's that mony enquiries we thocht we micht need mair than one.'

'Aye,' said Bob. He felt a pulse of nervous excitement in his chest. He could never decide whether he enjoyed these moments of tension or hated them. Mostly, he thought, it was both.

*

Sandy Disdain strode uphill from the Comrie road at Ardvreck towards Culcrieff, shotgun broken over his arm and empty gamebag set across his shoulders. He pulled on his Capstan as he reviewed the events of the past couple of days – that dead body in the tent was a gey queer affair, and all these thousands of laddies from around the world camping at Monzie. And thon shy lassie, Pat the postie's bairn, a nice wee thing but about as animated as his wee sister Moira's wooden doll, Camilla. He wasn't sure he'd even heard her speak.

'Ho there, Sandy.'

Johnno Douglas appeared through the early morning mirk, trundling his aged Victorian perambulator, loaded with sticks, down the hill towards him.

'You were in a dream there, son,' he continued. Johnno lived in a cottage at the foot of Milnab Street but was originally of traveller extraction, his family summer walkers who travelled the highlands and lowland Perthshire hawking and tinsmithing until his faither, Douglas Douglas, took ill with the cancer and broke with tradition by taking the cottage in Crieff. Johnno, as a result, was a perpetual

40

outsider, neither traveller nor scaldy, never wholly trusted by either community.

'I was, aye,' said Sandy, throwing his cigarette butt into a damp clump of sedge by the trackside.

'Thinkin aboot the lassies, judging by the look on your fizzog.'

'Ach, you ken me too weel, Johnno.' He offered the older man one of his Capstans and lit one for himself, and they stood and examined the press of trees lining the path all the way downhill towards the main road to town.

'I was wonderin,' said Sandy. 'I saw a curious thing, couple of days syne, a burnt-oot bow tent on the Monzie estate …'

'The Monzie estate?'

'Aye, exactly. Wha would pitch a tent on the Monzie estate? Wi Jamesie Kerracher the factor …'

'A nasty piece of work.'

'Threatened to shoot the arse off me ae time. I'd hae been thirteen at maist, just oot of school.'

'Shan brute.'

'I was wonderin, ony ideas wha micht hae done that?'

'A traveller's tent, you think?'

'Looked like ane, aye.'

Johnno sucked his cigarette as though pondering, but Sandy was certain he already knew something.

'Doesnae seem likely.'

'I agree. But I saw it wi my ain eyes …'

'And … was there onythin unusual … aboot the tent?'

Sandy knew two things: firstly, the dead man in the tent wasn't common knowledge; and, secondly, Johnno Duncan knew about it.

'No, no,' he replied. 'Just a tent. But abandoned, like.'

'Must hae been running awa fae the factor.'

'If he'd ony sense, aye. But why pitch a tent there in the first place? Askin for trouble.'

41

'Aye, it's curious, richt enough.'

Sandy shifted his gamebag. He fumbled for his cigarette packet and, watching Johnno, pulled out another Capstan. Johnno waited, impassive. Sandy pulled out a second. Johnno's expression didn't alter. Sandy pulled out a third and saw the vaguest twitch from the corner of Johnno's mouth.

'For the road,' he said, handing the cigarettes over.

'Awfae kind of you, son.' Johnno secreted the cigarettes in a side pocket inside his jacket. 'I couldnae help you wi your bow tent,' he continued, 'but you micht speak to Habbie Goudie …'

'Fae Duchlage?'

'Yon's the man.'

'The tent's his?'

'No, no. Habbie's got a hoose in Sauchie, noo.' Johnno flung his spent cigarette to the ground and stood on it. 'But his cousin, Chic, he was in toon the ither day …'

'And?'

'And noo he's no.'

'Aye.' Someone who had been in town and now wasn't didn't sound like three cigarettes' worth of information to Sandy, but he knew he would get nothing further out of Johnno. 'Grand,' he said. 'I'll maybe go and hae a word wi Habbie, richt enough.' He hitched his gamebag further up his shoulder.

'Guid seein you again, son. Be sure and let me ken if there's mair information you're efter, ony time.' He patted his inside pocket and winked, then picked up his perambulator and trundled it downhill towards Crieff.

*

It was an hour before Bob was challenged. Brigadier Ross spotted him crouched over a wooden pallet at the rear of the tent, scribbling onto a piece of paper.

'You, man, what are you doing?'

42

Bob cursed. He knew discovery was inevitable but he'd hoped the length of the queues of Rovers might have kept everyone busy for a while longer.

'Morning, sir,' he said. 'I'm from the ARP in Perth. Doing some research for Lord Kellett. He knows me, asked me to help him.'

'By doing what?'

'Checkin the names of the group leaders. Cross-checkin against our files, seein if they've volunteered. A rich source of men, don't you think, Rovers? Good discipline. Sensible.'

'And who let you behind here?'

Bob could see Annie at her desk, busy with an Indian Rover Scout. 'One of your young ladies, sir. I don't recall which one.'

'You can't stay here. It's not authorised.'

'Lord Kellett ...'

'Yes, I know Lord Kellett. I'll speak to him about this.'

'Yes, sir.' Bob tried not to display any nervousness. 'I'm sure it's just a communications breakdown. Out here, must be terribly hard to keep in touch with everythin.'

'Well, it's hardly a war zone. I must ask you to leave. And leave behind any paperwork you were compiling.'

'Of course, sir.' Bob handed over two pieces of paper, each with about a dozen names on them. Inside his jacket were another five pieces. He saluted and stepped quickly out of the tent, making sure not to let Annie see him in case the Brigadier saw her waving to him. He emerged into rain that was even heavier than before.

'Well,' he said to himself. 'It's a start.'

*

'Miss, where can I find the Witch Crag? Kate McAnavie?' Annie suspected the Rover in front of her, young and skinny, smiling, was possibly French and she couldn't fully decipher what he had asked.

43

'Witch Crag?' she said uncertainly. 'Is it near here?'

'I think so, yes. Someone told me about it last night.'

Annie looked around, as though in search of inspiration, and noticed a young woman hovering close by. After a moment, she recognised her as Pat the postie's nervous daughter, Mary Kemp.

'Sorry,' said Mary, 'I heard your question. It's called Kate McNiven's Crag. She was a witch, burned to death twa hundred year ago.'

'Yes, that is the one,' said the Rover. 'The site? It's here?'

'Aye, just follow the path past the castle uphill. It's no even half a mile. There's no much to see, mind, just a hill and a big stane in the ground.'

The Rover doffed his cap and thanked her and departed.

'Thanks,' said Annie. 'I've been bidin in Crieff twa year and I havenae heard of Kate McNiven's Crag.'

'It's probably just an auld wives' tale. There's a steep hill and they say they put Kate McNiven in a barrel of boilin tar and hurled her doon the slope. Then at the bottom they set fire to her, just to mak sure.'

'Aye well, Crieff folk can get richt bad-tempered sometimes.'

Mary laughed but she still appeared nervous, struggling to make eye contact, looking around the tent at nothing in particular. Annie got the feeling she wasn't used to company.

'What brings you here?' she asked. 'Helpin your faither again?'

'Aye, we had another bumper pile of post but now he's gone aff somewhere. Looking for a bar, probably. I've nae place to go and it's pourin ootside.'

'Bide wi me, if you like. If I get any mair difficult questions you can help me oot. And when I get my denner break Bob and I are goin for a walk roond the camp, as long as that blessed rain's stopped. You can join us if you like. We'll show you roond.'

Mary broke into a smile as though a weight of worry had been released from her. 'Grand,' she said.

*

Their first attempt to speak to group leaders did not go well. Annie and Mary followed as Bob went from group to group, enquiring after the leaders named on his scribbled list. Most weren't around. Those who were didn't want to talk.

'It's the grand opening in an hour,' said a white-haired Welshman, clearly in his fifties but dressed, like the rest of the Rovers, in shorts and pullover. 'I've no time now, see? Come back later.'

'I only want to ask them one question,' Bob complained to Annie half an hour later as they retreated in defeat to the sanctuary of Meikle's Nook.

'What is it you're tryin to find oot?' said Mary.

Bob measured his words. 'There's somebody we're tryin to find,' he said. 'Who he was.'

'Is it that deid body in the tent?'

Bob stared at her. 'How did you ken aboot that?'

'My faither telt me.'

'And how did he ken?'

'Nae idea.' Mary saw how exercised Bob and Annie had become and immediately retreated into herself so that Annie could have sworn she had become smaller. 'I'm sorry,' she continued. 'I didnae mean to cause trouble.'

'Nae trouble," said Annie gently, touching her arm for reassurance. 'D'you think you could ask him? How he heard aboot it?' Mary appeared reluctant but Annie insisted. 'It could be important.'

'Was he … is it suspicious, the death?'

'It is, aye.' Annie braced herself for further questioning but Mary pulled an escaping lock of hair from her eyes and said no more. Annie was well used to Bob's awkward manner in company, had learned to smooth over it, but

Mary's discomfort was of a different magnitude, her anxiety almost physical in its manifestation. The three watched the rain from Meikle's Nook for half an hour. Bob raised his hand in the air to feel the wind direction and checked the advancing clouds for a glimmer of respite. None came.

'We'd best get doon,' he said. 'They'll be startin the openin ceremony soon.'

'Will you join us?' Annie asked Mary.

'I wouldnae want to be a scunner.'

'You wouldnae be.'

When they returned to the main area, visitors were streaming uphill from the car and coach park to the Moot parade ground on paths that had been covered in cinders to counteract the rain. Under the pressure of thousands of feet the cinders had metamorphosed into a black glaur. Despite the weather, a steady flow of buses was ferrying to Monzie the crowds that had descended on Crieff Railway Station, while organised coach trips and magical mystery tours were arriving from all over Scotland. By nightfall, more than ten thousand visitors would have paid a shilling for entrance.

'Jings,' said Bob, 'this is busier than Crieff Games day.'

Young couples, the occasional spinster or widow, groups of youths, families, everyone seemed determined to ignore the rain and have a grand day out, to put aside for a while the threat of war and relax in the Perthshire countryside. Crowds began to congregate around the amphitheatre that had been identified for the opening ceremony, marked off by ropes attached to wooden stakes lining its circumference. On makeshift flagpoles, twenty feet high, running the extent of the arena, the flags of the forty-eight nations represented at the Moot were tightly knotted, waiting to be broken as the ceremony progressed. A heady thrum of laughter and chatter filled the air, children running and skipping and yelling with excitement. Bob, Annie and Mary walked round the perimeter in search of a vantage point.

At one o'clock, the Rovers began to gather on the slopes of the rallying point. The Glasgow Rover Pipe Band struck up *Scotland the Brave*, and at a quarter past the hour they marched into the arena and completed a full circuit before halting to the right of a dais set on higher ground overlooking the arena.

The dignitaries took their places. Lord Somers, the Deputy Chief Scout presiding over events in the absence, through illness, of Lord Baden-Powell, took the centremost position. Around him, John Colville MP, Secretary of State for Scotland, Lord Rowallan, Prince Gustav Adolf of Sweden and Colonel AG Johnston DSO, the Moot organiser, took their places. All but John Colville and Prince Gustav wore kilts. The Pipe Band played again until half past the hour and then momentarily fell silent while the crowd hushed, patient at the start of events.

This stillness was broken by a maroon sounding, a coarse boom reverberating around the Scottish hillside. As the noise faded, the Pipe Band began again. Up on the rallying point, the starting official gave the signal for the first contingent of Rovers to begin their procession. Rovers from Armenia, alphabetically the first of the forty-eight nations, marched into the arena and made an anti-clockwise circuit before stopping to take the salute of the dignitaries. Moot officials marched to the flagpole bearing the Armenian colours and, with a brief ceremony, broke the flag. The red, blue and orange tricolour fluttered limply in the rain, draping itself around the flagpole. Salutes exchanged, the Armenians marched away to take up their position in the far corner of the arena. As soon as they were settled, the Belgian contingent began their tour of the arena, the crowd clapping them all the way. Occasionally, a Rover would break discipline and wave back. He would be rewarded by even louder cheers. At the end of their circuit they took up their position next to the Armenians and the two groups mingled and shook hands and

47

chatted in whatever shared languages they could discover.

The British contingent followed, by far the largest, with fourteen hundred English Rovers and seven hundred Scots. Bob waved at James and the Pollokshields gang from Meikle's Nook and they waved back nonchalantly. The countries of the Empire followed, the Indians causing a huge ovation when they doffed their hats and cheered as they passed the dignitaries. The Rhodesians startled everyone with their "veldt yell", a sustained, high-pitched sound, something like a yodel. Eire and Ulster followed, the Eireans splendid in their green kilts. Two hundred and fifty French Rovers raised their caps in unison in appreciation of the acclaim from the crowd.

'Mercy,' said Annie as fifty Hungarians entered the arena, goose-stepping in a style reminiscent of the German Nazis. 'What a sicht.'

'I tell you what,' said a man standing next to Bob, 'that just puts the tin lid on it. I was already thinking this is just like one of those damned Nuremberg Rallies.'

'I've seen them on the newsreels,' said Bob.

'I've seen them in the flesh. Last year, I did a tour of Europe. Made a detour to Nuremberg to see what it was like.' He was well-spoken, a young man of perhaps twenty-three or -four, wearing a pinstripe suit and homburg. 'Marvellous spectacle, I grant you. But sinister.'

'Aye,' said Bob. The man's observation chimed with an unease that had been bothering him since the start of the display. The Moot was a festival of friendship and solidarity, and yet the centrepiece was this, phalanxes of young men marching like soldiers and saluting. 'You dinnae beat somethin by impersonatin it,' he said. The man cocked his head in agreement.

Annie pointed to a short man at the rear of the Hungarian contingent. 'I met him yesterday,' she said. 'Ivan, or something like that. Funny little man.' Almost as though he had heard them, István Kedály looked in their direction and waved.

'I wonder if he found the laundry,' she said and explained to Bob about her conversation with István. The parade continued and the arena began to fill with Rovers, each of them standing patiently in the rain until all forty-eight countries had paraded and their flags had been broken. As the United States of America, the final country to march, took their place in the gathering, the British national anthem rang out and the crowd sang along.

Bob was struck by the strangeness of the scene. Three-and-a-half thousand Rover Scouts gathered in international harmony, but among them was probably a murderer. Evil prospers by masquerading as good. Good becomes infected. The law of averages dictated that there would be more men among the crowd gathered before him who at some stage in their lives would murder or rape or rob or cheat. Hidden in plain view. Waiting. It was a scourge of humanity.

Lord Somers tapped his microphone and waited for a moment, surveying the young men before him. He began to speak.

'We hope that you Rovers will get to know each other during the next ten days and that many friendships will be formed. We hope that you will all talk freely of your lives and aspirations, and let us learn something through you of the countries in which you live. It is through these methods that the purpose of the Moot will best be accomplished. That purpose, of course, is the promotion of mutual understanding and brotherhood. This is, at any time, a noble and honourable pursuit. In these times of international tension, it seems that only by these means can international peace be established. Rovers will be in the vanguard. This is your solemn duty.'

Solemn duty, thought Bob. *And how could such a duty be exercised? Really? When men older and harder and more cynical than them operated the levers of power?* He felt a

49

curious sense of indolence, a kind of melancholy. It was, in truth, a common feeling for him. *Sometimes I just think too much,* he chided himself.

'It's odd,' said Jozef afterwards. They were sitting around the campfire at Meikle's Nook, Jozef, Bob, Annie and Abdalla, eating roast pigeon. Mary had found her father and gone home. 'A day of friendship and all that, but who knows what is coming? When war begins, who will be on which side? You and me, Bob, we will fight hand-in-hand. But Abdalla? What side will Egypt be on?'

Abdalla clasped his hands in front of him. 'I believe Egypt will not support Germany. But I cannot say that we will support England either. There are still wounds there. England is not popular with our people. I think we will stay neutral. I hope so.'

'But the Nazis must be stopped.'

'They are bad people, yes. They are seeking to build an empire. But it seems to me this empire is only in Europe. Not like Mussolini, who wants his African empire. Or England, too, which already owns much of Africa. Hitler seems to me to have no interest in Africa.'

'So it's not your war?'

'No.' Abdalla caught the look of irritation on Jozef's face. 'You are turning this into a moral question, my friend. The Nazis are evil. I agree. They are killing innocent people. I agree. They should be stopped. I agree. But by who? Does the whole world become evil, to stop evil? Is that how it should be done?'

'If there is no other way.'

'And you believe there is no other way?'

'No.'

'Your trouble, my friend, is that you are looking for instant solutions. Fix the Nazis now. That cannot happen. But they will be fixed. In time. Evil will collapse under its own weight. It always does.'

'So we have to wait?'

'Yes.'

'Meanwhile, thousands of Jews suffer. Gypsies. Communists. My country will be invaded. My people will be made slaves. Europe will be turned into a German state. Is that what you want?'

'Jozef, what Abdalla Ben Salah wants is of no importance to anyone. Not even to me. I do as I am guided by Allah, *subhanahu wa ta'ala*.'

Jozef leaped to his feet. He threw the dregs of his tea into the campfire and it sizzled and cracked and sparked for an instant. 'I tell you,' he said, 'Danzig will be next to fall, and I will fight every step of the way to win it back.' He pulled on his cape and buttoned it round his neck. He glowered at Abdalla. 'And cowards can rot in hell.' He marched away from the campfire, muttering as he went.

'I am sorry,' said Abdalla. 'I upset him.'

'He's worried,' said Bob. 'The Polish corridor is likely to be the next place the Nazis annex. And he was tellin me earlier about his parents. They live on the German border. If there's an invasion, he thinks it'll probably start there.' He stood up and shook grass from his trousers, then reached for Annie's hand. 'I think we'll hae a wee daunder as well,' he said.

They walked through the campsite towards the now empty arena. Darkness was settling but all around campfires lit up the night. The rain had finally stopped. Shouts and laughter rang out. Music from half a dozen different groups mingled around them, pleasant cacophony. *Alouette, gentille alouette*. The smell of woodsmoke filled the air, that and the smell of soil reviving after the rain.

'Jozef's right,' Bob said. 'War's comin. And we'll all have to decide.'

'Decide what?'

'What to do. How to fight.'

'It winnae come to that.'

'Annie.' He stopped and took both of her hands and kissed her. 'I'd love you to be richt, and usually you are. But no this time.'

They wandered down the central pathway to Moot HQ. A hoolet hooted nearby. The evening was cooling rapidly. Approaching them, head down, kicking at stones on the path, was Jozef. He looked up and smiled.

'Sorry,' he said. 'I sometimes get too excited.'

'You have cause.'

'I do, yes.'

'Let's go back, see if there's any of that pigeon left.'

As they passed a tent that was operating as a branch of the Bank of Scotland, in the darkness between it and a nearby tree they heard voices in a language Bob and Annie could not understand.

'*Triff mich um zehn Uhr am See.*'

Jozef froze. He pulled Bob and Annie off the track, into shadow and, as they watched, a man strode past, walking in the direction of the castle. A moment later, a second man emerged, cigarette glowing in the darkness, and walked in the opposite direction.

Jozef's hands were resting on Bob's and Annie's backs, cautioning them to remain quiet. They waited until both men were out of sight.

'What was that all about?' said Bob.

'You know what language they were speaking?' said Jozef.

'No.'

'German.'

'Do you know what they said?' said Annie.

'I do. I understand German very well. One man said: "Meet me at the lake at ten." And the other man said "Ja".'

'Lake?' said Annie.

'They must mean Loch More,' said Bob. 'It's just along

the wey, there.'

'There are no Germans at the Moot. Why would anyone be speakin German?'

'A shared language?'

'Maybe. But why oot here? Oot of the wey? In darkness? Awa fae the path, hidden fae sight?'

Jozef lit a cigarette. 'It is very suspicious, I think. And we have reason to be suspicious. With our dead man.'

'You're right,' said Bob. 'We already agreed that the dead man was probably from this camp. That means the man who killed him is probably from this camp, too. So anyone who behaves in ony wey suspiciously should concern us.'

'But we've no idea who they are,' said Jozef.

'I do,' said Annie. 'At least, I ken wha one of them is.'

*

Back at Meikle's Nook, they relayed details of the event they'd just witnessed to James and Abdalla.

'He's Hungarian,' said Annie. 'Ivan somebody. He asked me about a laundry yesterday. Said the on-site laundry wasnae good enough. He had a lot of stainin on his claes.'

'What kind of staining?' asked Jozef.

'I dinnae ken, but I ken what laundry he went to. So we can go and ask them the morn. If he really is our man, that stainin could be blood. There would hae been blood fae a blow to the heid.'

'No much,' said Bob.

'No. But enough to be noticeable in a laundry. What time is it noo?'

Bob checked his time piece. 'Nine o'clock,' he said.

'An hour to wait for the rendezvous by Loch More.'

'We cannae go to the loch.'

'What d'you mean we cannae go?'

'Only Rovers are allowed on site after half nine. We need to get hame.'

'Not on your nellie.'

'He's right,' said James Meikle. 'We could probably get away wi smugglin Bob in after hours, but you – well, ye're gonnae stand out a bit in a camp with three-and-a-half thousand boys and no wummin.'

Annie fumed and folded her hands over her chest but she knew he was right. 'So who's goin, then?' she said.

'I will go,' said Jozef.

'And I will go to the Hungarian Rovers' tents,' said Abdalla. 'Sit with them a while, introduce myself. Check to see who leaves before ten o'clock.'

'You see?' said James. 'We'll probably huv it all solved by the time ye come back the morra.'

'Aye,' said Annie, scowling. 'Like enough.'

Monday 17th July

A Day of Suspicions

It was a little after six in the morning when Miško Čurović watched Bob trudging uphill with his bagpipes. He shook his head. These Scottish pipes were infernal beasts, all din and stridency. Even worse than the bagpipes from his homeland, the *Svrljiške gajde*. His uncle Cvetko, dragged into the Balkans War and too stupid to know he was on the wrong side, kept the idiots of the Serbian Army happy as they marched through the Albanian mountains on a fool's errand by playing the *gajde*. Miško had hated the *gajde* all his life because of the way his elders told that story, displaying pride and foolishness in equal measure. Yugoslavia's future wasn't in those ancient stories and animosities that looked southwards into the Balkan peninsula; it was north-facing, into the heart of Europe, the new world, a Europe that wanted to become one. *Ein Reich.*

That Scottish buffoon, Miško thought as he watched Bob join his piper comrades, would probably have found much in common with Uncle Cvetko.

Herd animals, both.

Miško turned towards the Makgill camp and the Hungarian enclosure. He selected a tree, stood behind it, and watched.

*

55

Despite Bob's promise of a later start, the morning provocation of the London lads started as early as previously and aroused the same sentiments. However, Bob was in no mood to enjoy the Londoners' mock fury. When they had finished, he and Annie hurried to the Polish tents in search of Jozef and news of last night's rendezvous.

'Nothing happen,' said Jozef. He was shaving in front of a tiny, cracked mirror propped against a block of wood, his face half-covered in lather. 'I stay for an hour. There were a few Belgians swimming. One nearly drowned and had to be rescued by a Rhodesian fellow. That was all. Our man not show.'

'How did Abdalla get on?'

'I not see him this morning.'

When Jozef had finished shaving they strode across the camp to the Egyptian enclave, the boundary of which was marked by a representation of symbols from the Egyptian flag. The crescent was turned on its side and fashioned into stylised, curling pillars expertly carved from wood, and hanging from them were the three stars that made up the rest of the flag. Half a dozen men in fezzes and overcoats were milling around their fire, eating from tin pans or holding pots over the flames. Among them, Bob recognised Mustafa Mansour, goalkeeper for Queen's Park football club.

'My friends,' said Abdalla, 'is this not a beautiful morning?' There was, indeed, bright sunshine from a cloudless sky, although the air was unseasonably cold.

'How did you get on last night?' said Bob.

'The Hungarian boys are most friendly. I stayed with them all evening.'

'And did anyone disappear before ten?'

'I would say no, but I cannot be certain. They are a large group. Fifty or more. I couldn't watch them all.'

Bob sighed with frustration. He had no idea what he'd expected to happen the night before, what the rendezvous was for, whether it was innocent or suspicious, but nothing had transpired and now they were back where they started. Back with a dead man about whom nobody but them seemed to care.

'We have to find Ivan,' he said. He pulled his list of names from his pocket and studied it, hoping the Hungarian Rover Lead would be one of the names he'd recorded before being expelled by Brigadier Ross. It was.

Zoltán Tóth.

'Right,' he said. 'Let's see if we can find Mr Tóth. Twa birds wi one stane. Anyone missin in the group and anythin aboot our man, Ivan.'

Zoltán Tóth was a man of around forty. Although Rovers were mostly aged between eighteen and twenty-four there was no upper age limit and most of the group leaders were much older men. Zoltán offered Bob and Annie tea from a large urn resting on a trivet above the campfire.

'Most of our Rovers have gone out,' he said. 'Today is the first day of the tours around your beautiful country.'

'Aye, a friend of mine is takin one of the groups.' Bob knew that Sandy Disdain was leading a trip up Ben Lawers, about twenty miles distant, each day for the next week. 'We're from the information centre,' he continued. 'We're goin round all the groups checkin up that everyone who was due to be here has arrived. Is there anyone missin?'

'No. We are all accounted for. There are fifty-one of us and most came across together on a ferry from Rotterdam to Hull.'

Bob tried to look as though he was satisfied with this news. 'What about a man called Ivan? Is there an Ivan in your group?'

'Ivan? That's not a Hungarian name. Do you mean István? István Kedály?'

'That's it,' said Annie. 'I remember the name now.'

'István. Yes, indeed. You asked if anyone was missing.

István is the opposite. He was a late addition.'

'What d'you mean?' said Bob.

'He wasn't in the original group.' Zoltán took a list from his pocket. 'These are the names of everyone from *Magyaroszág*. Fifty of us. István arrived by himself. He had all his paperwork but he was not on my list.'

Bob and Annie exchanged glances. First, his clothing needed heavy laundering, then he made a late-night rendezvous, and now it seemed that he was a late arrival at the Moot. None of these events, taken individually, were especially significant, but together?

'How do you think that happened?' Bob asked.

Zoltán shrugged. 'A simple mistake, I think.'

'Where are your men going on their trip today?' Annie asked.

'I believe most have gone to Ben Chonzie.' He pronounced the second word with a hard "ch" sound.

'Ben Chonzie,' Bob corrected, softening the "ch".

That was good. Some of the trips were to distant spots – there were even two excursions to Ben Nevis planned in the week – which would result in the Rovers not returning to camp until late. Ben Chonzie was only a few miles away and they would be back by early evening.

'I've a café in town,' he said. 'You'd be most welcome to come by this evening for somethin to eat. A wee bit of Scottish hospitality.' Bob tried not to estimate how much that Scottish hospitality might cost him. He could see his profits from the Moot week disappearing in a single evening, but the chance to speak to István Kedály was worth the expense.

'We would be honoured,' said Zoltán.

*

'Hello, Elsa.' Annie smiled at the woman in the blue pinafore behind the counter of the Strathearn Steam Laundry.

'Your coat'll no be ready till the morn,' Elsa replied.

'That's no what I'm here for.' Annie explained about István Kedály, about giving him directions to the laundry, his need to clean his clothing. 'Did he come in? Seturday, it would hae been, late on.'

'Seturday? Nut. I was on Seturday efternoon. Nae foreign bloke came in. I would hae minded.'

'You sure?' This wasn't what she expected at all. She had steeled herself for discovering the staining was just grass or dirt rather than blood, but she hadn't anticipated István not even showing. 'I gave him clear directions. He seemed awfae keen.'

Elsa turned to the door behind her. 'Jean, did you see a foreign mannie, Seturday efternoon?'

Jean, a plump woman of around sixty emerged from the back. From the way she squinted it was clear she had poor eyesight but she did not wear spectacles.

'There was a bioke, aye. Ane of thae Rovers, wearing shorts and a stupit hat. Looked like he'd a clump of grass stickin oot of his heid.'

'I didnae see him,' said Elsa.

'He didnae come in. He was hingin aboot ootside for half an hoor, then just went awa. I telt you aboot it.'

Elsa raised her hand. 'I mind, aye. I didnae hear you say he was foreign.'

'Well, I dinnae ken he was foreign but he wasnae fae here, that's for sure. No dressed like a ninny.'

'What d'you want to ken for?' Jean asked Annie.

'Oh,' Annie sighed. 'Nuthin. Thanks onywey.' Outside, she leaned into the steep incline back to the High Street, her mind whirring. So, István Kedály had come to the laundry as he explained to her he would, but had stood outside for half an hour. Why? Plucking up courage to go in? Again, why? That made it more likely that the staining on his clothing was indeed suspicious. Something he wasn't sure he could show the staff in the laundry. Blood, perhaps. But wouldn't he have thought of that before? He would have known he would have to hand over the garments. Was there something about the laundry itself that deterred him? She looked back the way she had come, as though studying the outside of the laundry would somehow furnish her with answers.

'Women,' she said aloud. They were all women working there. Maybe he couldn't speak to a woman about it. Maybe he thought they were too delicate. Or would gossip. Or couldn't be trusted. She turned onto the High Street and walked downhill distractedly. So what would he do next? If he couldn't go to a laundry, how could he get his clothing cleaned?

'Do it himsel,' she said.

'Eh?' said a woman with a grey headscarf draped round her head and a cigarette in her mouth.

'Sorry, talkin to mysel.'

'There's a place for folk wha do that.'

'Aye.'

'Gilgal. That's where Agnes Harrison ended up. She talked to herself for years. Completely doolally, noo.'

'Aye well,' said Annie, 'what's for you'll no go by you.'

She stopped outside Turnbull's the butchers and stared at the array of meats on display. Yes, she thought, maybe he would just clean the blood himself. But couldn't he have done that at the camp? The Shaggie Burn ran right through it. He could have used that. Maybe he tried, but it didn't work. Cold water wouldn't clean blood, would it? Through the window, Mr Turnbull was staring at her, waiting to see if she was going to enter. He wore a white apron tied almost under his chest.

There were bloodstains on the front.

Annie entered and smiled at Mr Turnbull. 'I've a strange question,' she said.

'No, I dinnae put sawdust in the mince. That's Erchie McLagan started that rumour and I'll hae him in the court if he says it again.'

'Nae doot. What I wanted to ask was, did a foreign mannie come in last Seturday and ask aboot how to get blood oot of claes?'

'Well, I'll grant you, lass, that's a question I've no been asked afore.'

'But was there?'

'No.' Mr Turnbull straightened his back and folded his arms. 'You gonnae buy onythin, or d'you juist want to admire it?'

She made to look at the meats and sniffed. 'They're no as good as Roy's,' she said and turned and walked out. She stopped outside Frank Thomson's the ironmonger's to collect her thoughts. She had imagined she was so clever, working out what István Kedály would have done. She'd convinced herself she'd cracked the mystery, and now she was back where she started.

'Roy's,' she said. Roy's the butcher's was further down the High Street. She crossed the road at the cinema and hurried downhill.

'Mrs Kelty,' said Mr Roy as she entered. 'Didnae expect to see you the day. Friday's your day, is it no?'

'You didnae hae a foreign mannie in on Seturday, did you ...'

'I did aye. Askin aboot gettin blood stains oot of clothin.'

Annie felt her pulse race with excitement. She'd done it. She'd worked it out. She tried to concentrate. 'What did he look like?' she said.

'Ain of thae Rovers. Funny hat on his heid ...'

'Grass stickin oot of it?'

'Aye. An shorts. Peltin doon wi rain. He was soaked through.'

'Did you see the clothin?'

'What, wi blood on it? No.'

'What did you tell him?'

'Milk.'

'Milk?'

'If you want to get blood oot of clothin, soak it in milk for five minutes, then rinse it oot thoroughly.'

'Does that work?'

'Like a treat.'

'I'll hae to mind that.'

'It's easier to juist no get blood on your claes in the first place.'

Annie looked at his apron. Like Mr Turnbull's it was heavily stained. Mr Roy saw her looking and smiled.

'Lass, if you're cuttin up as much fresh meat as I am every day I'd be gey worried aboot you.'

Annie laughed. 'What did he do next?'

'Asked where he could buy a pint of milk.'

'And did you tell him?'

'Lipton's.' He cocked his head to the left, indicating up the street. 'What are you interested in this man for? What's the blood all aboot? Has he done somebody in?' He spoke in a jocular fashion and Annie chose to take his question that way.

'Ach,' she said. 'There's nae tellin what these Rovers get up to.'

*

It was six o'clock before Bob returned from the Moot. James Square was much busier than normal, most of the shops open long after their usual closing time to cater for the Rovers, and weary groups of Rovers themselves descending from buses outside the Drummond Arms, returned from their day's exertions. Muir's the ironmongers, uphill from Cloudland, was doing a rare trade in gas and camping equipment. Bob studied the scene through the window, puffing on his pipe.

'It's been busy all day,' Leslie told him and, indeed, she looked trauchled. 'Quite a few of the Rovers came back early and dropped in here. You've a grand location. It's the first place folks come to when they get aff the bus.'

'When I bocht it, aabody telt me nothin lasts here.'

'Well, you've proved them wrong, eh? This place'll be here in fifty years.'

'Maybe so, but will we?'

'Ach, you're just bairns yet.'

Annie shouted from the kitchen. 'If you dinnae get through here and help me, Bob Kelty, you'll no see the end of the day, far less fifty year.'

Bob laughed and joined Annie in the kitchen. By now there were three large chicken pies cooking in the oven and four pounds of peeled and chapped tatties in three pans of gently bubbling water on the stove.

'Looks like you've got aathin under control,' said Bob. 'I'll awa upstairs and put my feet up a while.' He dodged Annie's flailing dishcloth and turned the heat up on the gas rings on the stove under the potatoes. The water started to boil violently.

From outside they heard the door of Cloudland open and the place was suddenly filled with excitable chatter. Bob looked round the corner and saw a room that seemed to be full of lightly swaying grass as the Hungarian Rovers removed their hats and placed them on the tables.

'They're here,' he said. Leslie went out to greet them and Annie turned to Bob. 'I dinnae ken what to say to him.'

'Me neither. This detectin lark's easier in the books.'

They joined Leslie in the cafe. Zoltán grabbed Bob's hand and shook it vigorously.

'I have brought twenty of our men,' he said. 'I hope that isn't too many?'

'No,' said Bob. 'That's grand. There's plenty to go aroond.' He looked at Annie and she knew what he was thinking: please let István Kedály be among the twenty. She scanned the faces of the men and there he was, nearest the door, seated by the window. He had the same expression as the first time she'd seen him, slightly smug, knowing. She inclined her head towards him and Bob followed her gesture.

'Let's sit,' he said to Zoltán and manoeuvred his way through the room to István's table. 'May we?' he said, indicating the empty seats next to István.

'Did you find the laundry alright?' Annie said to him. He looked at her curiously, then recognised her and smiled.

'Ah yes,' he said. 'Very good.' He gestured to a spot on his shirt. It looked exactly like the shirt he had worn when he came into the information centre. 'Clean as new.'

'Aye,' said Annie. 'They're very good at Strathearn Steam.'

'Very helpful.'

Annie nodded as though in agreement. 'Richt,' she said, 'I'll go and start platin up. Bob, you can help me.'

'Aye,' said Bob but he remained seated. 'It must tak a richt lot of organisin,' he said to István. 'Comin to a foreign country. You must have been plannin this for ages?'

'Yes,' said István. 'It take time.'

'When did you start bookin everythin?'

'Oh, months ago.'

Bob looked at Zoltán. From what Zoltán had said this morning, that couldn't be true. 'That's odd,' he said. 'I'm sure Zoltán told me you were a late arrival.'

Zoltán nodded. 'I only got told your name when I arrive here.' He pulled out his list of attendees once more and laid it on the table. 'You weren't on my list.'

István made a show of looking at the list and Bob was sure he saw a momentary flash of apprehension in his expression. As quickly as it appeared it was gone, but in its place István suddenly looked startled, as though he had seen something terrible. Bob turned to see what had alarmed him. Peering at them through the window of Cloudland was a Rover in shorts and overcoat, and Bob recognised him as the Yugoslavian who had been searching for a horse. Miško Čurović spotted Bob and gave an excited wave. He strode to the entrance of Cloudland and the bell jangled as he entered.

'My most helpful friend,' he said. 'I got horse at the estate as you said. Thank you so much. I have been riding these last two days. Truly the best way to see your wonderful country.'

Aye, thought Bob, as long as the gamies and factors dinnae see you. 'Braw,' he said. 'We're just about to eat if you'd like to join us.'

'Are you sure?'

'Aye, there's plenty.' Bob stood up and the Yugoslav immediately took his seat next to Zoltán and István.

'Miško Čurović,' he said, 'from Yugoslavia.' He smiled broadly and pressed his hand towards first Zoltán and then István. Zoltán greeted him politely but stared at him as though puzzled. István shook hands in silence, giving only the merest inclination of his head, not making eye contact. Bob departed for the kitchen.

'The mad horseman from Yugoslavia's here,' he said to Annie. She peered round the door frame at him.

'Did he get his cuddy?'

'Aye, been ridin it for twa days.'

'In shorts? His thighs must be chafed to ribbons.'

'Must breed them tough in Yugoslavia.' Bob drained the boiled potatoes and mashed them as Annie cut the chicken pies into portions. Leslie drained the peas in a colander and the three ladled their produce onto a selection of warmed plates that mostly matched.

'Smells braw,' said Leslie.

'Magic ingredient,' said Bob. 'Nutmeg. Just a tiny pinch. Cannae beat it.'

They ferried the meals into the front and were greeted with a rousing cheer. The Rovers, tired and hungry after their excursion up Ben Chonzie, fell on the food with gusto and the main course was devoured quickly, followed by Annie's apple pie and custard. The café was alive with noise and bustle.

'That was superb,' said Miško. 'How lucky I was to be passing.'

'Lucky indeed,' said Zoltán. 'Did I not see you this morning as well, in our camp?'

Miško smiled, flashing his white teeth. 'I do not think so. This morning I was out on horseback.'

'This was very early. Six o'clock.'

Miško shook his head expansively. 'You must be mistaking me for someone else, my friend. I have a common face. A very plain man.'

A number of the Hungarians laughed at his self-deprecation but Bob noticed that neither Zoltán nor István joined in. There was a palpable tension surrounding these three men, their various utterances followed by silences just a fraction of a second too long. The way they looked at one another, tried to smile, engage, everything seemed slightly out of kilter. Bob felt awkward, as he always did when he sensed conflict. He was relieved to hear the door of Cloudland jangle open and looked up as a man peered around the door frame, fedora firmly fixed on his head, brown mackintosh belted around his waist.

'Andrew Wood,' he said. '*Moot Pictorial.*' I saw you boys as I was passing. Wondered if I could have a photograph for the paper?' The *Moot Pictorial* was the daily paper written on the Moot site and published each morning by the *Perthshire Advertiser* in Perth and distributed on site before seven o'clock. 'We're very keen to get photographs of the Rovers integrating with the locals, so this would be grand.'

'Come awa in,' said Bob.

Andrew Wood organised the men into two rows, one seated, one standing. Bob watched István, thought he looked uncomfortable. Zoltán stood next to Miško and, like Bob, appeared to be studying his man intently. Bob indicated to

Leslie and Annie to join them and they perched at the end of the back row self-consciously. Andrew took a couple of photographs and raised his fedora. 'It'll probably be in on Wednesday,' he said. 'Front page, if I get my way.' He made his farewells and the Rovers settled back, still digesting their meals.

Zoltán pointed to Bob's piano in the corner. 'Would it be possible to play something, please?' he said.

'Aye,' said Bob. 'Be my guest.' He opened the piano lid and set a chair in front of the piano and Zoltán took his seat.

'This is Lizst,' he said. '*Magyaroszág*'s most famous composer. This is the *andante sostenuto* from his *Piano Concerto in B Minor*. Do you know it?'

'I'm mair of a jazz man.'

He started to play, soft and slow, initially so quietly everyone had to strain to hear but gradually becoming louder as the tune asserted itself and took beautiful form. The Rovers and the Scots listened in silence. Zoltán was clearly an accomplished pianist and when he finished Bob led the applause.

'My,' he said, 'that piano's never been played as fine as that afore.'

'You play?' said Zoltán.

'No like that.'

'Play us something.'

'Go on, Bob,' said Annie, caressing his shoulder. Bob took Zoltán's place at the piano and stared at the back wall, creating a barrier between him and the world.

'This is the *Weeping Willow Rag*,' he said. The tune was slow and melancholy but the ragtime rhythm, steady, insistent, gave it a rolling certainty. It felt like life itself, Bob always thought, inevitable, unstoppable, full of minor key beauty and major key calamity. He played it through and by the time he was finished he had transcended Cloudland and entered his own world and the audience no longer existed.

67

He launched into *The Entertainer* and revelled, as he always did, at the way the same set of notes, the same style, the same composer could create two tunes so different from one another. Melancholy became joy. Hush, noise. Despair, hope. Music was what kept Bob Kelty sane, what kept him alive. Without it, he knew, there would be no Bob Kelty. There would be no point.

He finished the tune and his fingers rested on the keys of the piano. Behind him, Cloudland cheered. He turned as though suddenly remembering they were there.

'I think you were not telling the truth about the piano never having been played so well,' said Zoltán, smiling.

'Very impressive,' said István. 'Did I not see you playing bagpipes at the Moot, too?'

'Aye. And fiddle. And guitar.'

'And a brilliant chef! What can't you do?'

Bob couldn't decide whether István was being genuine or facetious. There was something about his expression – too smiling, too forced – that seemed false. He thanked him anyway.

'You must bring your fiddle to the Moot,' said Miško. 'In Yugoslav camp we have some excellent fiddle players. You could join us. Teach us some Scottish tunes.'

István drained his tea noisily. 'Yes indeed. You are not even a Rover and yet you are one of the best-known faces on the camp, I think. You get everywhere.'

'No everywhere,' said Bob. 'I havenae been to Loch More yet.' He studied István closely. 'I hear it's grand.' He paused. 'Especially at night.'

If he did have a secret, Bob thought, he concealed the fact well. There wasn't a flicker of emotion on his face. He made no reply. Instead Miško spoke.

'The water is very, very cold,' he said. 'I recommend you jump straight in. You get used to the cold quicker that way.'

'Aye, I'll maybe do that,' said Bob. 'What d'you think?'

He turned to István. István looked at Miško and then at Bob and pasted on his smile again.

'I am not a good swimmer,' he said.

The doorbell of Cloudland jangled once more and Abdalla strode in, his face set in his usual beaming smile. He gestured to Bob excitedly and said good evening to the room and navigated his way through the tables. He crouched down beside Bob.

'I have found something,' he said. 'I have been making enquiries.'

'Aye,' said Bob, rising and pointing to the kitchen. Abdalla, however, ploughed on.

'I find a tent. In the Norwegian camp.'

The effect on István was instant and unmistakable. With eyes wide open he stared at Abdalla, his face colouring. He fisted his right hand and then released it slowly. As he did so, his usual smile returned. He turned to a Rover at a neighbouring table and spoke to him in Hungarian, some form of small talk as though he were completely unconcerned, but it was too late. Bob had seen his reaction. He grabbed Abdalla's shoulder and stood up.

'Through the back,' he said and guided him into the kitchen. Annie greeted him with a broad smile, but immediately noticed the men's excited expressions. Bob looked back at the group he had just departed. István had regained his composure and was now speaking to Miško, who smiled politely at him as he played with a cigarette lighter. Zoltán was studying Miško intently.

'Did you see his expression?' Bob said to Abdalla.

'He seemed shocked.'

'He certainly was. As soon as you said "Norwegian". Tell me, what have you found?'

'I ask around. A couple of Norwegian boys I met the other day. They tell me. There is a tent. No one has slept in it for four days. Someone put it up but no one knows who he is.' He gestured expansively with his hands. 'Or where he is.'

'Is there stuff in the tent?'

'Oh yes. Clothes. Equipment.'

'Anythin that identifies who he is?'

'Nothing. They have checked three times now.'

Bob looked back outside again. István was staring at him. Zoltán was still staring at Miško.

'What do we do now?' said Annie.

'Speak to Geordie Macrae again.'

*

The Rovers were in fine spirits as they gathered their belongings and sauntered into James Square, preparing for the two mile walk back to the campsite. Miško walked ahead, bending into the slope. István speeded up and grabbed his elbow.

'What are you doing here?' he hissed.

'Orders.'

'What orders?'

'You don't need to know.'

'Was *he* orders? The Norwegian?'

Miško turned to him and smiled. 'I do not know what you are talking about,' he said. He pulled his elbow from István's grip and tapped his own forehead twice, then turned and walked away.

Tuesday 18th July

A Day of Inquisition

Annie and Bob talked tactics over breakfast. Their belief that the body was not that of a traveller had been hampered by the lack of any reasonable alternative, any missing person. Now, they had evidence of somebody who *had* apparently gone missing.

'And Norwegian,' said Annie, spreading butter on her toast. 'Norwegians have light-coloured hair. Our body was light-haired.'

'That could be a coincidence,' said Bob.

'Aye, it could. But it's still mair likely than the idea a blond tinker would set up camp on the Monzie estate, would mak a hash of erectin his tent, would light a fire inside the tent, bang his heid on a stane and fall into the fire and kill himsel.'

'When you put it like that ...'

'Even Geordie Macrae must see that.'

'Well, we can gie it a try.'

Breakfast concluded, Bob sat down at the telephone in the hallway and asked the operator to be put through to the Macraes' house in Longcauseway, Perth. Mrs Macrae answered, her telephone voice turning to ill-graced iciness when she heard it was Bob, of whom she had never tried to conceal her dislike.

'Hullo?' came Geordie's voice eventually. He sounded as

71

displeased as his mother.

'I'm askin you to open an investigation ...'

'Nice to speak to you again, too ...'

'It's ay a pleasure speakin to you, Geordie ...'

'It's no even half past seven yet, man.'

'I kent you're an early riser. Now, you need to open an investigation ...'

'I telt you I cannae do that.'

'We've identified a missin person.'

There was silence for a moment. Bob waited, hoping Geordie would take the bait.

'What missin person?'

Bob explained about the missing Norwegian. 'And they usually have light hair, like oor deid body. Which tinkers don't. Have you ever seen a blond tinker?'

'Alec Patterson.'

'Fae Blair? He's no blond, he's white. The man's seventy.'

'Have you an identity for this missin Norwegian?'

'No.'

'So how d'you ken he's missin?'

'He set up a tent four days ago and hasnae been seen since.'

'Maybe he's found himsel a lassie. Livin it up in Crieff.'

'Or maybe he's lyin in the mortuary in Perth.'

Geordie sighed. 'Bob, I cannae help you. I'm sorry. Juist let it go, man.'

'I cannae.'

'Let me explain ...'

'Geordie, save your breath to cool your porridge.'

Annie was seated on the top step of the stairs down to Cloudland, her chin resting in her hands. She shook her head when Bob hung up the telephone.

'Nothin?'

'Nothin.'

'What now?'

'Now? We need reinforcements.'

'Who?'

'Your man Brigadier Ross. You need to speak to him.'

'I do?'

'Well, I cannae. He's already got my cards marked.'

*

As Bob and Annie walked up the cinder path to the Moot site, they saw Sandy Disdain sitting on a dyke, smoking a cigarette, arms folded. He glowered at them in silence from beneath his deerstalker. Greetings were not on Sandy Disdain's list of approved niceties.

'What are you doin here?' asked Bob.

'Waitin for the day's collection of Rovers. Walk up Ben Lawers.' He nodded to a coach waiting in the car park, its engine running. 'What was the name of that bloke you're suspicious of? Hungarian or somethin?'

'István Kedály,' said Annie.

'Sure it's no Kedaly? Sandy pronounced it with three syllables, Ke-dah-lee.

'That's how you spell it. They pronounce it Ked-aye.'

'Bloody foreigners. Can they no speak properly? Well, he's noo on my list for the morn's trip. He was in the HQ tent this mornin, makin a richt scene, demandin to be let on it, even though he was telt the bus was fu.'

'How?'

'How should I ken?'

'Wha else is goin the morn?'

Sandy took a sheaf of papers from his inside pocket and opened them out. He pointed with a huge, grubby finger. 'Abdalla,' he said. 'And Jozef.' He stared at Bob. 'Coincidence, eh?'

'So he specifically wanted to go wi oor twa friends?'

'Seems like. There was space on the day's trip. Or the day efter. He could hae gone either of them days, but he wanted the morn.'

Bob looked across the camp towards the hills beyond. István Kedály was growing more suspicious by the day.

'Right,' he said. 'I'm goin the morn as well. Add me to your list.'

'It's fu. I've juist telt you that.'

'Surely you can find room for me?'

'No.'

The Rovers for that day's trip were beginning to arrive, and Sandy threw down his cigarette and walked off to meet them. Farewells, similarly, were outside his sensibilities. Annie and Bob watched as he climbed on the bus without speaking to anyone, then they walked uphill to the site. Bob kissed Annie outside the information tent.

'Good luck,' he said, and turned towards his canteen to see what damage James and the Meikle's Nook lads had wrought during breakfast.

Back in the information tent, Annie hung her swagger coat on the coat stand and made tea. The centre didn't open for half an hour and only she and the Brigadier had arrived. She poured two cups of tea and took them to the Brigadier's desk.

'I wanted to ask you somethin,' she said.

He looked her up and down and Annie knew he was appraising her attractiveness. Such things mattered, apparently.

'How intriguing,' he said finally. His eyes lingered on her chest. Instinctively, Annie drew her hand across it. His gaze didn't waver.

'I need your help.' She cursed herself. She didn't want to seem beholden to this man even if, realistically, she was. She didn't want him exerting any more power over her. 'My husband and I need your help.'

'I won't know if I can help you and your husband unless you tell me what it is you want.'

74

Annie lifted herself onto the balls of her feet for a moment and swung her arms behind her back. She took a deep breath and explained about the dead body, their conviction that he'd been murdered, the police's reluctance to investigate.

'We're sure the man's no a tinker. Everythin says he's no. And a local man wouldnae need to be campin, would he? That means he must be an outsider. And since we've thoosands of outsiders here, it seems logical that the deid man is someone fae the camp.'

'But why would one of the Rovers be in a tink's tent?'

'That we dinnae ken.'

'Pretty major flaw in your reasoning.'

'It's no a flaw. A flaw would mean our reasonin was wrong. This is juist a gap. Somethin that still needs to be explained. It doesnae prove anythin either way.'

'Alright, little lady, carry on.' Annie couldn't decide whether his raised eyebrow was patronising or lascivious. Either way, she hated it. Ross sat back and drank his tea, staring at her all the while.

'We've been doin some investigation, Bob and me and some friends fae the camp. Tryin to find if onyone was due here who hasnae turned up.'

'Ingenious. How did you go about that?'

Annie faltered. This was where she knew things might prove tricky. 'Speakin to the group leads for each delegation,' she said.

'I see. And how did you identify who they were?'

'We had a list.'

'And where did you get the list?'

Annie faltered again. 'Fae here.'

Ross nodded firmly as though this confirmed what he had suspected all along. 'That chap the other day ...'

'My husband.'

'Why didn't you tell me about this then?'

'Well, what we're doin is ... unofficial.'

'Illegal.'

'No. It's a genuine investigation and we're no doin anythin untoward. All of us who saw the scene, we're convinced ...'

'Stealing my information was illegal.'

'I'm sorry. We juist needed the names. For a good cause.'

'Very well.' Ross's tight expression gave no indication whether or not he had accepted the apology, or believed her story. 'From this information, have you gleaned something useful?'

'One of our friends has found out that a Norwegian Rover turned up on the first day, pitched his ain tent and hasnae been seen since.'

'And this would be the day you discovered the body?'

'Aye.'

'You think he's your man?'

'He had blond hair. Our deid body was blond.'

'Why would he pitch a tent in the camp and then go out and pitch another tent outside the camp?'

'It wasnae his tent. It was a tinker's tent.'

'So the tink's done him in?'

'We dinnae ken.'

Ross scowled. 'All supposition. No evidence.'

'Exactly. That's why we need your help.'

'How?'

'The man's face. He was badly burned on ae side but no on the other. We think we might be able to identify him, if we could somehow get a photograph of the missing Norwegian. See if it's the same person.'

'How do you propose to do that?'

'We'd have to go through official channels. To the Norwegian Rovers' organisation in Oslo. Request their assistance. I couldnae do that myself, obviously. But you ... as part of the Moot organisation ...'

'And why would I do this?'

'Because I'm convinced a man's been murdered. And it's

oor duty to find out wha he is. To tell his faimly. If you came across a dedd man on a battlefield, would you no want to find out wha he was? Report it? Let his faimly ken? Finish things respectful, like?'

Brigadier Ross, a veteran of Flanders, had seen enough dead men on battlefields, had seen bodies so maimed there was no earthly way of providing any identification, to know that what Annie was suggesting was not always possible. He had seen destruction. He had been to hell. Like most men of his generation, death remained a painful fact of life for Herbert Ross.

'This husband of yours, he spun me some ridiculous story about being an acquaintance of Lord Kellett.'

'Chairman of the Police Committee. And now the ARP.'

'You're telling me that's true?'

'Aye.' Lord Kellett was one of the most prominent men in Perthshire, Police Chairman when Victor Conoboy was an Inspector in the force and a good friend of Victor and his wife Bella. He had always looked out for Bob, too, for reasons Bob couldn't fathom.

Ross ran his finger across his moustache. 'Very well,' he said. 'I will telephone Lord Kellett this morning. If he confirms what you say, I'll assist with your investigation.'

Annie felt a mixture of exhilaration and dread. What if Lord Kellett didn't back them up? The nobility could be capricious. And Bob had once turned down Lord Kellett's offer to join the Perthshire Police. Had lost his temper and argued with him. Would the Lord bear a grudge?

'But I'll tell you this,' Ross went on, 'if he doesn't confirm what you say I'll make sure neither you nor your husband set foot in this camp again. And I'll have your husband prosecuted.'

'That winnae be necessary,' Annie said.

She just hoped that was true.

*

77

James Meikle was sweeping the inside of his Nook with a besom when Bob arrived.

'Too late for breakfast,' he said.

'Had it twa hours ago, man. Cauld porridge, straight fae the drawer.'

'Bloody teuchter.'

Bob explained about Abdalla's discovery of the missing Norwegian. 'I'm goin to see if I can hae a keek in the tent. See if I can see onythin. Comin?'

'They'll huv searched it already, surely?'

'Maybe so but – no to blow my ain trumpet – I once solved a murder and rape case by searchin a tent.'

'Come oan then, Sexton Blake.'

The morning was already warm. The campsite was quiet, most Rovers having already departed on their day's excursion. A peewit swung through the sky, green and blue, almost swifter than the human eye. Long grass beneath the trees swayed in the wind. There was a sigh in the treetops, a gentle wind blowing through the day. In the Netherlands area, three Rovers were putting the finishing touches to a half life-sized wooden windmill. Bob and James passed the French area, with the cathedral of Notre-Dame painted on the outside of every tent, and then the Polish area. A young man was rehearsing for a performance at the open session in the main auditorium on Sunday, singing an extract from the libretto of Paderewski's opera *Manru*.

Jozef called them over. 'This is Hildebrande,' he said, introducing them to the young man. 'From Pozńan. He's going to be a world-famous opera singer one day.'

When James explained their plan, Jozef insisted on joining them. Bob wasn't convinced this was the best idea, given Jozef's short temper, but he chose not to argue. On the way, he expanded on events the previous evening in Cloudland, István's suspicious behaviour, the way he reacted when Abdalla mentioned the Norwegian tent.

78

'I not like the sound of this man,' said Jozef.

'We've nae proof of onythin, mind,' said Bob warily.

There was a single Norwegian still in the Norway enclave, a middle-aged man, bespectacled, lamp post thin with a shock of greying, light brown hair flopping over his eyes. He wore a cool, blue-grey uniform with a yellow woggle and he greeted them cheerily.

'Are you the group leader?' Bob said.

'Knut Larsen. Pleased to meet you.'

Bob introduced himself and was met with cool politeness, a brisk handshake, business-like nod of the head. 'I'm a friend of Abdalla,' he continued.

'Abdalla! Is he not with you? What a wonderful man.' Bob was coming to realise that Abdalla's name was a tool that could fashion an opening in most situations. He allowed Knut Larsen to eulogise their friend some more, then came to the point.

'Abdalla mentioned you had a lad who appears to have gone missin?'

'Yes. A curious thing. He arrived. Pitched his own tent – and that is quite unusual, most Rovers share the communal tents put up by the organisers …'

'Why would he do that?'

'You tell me. Perhaps he's shy. Or snores a lot. He pitched his tent on Thursday morning, chatted to some of the boys, then went off on his own. He hasn't been seen since.'

'Do you know where he went?'

'I don't. He went in the direction of the main area the last time time I saw him.'

'What was his name?'

'Erling Hagen.'

'And do you know where he was from?'

'Alna. Just outside Oslo.'

'What did he look like?' said James.

'Norwegian.' Knut laughed. 'We all look the same,

79

people tell us. Blond. Worried. Complexion like a fish.'

James and Jozef laughed loudly.

'Can we see his tent?' Bob asked

Knut led them to the edge of the Norwegian enclave, to a single tent made of white canvas, pitched beside a hawthorn bush.

'Would you mind if we had a look?' said Bob.

'Why? Why are you interested in Erling?'

'Well, maybe nothin. We're actually lookin for another mystery man, in another tent we found a few days ago. But there's just a wee possibility they might be one and the same.'

'One person, two tents?'

'Maybe.' Bob hoped Knut didn't question him too closely because he had scant evidence to back up his theory. 'It's just a hunch.'

Knut shrugged, clearly not understanding. 'There's nothing much there anyway,' he said. 'We looked already, but help yourself.'

James gestured to the tent. 'On you go, Bob,' he said, 'let's see if the famous detective can work his magic again.'

Bob got on his knees and crawled inside the tent. Even this early in the morning, the air was growing stuffy. As Knut had said, the tent was almost empty. A sleeping bag was still rolled up, and a small rucksack sat upright beside it. Bob checked inside. Underwear, spare trousers, shirt, a toothbrush and toothpaste. This was a man travelling light. He would undoubtedly have kept money and valuables with him, but Bob was surprised his passport wasn't secreted in a pocket in the rucksack. He checked again to make sure. There was no requirement for him to carry a passport with him and Bob felt sure he would have left it securely in the tent. He looked around. There was nothing else. He scrambled back into the sunshine outside.

'Well?' said Jozef.

'Have you got your passport on you? Now?'

'No. It is in my tent.'

'What about you?' he said to Knut. 'Do you carry your passport with you when you're out and about?'

'No. Our instruction is not to. Mine is under my pillow.'

Bob frowned. Something felt wrong, but he couldn't see any meaningful pattern.

'Hello.'

István Kedály sauntered towards them, smiling. He reached out his hand and Bob shook it. Jozef did not. 'Did I not say last night,' he said to Bob, 'that you get everywhere on this site?'

'I could say the same about you.'

'I miss my trip this morning. My own stupid fault. I sleep in. So I have a day of leisure today.'

'You slept in? I heard you were up at HQ early on, makin a fuss …' Bob was about to mention the reason for the fuss, István booking a place on the trip tomorrow, but he looked at Jozef and decided it would be best if his excitable Polish friend remained unaware of that development.

'You hear everything, don't you?' said István.

'I try to. What brings you here?'

'Oh, I was going to look at the lake you mentioned last night. You made it sound very nice.'

'Loch More's that wey.' Bob hitched his thumb back the direction István had come.

'Then I shall return.' He looked around, studied the Norwegian flag billowing gently in the breeze. He pointed to it. 'This is the Norwegian area?' he said.

'Aye.'

'This is where you said there was a tent of a missing person. Last night. Is that right?'

Bob thought back to what Abdalla had said in Cloudland, before Bob took him into the back. "I find a tent. In the Norwegian camp." Wasn't that what Abdalla had said? Did he say anything about a missing person? Bob couldn't remember. Not for the first time in his life, he cursed his fallible memory.

'So this must be the tent,' continued István.

'Why you think that?' Jozef barked at him.

'Because Bob has just been in it. Why would he be in another man's tent, unless it was the one he was so interested in last night?'

'I wasnae the only one interested,' said Bob. 'So it seems.'

'Me?' said István, feigning innocence. 'I have no interest in such matters.'

'In that case,' said Jozef, advancing towards him, 'why you no leave?' He waved his arm menacingly in front of István's face. 'Go!' he shouted.

István smiled like a patient uncle indulging an over-excited nephew. He bowed his head and raised his palms towards Jozef. 'I go find the lake,' he said. 'Will be hot soon. Maybe I will even try a dip in the water.' He looked directly at Jozef. 'It does not do to get hot under the collar.' He turned and walked away jauntily. Bob glowered at Jozef.

'What?' said Jozef.

'Man, you dinnae half get your dander up easy.'

Jozef turned to James with a baffled expression.

James shrugged. 'What can I say? He's a teuchter. I dinnae understand what's he's on aboot half the time, either.'

*

As they walked past the arena, they noticed a new tent had been erected beside the dais on which the dignitaries had stood for the opening ceremony. Men prowled at the entrance, smoking pipes and frowning, large sets of earphones perched on their heads.

'BBC,' said James. 'They're goin to do a live recording of the afternoon concert. The Rovers tak it in turns to do a show every day in the arena. BBC's here for it the day.'

'What, as it happens?' said Bob. 'How do they do that?'

'God knows.'

They headed over for a better look. The men in earphones were bellowing something incomprehensible at each other and Bob wasn't sure if this was because of the earphones or if these were just their normal voices. A wooden plinth had been erected in the arena before the dais and half a dozen Rovers in Highland dress were preparing to do a demonstration of Highland dancing. The Glasgow Rovers Pipe Band, or at least half of them, were waiting to provide accompaniment. Behind them, on the edge of the arena, Zoltán Tóth was marshalling a group of around twenty of the Hungarian Rovers who were providing a concert of Hungarian folk songs after the dancing. István was not among them.

'I say,' said one of the BBC men. 'Are you James Meikle? Of Meikle's Nook?' His voice was impossibly posh. Bob felt himself bristle.

'Aye.'

'Thought I recognised your picture from the paper.' He waved a copy of the *Moot Pictorial*. Meikle's Nook had featured twice so far. 'Come in. We have five minutes to fill. We'll do an interview.' He looked at Bob and Jozef. 'You too.'

James rushed inside without further bidding and Jozef followed. Bob stood for a moment, while his mind invented every catastrophe that might befall him live on national radio.

'Come along,' said the BBC man, waving his arm like a school dominie remonstrating with a troublesome child. James was being fitted with a set of headphones and ushered into a seat beside another man in headphones. Next to him, sporting a giant moustache, was a man holding a new style telephone. In front of them was a round microphone, bigger than a human face. Another man was turning a knob on what looked to Bob like a chest of drawers but with the drawers

83

running vertically instead of horizontally. Behind him, yet another man was turning knobs on an instrument panel that was similar to Bob's wireless at home, but much larger. However they did a live broadcast, Bob reflected, it took a lot of them.

'On air,' the man with the telephone said.

'We have with us this afternoon Mr James Meikle, famous in these parts as Meikle of Meikle's Nook. Good afternoon, Mr Meikle.'

'Hullo.'

'I understand you were responsible for erecting the majority of the tents on site?'

'Aye, me and the Pollokshields lads.'

'That must have been quite an undertaking?'

'Ach, you just start wi the first wan and keep goin till you've done the last.'

'And you also dug most of the latrines?'

'Aye.'

'A site this size, that must have been jolly hard work.'

'Well, we had Sir Lancelot to help us.'

'Who's Sir Lancelot?'

'No who. Whit. Sir Lancelot is David Maitland-Makgill-Crichton's jalopy. A 1909 Sunbeam, 4 cylinder. Some car, by the way. He's lent it to the Rovers for the week. We used it to carry aw the gear.'

'Very beneficial, I'm sure. And I believe you also offer nourishing breakfasts and dinners at Meikle's Nook for the men?'

'Aye, but we wash oor hands first.' The interviewer laughed politely, clearly not fully understanding the joke. 'And see him?' James nodded to Bob. 'He does the best scran on site.'

'Really? And who is this gentleman?' The man gestured to Bob to speak into the central microphone.

'Eh, Bob Kelty.'

'And you're a Rover?'

'No, no, I'm fae Crieff. I hae a café in town and I'm runnin one of the caterin tents on site here.'

'And how are you finding the week so far?'

'Busy.'

'What's been the most exciting part so far for you?'

'Well, excitin's maybe not the word, but findin a dead body on the first day was certainly out of the usual.'

The BBC reporter stared at him, aghast. 'A dead body? On the site?'

'No, just up the road there.' He pointed in the direction of the Knock, saw the microphone, realised the ineffectiveness of his gesture and shrugged.

The reporter's expression had shifted to something nearer panic. He turned to Jozef. 'And what is your name?' he said.

'I am Jozef Kawala, from Danzig.'

'I can see, from your colourful uniform, you are a Rover. How long have you been here?'

'Since Thursday. I was with Bob when we find the body. We think it suspicious, for sure, but your police, they not interested.'

The reporter pawed at his headphones as though they were stabbing him through the ear. 'I think we'll go back to the studio in Glasgow until the afternoon performance is due to begin,' he said. He pulled off the headphones and rose to his feet in front of Bob. 'What the hell do you think you're playing at?' he shouted at him.

'What? You asked me a question. I answered it. What more d'you want?'

'I'll kindly ask you to leave. All of you.'

James removed his headphones, his shoulders heaving with laughter, as he and Jozef and Bob were bustled out of the tent. They emerged into sunshine so bright it made them blink. James let out a roar and clapped Bob's back.

'Christ, if it's no Jozef rilin people, it's you. Right pair of wallopers you are, eh?'

They headed back to Meikle's Mount. One of the BBC men watched them until they were out of sight. Frowning, he returned inside the BBC tent.

*

The telephone in the information centre rang and Annie rushed to answer it.

'I have a call for Brigadier Ross from Lord Kellett,' the operator said. Annie's heart lurched.

'Grand,' she said. 'Put him through. I'll get the Brigadier.' She heard the connection being made. 'Lord Kellett?' she said. 'Annie Kelty here. I'll just get Brigadier Ross for you.'

'Are you two up to your necks in intrigue again?' Lord Kellet's voice did not sound angry, at least.

'We think there might be something important,' she said. 'We'd appreciate your help, my Lord.' She went in search of Brigadier Ross and found him outside, smoking a cigarette. 'Lord Kellett's returned your call,' she said. Ross threw his cigarette onto the grass and strode inside. Annie stubbed it out with her shoe and followed.

'Lord Kellett,' Ross boomed. 'Thank you for returning my call and giving me your valuable time. I know you must be up to your neck in ARP work. I have a very quick question to ask you.' He outlined Bob's and Annie's story of the burned-out tent and the dead man and there was silence as he listened to Lord Kellett's response. Ross's face was impassive.

'I see,' he said. 'That's most helpful. That gives me everything I need to know. Thank you again for your time, my Lord.' He hung up and stared ahead.

'Well?' said Annie. She tried to interpret what Ross's stern expression might mean.

'Lord Kellett confirms that what you're doing is not any part of an authorised police investigation.' Annie's head throbbed with tension. Her palms were sweating and her fingers tingled.

'However,' Ross continued, 'he also said that if Bob Kelty was investigating something, that means something needs to be investigated. Spoke very highly of him.' He paused. 'And you.'

Annie clapped her hands with relief. 'Oh my,' she said. 'So will you help us?'

'What do you need me to do?'

*

Eight o'clock, and Bob, Annie and Leslie Comer sat in Cloudland drinking tea. Bob and Annie had just returned from the Moot, and Leslie was enjoying a seat after a frantic afternoon and early evening in Cloudland, feeding the sundry Rovers who had alighted from buses outside the Drummond Arms. Today, around twenty Indian Rovers, most in coloured turbans, had crowded into the café and their infectious good humour and incessant chatter made Leslie forget how weary she was. Now that they were gone and the day's work was done, fatigue had swept over her. Annie too, her feet swollen and ankles puffy after a day mostly spent standing, was slumped in her chair.

'So the Brigadier's goin to help?' said Leslie.

'Aye, he's sent a telegram to the Norwegian Rover Association to ask for their assistance. Send us a photie of the missing lad.'

'It'll tak a few days, mind, but it's grand news,' said Bob. As he was about to take a sip of tea, there was a loud knock on the door of Cloudland.

'We're shut,' said Bob, but he rose stiffly and opened the door. Standing before him was Bailie Bruce, the number two public official in town behind Provost Hunt, a short and amiable man with a tidy moustache and a combover hairstyle even more drastic than Bob's. Bob was on speaking terms with him from his voluntary work with the Air Raid Precaution which had been set up by the Bailie the previous year. He invited him in.

'Mrs Kelty, Mrs Comer,' said Bailie Bruce. 'I'll no detain you long.' He declined a cup of tea and sat at an adjoining table. 'You were on the wireless earlier,' he said to Bob.

'I was, aye. Up at the Moot. It's amazin what they can do, nooadays.'

'Is it no just? But you've caused a wee bit of consternation.'

'Aye?'

'Aye. The polis are fair vexed. Sergeant Rudd's been on at me. No a happy man.'

'He seldom is.'

'That's true. The gout's a terrible thing. But the day he's *very* unhappy. Wi you.'

'I have that effect on the polis.'

'Why did you say it?'

'What, that we found a body? Because we did.'

'It's a polis matter. You shouldnae be gabbin aboot that on the wireless.'

'Either it's a crime, in which it's in the public interest to talk aboot it, or it isnae a crime, in which case there's nothin wrang wi talkin aboot it.'

'Or … the nature of the incident is still to be determined.'

Bob raised an eyebrow. 'You mean they're still investigatin it? That's news to us.'

'I'm no sayin anythin. I don't know anythin. But I do know the polis arenae happy. And neither is the Provost. The Moot is the biggest thing in Crieff in decades. We've another week to go, and people are comin in their thoosands to see it. I've never seen the toon this busy. We cannae hae anythin tarnishin the Moot or affectin its success. It's vital for the toon.'

'Anythin? Even a murder?'

'Wha said anythin aboot a murder?'

'The man didnae clobber himsel ower the heid wi a stane.'

'I've no idea the ins and outs of this. I trust the polis to have investigated properly, and if they tell me there's nothin of concern then there's nothin of concern.'

'Even if there is?'

Bailie Bruce gave an exasperated shake of his head. 'Listen Kelty, you're a grand chap but sometimes you can be a richt scunner. The Provost's asked me to ask you – in the firmest possible way – to keep oot of this from now on.' He rose and picked his hat from the table and placed it on his head. 'Tak a tellin, son,' he said. 'You've no long joined the ARP. You wouldnae want anything to spoil that, would you?'

Bob studied the Bailie. He was a good man, kind and generous, and passing on idle threats clearly sat ill with him. 'No offence Bailie, because I like you weel enough, but see next time the Provost asks you to do his dirty work, tell him to come and do it himsel.'

The Bailie shook his head. He raised his hat to the ladies. 'I'll see mysel oot.'

They watched him leave and turned to one another.

'For somethin that isnae a crime, they're awfae nervous aboot it,' said Annie.

'Are they no juist?'

Wednesday 19ᵗʰ July

A Day of Attack

The Alexander's bus was waiting in the car park at the foot of Monzie Castle estate when Bob arrived at eight-thirty. Abdalla was already on board and Miško Čurović was about to embark when he saw Bob coming behind him.

'Are you joining us today?' Miško said.

'I hope so,' Bob replied.

Miško clapped his shoulder. 'I am happy to give up my horse for the day,' he said. 'To tell the truth, I have a sore arse. Is that the right word?'

'Well, maybe don't say it to the minister,' laughed Bob. Even this early, the sun was growing hot. There was no wind. The ascent of Ben Lawers was going to be thirsty work. Bob had been brought up a country lad, working the horses on the farms, but since he moved to Perth aged twelve and then Crieff just over two years ago, he'd become less used to outdoor exercise. Soft, he described himself to Annie. Noticeably, she hadn't argued. He paused at the entrance to the bus.

'May I come on board?' Bob turned. Standing behind him was István Kedály. Although watching this man was the reason Bob was here, he still felt a jolt of apprehension on seeing him. *He could be a murderer.* István fixed him with a supercilious smile. He had a rucksack on his back and new-looking hiking boots. He was short and thin and weaselly and his posture was crabbed. Bob got the impression that, like himself, István was not a seasoned hiker. He stood aside and watched as István climbed aboard and sat on one of the few remaining empty seats and stared out of the window at the castle in the foreground.

'Hoi,' came a voice from behind him and he turned to see Sandy Disdain striding towards him, cigarette in mouth, deerstalker on his head. As usual, he was frowning.

'What did I tell you?' he said. 'There's nae room on the bus for you.'

'I'm just wee.'

'And I'm just tellin you, we're fu.'

'Come on, man.'

Sandy stood his ground, scowling. Bob looked back at the packed bus, and then at Sandy, understanding finally that this was not a man given to changing his mind. 'You're a hard man,' he said. He stared into his eyes, one final attempt at exhortation. No response. Accepting defeat, Bob tugged at Sandy's sleeve and drew him away from the bus.

'You win,' he said. 'But you need to keep an eye on István. There's somethin queer aboot him.' He explained how István had conveniently turned up yesterday when they were at the missing Norwegian boy's tent. 'And now he's here …'

'Keepin an eye on you lot …'

'Seems like. Wants to see what we're up to.'

'And how much you ken.'

'Which, fortunately for him, isnae awfae much.'

The bus was filling up rapidly. Jozef approached, smiling broadly, and he was about to board when he spotted István through the window.

'What is that man doing here?' he hissed at Bob. In an instant, he appeared to have become furious.

'On a day trip, same as you …'

'I don't trust this man …'

'Just leave him be. Please.'

Jozef muttered to himself and punched his fisted hand into the palm of his other hand. He clambered on board and took the seat nearest the driver and turned and glared at István. Bob sighed.

'Keep your eye on him an aa.'

*

Ten minutes later, Bob waving them off, the bus turned out of the car park and began the steady ascent through the Sma Glen towards Amulree and Aberfeldy and on to Kenmore. Heather blanketed the hillside, patches coming into bloom, pale pink flowers rising up the stems. Loch Tay was still and dark in the morning sun as they skirted its edge as far as Kiltyrie before turning right onto a road that was little more than a rough track. The bus groaned and began to tilt to left and right as they navigated the rutted ground. They rolled to a halt as the expletives of the driver, Jimmy Wright, resounded the length of the bus. One by one, the Rovers disembarked, grabbing their rucksacks and looking around wide-eyed at the expanse of mountains and valleys surrounding them.

'You can come wi us, if you want,' Sandy said to Jimmy.

'No, you're fine, son. I need to cut my toenails.'

The Rovers congregated around Sandy, anxious to be off. Jozef was still glowering at István, who was taking in the scenery, unconcerned. Abdalla stood next to Miško, chatting mildly.

'Right,' Sandy said, 'I'm sure you're all used to hikin in your ain countries, but stay wi me and dinnae wander off. The weather can turn in an instant up on the mountain. It can be beautiful one minute and you cannae see your hand in front of your face the next. Bide thegither. Stay together, I mean.'

'Thank you,' said Miško. 'Sometimes, I think you Scotch are more difficult to understand than foreign people speaking

English.'

'We're no speakin English,' said Sandy. 'We're speakin Scots. Different language aathegither.'

He marched uphill, bending into the slope, arms pistoning, his strides long and regular. This was a man in his natural habit, that much was evident. They made steady progress, the lower slopes gentle and easy and the Rovers chatting amiably amongst themselves. As they made their ascent, Sandy stopped at various points to show them items of interest.

'Dung beetle,' he pointed out, indicating a round, black insect perched on a ball of sheep droppings, its black carapace gleaming in the sunshine. 'See that yellow flower, that's saxifrage. Grows near streams, so if you're ever needin water, look oot for it.' And right enough, a few feet away the tiniest stream trickled down the mountainside. At one point, he stopped and gestured excitedly to a small clump of delicate, pale-blue flowers colonising an area of exposed stone. 'That's alpine forget-me-not,' he said. 'Forget-me-nots are ten a penny, but the alpine is very rare. I've only ever seen it a puckle times, mysel.'

They walked on and the way became steeper and stonier, the Rovers reduced, at times, to scrambling on their hands and knees. They were all relieved when they came to a gentler area of marshland. Sandy pointed to a peak that looked impossibly distant.

'Up there, that's Ben Ghlas. It's a Munro in its own right. We have to climb that to get to Ben Lawers. Be there in aboot an hour.' He looked at the reddened faces of some of the Rovers and laughed. 'Maybe,' he added. He walked on.

For the first hour, Jozef and István studiously ignored one another. Jozef took up the rear and István tracked Sandy at the front but, as they skirted a steep expanse, István slowed and walked alongside Jozef. 'I think maybe I annoyed you yesterday,' he said. He offered him a cigarette but Jozef declined. 'I did not mean to be rude or cause a fight. I was just curious. My mother always says I am too nosy for my own good. I mean nothing by it. I did not mean to upset you or Bob.'

Jozef studied the ground in front of him, the heather and moss and sedge. He wanted to shut István out but, in truth, his tempers disappeared almost as quickly as they appeared and he could never stay angry with anyone for long. 'Is okay,' he said.

'If I may ask, why are you interested in a missing Norwegian?'

Jozef pondered a response. 'We want to make sure he's okay.'

'But you were already looking for someone else who was missing before this Norwegian boy?'

'No.'

'Then how did you find out about the Norwegian boy?'

'That's Abdalla for you. He get everywhere.'

István drew on his cigarette and studied the glowing ember. 'I wish you luck looking for your missing people,' he said.

'Missing person.'

'Only one missing person?'

'Only one.'

Ahead of them was a stand of alders. A full sun was shining directly above them, making the trees appear the blackest black. In the middle of verdant countryside beneath such a bright sky, the effect was mesmeric, as though the place was some form of alien portal planted in the landscape. Jozef looked at István, tried to understand the man.

'Why are you so interested in what we're doing?' he said.

István shrugged and gave a brash laugh. 'Everyone likes a mystery.'

'Do they?'

'They do. And thank you. By asking, you've confirmed

you are doing something, you men.'

Jozef felt his temper rise once more. 'Yes. And you confirmed you have an interest in us. What is that, eh?' He strode on, leaving István behind, then stopped and turned back to him.

'I'm watching you,' he said.

*

The Moot campsite was quiet, with the majority of Rovers already embarked on one of the daily excursions. When all of the Hungarian contingent had departed, Zoltán Tóth made a quick and fruitless search of István Kedály's tent, then walked uphill, past Meikle's Nook, past the painted Loch Ness Monster, upwards almost as far as the tree line, where the Yugoslavian Rovers were camped. In so doing, he was retracing his steps of the previous evening, after nightfall, when he had followed Miško Čurović from the main ring where Australian Rovers had been performing their Corroboree and, unseen, had watched him entering his tent. Zoltán looked around now, reassured himself that he was once more unobserved, and crawled into Miško's tent.

He did not know what he was looking for, but he felt sure he would uncover something unusual about this man. In real life, Zoltán was a solicitor, increasingly busy representing Jewish people against whom there was rising animosity in a country that was drifting steadily rightward. His years of legal training had taught him that coincidences which came in threes should be regarded with great suspicion. First, a stranger called István Kedály had arrived in his group, his accreditation all seemingly correct but not included in the documentation with which Zoltán had been provided as group leader. Then, a stranger stood beneath an oak tree and watched the Hungarian encampment for a full half hour the following morning, just after dawn. And then that selfsame person, Miško Čurović, chanced on the Hungarian

Rovers as they dined in Cloudland, wangled an invite to join them and proceeded to spend the evening talking to István Kedály. Two strangers. Acting as though they didn't know one another. Both noticeably uncomfortable in each other's presence. Conspicuously polite. Something wasn't right.

He searched the tent quickly. There was nothing under the pillow or in the sleeping bag. A rucksack was propped against the side of the tent – a greenhorn mistake no seasoned Rover would make because, if it rained, the rucksack would get wet – and he dragged it onto the sleeping bag, opened it and rummaged inside. Trousers, shirt, underwear, a wallet containing English pounds, Serbian dinars and, beneath them, a bundle of German Reichsmarks. Zoltán counted them – 100 Reichsmarks, a huge amount of money, far more than Miško had in pounds or dinars, currencies that would have seemed to be of most use to him. Behind the currency was one half of a postcard that had seemingly been ripped in two, featuring a street corner in what looked like a major city, with a five-storey building occupying both streets. Written on it was "Ecke Seilerstraße und ...". Ecke meant "corner of" but the name of the second street was presumably on the missing right-hand portion of the postcard. Zoltán studied it for a moment, wondering why anyone would use such a prosaic image for a postcard, and why it should be ripped in two. He replaced the money and card and dug deeper into the rucksack, feeling an oblong object, small and compact and metallic. He pulled it out and held it in the palm of his hand, a tiny camera about the size of a packet of cigarettes. On the back it read "Minox Riga". Beside the camera in the rucksack was a roll of film, impossibly small, looking like a set of miniature binoculars. Zoltán had never seen anything like it. He replaced the camera and film in the rucksack and searched further but found nothing else of interest. No passport. Nothing which mentioned his name, or his background.

'Who are you?' Zoltán said.

*

During her mid-morning break, Annie sauntered through the camp to the *Moot Pictorial* office. She saw in the distance, trailing morosely behind her father, Mary Kemp, and she shouted but Mary either didn't hear or feigned deafness. Annie went inside the office and bought three copies of the *Moot Pictorial*.

'My picter's in it,' she explained to the lad behind the counter.

'Can I hae your autograph?' he joked.

Annie opened the paper and there, on page five, was the photograph from Cloudland on Monday evening, Annie and Leslie at the rear like afterthoughts, and Bob standing beside Zoltán Tóth and István Kedály and the mad horseman, Miško Čurović.

'Looks like the photographer lad didnae get us on the front page efter all,' she said.

'If it was up to me,' said the lad, staring at her up and down, 'I'd hae had you on the front page and no mistake.'

'Ach, awa wi you.'

*

The high summer air all around had a freshness, a lightness, that didn't exist lower down, in the towns, the streets, a freshness that made you conscious of every breath cycling through your body. As Sandy and the Rovers pressed on, Perthshire lay in beauty around them, serene like the touch of perfection. Spread of mountains, the noble loch, field on field, moor on moor, birds above, predators hovering, peewits coasting, the hum of existence. Pulse of wind, growing stronger. Days like this should last forever. They marched on. Ben Ghlas was reached.

'Well done, boys,' said Sandy. 'You've climbed your first

Munro.'

'What is Munro?' asked Abdalla.

'Mountains in Scotland over three thousand feet are called Munros. There's nearly three hundred of them.'

'How high is this?'

'About three thousand six hundred. Ben Lawers is four thousand. Over there.' He pointed eastward to a nipple-topped peak in the near distance.

'Where exactly are we?' said Abdalla studying the canvas of life surrounding them.

'Loch Tay's ahint that peak. It goes up to Kenmore. Then Aberfeldy. Then you're gettin towards the Cairngorms. If you think this is high, try the Cairngorms.' He sat on the heather, legs stretched wide apart. 'We'll bide here a while,' he said. 'Catch your breath. It's another hour to the summit of Lawers.'

He sat on a patch of heather and lit a cigarette. Until now, the weather had been perfect but, as they sat enjoying the view, a fierce wind started gusting every thirty seconds or so. Sandy looked to the east, where the weather was coming from. Abdalla crouched next to him.

'In Egypt,' he said, 'we have desert. This ...' He gestured around him. 'This is like we have climbed to heaven. How lucky you are to live here, my friend.'

Sandy inhaled from his cigarette and nodded in agreement. The view was, indeed, extraordinary but he had other things on his mind. István was seated beside Miško and Jozef twenty yards down the slope. An uneasy conversation was taking place, no eye contact, long pauses after each utterance. Sandy, a man used to conflict, recognised the tension between the men.

He stood up and stretched his back, 'Right,' he said. 'On we go. It'll be three before we get to the top of Lawers. Six afore we're back at the bus.'

'Sandy, what is this plant, please?' Abdalla pointed to a

carpet of tiny, deep red flowers threaded through a moss-covered stone at his feet. Sandy bent down and studied them for a moment.

'Dwarf willow. One of the smallest woody plants you can get. Only grows on high ground like this.'

A single cloud passed in front of the sun and the warmth of the day instantly dissipated. A solitary shadow crossed the valley below, the patchwork of fields and moors falling into and then sliding out of momentary adumbration. Sandy looked back the way they had come. Cloud was building and it was being driven towards them by an easterly wind that was growing ever more insistent.

'You think it will rain?' Abdalla asked.

'No. They're no rain clouds. But they're gey low. They'll be on top of us by the time we make the summit.'

'Do not say that. We have not come all this way to not see a view at the end of it.'

'Aye well. The quicker we march, the sooner we get there.'

They made the summit a little before three, tracked all the way, as though in a race, by billowing cloud. The wind was distinctly cool on their faces. The Rovers looked around them in wonder. Abdalla inhaled a lungful of fresh air. Miško smiled at István. István looked away. Jozef glowered at him, and then at Miško. Sandy watched all three.

'Enjoy the view,' he said. 'In aboot ten minutes that cloud'll be on us and you'll no see a thing.'

'Will it be dangerous?' said István.

'No, once we're on the way doon we'll soon dip below the cloud level again.'

'This is the most beautiful thing I have ever seen,' said Abdalla.

'Aye,' said Sandy. 'Think of all these fools and warmongers doon there. If they'd just come up here and look around them, see the beauty of this world, understand how small we are, they'd soon stop their bloody nonsense.'

As Sandy predicted, the cloud grew thicker. Wisps floated in the air around them. Abdalla tried to capture them but they disappeared into nothingness in his hands. The light dimmed, like an afternoon in October. Before long, they were enveloped by cold and damp and cloying cloud. Along with it came a silence that was almost physical in its intensity.

'I remember once,' said Miško, 'many years ago, when I was only a boy, and my younger brother would have been maybe seven, eight years old. We were hiking in the Carpathian Mountains, my mother and father and Dragan and me. My father liked to do that kind of thing. All of a sudden, the cloud came down, just like this, and we could not see a foot in front of ourselves. And we were on the side of the mountain, sheer drop on one side, hundreds of feet. We walk very slowly, and it seem to take hours. After a while, Dragan starts to chant his name over and over, "Dragan, Dragan, Dragan." And my mother, she say to him, "Dragan, why you do this?" And Dragan say: "Mummy, stop talking. This is my dream, you can't be in my dream." He was so scared he convinced himself none of it was real and he was only dreaming. His way of coping with the fear. To this day, he still does not believe he was ever on that mountain.'

'No a bad approach,' said Sandy. 'Best be gettin doon noo, though. There's nothin to see onywey. Just ca canny aabody. Be careful. Watch where you're puttin your feet. We'll be oot of this in ten minutes.'

It was fifteen minutes – and a very long fifteen minutes – before they dropped beneath the cloud level and the valley returned to view, colours now muted compared to earlier without the brightness of the sun. Somehow, that made the scene even more beautiful. Less gaudy, quieter, unassuming. A single train of cloud, perhaps thirty feet wide and a hundred feet long, was settled a few hundred yards to their right but below them. It looked strangely substantial, quite unlike what they had been walking through. Sandy wondered at being able to look down on something which was supposed to be above you. Perspectives. Impressions.

He made a point of walking alongside István. There had been no incident so far, but Sandy was conscious of how often István seemed to talk to Miško, and the efforts Miško made to avoid conversation. They were an odd couple, for sure. Sandy and István walked in silence until, as they slowed to find a way through some stonier ground, they were joined by Jozef.

'It is strange,' Jozef said to István, 'how you keep appearing. At the tent yesterday morning. Now here. It feels like you are following us.'

'Yesterday, I was just passing. Today, I booked my place like everyone else.'

'Why this trip? Why not any other?'

'I sometimes get sick travelling on buses. I wanted somewhere not too far away.'

'Ben Chonzie is closer than Lawers,' said Sandy.

'I did not know that.'

'And why today?' Sandy continued. 'Today's trip was already full. Other days had spaces. But you insisted on today. Why?'

István smiled and shrugged. 'I saw Abdalla's name. He is a good man. I am shy, I don't make friends easily, so I thought I would join Abdalla's group.'

'Why not stay with your Hungarian friends?'

'You heard Lord Somers at the opening. Talk to each other. Learn from each other. That's what I try to do.'

Everything István said seemed plausible, yet doubt still filled Sandy's mind. There was something about the man, something untrustworthy. Sandy, a solitary man, did not often consider the motives of other people, but with István he had no choice. And he could tell, from the expression on his face, that Jozef was thinking the same thing. Sandy tensed, aware of Jozef's quick temper. Indeed, in a mere instant he could see anger overtaking the man's features.

'I do not believe you,' Jozef said. 'You are a liar.'

'I am sorry you think this.'

Jozef grabbed István's lapel and swung him around. He punched him hard on the jaw, the sound echoing around the mountainside. Before István could react, he punched him again and this time István staggered and tried to squirm free of Jozef's grip. He flailed at Jozef and caught his shoulder, then rose up and punched his face.

'Stop it,' Sandy shouted. He forced his way between the combatants and separated them, glowering at each in turn. Blood was oozing from Jozef's nose. István's cheek was reddening. He would have a black eye by nightfall.

'Keep that man away from me,' István said. 'Crazy Polack.'

'Belt up,' said Sandy. 'Walk on. Out the front. And you ...' He turned to Jozef. 'You stay at the back wi Abdalla. Like a pair of bairns, fightin in the playgroond.' He adjusted his deerstalker and strode down the hill after István.

The Rovers proceeded downhill in silence, the bonhomie of the day broken. Abdalla clapped Jozef's shoulder and smiled. Jozef, already ruing his outburst, smiled back. Miško speeded up until he reached István's shoulder. István glared at him and carried on walking.

'You cannot go around causing scenes like this,' Miško said. 'You know this.'

'I did nothing. He attacked me.'

'You must have given some cause. Even Poles don't hit people for no reason.'

István strode on for some moments, his irritation growing. '*You* are the reason,' he said.

'Me? I've never spoken to the man.'

'He thinks I'm involved with the missing man.'

'What missing man?'

'You know what missing man. The Norwegian.'

'That's twice you've mentioned him. How do you know about that?'

István laughed. 'It's my job to know.'

Miško stopped and grabbed his arm. 'It is not your job to keep tabs on me, my friend. We are on the same side.'

'Are we?'

'You know we are.'

'I know what side I'm on. I know what side you say you're on.'

'And they are the same.'

'We'll see.'

'What do you mean?'

'I have made contact with Uncle.'

'You are a bigger fool than I thought.'

'I'm a fool? I'm not the one killing people on foreign soil.'

'What have you said to Uncle?'

'I asked them if they know whether friend Miško might have another Uncle. An *Onkel*, maybe.'

'You think I'm a double agent?'

'How else to explain your behaviour? Or are you just incompetent, my friend?'

Miško let go of István's arm and stood back. He appraised him, as though trying to determine whether he had spoken the truth. 'You lie,' he said. 'You would not contact Uncle. Not here, in the field. London doesn't like that. Only in emergencies.'

'And you think this isn't an emergency? A dead man?'

'Emergency? No. The damage of war.'

'We are not yet at war, my friend.'

Miško laughed. 'Of course we are. To the death.' He broke his gaze and strode down the hill. István watched him go, then followed, more slowly.

*

That evening, they gathered on the steps of the Murray Fountain, Bob and Annie, Sandy, Mary Kemp, James, Jozef and Abdalla, with sundry others from Crieff and from the Moot, forty or more people plucked from their day-to-day existence and the threat of war and the blight of poverty, forty or more people released for an hour or two from reality and given licence to enjoy the moment. Pipey Oldham, friend of Sandy and Bob and stalwart of the Pipe Band, took the lead, becoming *compère* for the evening, ensuring everyone joined the celebration. Into the mild summer evening they played music and sang songs and told stories. They heard about Egypt and Danzig, and a song from Nigeria raised hairs on the napes of every listener. *Green Grow the Rashes O, Danny Boy*, songs in languages so exotic they'd never been heard in Crieff before. Bonds were made, friendships cemented. Sandy Disdain and Mary Kemp side-by-side. Glancing eyes on glancing eyes, shy smile, gentle frown. And Bob and Annie, hand-in-hand, drinking the joy of the evening, gazing down at Cloudland, knowing this was now, this was them, this was theirs forever and ever.

This is the way that love grows. Jock Tamson's bairns an aa an aa.

Thursday 20th July

A Day of Illustration

Sandy attacked his bacon butty and swallowed it in three mouthfuls, almost without chewing. He hadn't eaten the previous day, and he wasn't sure if he'd had anything the day before either. Bob took his plate, made him another and placed it before him.

'Hungry?' he said.

'Peckish.'

Bob sat astride a wooden chair and pulled his pipe from his pocket. 'You're sure it wasnae István wha started it?'

'They had some argy-bargy early on and Jozef stormed aff, yellin "I'm watchin you". Then later they started again. Jozef just went for him. Accused him of bein a liar and punched him ower the heid.'

'And István didnae do onythin suspicious?'

'No that I saw.' Sandy wiped his mouth with the back of his enormous hand. 'I spoke to Jozef efterwards and he said that Ivan was pumpin him for information. Aboot the tent. Why we were interested.'

Bob pulled out his matches and tamped down his pipe. 'That's it, you see. István, he's just too interested.'

'You could say that aboot maist of the boys on the walk. Abdalla. Jozef. Especially Jozef. You say Ivan's too interested in all this. Strikes me Jozef is an aa. And he's got a hellish temper on him.'

'He was there when we found the body. That *would* make him interested.'

'And maybe suspicious.'

'Why would a killer lead people to where he'd done the crime?'

'The crime didnae happen there, mind? We found another bloody stane on the path. And it was *you* wha took them that wey, no him. Think aboot it – he could be playin us for fools.'

Bob lowered his pipe. That was true. The first day, when Jozef and Abdalla were looking for firewood, it was Bob who had taken them up the Knock path. Jozef had been heading in the opposite direction.

'And,' continued Sandy, fishing in his jacket pocket for his cigarettes, 'wha is it that's ay talkin about Ivan, bad-moothin him?'

'Jozef.'

'Jozef.'

'I suppose you're richt. The trouble is, we've nae idea what the motive is. And until we can identify wha the body is, we've nae wey of finding oot the motive. So we're stuck.'

*

'Hello.'

Mary Kemp looked round in surprise. She was holding her dad's post office bicycle on the Moot concourse outside the information centre, where Pat the postie had delivered that morning's post. That had been quarter of an hour ago and it seemed that a cup of tea had been offered and accepted, leaving Mary on her own outside. This wasn't how she had planned to spend her day off.

'You look scunnert.'

That strange poacher man with the deerstalker hat was towering over her. He'd been looking at her the previous evening, at the Murray Fountain and it had made her feel strange. Mary gave him a brief smile. 'Waitin for my faither,' she said.

'Aye, that's faithers for you,' said Sandy. 'Ay waitin for them to do somethin or other.'

'Story of my life.'

'You should strike oot, leave hame.'

'I wish.' Mary didn't wish at all, but she wanted to sound grown up. She worked as a maid in Dr McNeill's house on Turretbank Road and the only thing she didn't like about it was that her hours were usually twelve midday until nine in the evening, which meant that her father regularly dragooned her into helping him with his morning rounds. At seventeen, she wasn't a lassie but she didn't feel like an adult. The thought of marriage, leaving the family home, being a responsible person, terrified her. She looked up at Sandy Disdain, his deep-set eyes. He was frowning at her again. Maybe that was just the way he looked. Maybe he wasn't always angry.

'I thocht you were runnin bus tours up Ben Lawers this week?' she said.

'Supposed to be. Had to cancel the day. The bus broke doon.'

'It must be grand goin on one of those tours,' she said. 'I've lived here aa my life but I havenae seen much of the country ootside Crieff.'

'We can fix that,' said Sandy. And he started to march downhill towards the Monzie estate car park. Mary watched him go. He turned. 'C'mon.'

'I cannae,' she said, her voice rising. 'My faither …'

'I've just seen him nip oot the back wey of the information tent wi Broon the baker and a half bottle of Bell's. If I ken Pat, they'll be at it till denner time. I'll let him ken whaur you've gone.'

Well, that explained her faither's disappearance, Mary thought, and because of something stronger than tea. Again.

'But these trips, they're for the Rovers …'

'Ach, there's spaces on lots of them.'

'I need to get back …'

'What time do you start your work?'

She thought about lying but knew she wasn't up to it. 'I'm no workin the day …'

'So you've nae need to get back.' He marched on, long strides eating up the ground, and Mary followed, struggling to keep pace. This was what her life was like. Every time she offered what she thought was a cogent argument, somebody else swatted it away. She could never compete with the certainty of others.

There were still half a dozen buses in the car park, at various stages of embarkation. Sandy scanned them and spotted a driver he knew, Derek Muir from Lauchlan. His bus looked ready to depart but contained no more than a dozen Rovers.

'Now then, Derek,' he called. Derek Muir threw his cigarette out of the window and waved at him. 'Whaur you goin the day?'

'Loch Rannoch. Power station.'

'Okay for a lassie?'

Derek looked at the shy wretch standing next to Sandy. 'Aye, nae problem. It's easy hikin.'

Sandy boarded the bus and spoke to Pelly Duncan, the tour guide, usually an engineer with the electricity company, and after a brief negotiation he beckoned through the window for Mary to come on board. Mary groaned.

'I dinnae want to,' she said under her breath. She climbed onto the bus and took a seat on the right-hand side, hoping she wouldn't get travel sickness and resolving not to engage with any of the Rovers. But as soon as Sandy Disdain had disembarked, waving back at Mary, she felt someone slide onto the bench beside her.

'Good morning, miss,' the Rover said. 'My name is

Miško Čurović.'

*

'We've just heard from Norway.' Brigadier Ross waved a telegram at Annie. 'They put a photograph of their Rover in the post yesterday morning.'

''My,' said Annie. 'That's wonderful. We should get it tomorrow, hopefully. Thank you very much, I cannae tell you how grateful we are.'

'A pleasure. Is it so important that you identify the chap?'

'Aye. As long as the authorities think it's juist a tinker that's deid, they dinnae seem inclined to interfere.'

'That doesn't seem right.'

'It seems totally wrong. But what can we do aboot it? We're juist the little people.'

Brigadier Ross studied her features, and for the first time Annie felt he was appraising her as a person, not an object. She smiled.

'Little people can change the world,' the Brigadier said. 'Step by tiny step.'

*

Zoltán Tóth collected a telegram pad from a side counter in the Moot post office and took a pen from his jacket and, resting against an upturned barrel outside, composed a telegram to the Hungarian Rover Scouts headquarters in Budapest:

PLEASE PROVIDE INFORMATION ON RS ISTVAN KEDALY CURRENTLY AT MOOT STOP AGE ADDRESS OCCUPATION HOW LONG MEMBER OF RS STOP ANY DISCIPLINARY ISSUES STOP

Zoltán was forty-three, had been a Boy Scout and then a Rover Scout. Scouting had been his life. He was at the first World Rover Moot in Kandersteg, Switzerland in 1931 and

109

the second, in Ingarö, Sweden, in 1935. Monzie was the third – and who could say when the fourth might take place, when the world might be temperate enough to allow young men to meet in peace rather than conflict. Hungary was becoming a dangerous country and thoughts of war were a constant in Zoltán's consciousness. He resented the way that István and Miško, those suspicious – and, frankly un-Rover-like – young men were affecting his enjoyment of the Moot. In Zoltán's reasoning, scouting was almost as important as religion, a way of instilling the virtues of Christianity through brotherhood and comradeship. The one area where he disagreed with Lord Baden-Powell, their Chief Scout and leader, was in the question of patriotism. Baden-Powell tended to bracket the desire to serve one's country and one's fellow man together, as though they were indivisible. That, Zoltán knew, was naïve. Patriotism becomes nationalism, and nationalism too easily degenerates into narrow and isolationist jingoism, brutish and vicious. This was what was overtaking his own country, and this was what he recognised in Miško Čurović, a man who did not appear to understand or respect the Scouting ethos.

Miško wasn't alone in that, Zoltán reflected. He saw the same thing in his own nephew, Adorján, fourteen years old but with no interest in Guiding and an unhealthy enthusiasm for some of the unsavoury nonsense emanating from Germany. All the young ones did, and Zoltán foresaw trouble. His intuition rarely failed him.

He took the telegram inside and queued to have it collected and despatched by a young woman with a radiant smile. Zoltán tried to return her smile but couldn't.

*

On his way to the Pretoria Bar from John Low's where he'd just sold thirty rabbits snared at Culcrieff that morning, Sandy Disdain tipped his deerstalker to the town stocks, aware he

110

was only a few generations and a couple of misdemeanours away from their summary justice. He stopped to inspect the intricate Celtic carvings of the Burgh Cross. His ancestors, his history, carved for eternity.

He swung open the door of the Pret and bought a pint of heavy from Maisie Hill and navigated his way past a couple of darts players to a bench beneath the window facing the High Street.

'Can I?' he said, gesturing to an empty wooden chair.

'Dinnae often see you in here this time of day, Sandy.'

'Just been to Low's. Been a hot day. Thirsty work.'

Habbie Goudie sipped from his wee half and followed that with a swig from his half pint.

'It'll be the hairst soon,' Sandy continued.

'Aye. Month or so. I'm hopin the weather holds. We've a grand barley crop this year, I'm thinkin.'

'You've plenty manpower on the fairm?'

'Why, you lookin for work?' Habbie seemed surprised. Sandy Disdain's independent spirit was weel-kent among the country workers of Crieff.

'No me. I'm plenty busy my lane.' He gestured to his now empty gamebag.

'We could aye use mair. The traivellers'll be rollin in afore lang.'

'Aye.' Sandy supped his beer. 'Was that your Chic I saw in toon the other day?'

'Bloody waster.'

'He ay was a bit feckless.'

'Ken what he's done noo?'

'Naw.' Sandy sat up, trying not to reveal the extent of his interest in Chic Goudie.

'Came hame the other day, Thursday efternoon this would be, wi a brand-new girdle. Fancy like, fae Frank Thomson's. Shiny, never used. Still had a label on it, twelve and six. For a girdle? I'd be wantin a couple of pans thrown in for that

111

price.'

'So how did he come by it?'

'Well, there's the thing. Mammy asked him that. "Chic, son," she says, "whaur did thon come fae?" And he says, "I bocht it." "Fae Frank Thomson's?" she says and he says no. "Fae a mannie," he says. "Whit mannie?" "I cannae mind his name." And he's lookin shifty, ken? "How much did this mannie sell it for?" Mammy asks him. "Five bob." "Five bob?" says Mammy. "Wi a price tag on it still for twelve and six?" "Aye," says Chic, "it's a wonder, is it no?" "You'll be thinkin I've only the sense I was born wi," says Mammy, and she gets to her feet and Chic kens trouble's comin. "No, no, Mrs Goudie …" he says, but Mammy swings up her besom and clouts him ower the heid wi it. "Aff wi you," she says. "I'll no hae thieves and vagabonds in this hoose." And she chased him all the way doon to Milnab Mill, yelling at him all the while, "You brute, you brute".'

Sandy pondered for a moment. 'He'll no be back for a while, then?'

'No if he's ony sense. Which, come to think of it, he hasnae.'

'D'you really think he bocht the girdle off a man?'

'I do. Chic hasnae the sense to mak up a story like thon.'

'D'you ken wha it was he bocht it fae?'

'I couldnae say, but while he was here he did say he was goin to meet up wi ane of the Williamsons …'

'Tinker Williamsons?'

'Fae the Western Isles, aye. They're often here this time of year, ready for the hairst, then the apple hervest and the tatties.'

'Which ane of the Williamsons?'

'Nae idea. Onywey, Mammy thinks Chic stole it fae Frank Thomson's himsel. I'm haein the deil of a job stoppin her fae takin it back and peyin for it. "It's the richt thing to do," she says. Maybe it is, I dinnae ken the rights and wrongs of sic things, but what I do ken is we're hand-to-mooth as it is these days, and there's a war comin. We cannae afford to go peyin for things we never bocht in the first place. I'm worried sick aboot it. Bloody waster.'

'Aye,' said Sandy. 'It's a sair fecht.'

*

'Please note,' said Pelly Duncan, 'you can take photies of the loch nae problem, but you're no allowed to take a photie of the power station itsel. I dinnae ken why, I'm just relayin orders.'

The Rovers and Mary Kemp trooped off the bus. The journey had been magical, Mary thought, the colours so vivid, green and purple beneath the clearest blue sky, and with no hint of the travel sickness she was convinced would assail her. They had driven the length of the southern shore to Bridge of Gaur and round to the northern shore road as far as the Loch Rannoch Power Station. Mary could not process how big the loch was, how it stretched all the way into the distance. It must be like the sea itself, she thought, although she had never seen the sea. The man who had sat beside her, Miško Čurović, had been polite throughout, chatting occasionally but mostly leaving Mary alone to enjoy the views. Now, though, as they stood in front of the bus facing the loch, he appeared to be attaching himself to her.

'We walk?' he said, indicating the path in front of them with a flourish of his hand. In front of them, Pelly Duncan was describing the loch to the Rovers, nine miles long and one mile wide, four hundred-odd feet deep, but Miško walked so slowly he and Mary began to fall behind and Mary couldn't hear most of Pelly's description. Not that she was much concerned. Facts and figures did not impress her, they made no difference to day-to-day living. The loch was huge. That was all she needed to know.

As they walked, Miško kept stopping to take photographs

113

of the lake with what appeared to Mary to be the smallest camera ever invented, no bigger than a make-up compact. She wondered where the spool could possibly go. Miško noticed her admiring it.

'Is good, no? Top of the art.' He handed it to her. 'Try.'

Mary had never held a camera before, seldom even seen one, apart from a Kodak belonging to her cousin Agnes who had married a banker from Glenrothes and seemed to own one of everything. She raised it to her eyes and looked through. She could see nothing.

'Close your left eye,' Miško said. 'Look through with your right.' She did and the loch came into focus. 'Now,' Miško continued, taking her hand and guiding her finger onto the shutter, 'press here when you're ready.' Mary took a photograph without really examining what she was filming and handed the camera back.

'No,' said Miško. 'Keep it. Here …' He moved to his right, with the power station rising behind him. 'Take my photograph.'

'We're no allowed to film the station, the mannie said.'

'Is okay.' Miško looked around. The others were some yards ahead, oblivious. 'Is just a photograph of me. The station is just to show where I was.'

Mary knew this was somehow wrong, but she took the photograph anyway and passed the camera back to him as though handing over stolen goods. Miško put it in his inside pocket and smiled and looked up once more at the station. 'Come,' he said, 'let us not get left behind.'

They caught up with the group and re-boarded the bus for the tour along the remainder of the north shore, into Kinloch Rannoch. Pelly stood up as they came to a halt.

'Over here is the weir. That controls the flow of water from Loch Rannoch and channels it into Dunalastair Water, juist over there. Dunalastair Water's completely man-made, only about five or six year ago, to provide hydro-electric power. The wonders of modern engineerin. Again, sorry but you're no allowed to tak photies of the weir.'

Mary felt a lurch of concern at his words, certain that she would once again be called on to do something illicit by the man sitting next to her. She wasn't wrong.

'Here,' Miško said a few minutes later, after they had disembarked and the Rovers had begun to explore the area. He positioned himself in front of the weir and handed the camera to her. He winked conspiratorially. A pulse was throbbing in Mary's throat. She looked around, then held the camera in front of her and steadied her hand as she tried to focus on Miško but before she could take the photograph she heard a shout from Pelly. He rushed towards them but Miško deflected his ire with a broad smile and a wave of his hand. 'Is only a photograph of me,' he said, 'to take home to my mother and father. Is very small camera, as you see. Does not show much detail.'

'Aye,' said Pelly, 'just keep the weir oot of it, though.'

'Of course, of course.' Miško continued to smile throughout, a paragon of reasonableness. When Pelly left them, he turned back to Mary. 'Now,' he said. Mary tried to frame him in the camera so that the weir was out of shot but Miško kept sidling to his left until it could be plainly seen. Mary felt frightened, aware she was doing something she had been instructed not to. Holding her breath, she clicked the shutter.

*

'There's someone waitin for you.' Leslie Comer jerked her head towards a man in a grey overcoat seated in the corner of Cloudland. Bob crossed the floor and took a seat beside him.

'Mr Kelty?'

'Aye.'

'Gordon Phillips. Editor of the *Strathearn Herald*. I heard an interesting story today about you. You were speaking on the wireless a couple of days ago.'

'I was, aye.'

'Something about a dead body.'

'A murder.'

Mr Phillips took out a notepad and a pencil. 'Would you care to tell me about it?'

'I've been warned aff. Bailie Bruce.'

'And are you going to let that bother you?'

'What d'you want to ken?'

*

Sandy hid half a dozen dead rabbits in undergrowth near the Knock path and headed for the Castle car park. On the way, he saw Mary Kemp and a handful of Rovers heading out of the camp and he whistled to her. She stopped and turned and Sandy was sure he saw her shoulders droop with resignation.

'How was your day?' he said.

'Grand,' she said, but she spoke with little enthusiasm.

'We had an excellent day,' said Miško, walking beside Mary. Sandy immediately sensed tension and looked at Mary's face. *Help me*, it said.

'I think your faither's still at the information tent,' he said. 'I'll walk you back up.'

He turned and Mary followed. So, a moment later, did Miško.

'I walk with you,' he said.

'No, you're fine. We're only goin to find her faither. I'll see you around.' He walked away purposefully with Mary by his side.

'Thank you,' Mary said. 'He's a nice mannie but he's bit of a scunner.'

'Sorry, did I lumber you wi him aa day?'

'No. The day was grand, thank you. I enjoyed it.' And Mary thought, yes, I really did enjoy it. All the same, at the back of her mind there remained the nagging fear that she

116

had done something wrong with all those photographs.

*

Both Annie and Bob felt in a state of limbo. They wanted to progress their investigation but, until they received the photographs from Norway, there was nothing they could do. They sat in the quiet gloom of their living room, reflecting on the day. The BBC was broadcasting live from the Moot and it felt strange to hear the sounds of a place and an event at which they had, not an hour before, been present. Rovers from Eire were playing tunes, their jigs and reels bringing whoops of approbation from the men around the campfire. Bob could picture the scene, the mellow light, hills dissolving into nothingness while the Rovers, eyes gleaming in the flames of the giant campfire, listened and chatted and relaxed. This was how the world should be, he thought.

He picked up the newspaper. The situation was tense, as ever. Poland had delivered a warning to Germany that it would protect its borders from invasion, following suggestions that Hitler would be elected President of the Nazi-dominated Danzig Senate. This would be "an inadmissible violation of the present political and juridical state of affairs and would evoke the appropriate response", he read. There were reports of a German battalion with horse-drawn light artillery doing exercises in Danzig. The week before, Arthur Greenwood, deputy leader of the Opposition, responding to complaints that British people would not fight for Danzig, said that nobody would ever ask them to fight for Danzig. They would be fighting against dictatorship to make peace forever certain and that was an entirely different proposition. But was it, Bob pondered. How could peace be achieved through war? It was like countering hunger by not eating, or rehabilitating criminals by placing them in jail with other criminals. On Monday, General Ironside, Inspector-General of the British Overseas Forces, arrived in Warsaw on a four-

117

day visit, demonstrating British solidarity with Poland. The first batch of militiamen, conscripted earlier in the year, were being issued with battle dress.

It sounded to Bob like decisions had already been made. The future was writ, at least in outline. The consequences of those decisions would not be felt by those who made them – the men in suits and in uniforms with shiny buttons and braids – but by young men the world over. The pawns were being manoeuvred into position. Slaughter imminent.

'Dinnae read it,' Annie said. 'It just upsets you.' She was studying the latest government public information leaflet, the fifth to be distributed to households in the past month, this one detailing fire precautions in wartime. Others had covered evacuation, food, gas masks and the covering of windows. In the corner, on a wooden seat beside Annie's knitting, was a pile of blackout curtains purchased from Salmond's in King Street. The idea of that, of living in darkness, waiting to be attacked, was horrifying. Annie and Bob listened to the Eireans playing their joyous music, the casual murmur of hundreds of Rovers in the background, and pondered the incongruity of it.

'I wish I could just ignore it,' he said, laying down the paper and picking up his pipe. 'I see these lads, the Rovers, and grand lads they are. They're fun, and they're happy, and they're kind. They're the future, that's what Lord Somers said. But are they? Is everything what it seems? There's a killer among them. There's an infection there. They're already tainted, even if we cannae see it. Is that what's become of all of us? We're tainted?'

'We're not tainted. We're what we ay were.'

'Maybe. But wait. This war, it'll be hell, worse than anythin we've seen afore, worse than the last one and dear God, that was bad enough. It's no goin to be men fightin men on a battlefield this time.' He gestured to her leaflet. '"Fire precautions in wartime". We live in Crieff, for God's sake.

Why the hell should we need to tak precautions? I'll tell you why, because the war is comin here. And it's goin to be total. Nae distinction between soldier and civilian, just enemies to be killed. People to be destroyed. We'll never be the same again.' He laid down his pipe and sighed and switched off the wireless. They sat in the gloom, in silence, in dread.

Friday 21ˢᵗ July

A Day of Identification

After their early morning pipe band tour of the campsite, with the now customary extended stop outside the London enclosure, Bob and Jozef sat drinking tea at Meikle's Nook. 'I have good news,' Jozef said as he whittled a piece of wood into the shape of a bird. 'My old school friend Wladyslaw is due to arrive tomorrow.'

'He's a bit late,' said Bob. 'We're half way through.'

'He sail from Australia to be here, with two friends. It take them a year. They leave Gibraltar three weeks ago and we hear nothing again until they arrive in England yesterday. We were very worried, but they will be here tomorrow. We will give them a big welcome.'

'Big welcome? It's a medal they're needin after that. Let's get Sir Lancelot to parade them roond the site.'

'Excellent idea.'

James Meikle approached, grinning, and bent and sat cross-legged beside Jozef and Bob. 'You owe me five bob,' he said.

'What for?' said Bob.

'Services rendered. Me and the lads huv been round the camp drummin up support for your haggis evenin.'

'Is that right?' Bob had arranged to sell haggis suppers that evening to introduce the Rovers to the great Scottish feast. He only had three haggises, though, and he wasn't sure that drumming up support was in his best interests.

'They're avid for it. Ye'll be turnin folk away.'

Sooner than you realise, Bob thought. He looked at his pocket watch, calculating whether he had time to get back to town and visit Roy's the butchers.

'Ye'll never guess,' James went on, oblivious of Bob's concerns, 'Edinburgh huv had the "r" and "h" nicked aff their sign. They're "Edinbug" now.'

'Nae prizes for guessin whaur they'll be,' said Bob, pointing downhill in the direction of the London enclave. 'Serves them right. Should have spelled it properly in the first place.'

'This is not how you spell Edinburgh?' said Jozef.

'Embra,' said Bob. 'E-m-b-r-a.'

'Embra,' said Jozef. 'I not know this.'

'Don't go teachin him bad ways,' laughed James.

'What's bad aboot that? That's how you say it.'

'There you are.' Annie stood above Bob, studying him solicitously. She spoke lightly but Bob sensed tension. 'You left withoot sayin goodbye.'

'You were fast asleep.'

'What time did you go?'

'About half four.'

'How?'

'I couldnae sleep.'

'Are you okay?'

'Grand.'

'D'you want some tea, missus?' James asked her.

She checked her watch. 'Aye, alright,' she said. 'I've a while afore I start, thanks to Thomas Edison here, the man wha never sleeps.'

'Damn,' said Jozef, indicating down the hill, 'here he comes again.' Approaching them, with his familiar jaunty walk, was István Kedály.

'Dinnae hit him this time,' said Bob.

121

'He provoke me.'

'Bite your tongue. D'you ken that phrase?' Jozef shook his head. 'Count to ten.' Jozef still looked blank. 'Ca canny.'

'Just keep calm,' said Annie, stroking Jozef's shoulder.

Bob studied Jozef closely. Sandy had questioned his role in the matter. *He's too interested in all this.* Was that right? Did Jozef need watching? But before he had time to delve further into his thoughts, István arrived. His black eye was turning reddish-brown. It made him look even more weaselly.

'Good morning, my friends,' he said. Only Bob returned the greeting. 'I hear about your haggis special,' he said to Bob.

'Freshly shot the day.'

István faltered. 'Haggis is an animal?'

'Member of the hedgehog family,' said James.

'I think you are fooling with me.'

'Come along the night and find oot,' said Bob.

István turned to Jozef. 'Will you be trying this Scottish delicacy, too?'

'That is none of your business,' Jozef replied. 'Like everything else we do.'

'Why are you so nasty with me? What have I done to you?'

Jozef jumped to his feet and Bob rose as well, ready to prevent another fight.

'Who are you?' Jozef said. 'You turn up here not on any list. Wherever we go, there you are, following us. You had blood-stained clothing you wanted to clean ...'

Now it was István's turn to raise his voice. 'What? Blood-stained clothing?' He turned and pointed at Annie. She shrank backwards. 'You!' he shouted. 'You start all of this, with your gossip, your idle chit-chattle!'

'Leave her alane!' said Bob.

'No! I make a complaint about this. You have no right

to talk behind my back. I have you lose your job, lady.' He threw his hands in the air and marched downhill.

'Good riddance,' said Bob.

'He winnae do that, will he?' Annie asked.

'Course no.' Bob squeezed her hand, hoping he was right. 'Whaur's Abdalla onywey?' he said, more out of a desire to shift the conversation than any genuine curiosity.

'Perth,' said James.

'How?'

'Invite fae the Town Council. Lord Provost, local MP, JP, mair bigwigs than you can shake a stick at. Lord Somers and Prince Gustav and Makgill-Crichton himself – and Abdalla.'

Bob whistled. 'How does he do it? I tell you, before this Moot's ower he'll be takin tea wi the King.'

*

Just before nine, with the sun rising high in the sky, Bob and Annie walked hand-in-hand through the site. Bob could sense Annie was still tense about István. He was sure nothing would come of the argument, but he walked in silence. It was a week since he had first arrived on the Moot site and everything that had seemed so exotic seven days before was becoming commonplace. The carved Nessie grimaced at them as they passed. The crescent and stars adorning the entrance to the Turkish enclosure gleamed in the sunshine. A giant cross fashioned from a single fir tree soared high into the morning sky in the Hungarian area. The concourse by the main arena was busy, queues already forming outside the bank and the post office and, oddly, the barber's. Pushing his bicycle away from the post office was Pat Kemp. Bob squeezed Annie's hand.

'If Pat the postie's just delivered the post ...' said Annie.

'We micht hae oor picters fae Norway.'

They rushed to the staff entrance at the rear of the tent and, inside, Annie threw her swagger coat on the coat rack. She

123

approached the desk where Brigadier Ross had deposited the post delivered by Pat Kemp.

And there it was, a large letter with foreign stamps, the address hand-written in a curious, angular script, clearly not the handwriting of a British person.

'Open it,' Bob said.

He handed her a penknife and Annie slit open the envelope and drew out a single, folded sheet of paper, inside which were two photographs. The letter confirmed the Rover was called Erling Hagen, aged twenty-seven years old.

'Old for a Rover,' said Bob. 'And he wasnae one of the leaders. It's usually the leaders who're the older anes.'

Annie turned to the first photograph and studied the face staring out from it. She looked at the second one. 'I dinnae ken,' she said, handing the photographs to Bob. 'You saw his face better than me.'

Bob took the photographs and studied each in turn. Erling Hagen was a handsome young man with blond hair and rugged features, a broad nose and wide lips drawn back in a light smile. Deep-set eyes stared at the camera lens. A confident man, assured.

And – without question – the man they had discovered in the burned-out tent. Bob felt a surge of elation that the first of their imponderable questions had been answered, but instantly that was replaced by a deep-rooted sorrow. A sorrow for this young man, bright, happy, newly arrived in a foreign country on a grand adventure, only to be murdered and left like detritus hundreds of miles from home and family. A mystery, unwanted, unmourned, unconsidered by authority, not important enough to even have his death acknowledged, far less investigated.

'Erling,' he said. 'I'm awfae sorry.'

'It's him?' said Annie.

'Aye.'

'So we ken wha he is.'

'And noo we want to ken what he deed for.'

'Holmes and Watson.' Brigadier Ross's surprisingly soft voice interrupted their conversation. 'Which is which, I wonder?'

Annie and Bob pointed to each other and said, 'Holmes'. They laughed. The break in tension was welcome, particularly for Bob, who could easily have fallen into a cycle of fretting over what to do next and feeling vexed about the fate of Erling Hagen.

Brigadier Ross indicated the photographs in Bob's hand with a brief incline of his head. 'The Norwegian?' he said.

'Aye.'

'And?'

'It's him.'

'The body in the tent? You're sure?'

'As we can be.'

'What do you plan to do next?'

'I guess we need official confirmation.'

'Indeed. And how can you get that?'

Bob waved the photographs at the Brigadier. 'We need to get these to the authorities. In Perth.'

'Quite.'

Bob gave Annie a resigned look. 'Time for a trip to the polis station,' he said.

'Good luck,' said Annie.

'Good luck,' said Brigadier Ross.

*

First in the queue at the post office at nine o'clock was Miško Čurović. He chatted politely to a couple of Rovers from Iraq, the three of them alternating between English, French and German and somehow making themselves understood. When he reached the head of the queue he approached the teller briskly, smiling his usual warm smile.

'Good morning,' he said, handing over a neatly wrapped

and tied parcel containing the tiny spool from his pocket camera. 'I wish to post this please. Your best delivery. First class, yes?'

The teller, completely bald and wearing a suit apparently two sizes too large for him, took the parcel from Miško. It was addressed to "Sanders, Post Box 629, Hamburg 1". The teller looked at the parcel and then at Miško. Miško smiled once more.

'Of course, sir.'

*

By nine-thirty, the Hungarian encampment was mostly empty, only Zoltán Tóth and a few stragglers not yet embarked on their day's excursion still ambling between the tents. Among them was István Kedály. Zoltán grabbed his shoulder.

'A word, please," he said. István tried to pull free but Zoltán gripped him more tightly. He lowered his shoulder to escape and a furious expression overtook him but, in an instant, it was replaced by his customary smile.

'I will be late for my trip,' he said.

'I won't keep you long. A little chat, just as soon as the others have gone.' They both looked at János and Lörinc, bent over their rucksacks and fiddling with the straps.

István clapped his hands. 'Hurry,' he said. 'Your bus will leave without you.'

'Are you coming?' János asked him.

'I'll catch you up. Go.'

István and Zoltán watched as the young men hitched their rucksacks over their shoulders and, with a brief wave, headed in the direction of the car park.

István flashed a smile of pure reasonableness and stretched out his hands, palms upwards, fingers splayed.

A parody of sincerity, Zoltán thought. 'Who are you?' he said.

István feigned surprise. 'I am István Kedály.'

'I've sent a telegram to headquarters requesting more information about you. I should have an answer today or tomorrow. What do you think they will say?'

'That I am István Kedály.'

'From?'

'From Köszeg.'

'Age?'

'Twenty-four.'

Zoltán studied his face. 'Twenty-four? Life must be hard in Köszeg.'

'A border town. We are very poor there. Not like where you come from. Budapest? You pluck money the way I pluck apples, no?'

'Why are you here?'

'For the Moot. I wouldn't miss it for the world.'

'Been a Rover long?'

'Boy Scout first. Then Rover.'

'Liar.'

István raised an eyebrow. His mouth slid into its customary supercilious pose. 'And why do you say that?'

'Because you've never been camping in your life. You have no idea. I've been watching you. You wait, every time, to see what someone else does, how they do it. And then you copy them. You don't know how to pack a rucksack. How to cook over a fire. You walk like a town boy. You ignore nature …'

'Such hostility,' István said. 'You must have a reason for this?'

Zoltán considered how to answer. Should he mention Miško Čurović, the way they seemed to know each other, though they assiduously tried to pretend otherwise? He thought not. Keep some powder dry.

'I don't like you,' he said.

'Very well,' said István. 'In that case, I shall leave.' He

127

picked up his rucksack, slung it over his shoulder and walked away from the camp towards the car park.

*

Bob sat in the grimy police waiting room for ten minutes until Sergeant Rudd slouched in and slid onto the chair opposite him. He looked hungover, his eyes glassy, his breath pungent. Bob laid the two photographs on the table, facing Rudd.

'This is the man in the tent,' he said. 'Erling Hagen. I saw enough of his face the other day to recognise him.'

'And who's he when he's at hame?'

'A Norwegian Rover. Last seen last Thursday.'

Rudd stared at the photographs for some moments, then looked around the spare, grey-painted room. Then he looked at Bob.

'There's no wey you could recognise him. His face was burnt aff.'

'Only half of it.'

'And you think you can match half a face with a couple of black and white photies?'

'Aye.'

'Leave them wi me.'

'No. No offence, but I'll hing on to them.'

'What did you come here for then, if you dinnae want to leave the photies?'

'I want you to do somethin for me.'

'What?'

'Telephone the Procurator Fiscal.'

'Are you mad?'

'The Perth boys winnae touch this case. They've made that plain. But you ken I'm right. You ken I'm no makin this up. You're a good polisman, sergeant. You ken right fae wrang. So bypass them. Go to the main man.'

Rudd stared at him again. There was a barely discernible

nod of his head. 'On you go,' he said, indicating the door.

'Thank you.'

*

Abdalla and Jozef, walking down Crieff High Street, were opposites in almost every regard. Jozef, short and squat in his over-long cape, pale and made paler by the shock of black hair that encased his face, walked briskly, every part of his body apparently in motion, like a poorly-functioning automaton. Beside him, Abdalla kept pace seemingly without exerting any effort, tall and lean, elegant, his movements an exercise in streamlining, like a production line made human. While Jozef ignored the locals, Abdalla sought them out, made contact, made acquaintances.

'You have a beautiful daughter,' he said to a harassed mother in a purple headscarf. 'I can already see her mother's beauty waiting to bloom in her face.' To an old man, smoking a pipe outside Harley and Watts, he said, 'One day, like you, I hope to have gained the wisdom to watch the world and learn.' Even the inevitable rebuffs seemed not to fluster him.

'If I'd gained ony wisdom in my life, d'you think I'd be hingin aboot this shitehole? Those that lairn are the anes in their fancy hooses, drawbridges up, keeping the rabble oot.'

'The trouble with a drawbridge, sir, is that as well as keeping people out, it keeps you in. Who wants to live entirely on their own?'

'You havenae met the wife, have you, son?'

They were still laughing as they entered Cloudland and Abdalla greeted Leslie Comer. Jozef had previously wondered at Abdalla's ability to remember names. It was a skill he singularly lacked and he was convinced there must be some trickery involved. They ordered tea and scones and watched Crieff life unfolding outside.

'You seem a very happy man,' Jozef said. 'I not know how you manage that.'

129

'You are not happy?'

'This world …' Jozef threw up his hands helplessly. 'It's running away with itself. Out of control. I was in a car crash once. Not serious, not hurt. The steering wheel stopped turning, or it turned all over the place, but the wheels didn't turn with it. I panicked. I could have used the brake to stop, but I saw a car parked on the street ahead of me and I couldn't think and I knew I was going to hit it. I could do nothing to prevent it. That's how I feel now. My country … Disaster. I'm not even sure a communist revolution can fix it, now.' He lowered his head and appeared to study the grain of the wood on the table top. 'I envy you. Your certainty.'

Abdalla patted his hand. 'My friend. You never know what people are thinking. What bothers them. You think I am certain? Happy? Yes, in a way. But my country is in danger, too. We have a new king. Very young. He is trying to change too quickly. Bad things will happen. Not now, not next year, but sometime. In my lifetime. Egypt will turn away from the West. That will be good for Egypt, but not for everybody else. The next war will be European. The one after that will not.'

'And you do not try to do anything to stop it?'

'This – and this alone – is where I am a happy man: I know I can do nothing and so I do nothing. You know you can do nothing but still you torture yourself.'

'But evil …'

'The evil will come. With or without you. People will do what people do. Look after their own. Your communist paradise, it is a mirage, my friend.'

'Tea.' They looked up. Leslie Comer, a woman who knew all about evil, and about what can and cannot be done to counter it, stood in front of them holding a tray of tea and scones.

Abdalla beamed. 'My dear Mrs Comer, thank you so much.'

Unknown to him, Abdalla and Jozef were still in Cloudland when Bob stopped on the way from the police station at Roy's the butcher's to collect his order of haggis.

'Must be a hell of a party you're haein,' Mr Roy said. 'I've had to get some haggis fae Turnbull's and Stephen's to mak up your extra order.'

'Aye? I'm sure they'll be fine.'

Mr Roy looked at him sharply. 'They'll no be as good as mines.'

'Of course no.'

'D'you need a hand loadin them into your van?'

'What van? I'm on my bike.'

Mr Roy looked at him incredulously. 'Six eight pound haggises? On a bike? What are you goin to put on the other handlebar? A couple of anvils?'

'Are they that heavy?'

'Forty-eight pounds? That's ower three stane. All the way to Monzie? Round thae bends? You'll never be able to steer it, man.'

Bob frowned. Could he do it in relays, he wondered, two at a time? Would that leave long enough to cook them? But even as he framed the question he knew the answer was no. And then the solution came to him.

'Could I use your telephone?' he asked. He was invited into the back and he asked to be put through to the Information Centre at Moot Headquarters.

'Annie?' he said, 'I need you to get James. We need a car ...'

*

It took James Meikle an hour to secure the use of Sir Lancelot and negotiate the Gilmerton bends into Crieff. He parked outside Roy's and Bob ran to greet him.

'What's the tearin rush?' said James.

'This,' said Bob, holding up one of the eight pound haggises.

'Christ almighty, that's enormous. How long's it gonnae take to bile that hing?'

'Exactly. That's your tearin rush.'

They loaded the haggises into the rear of Sir Lancelot and James turned on the High Street and headed back to the campsite. Annie was waiting at the catering tent and the three of them set the haggises to boil, peeled and chopped the tatties and neeps and steeped them in water ready to cook later, then sat on the grass by the Shaggie Burn. Smells of haggis began to permeate the campsite.

'That's a hellish lot of haggis,' James said, drawing on his cigarette. 'Hope to God everybody who said they were comin turns up.'

'It'll be grand,' said Bob, but the same concern was filtering through his mind. Too many, too few? Ach, why did planning always have to be so difficult?

*

While the haggis continued to cook, Bob sat at a bench in the catering tent and smoked his pipe, reflecting on the past few days. The sound of canvas being pulled back alerted him to someone entering the tent and he looked up, expecting Annie. It was Zoltán Tóth.

'Hello,' said Bob, rising and extending his hand. They exchanged small talk for a couple of minutes but Bob sensed something was on the older man's mind. He waited.

'I wanted to ask,' Zoltán said finally, 'I sense you are looking for something. In the camp.'

'Well,' said Bob, trying to be as non-committal as possible, 'there's been one or two queer things happened recently.'

'And they involve István Kedály?'

Bob faltered. 'What maks you think that?'

'I notice, that evening in Cloudland, there was something odd happening. Everybody watching everybody else. And István, he was at the centre of it. The first time we met, you were asking me about him. He wasn't on the original party. There is something strange about him, I think.'

'I think so, too, but I don't know what.'

'I ask him today.'

'And what did he say?'

'He deny anything strange. But I do not trust him. Nothing he says is true. He says he comes from a small village. I not believe that. He says he is twenty-four and I look at him and think he must be older. He says he has been a Scout since childhood. That is not true. I tell you, my friend, that man is trouble.'

'Aye.'

'No. I don't think you understand me. István Kedály, I think he is dangerous.'

*

Bob didn't have time to reflect on Zoltán's warning because the publicity drive by James and the Meikle's Nook boys that morning, along with the efforts of dozens of Scotsmen throughout the day to sell the mysterious allure of Scotland's national dish, saw a queue of over a hundred Rovers forming outside Bob's catering tent by seven o'clock.

'We'll hae to start,' he said.

'They've only been on the simmer twa hoors,' said Annie. 'And look at the size of them. Will they be done?'

Bob checked his pocket watch. 'Nearer two-and-a-half hoors,' he said optimistically. 'That's fine.'

'We dinnae want to gie onyone food poisonin.'

'Wi a Roy's haggis? No possible. All finest ingredients.'

'What about Stephen's? Or Turnbull's'

'Dinnae fash. It's grand.'

133

They set up their serving station on a trestle table by the entrance and Bob, Annie and Leslie Comer, newly arrived from Cloudland for her first visit to the site, took their places behind the haggis, tatties and neeps respectively.

'Let them in,' Bob said to Annie and she untied the tent flaps and spread them open. One by one, the Rovers filed in, banging their spoons on their tin plates.

'This is your true Scottish tucker?' a young Australian asked.

'This morning it was still loupin aboot ower yonder.' Bob indicated towards the woods rising above the campsite. He deposited a serving of haggis on the plate and winked as the Rover passed to Annie for his tatties and then to Leslie for his neep. The lad looked at his plate dubiously. He sniffed it, looked at Bob, looked at the plate again.

'It'll put hairs on your chest,' Bob said.

James and the lads from Meikle's Nook arrived, along with Abdalla and Jozef. To no one's surprise, István Kedály arrived moments later, followed by Miško Čurović.

'Are you sure I am allowed to eat this, Bob?' Abdalla asked him. 'I am Muslim.'

'To be perfectly honest, I've nae idea.'

'Does it contain pork?'

'Naw. Sheep. Liver, heart, lungs. All wrapped up in sheep's intestine.'

Abdalla raised an eyebrow. The Rover behind him in the queue, another Egyptian, stepped away and fled the tent. Abdalla laughed. 'I'll have his serving too,' he said.

A volley of shouts in loud cockney accents heralded the arrival of Mickey Peterfield and the lads from the London enclave. They were universally scrawny, Bob thought, in need of a proper feed.

'Cannae get enough of oor Scottish culture?' he said to Mickey as he ladled a portion of haggis onto his plate.

'Our barrow's got a hole in it. Thought this might seal it

up.'

'It probably will, an aa.'

'And what's in it, again?'

'Trust me, you dinnae want to ken.' He paused. 'Mind, you lot eat jellied eels, don't you?'

'Never eaten a jellied eel in my life,' Mickey said, laughing. 'Don't believe everything you read.'

They sold out over one hundred and twenty portions in fifteen frantic minutes, with just enough left over for the three of them. Annie counted the takings – four pounds and seventeen shillings. They collected their plates of haggis and went in search of the others, finding them lazing beneath a sycamore tree by the side of the Shaggie Burn.

'Bob!' shouted Abdalla, springing to his feet and shaking Bob's hand. 'Thank you, my friend.' He turned to Annie and Leslie and kissed their right hands. 'And thank you ladies. I never eat anything like that.'

'Glad you liked it,' said Annie.

'Actually,' said Miško, 'he did not say that exactly. He only say that he never eat anything like it.'

They all laughed but Abdalla, ever conscious of giving offence, raised his arms. 'It was truly amazing,' he said. 'Delicious.'

The caterers sat down and ate their suppers while the others chatted and joked and smoked. Sounds from the campsite drifted towards them.

'There's that song,' said Annie. 'I've been hearin it all week.' They listened and from a campfire about a hundred yards downstream they could hear a group of men singing a jaunty song which Bob, too, recognised. Everybody, it seemed, was singing it.

'Can anyone work out what they're sayin?' he asked.

'It is in French,' said István. 'I was with a couple of French boys last night and they sang it.' Oblivious of the antagonistic stare of Jozef and the suspicious glances of the others, he began to sing.

Allouette, gentile allouette
Allouette, je te plumerai

He taught the others the words phonetically and they joined in and after a few minutes they were in full voice, singing the refrain, and all around other Rovers joined them until hundreds of voices could be heard, the length and breadth of the campsite, some of them slightly out of sync, all singing *Allouette*. The sound seemed to reach through the darkness, a web of music threading together the moments of these hundreds of young men and two women, creating a unity, a fragment of peace.

'Such a pretty tune,' said Annie. 'What do the words mean?'

István smiled. 'Like the ingredients of the haggis,' he said, 'it's probably best you don't know.'

Behind them, the Shaggie bubbled gently. Wind soughed through the sycamore leaves. Sundry fires around the camp lent scant light and the group were mostly shrouded in darkness. The night was cooling. Bob's bare forearms were beginning to goose-pimple and he rolled down his sleeves. He filled his pipe and lit it. In the flare of the match he studied István's face. Was this really a murderer? Bob didn't care for the man, thought him slightly creepy but, for all Zoltán's warning earlier, when he looked at him he didn't feel as though he were in the presence of evil.

'István,' he said, 'you've a fine voice. Would you sing us somethin else?'

István shook his head but after a moment he looked up and smiled and said he would. He counted himself in – one-two-three-four – and started to sing: '*Végig mentem a tárkányi sej, haj, nagy uccán*'. The tune was strident, almost martial and the lads from Meikle's Nook started to piston their arms up and down as though they were marching.

'Braw,' said Bob when he'd finished. 'What was that?'

'It is by Béla Bartòk. *I Walked to the End of the Great Street in Tárkány.*'

Bob was going to enquire about the meaning of the song but he was put off by the arrival of Sandy Disdain. He was smiling, something which seemed to Bob almost sinister.

'There's a richt steer up at the campsite,' he said. 'The London laddies hae had their sign nicked.'

'Bugger. We'll get the blame for that.'

'How?' said Annie.

'It'll hae happened this evenin. When we were puttin on the haggis supper. They'll say that was a diversion, so James's lads could get roond there and do the dirty business.'

'But it was nothin to do wi us.'

'Absolutely nothin,' said James too quickly.

Bob grinned and sucked on his pipe. 'Was it you done it?' he said.

'Ah know nothin aboot it,' James replied. He paused. 'But if they're wantin their sign back they might huv a swatch behind Nessie up the hill.'

'You're a bad man.'

'Am are.'

*

The telephone was ringing in the hallway when they returned home and Bob ran upstairs as fast as his still sore legs and blistered feet allowed.

'Crieff 364,' he panted into the receiver.'

'I have the Procurator Fiscal for you.' Bob stared at the phone in amazement, his heart instantly throbbing.

'Kelty?' came a male voice on the other end of the line.

'Bob Kelty, aye.'

'It's Malcolm Harman here, Procurator Fiscal. I expect you in my office tomorrow morning, nine o'clock sharp.'

'Tomorrow's Saturday.'

'Exactly. And my day off. Which may indicate the urgency

137

with which I require to speak with you. Nine o'clock.'

And the line went dead.

Saturday 22nd July

A Day of Meetings

Bob paced the draughty waiting room of Crieff railway station. The 7:04 from St Fillans was late, and he could foresee an almighty dash from Perth's General Railway Station across the city to the Procurator Fiscal's office on South Street. At least the adrenaline would stop him feeling nervous.

When the train arrived, he plumped for second class and took a seat by the window. They puffed out of the station and past the Market Park and the slaughter house towards the burgh boundary, beyond which was the Pittentian crossing and a ripe smell emanating from the Manure Works. Bob opened *The Courier* and braced himself to read the news. Poland had protested to the Nazi-controlled Danzig Senate over the death of a customs officer in a frontier incident. Poland would fight for Danzig if all diplomatic means failed. It depended on Germany's decisions, they warned, "whether or not the fields of Europe are to be littered with millions of dead". Meanwhile, in Britain a national medical service was being established to cater for injuries in the event of war. Conflict was drawing ever closer, it seemed. It was even impinging on sport: Robert Wilson, St Johnstone's outside-left, was on military service and likely to be posted outside the city. Three other players were expected to receive call-ups soon. In good news, there was a large feature on the

Australian sailors and Jozef's friend arriving in Scotland following their year-long journey. The city of Dundee was apparently empty after the introduction of the Holidays with Pay Act saw a mass exodus by bus, train and car of people able to afford holidays for the first time. There was a photograph of the Moot campfire and Bob fancied he and Annie were on the very edge of the scene, beside Abdalla and Jozef, although the picture was too grainy to be certain.

By the time he'd finished the paper, the train was rolling into Perth and Bob queued to disembark at the General Station, from where he walked into the city. Although he'd lived there from the age of twelve until he moved to Crieff two years before, Perth had never felt like home. Too big. Too busy.

He marched uphill onto Leonard Street and then South Street. One of the front windows of the Salutation Hotel was boarded up and Bob felt sorry for the poor polisman who would have had to intervene in whatever ructions had caused that. He was five minutes early when he arrived at the Procurator Fiscal's office and he lit his pipe to settle himself. He had never met Mr Harman but knew of him. Marjory Fenwick, whom Harman had precognosced in relation to the Cuddies Strip crimes, spoke of how intimidating he was. And now he wanted to speak to Bob. On a Saturday. Bob didn't anticipate the meeting would be an easy one.

'Ach, come on,' he chided himself aloud. 'What's the worst can happen?'

A secretary in a loose blue frock that seemed rather daring for such an austere setting asked Bob to wait in a dark, wood-panelled side room while she knocked on the Procurator Fiscal's door and entered, pulling the door closed behind her. Bob waited for minutes that seemed twice as long as they actually were, all the while aware of the pulse hammering in his ears. Finally, the door opened.

'This way,' the secretary said and Bob followed her

into the Procurator Fiscal's office. Mr Harman was seated at a mahogany desk, a tall and thin man with thick-rimmed spectacles and his greying hair combed into a side parting. His back was to the window overlooking South Street. Beyond, Bob could see activity at the Sheriff Court, his old friend Eck Thornton escorting a group of half a dozen men inside. Sitting on a Saturday? This was probably the ruckus that had ended in the Sally's window being smashed. Bob remembered with a shudder being sent to the Sally on a Friday night, when his superiors thought that giving him a badge and a helmet and a truncheon somehow bestowed on him a sense of authority. Bob knew, and so did the denizens of the Sally, that this was never the case.

'Kelty?'

Bob became aware that Mr Harman was speaking to him. The Procurator Fiscal's expression seemed to exude contempt.

'I said, take a seat.'

Bob sat. He took off his bunnet and ran it through his fingers.

'You know why you're here?'

'The body, I imagine.'

'The dead tinker.'

'He wasn't a tinker.'

Mr Harman clasped his hands on the desk in front of him as though they were pointing at Bob. 'I had a peculiar telephone call yesterday, from Sergeant Rudd in Crieff. I asked him why he had telephoned me directly rather than going through County Headquarters. Most improper. He suggested that you intimated that might be the best course of action. Is that true?'

'Yes.'

They faced each other across the desk. Bob generally felt terrified when dealing with authority but he'd learned to conceal the fact. As a result, they no doubt thought him arrogant. He didn't care. Mostly, he found them obnoxious. That seemed a fair trade.

'Why did you say that?'

'Because I knew HQ wouldn't do anythin about it.'

'How could you know that?'

'Geordie Macrae – Sergeant Macrae of CID – already told me he wouldn't investigate.'

'And did he explain why not?'

'He said, unless he was sure it was murder, and he was sure it wasn't a tinker, he'd been told not to.'

Harman winced. 'I suspect that may be a paraphrase of a paraphrase.'

'If you say so.'

'Sergeant Rudd mentioned some photographs.'

'Aye. I brought them with me.' Bob felt in his inside jacket pocket and pulled out the envelope containing the photographs of Erling Hagen. He pushed them towards Mr Harman. Mr Harman pushed them away again.

'I'll consider these in due course. Why don't you take me back to the beginning.' He lit a cigarette and sat back in his chair, folding his right leg over his left and resting his hands on his thighs. Bob relayed the events of two Fridays before, the discovery of the body, the arrival of the police.

'And you intimated your misgivings to the police officer at that point?'

'We said it was gey suspicious, aye.'

'When did the CID officer come on scene?'

'That night, apparently, though I didn't speak to him till the next day.'

'But he actually saw the scene of the incident?'

'The murder, aye.'

Harman flicked ash from his cigarette. 'Why do you insist this was murder?'

'We found another stone covered in blood and hair. A hundred yards or so from the tent. Somebody could fall and

142

hit their head on one stone, in one place. But two? In two different places? The tent was a tinker's tent, but the man in it wasn't a tinker. It had been erected by someone who didn't how to erect a tent. And a tinker would never have set up a tent there, anyway. The Monzie estate don't like tinkers on their land. The body had no shoes. His clothes didn't fit. Nothin about that whole scene makes any sense.'

The more Bob talked about the case, the more incensed he became by the lack of police interest. What he was saying seemed so obvious he couldn't understand why the authorities could not reach the same conclusion. And now the Procurator Fiscal would probably refuse to give his summary any credence either. Harman played with his cigarette case, turning it round and knocking each corner in turn against the desk.

He inhaled and blew smoke towards the bare lightbulb in the centre of the room. 'I attended the post-mortem,' he said. 'One of my duties. A curious case. Doctor Murphy said to me right at the start, "Some post-mortems write themselves." That's true, in some cases, but it didn't seem that way to me in this particular case. However, Doctor Murphy was quite adamant on the point.'

'Why didn't it seem that way?'

'There were two fractures on the man's skull. Together, certainly, as though someone wanted to make it look like a single fracture, but even as a non-medical man I could see that quite clearly.'

'Did you challenge the doctor?'

'I aired my opinion. Doctor Murphy said I was wrong. His diagnosis of death was intracranial bleeding from a single blow to the head.'

'And what did you do?'

'I deferred to his medical knowledge, of course. I respect his professional integrity.'

'You're the Procurator Fiscal. Where's your professional

integrity?'

'Don't overstep the mark, Kelty.'

'Mr Kelty.'

Harman smiled and raised an eyebrow. 'You were involved in the Cuddies Strip murder weren't you?'

'Murder and rape. Two crimes.'

'I remember it very well. I came under considerable pressure to effect a speedy outcome in that case. From high up.'

'I mind Inspector Conoboy telling me that.'

Harman pursed his lips as though debating with himself whether to continue. 'The pressure I came under then was nothing to the pressure I have come under for this case. Not by a factor of one hundred.'

'They told you what to say?'

'They made clear how they thought the case should be concluded.'

'And who's they?'

'Honestly? I have no idea. Home Office. Intelligence. I couldn't say. But I do know there are some battles that shouldn't be entered into because there's only one outcome. I like you, Mr Kelty. You're clever and principled. You're a breath of fresh air, in many respects. But you're naive. People will take advantage of that, be assured.'

'Aye, I've already noticed that myself. Thing is, I don't care what folks think about me. Whether they want to take advantage. I just do what I do. I don't know any other way. That's what I told the man from the *Herald*.'

Harman looked immediately concerned. 'What man from the *Herald*?'

'Mr Phillips. Editor of the *Strathearn Herald*.'

'You spoke to him about this?'

'Aye. It'll be in the paper next week.'

Harman fell silent. He blinked slowly and stared at Bob. He gestured to the photographs. 'Tell me about these.'

'This is Erling Hagen, a Rover Scout from Norway who arrived at the Moot last Thursday and hasn't been seen since. That's because he's also the man we found in the tent. I recognised him ...'

'Even though half of his face was burned?'

'Half of it wasn't ...'

'And you believe that is sufficient grounds for identification?'

'No, that's why I wanted to get in touch with you. You've got the body. I've got the photies. So I thought, if we can look at the body again now, make a positive identification ...'

'It doesn't work that way, Mr Kelty.'

'In general, or just in this case?'

'I've already told you, I've come under ...'

'Pressure. Aye, you said. Meanwhile this boy – his mum and dad will be back home in Norway, brothers and sisters maybe? Thinkin he's havein a rare time in Scotland, makin friends, seein the sights. And he's in your mortuary ...'

'I understand your sense of compassion ...'

'It's not hard, is it? Compassion? It's basic human decency, man. All I'm askin is that you have another look at the body, see if it's the man in these photies ...'

'I'm afraid that won't be possible.'

The abruptness with which Harman spoke alarmed Bob. 'Why not?' he said.

'The body was cremated yesterday.'

*

On a morning stroll, Annie spotted Mary sauntering towards the arena, head bowed. 'Helpin your faither again?' she said.

Mary looked at her bleakly. 'I'll be glad when this camp's ower and we can get back to normal.'

'I'm sorry to chase you, but we ken wha the body is noo, so we'd sair like to ken how your faither fund oot aboot it.

145

Have you spoken to him yet?'

'I did, and he telt me to mind my ain business.'

'Oh.'

'And then, when he'd gone oot, my mither telt me it was Habbie Goudie telt him.'

'Habbie Goudie? Drinks in the Pret?'

'The very man.'

'But Sandy spoke to him. He never said onythin aboot the body.'

Mary shrugged. 'That's what my mither telt me.'

'Right.' Annie strode back towards the information office. 'Come on,' she said.

'Whaur?'

'To get my coat, and then we're goin to the Pret.'

'But my faither …'

'Your faither'll hae to do his ain work for a change.'

*

Perth's North Inch was criss-crossed with trenches, each four or five feet deep, preparations for war which had been dug the previous year on instruction from the government but abandoned when Perth's Air Raid Warden officials decided that public shelters would be more effective than trenches which, given the North Inch's proximity to the River Tay, would be prone to flooding. As if to prove the point, most of the trenches lay an inch deep in water, residue from rains last week that wouldn't drain away. Instead of these trenches, the basements of the new Art Gallery and the Sandeman Public Library had been identified as suitable locations for civilian shelters. Bob stared into one of the trenches. More than the steady drip of bad news in the papers, it was scenes like this that truly frightened him. The North Inch, a public park, place of recreation for generations, being prepared for war. Once, in 1396, it had been the site of a battle between Clan Chattan and Clan Kay, but that was ancient history and the

146

modern world should have had no place for such terrors.

He turned and headed towards the Conoboys' house on Rose Terrace. Mina, the new maid, opened the door and escorted him to the living room where Victor and Bella were, as usual, reading. Bella put down her book and rose and embraced Bob.

'Robert, what a delight. You haven't been to see us in simply ages. How's Annie? How's Cloudland?'

'Both grand, thanks.'

They settled into the rituals of tea and chatter. Bob told them about Cloudland, about the Moot, the influx of young men from around the world. Victor explained his new role, overseeing the Perth ARP for Lord Kellett.

'It's exciting work,' he said. 'I feel useful again. Retirement's all very well, but I like to feel like I'm contributing something.'

'As long as you don't overdo it,' said Bob. Victor's heart attack went unmentioned but all, simultaneously, knew this was on Bob's mind.

'It's only a few hours a week, and it's not physical work. The hardest bit's getting all the way out to HQ in the Fechney building.'

'Aye, that's a fair hoof from here.'

Bella passed her book across to Bob. 'You should read this,' she said. 'It'll become a classic.' Bob inspected the cover. It looked like a children's book, a naive painting of a man, woman and a child looking across a valley. *The Grapes of Wrath*, he read, by John Steinbeck.

'The evil that men do,' said Bella, 'in the name of progress.' She explained the plot and as Bob learned of the Joad family's travails he gradually felt himself relax. He could never understand why being with the Conoboys made him so nervous, given how kind they were, but somehow he always felt he had to be on his best behaviour with them. He generally found, though, that the longer he spent with them

147

the easier things became.

'What brings you to town?' Victor asked. 'St Johnstone playing?'

'No, the season doesn't start for a couple of weeks. Actually, I was summonsed by the Procurator Fiscal.'

Victor raised his eyebrows in surprise. 'Malcolm Harman? On a Saturday? What makes you so popular?'

Bob wasn't sure, given Victor's heart attack, whether he should tell him. He knew Victor, and he knew he would be appalled by the lack of police action and would immediately wish to become involved. All the same, he was so incensed by what the Procurator Fiscal had told him about the cremation he felt compelled to speak. He explained what had happened but tried to play down the significance. To no avail.

'A man's been murdered and the police are doing nothing about it?' Victor's outrage was instantaneous. Bob sat back in his chair uncomfortably.

'We don't know for certain ...'

'But a police investigation would provide that certainty. I'll speak to Lord Kellett.'

'He already knows. It was him who helped us get permission to contact the Norwegian Rovers in Oslo.'

Victor frowned. Instinctively, he reached for his cigarettes on the table beside his chair before remembering he had stopped on doctor's orders. Breathlessness wasn't good for heart trouble, he'd been told.

'What will you do now?'

'I don't see there's much we can do. They've cremated the body so we've literally nothing to go on.'

Bella put down her teacup. 'It's important you don't give up,' she said.

'We aren't. There's a couple of folks in the Rovers' camp we've suspicions about and Sandy Disdain is lookin into the tinker's tent, see if we can trace that, or who it belonged to. But apart from that we're at a loss ...'

'Nevertheless, you must persevere. There are those who hold that good government flourishes best in the dark, unseen and unknown by we common folk. They're wrong. If our representatives are making decisions on our behalf – which we elect them to do, of course – but those decisions affect life and death, honour and decency, right and wrong, trust and deception, then those decisions must be dragged into the light where they can be judged. For good or ill.'

'Indeed, ma'am.'

'This is what distinguishes us from the Nazis in Germany or Mussolini in Italy. We must maintain the rule of law, and that rule of law must be proclaimed in public.'

'You always make things seem so straightforward.'

'Because they generally are.'

*

Sandy Disdain marched down the narrow corridor of Frank Thomson's, flanked either side by all varieties of ironmongery and household utensils. At the back of the shop, behind a wooden counter, stood Frank Thomson himself.

'Sandy,' he said. 'Thocht you'd transferred your allegiance to Muir's?'

'They're cheaper …'

'Cheap rubbish, aye.'

'When you can do me a hank of snare wire for under twa shillins I'll be back.'

Frank Thomson gave an affable smile. 'You'll hae me in the poorhoose.'

'I'll no be far ahint you.'

'Aye, times are tough for us aa. What can I do for you?'

'Girdles. You havenae had ony stolen, have you?'

'Kitchen girdles or wifies' girdles?'

'What would I be interested in a wifie's girdle for? Kitchen. Metal.'

'Funny you should mention that.'

'You have?'

'No.'

Sandy's habitual frown deepened, his eyebrows descending to form a single crease across his forehead.

'But I did sell ane. Last Thursday.'

'Wha to?'

'Well, that's the surprisin bit, and it's why I mind. Eddie Williamson.'

'Tink Eddie Williamson?'

'The same.'

Sandy felt a burst of satisfaction. That chimed with what Habbie Goudie had told him about Chic meeting up with one of the Western Isles Williamsons. Eddie was part of that traveller family. 'What would he be wantin wi a shop-bought girdle?'

'My thocht exactly. And …' Frank paused for effect. 'That wasnae all. He bocht a pair of boots and a pair of troosers. And …' He paused again. 'Canvas for a new tent.'

'How did he pay for it?'

'Weel, that was the queerest bit of all.'

'How?'

'He paid for it in banknotes … English banknotes.'

'English banknotes?'

'Exactly. Fishy or what?'

'But you took it?'

'Course I took it. I'm no lookin a gift horse in the mooth. Even an English ane.'

*

Habbie Goudie placed his pint on the window shelf and eyed Annie and Mary warily. 'Alright, lassies?' he said.

'You were speakin to Mary's faither,' Annie began, taking charge. 'Aboot a deid man in a tent.'

Habbie thought for a moment, working through the permutations, assessing where the greatest risk to himself

150

lay. He had a feeling the feisty madam in front of him wasn't going to take any bluster from him.

'Aye,' he replied.

'How did you ken aboot it? It hasnae been made official.'

Habbie sipped his pint, pondered whether to try and inveigle a wee nip from the lassies to go along with it, saw the expression in Annie's eye and decided against it. 'Eddie Williamson telt me.'

'And how did Eddie Williamson ken aboot it?'

'This was last Thursday, like. Eddie was headin oot the Comrie bends at a fair lick and I asked him whaur he was goin in sic a rush. He said he was gettin oot the wey for a bit. How so, I said, and he said there was a deid man in his tent. Nothin to do wi me, he said, but the polis wouldnae see it that wey, no wi him bein a traiveller. So he was getting oot of toon. Winnae be back till the tattie-howkin, he said. If then.' Habbie's resolve failed him. 'I could fair go a wee hauf, if you're needin ony mair information.'

Annie rolled her eyes at Mary. 'Well, you ken whaur the bar is. How did you no mention ony of this to Sandy Disdain when he spoke to you?'

'He never asked me aboot it.'

'But he asked you aboot your cousin Chic. And you telt him Chic was speakin to the Williamsons. Did you no think to mention Eddie then?'

'He asked me aboot Chic. No Eddie.'

'D'you only ever answer exactly what you're asked?'

'I do, lass. It's a lesson I learnt when I was a bairn. Saved me mony a skelped arse.'

*

In the minutes before four o'clock the pipers began to congregate on East High Street at Leadenflower. Bob and Sandy, in the red Drummond of Perth tartan worn by the Crieff Pipe Band, stood with Pipey Oldham and their fellow band members. The pipers from Bob's scratch Moot Band stood behind them, most of them smoking. At the rear, in black kilts, were the pipes and drums of the Eirean Rovers' Band. Drum Major Salmond called the three groups together and ran through the order of tunes.

'It's goin to be hot work, this,' said Bob.

'Aye,' said Sandy. 'Whose daft bloody idea was it to wear the full bearskin in this weather instead of the tam o'shanter? All the wey to MacRosty Park? We'll melt. You'll get blisters.'

'Cheer me up, why don't you?'

The band settled into formation, five rows of three, pipers foremost, bass drummer on his own in the middle, tenor drummers bringing up the rear. Bob, Sandy and Pipey Oldham formed the first trio, behind Drum Major Salmond. The crowd was still sparse at this early point in the route and grew quiet as it became obvious the band were about to begin.

The Drum Major raised his baton high in the air, holding it by the ferrule and keeping it admirably steady. He paused, milking the moment. 'By the right, quick march,' he shouted and the tenor drummers played two tight drum rolls while the pipers filled their bags with air and they launched into *Leaving Port Askaig*. They began their march down East High Street, past the Temperance Hotel, Inglis's garage and the town cross. Drinkers from the Pretoria cheered, beers in hand. Habbie Goudie gave Sandy a wave. They passed the Post Office and Crolla's café and Bain's Emporium, on past the British Linen Bank, downhill to James Square. Flanked on the north face by a suite of temperance hotels, they stopped at the Murray Fountain and formed a circle. There were a couple of hundred people watching by now, laddies and lassies scrambling on the fountain, a couple of intrepid, tousle-haired lads wrapped around the Diamond Jubilee lamp posts until they were pulled off by Constable McAnuff.

The band played for ten minutes and Bob, gradually relaxing until he could admit to himself he was enjoying the moment, spotted Annie and Mary waving to him from the top step of the fountain. Just as he cocked his head in recognition, the band changed pace with *Lairig Ghru* and Bob focused on the work in hand. Although a slow air, he knew this was a tricky piece and he stared at a cobble in front of him to help him concentrate on his fingering.

Drum Major Salmond threw his baton high in the air and caught it and twirled it, indicating to the band to form back into rows and move on again. They marched down West High Street, the Strathearn band in strict time, the Rovers and Eireans behind less so. On Comrie Street, they passed the South Church and the *Strathearn Herald* office and continued as far as the war memorial, where they crossed Burrell Street onto Milnab Street. At the Milnab Mill they turned into the brand-new Taylor Park and up to the circular bandstand in MacRosty Park. Behind them, hundreds of Crieffites and visitors and Rovers followed, marching in time to the music, the bairns running and shouting and pretending to play either bagpipes or drums or, for the more adventurous, both. The band halted by the gardeners' huts between the bandstand and an ancient oak around whose mighty circumference a wooden bench had been built. Seated on it were three of the old maids of Crieff, the Misses Seaton, Beaton and Miller. They were gloved, coated and hatted despite the warm weather, as was the custom in the old Queen's day, before the world had turned to rack and ruin.

'They're no as good as they used to be,' opined Miss Beaton.

'No a patch,' said Miss Seaton.

'Look at that show-off,' said Miss Miller, pointing at the Drum Major twirling his baton. 'Go on, you brute, drop your stick.'

153

Abdalla approached them, smiling. 'But they are very good, are they not?' He doffed his fez and smiled. They stared at him in wonderment.

'Well, I cannae see what you would ken aboot it,' said Miss Miller. 'D'you hae music where you come fae?'

'Still livin in trees, I should think,' said Miss Beaton.

'Madam, I am from Egypt.' He saw blankness in their expressions. 'Mostly desert.' Their expressions remained blank. 'No trees.'

'Good for you, son. Now wheesht. We're listenin to the band.'

Jozef laughed. 'Your famous common touch has deserted you at last, my friend.'

Abdalla clapped Jozef's shoulder as they walked away, leaving the maids to their disgruntlement. 'But,' he said, 'that is the first bad word I have heard since I came here. Is that not amazing? So friendly.'

Jozef pondered. 'You are right. We have been made very welcome.'

'This is a wonderful country.'

'Even if some of its old women aren't.'

'You must have the same in your country?'

'Oh boy, you wouldn't believe some of our old people.'

By the bandstand, the enhanced Crieff Pipe Band played its final tune and Drum Major Salmond called them to a halt. Applause rang out across MacRosty Park. The band broke ranks and Sandy, Bob and Pipey Oldham sauntered towards the river Earn. Sandy took a Capstan from his jacket and lit it. Bob retrieved his pipe from his sporran.

'They werenae bad,' said Pipey, nodding towards the Rovers.

'Taught them mysel,' said Bob. 'Should have heard them three days ago.'

'Aye,' said Sandy. 'They were better.' He turned to Pipey. 'Ony idea how I could track doon a tink that was aroond here last week?'

'Which tink?'

'It micht hae been Eddie Williamson.'

'Micht hae?'

'Micht no.'

Pipey looked to see if he was joking, but Sandy frowned back at him with eyes deep-set beneath bushy eyebrows.

'Well, there's nane of Eddie's kin here the noo, far as I'm aware, so the only thing you can do is ask some of the other tinks in toon. There's some Robertsons working doon on Duchlage fairm. No that they'll tell you onythin but if it maks you feel like you're doin somethin useful …'

'Aye, you're a grand help.'

'Ony time.'

Bob spotted Annie and Mary Kemp bustling towards them down the shallow incline to the right of the gardeners' hut.

'We ken wha the tinker is,' said Annie between deep breaths.

'Eddie Williamson,' said Pipey.

Immediately, the excitement in Annie's expression dissipated. 'How did you ken that?' she said.

'I didnae,' Pipey replied. He jerked his thumb at Sandy. 'He did. Well, maybe.'

Sandy, his cigarette still in the side of his mouth, his left eye half closed to evade the smoke, addressed Annie and Mary. 'I dinnae ken for sure. Frank Thomson mentioned his name. Nae mair than that.'

'It definitely is him. Habbie Goudie telt us.'

A perplexed expression overtook Sandy's face. 'Habbie? But I spoke to him the other day …'

'Aye, but you didnae ask him the richt question. You hae to be specific wi Habbie Goudie, seems like.' She relayed their conversation, the story of Eddie Williamson departing in a rush.

'Did he say whaur he was goin?' Bob asked.

'No.'

'But he was goin oot the Comrie bends?'

'Aye.'

'Probably headin for the Western Isles,' said Sandy. 'His faimly's oot that wey. They usually spend the winter there.'

'The Western Isles? Hell's bells, we've nae chance of findin him, then.'

'Well,' said Annie. 'That's your job. Me and Mary, we found out wha it was. Now it's up to you to find him.'

*

From the colour of the baleful sky overhead, Miško Čurović estimated he had thirty minutes before the rain came. He spat on the ground in annoyance and pulled on the reins of his horse. The horse neighed. The address he'd been given – The Old Ploughman's Cottage, Laggan, Crieff – was proving every bit as troublesome to locate as he'd anticipated. The local people were either imbeciles or obtuse, but either way he could elicit no sense from them. Indeed, the old crone he had just spoken to was surely playing him for a fool.

'You know where the Old Ploughman's Cottage is?' he'd asked her, a woman of maybe seventy with a face like a Bosnian peasant.

'Dinnae ken him.'

'I not understand you.'

'You and me baith, son.'

'Do you know how I find this Old Ploughman's Cottage?'

'Never heard of him.'

'It's not a person. It's a place.'

'Oh aye? Where is it?'

'That's what I ask you.'

'How would I ken?'

'Because you live here.'

The crone looked around and gesticulated. 'This is a

156

wood. Does it look like I bide here? What am I, a squirrel?'

'You're a crazy woman.'

'And you're lost. So wha's the smart ane, eh?' She waved her arm dismissively and turned and walked away.

*

Bob, as he generally did, tried to review the day. He walked hand-in-hand with Annie towards Milnab Mill on the road home, considering what had happened. He remained incensed about the cremation of Erling Hagen, something he viewed as a dereliction of duty. And the news about Eddie Williamson had not improved their chances of solving the crime. Yet he did not feel the despair he might have anticipated. As ever, the humanistic optimism of the Conoboys had bolstered him. Drag decisions into the light, Bella had said. That had to be the way. They wanted to silence him, they wanted to bury the death of Erling, but Bob wouldn't let that happen.

'Mr Kelty.' Bob and Annie turned as Gordon Phillips from the *Herald* office hurried towards them, removing his fedora.

'Enjoy the band?' Bob said.

'Stirring, as ever.'

'All set for the article?'

'That's what I wanted to speak to you about.' Mr Phillips paused, as though measuring his words. 'I had a telephone conversation this afternoon. With someone from the government.'

'Government?'

'Have you ever heard of a D-notice?'

'No.'

'A D-notice is sent to the press by the government, asking them to desist from reporting any news which may affect national security.'

'And?'

'When I say "ask", I mean instruct. In all my career, I've

157

never been subject to a D-notice. We're a provincial press. Why would we?' Bob felt a tug of fear in his chest as he watched Mr Phillips try and fail to hide his bemusement. 'This morning,' he continued, 'I was subjected to a D-notice. About your body. I just wanted to tell you. The story won't be appearing on Saturday.' He gave an apologetic smile. 'Or any time. I'm sorry, Mr Kelty.'

He turned back the way he had come and Bob watched him retreat towards the bandstand. Annie squeezed his hand. He looked at the lade, the mill, the railway cutting in the distance. Good government? Drag decisions into the light?

This was darkness, darkness visible.

Sunday 23rd July

A Day of Accounting

Cobbles in the stable yard of the Crieff Hydro Hotel glinted in early morning sunshine as Miško Čurović approached a young woman in a short coat, riding trousers and wellingtons. A headscarf was tied round her hair. She looked tired.

'Good morning, Miss Carter,' he said. 'Here I am again.'

'Good morning, Mr Čurović. Are you wantin a ride again?'

'If that's possible.'

Nalda Carter looked across the yard to the office. Mr Black, the manager, wasn't around. She checked the time: nine o'clock – he'd be having tea with Shuggie from the vegetable gardens. 'I'm sure we can help you,' she said brightly. 'Meggie's all ready to go. She's the one you rode the other days.' She led him to the stable and clapped a chestnut mare on the back of the neck. The horse whinnied and shook its head. 'I'll get you a stool to climb on,' she said. But, by the time she returned with a three-legged stool, Miško was already astride the horse.

'Ninepence,' said Nalda, stretching out her hand. Miško fished in his jacket and pulled out a shilling.

'Is that enough?'

'Aye, that's just right.' She pocketed the money in her coat. Miško saluted and turned Meggie and trotted out of the stable yard uphill towards Ferntower. Nalda watched him go

159

before turning back to her chores.

'Miss.' She turned and saw another of those odd Rover gentlemen smiling at her. This one was much older, and he seemed to be wearing a field of grass on his head. Zoltán Tóth took off his plumed hat and bowed stiffly.

'I see you lend a horse to my good friend. I wonder, possibly, could I have one too?'

Nalda turned to the office again and was encouraged to see no activity inside. This was cutting things fine all the same. Mr Black would surely be back soon, especially on a Saturday. There was no fruit cake to detain him on a Saturday.

'A shilling,' she said.

'But of course.' He handed over a two-bob bit.

Nalda studied it. 'Just right,' she said. 'Jenny's ready to go.' As she had with Miško, she led him to the stables and offered the use of the stool to mount the horse. Zoltán, fifteen years older and twenty pounds heavier than Miško, took advantage of her offer and, in an ungainly manner which betrayed a lack of familiarity with horsecraft, hauled himself onto the waiting Jenny.

'Will you be alright by yourself?' said Nalda, already imagining a scenario where someone who had not officially hired one of the Hydro's horses had a mishap on it.

'Quite alright, Miss.'

'Miss Carter.' Nalda cursed and turned. Mr Black was striding towards her. 'Is this gentleman borrowing a horse?'

'Yes, Mr Black.'

'Have you collected the sixpence and written it in the book?'

'I was just about to.' She looked up at Zoltán. 'Sorry, what was your name again?'

Once more, Zoltán doffed his cap. 'Zoltán Tóth,' he said. He turned the horse and trotted out of the yard towards Ferntower. Mr Black escorted Nalda to the office.

*

After the morning's musical torment of the English in front of a London enclave which still lacked its sign, Bob sauntered back to Meikle's Nook where James handed him a pewter mug of tea and sat down beside him next to the burnt-out fire from last night. A few recalcitrant Rovers were frying breakfast in a skillet perched atop a smaller fire, squatting close as though urging the bacon to cook faster. Jozef and Abdalla sat in silence. Bob, attuned to such things, detected a tinge of melancholy in the air, the men more subdued than in previous days. The closing ceremony was on Tuesday, prior to the Moot relocating to Edinburgh for two final days of pomp and ceremony. James and the lads of Meikle's Nook were preparing to start dismantling as early as tomorrow. What had seemed, in the idealistic excitement of ten days before, like a huge expanse of time and adventure, had shrunk now into a few remaining hours. Alongside that feeling of impending loss, they were growing less confident that they could make any further headway into the mysterious death of Erling Hagen. Bob detailed the impasse they had reached regarding Eddie Williamson.

'It'd be hard enough to find any man in the whole of the west of Scotland,' he explained, 'far less a tinker. And far less a tinker who doesnae want to be found. There's naethin we can do.'

'What about the Norwegian boy's family?' said Abdalla. 'Surely they need to be told?'

This was concerning Bob, too. 'The Procurator Fiscal promised he would deal wi it. But he also said if I got involved he'd hae me arrested.' He stared at them bleakly. 'I believed him – on baith counts.'

'So he will contact the family?'

'I hope so.'

'You don't know?'

'No.'

161

Abdalla poked at the dead fire with a hazel branch. His usually smiling demeanour had clouded over. 'I thought England an honourable country. Standards. Goodness. Now, I am not sure.'

Bob didn't have the heart to correct his conflation once more of England and Scotland. He agreed with the Egyptian's sentiments. There was a sour taint to the whole experience and Bob was aware that it was caused by officialdom, by his interactions with the powers that be. He had been experiencing that taint since 1935, since the crimes at the Cuddies Strip and their aftermath. You were meant to trust the authorities, weren't you? Weren't they meant to have your best interests at heart? Meant to, aye. But, whatever Bella Conoboy said, it was a black world they inhabited, unregulated, irregular.

*

It took about ten minutes for Zoltán to catch up with Miško. Following from a safe distance, he could tell that Miško, like himself, was not an experienced horseman. He was too stiff in the saddle and would surely suffer backache by nightfall. Zoltán couldn't fathom what the Yugoslav was doing. For two hours he rode, sometimes venturing into new areas of Perthshire countryside before backtracking and circling the same areas again, stopping every ten minutes or so to study a map. On two occasions he encountered a local and spoke to them. All the pointing and gesticulating that followed, Zoltán noticed, came from Miško and not the local, and it was hard to imagine what exchange of information was being requested or, indeed, received. Four or five times Miško alighted at some remote property, a farm or bothy or smithy, where he dismounted and undertook a furtive recce. There was no question Miško's behaviour was, at the very least, peculiar.

But what was he doing?

162

Meanwhile, in front, Miško was growing increasingly frustrated. Some fool was following him, charging about with all the subtlety of a sow in heat, and it was all Miško could do not to turn and confront him. This was his fourth day riding around Crieff and its environs in search of the Old Ploughman's Cottage, and he was becoming desperate. He had widened his remaining search area after the first couple of days, because the area around the Laggan Hill, despite its name, seemed to offer little of promise, but now he was back there again, convinced he must have missed something. He retraced his earlier route from the rear of the Monzie estate, round by Glenturret and in through the Curroch Strips. Skirting the lower reaches of the Laggan Hill rather than heading towards Turret Lodge, as before, he came across a small cottage in splendid isolation just below the tree line. Thinking this could be the place, he dismounted.

'Can I help you?' A middle-aged woman, dressed entirely in grey save for a black pinny, was bent over a row of carrots in the back garden.

'Is this the Old Ploughman's Cottage?'

'Nae ploomen here,' said Mrs Disdain, Sandy's mother, eyeing the stranger warily. Sandy had told her about the exotic specimens at the Moot, but she hadn't thought to meet one face-to-face.

'Do you know where I might find it?'

This was too strange a question. A foreigner, asking about Norrie Smith's house? No good would come of that. 'Nae idea, son. Have a grand day.' She returned to her carrots, her legs spread wide and her back straight. Recognising there was nothing useful to be garnered here, Miško remounted and walked on. A couple of minutes later, Mrs Disdain watched as a second Rover, wearing a ludicrous hat, rode past, trying to make himself invisible and thereby drawing attention to himself, the daft galoot.

Miško rode on, arriving at the Laggan farm from a different direction than previously and spotting, as he passed, a single-track lane to the right that he didn't remember from before. It was bounded either side by overgrown vegetation, rosebay willowherb and whins lending a pink and yellow ambience, making the passage seem less claustrophobic. He hoped this might be a new route but couldn't be sure. Everywhere in this blasted country looked the same. The countryside with its fields of crops or sheep or cows, the heather hillsides, the squat, grey buildings of its settlements, the sour-faced people, identical, at every turn. He reached a fork in the path and knew that right must lead back to the Laggan farm, but the path to the left was unfamiliar. He pulled the horse's reins and directed it left, the rough track ahead of them dappled by sunlight threading through the heavy line of beech trees as though indicating the direction of their passage.

*

At the entrance to Monzie Castle, surrounded by cheering Rovers, the Laird of Monzie, David Maitland-Makgill-Crichton, himself a sailor of renown, greeted the two Australian and one Polish sailors. The Australians, David Walsh and Bernard Plowright, both tall and lean in dark green uniforms and wide-brimmed hats, shook his hand vigorously. Wladyslaw Wagner, shorter and stockier, bowed slightly as he shook the Laird's hand. They were guided to Sir Lancelot and took their place in the open-topped rear in which, two days before, Bob Kelty had transported forty-eight pounds of haggis. An Australian flag was draped over the driver's seat behind James Meikle, while a guard of honour comprising Australian, Polish and Scottish Rovers lined both sides of the vehicle and Bob's Moot Band took up position at the front. On Abdalla's signal they started to play and the procession wound uphill. Cheers rang throughout the grounds as they entered the Moot arena, all three men waving animatedly to the crowds of Rovers who were already gathering for that afternoon's performances. At the dais, they were greeted by Mr Howie, the Moot chief, Lord Rowallan and Lord Glentanar and, after they had posed for photographs for the *Moot Pictorial* and the local newspapers, Mr Howie gave a speech praising their dedication and seafaring skill after their year's journey to be here.

'And only three days late,' Jozef said to Wladyslaw afterwards, clapping him on the back. He introduced the newcomer to the group at Meikle's Nook, and Wladyslaw spent half an hour regaling them with tales of high danger and low boredom, a life on the seas alternately buffeted by storms and becalmed for days on end.

'A year on a boat,' said Bob. 'I couldnae do that, I'm sure.'

'Much longer than one year,' said Wladyslaw. 'I left Gdynia in Poland seven years ago. Bought a boat for ten zloty, sailed to Panama. The boat was ruined by the time I got there, so I build a new one – forty-eight feet ketch, beautiful boat. It sank in Fiji and I build a third boat, the *Zjawa III*. That take me to Australia where I meet these boys …' He pointed across the campsite to the Australian Rovers who were similarly entertaining another campfire gathering.

'So what will you do now?' said Bob. 'Sail aff into the sunset again?'

'No. Now, I go back home. I must do my military service. In the Polish Navy. This is very important, I think, with what happen in Germany right now.'

He was a canny man, Bob thought. Cheerful. Clearly resourceful. He would be grand company. Seven years on the ocean, adventuring, living, pitting his wits against all that nature could throw at him, and now he was keen, apparently, to give all that up and return home to rumours of war, threats, a world in jeopardy. A world in motion. Never

165

stopping.

But going where?

*

The rain started to fall about twelve o'clock, just as Miško alighted on the small cottage hidden a mile or so down a scrubby lane he had taken at the last junction. Miško felt sure, finally, he had found the Old Ploughman's Cottage. He sat beneath a beech tree and watched for half an hour. The curtains in the front were drawn but those in the rest of the house were opened. Finally, he concluded the house must be empty.

He circled the house twice and looked in a side window but there wasn't enough light to see properly. He splayed his hands against a window at the rear and pressed his head against them. A kitchen came into view, old and dingy. Empty. To his right was a door. He tried the handle. It opened. He let himself in and looked around. A Belfast sink sat beneath the grimy window he had just looked through. A range was beside it, and a rustic table and a single chair occupied the middle of the room. A sour and musky smell filled Miško's nostrils, unpleasant, stale, dirty. This was a man's house. No woman lived here. That tallied with the intelligence Miško had been given before his arrival at the camp.

'Who the hell are you?'

An old man, bald and toothless in frayed and greying trousers, a three-quarters unbuttoned shirt and cardigan, stood in the doorway pointing a pistol at Miško. The pistol looked as ancient as the old man, probably some relic from the Great War or even before, but Miško didn't fancy testing whether or not it still worked. He put his hands in the air.

'Steady, old man. I mean no harm.'

'What are you doin in my hoose?'

'I'm going to reach into my jacket, yes?' He shook his right hand to demonstrate it was empty. Slowly, he edged it

166

towards his jacket and reached inside. From his breast pocket he extracted the torn half-postcard with a view of a suburban German street which Zoltán had found in his rucksack days earlier. "*Ecke Seilerstraße und*" it read. Still making slow and deliberate movements, Miško presented the postcard to the old man, who took it and studied it for some moments as though unable to process what he was seeing. He lowered his pistol and laid it on the kitchen table. His already frail body seemed to diminish, like someone who knew an end was approaching.

'They said someone micht come ae day, but I never thocht it.'

He made to say more but stopped. He turned and walked into the living room. Miško followed. With the curtain drawn it was cloaked in gloom. It smelled of stale ale, tobacco and alcohol, with high notes of halitosis. Bottles of beer lay empty on the floor. A solid chest of drawers, a good four feet high and three feet deep, probably homemade, lined one wall, the surface littered with papers and bottles and detritus. Propped against an empty glass vase was a half postcard. The old man handed it to Miško, and Miško placed it beside his. They matched perfectly. The old man's half said: "*Sophienstraße*".

'"*Ecke Seilerstraße und Sophienstraße*",' Miško said. Corner of Seilerstrasse und Sophienstrasse. Sophienstrasse, home of the Hamburg offices of the *Abwehr*, the German intelligence organisation. Postcards of the building were ripped in two so that agents in the field, who were given one half, would know when they were speaking to their counterparts and not some double-agent.

'Why are you here?' the old man said.

'You have been behaving badly, Smith. It is Smith, yes?'

'Aye.' The young man before him had hard eyes, Norrie Smith thought. He'd dealt with these people before and he knew compassion was not part of their makeup. He realised that leaving the pistol in the kitchen had been a terrible mistake. An involuntary glance towards the kitchen door betrayed his thought. Miško laughed.

'You don't seriously think that old thing will fire anyway?' he said.

'I've no done nothin, son. Honest, I havenae.'

'No. And that is the problem, old man. The point of setting you up as a postbox is that you receive letters and *then you redirect them* to *Abwehr* headquarters ...'

'And that's what I do ...'

'For this we pay you £10 a month ...'

'And I'm very grateful ...'

'And we expect our orders to be obeyed ...'

'They are ... I do ...'

'But for some time we have been suspicious that not enough is reaching us from you. Especially since Jessie Jordan was arrested ...'

'I send aathin I get ...'

'So we do some tests. Send you something. Wait for it to reappear at *Abwehr* in Hamburg ... And guess what?'

'I send aathin ...'

'It never appear.'

The old man before him was a wretched creature, to be sure, much as Miško had expected. He'd read the file before coming to Scotland. Norman Smith, over eighty, married to Frieda Schloss, a greengrocer's daughter from Frankfurt. His son Edward was killed at Megiddo in Palestine in September 1918, aged forty. His grandson, also Edward, was executed by firing squad for cowardice, aged eighteen, at Arras three days later. When news arrived of both deaths, in mid-October, Frieda Smith went into the woods and hanged herself. In the years that followed, old man Smith, now without family, without purpose, blamed the British authorities and grew embittered, possibly insane. In the early days of Herr Hitler's rule, he contacted the German authorities and offered his services. *Would have been better all round if you lot had won the last war. You were gentlemen, at least.* Despite a suspicion that Frieda Schloss had had Jewish blood, the *Abwehr* took him on. Sleepers were always useful, they said, although Miško remained unconvinced by the worth of such self-referring spies. They were unreliable. *Nesposoban. Unbrauchbar.* The specimen in front of him was confirmation of his doubts.

He strode to the chest of drawers and, with a flourish, he swept the surface clear of rubbish, scattering it across the floor.

'So where are they?' he said. Again, Norrie Smith tried to proclaim innocence. 'Enough!' Miško shouted. 'Jessie Jordan, the last Scottish spy, she get four years for espionage. But she's a woman. They will be much tougher on a man, yes? A traitor? Working with the enemy …'

'I only pass on letters …'

'So you will be happy to explain this to the authorities? If I report you?'

'You wouldnae?'

'Of course I wouldn't. Don't be ridiculous.'

Finally, Norrie realised he was in mortal danger. Once more his glance towards the kitchen door betrayed him. Slowly, deliberately, Miško walked to the kitchen, picked up the pistol and returned to the living room. He pointed the pistol at Norrie.

'What do you do with them? The letters you don't send?'

Norrie indicated to a cupboard in the chest of drawers.

'Open it.'

Norrie crouched and opened the cupboard, revealing a mass of letters and parcels. There must have been eighty or more, a chaos of creased and tattered correspondence going back two years or so. All of them were still sealed.

'Why? We pay you well. All you have to do is receive the mail, redirect it and post it again. This is simple.'

169

'There was so much of it. Ever since that woman was caught.' Miško sighed. Jessie Jordan, as well as being a spy, had similarly run a *post restante* operation from Perth and Dundee for the *Abwehr* until she was arrested the previous year and convicted that May. She and Smith and a few others received mail from America and Egypt and other countries from where mail sent directly to Germany would be deemed suspicious and probably intercepted by the host governments. Sent instead to Britain, communications could then be redirected to Hamburg, with the British authorities – still desperate to appease Germany – operating far less stringent checks. Miško had warned his seniors, when Jordan was caught, that they needed to rebuild the capacity of the operation, but they had vacillated, as usual. Nothing had been done. And the old man had been swamped with mail. This was a problem of the *Abwehr*'s own making.

'Every time Pat the postie comes by, he mentions it,' Norrie continued. 'I get mair post than the town hall, he says. I was terrified I was goin to get caught.'

Miško shook his head. 'Would probably be better for you if you had, old man.' He gestured to the cupboard. 'Empty it. All the mail. Put it on that chair.' He pointed to a threadbare armchair beside the empty fire. The old man stooped and dragged a handful of mail from the cupboard, dropping it on the armchair. Dozens of letters and small packages, all addressed to the Old Ploughman's Cottage, Laggan, Crieff, in a plethora of writing styles, bearing stamps from across the world. When he was done, he stood up and straightened his back and had the effrontery to flash Miško a smile, as though to say "haven't I done well?" Like a dog. Like a sub-human, like a Bosnian. Like Miško's own father, a coward, too frightened, too stupid to recognise on which side victory stood. Too keen to serve the man before him, not the master behind. Bringing humiliation on his family, poverty, despair. Miško stepped forward, raised the pistol to the old man's head, pressed it against his ear and fired.

*

'It's a damned shame,' said Annie. 'Every time the public's allowed on the site it rains.' More cinders had been piled on the camp's footpaths but three hours of incessant rain had turned the site into a quagmire once more. Annie, Bob and Mary sheltered beneath a chestnut tree as Rovers from Finland gave a demonstration of their national dance in the arena. Despite the rain, a large crowd clapped and cheered. The Indian contingent were waiting to perform next, a show of singing and dancing that Bob had seen the other day, full of verve and rhythmic style although, Bob fancied, it might appear less effervescent today, in the deluge. Sandy Disdain approached, rain dripping from the brim of his deerstalker and his tweed suit sodden.

'I cannae believe the size of these crowds,' he said.

'This is the last chance to see the Rovers,' Bob replied, 'afore they decamp to Embra.'

Sandy looked towards the arena, to the hundreds hunched and shivering as they watched the bedraggled spectacle. 'I wouldnae pay a shillin for this.'

'Have you no paid?'

'Course no.'

'How d'you get in?'

'I walked fae Culcrieff. Roond the back of the loch.'

'Well, dinnae go tellin onyone or they'll all be at it.'

'I wouldnae.' He cupped an enormous hand around a Capstan and lit it. 'It's treacherous oot there, ken. You're liable to sink in the bog if you dinnae ca canny. Go under in there and you'll never be fund.'

'Michty,' said Mary. 'It's surely no that dangerous?'

'It is, aye.'

'Well, you be careful.'

Sandy stared at her for some moments. He gave the

171

merest nod of his head.

*

When the rain finally stopped, on a patch of waste ground a couple of hundred yards from the old man's house and on the edge of a wood, beside a field in which grazed a dozen morose cows, Miško Čurović gathered twiglets and small branches and arranged them one on top of the other. Above, he settled what dried leaves he could find. He took a match and lit the fire and fanned it gently until it took hold. Gradually, he added ever larger branches until a fire, insubstantial but the best he could achieve after the rain, burned in the late afternoon mirk. One by one, he threw the letters and packages on to the fire, ensuring that each was incinerated, that no incriminating fragments would remain. He watched over the fire for an hour after he had burned the last letter, then kicked over the remains in search of stray documentation. Finally satisfied he had obliterated any evidence, he went back inside the old man's house and sought to remove any trace of himself. He wiped door handles and surfaces he might have touched – the kitchen table, the chest of drawers. Had he touched anywhere else? No. He looked at the living room curtains, still drawn. Those could attract attention, he thought. He opened them, letting light flood into the room, showing up the dust and dirt more clearly.

He took the gun from the chest of drawers and knelt beside the dead man. Prising his fingers open, he placed the gun in the old man's gnarled hand and rearranged the body to suggest he had shot himself.

'Crazy old man,' he said aloud. 'Probably owed money. All get too much for him. Shoot himself. Tragedy.' He didn't believe that. Didn't believe the authorities would believe that. *But what's done is done. Pokazivati se. Vorrücken.*

He went outside, closing the door using the arm of his

172

jacket. He returned to his horse and clapped its flank, then looked up the path. There had been no evidence of his watcher for the past hour but he sensed his presence, all the same. And he had seen enough to know who it was – one of the Hungarian Rovers, those buffoons with the ridiculous headgear, like the pampas on manoeuvres.

The older one. Zoltán Tóth. He was going to be a problem. Miško climbed onto his horse and with a quick look back at the cottage, began to ride towards the Laggan.

Behind him, Zoltán watched from the cover of a stand of beech trees in which he had hidden when he heard the gunfire. He waited until Miško was out of sight, and then waited another ten minutes, before summoning the courage to move. He approached the house and entered, as Miško had, through the back door. Again like Miško, he used his jacket to avoid fingerprints. He did so on the way out again a few moments later, staggering, hand against his mouth. He made his way to a clump of bushes by the side of the house and vomited.

*

'There you fuckin are,' Pat Kemp said. 'Whaur you been? I'm needin hame for my tea.' He reached his hand out to Mary. 'Get me up.' Mary tried to pull him to his feet but she knew from experience she wouldn't have the strength.

'Get on your knees,' she said. 'Then let me help pull you.'

'I dinnae get on my knees for onyone, girl, let alone you.' He exhaled heavily as though it was him making the effort. Mary tugged, but she might as well have been trying to open a locked door.

'You alright?'

Relief flooded through her as she recognised Sandy Disdain's voice. There he was, staring at her faither with what she could only describe as pity.

'My faither's maybe got a wee bit too much sun,' she

173

said.

'Aye, that sun's been fair pourin doon aa efternoon.'

'Could you help me get him up?'

'I dinnae need any fuckin help,' Pat snapped. He threw his half-empty beer bottle beside the others and leaned on his left hand and tried to shift his bulk. Sandy gripped his right arm and yanked him upwards, pulling him into a crouching position and then on to his feet and finally – almost – upright. Pat staggered for a moment until he gained his balance.

'I think you need to get hame,' said Sandy.

'Dinnae tell me what to do, bairn.'

Pat became aware that Sandy's hand was still gripped around his bicep and he tried to pull clear but felt, instead, Sandy's fingers digging even harder into his flesh.

'Stop pawin me.'

Sandy ignored him and spoke to Mary. 'Get his bike. I'll walk you back to toon.' He altered his grip and additionally wrapped his left hand around Pat's wrist so that he was virtually frogmarching him. He nudged him with his shoulder and edged him downhill towards the car park and exit. He released him and the trio walked silently out of the camp and into Gilmerton and onto the bends, Sandy and Mary in front, Pat five or six yards behind, apparently in conversation with an invisible adversary, occasionally flailing his arm towards it and muttering.

'Keep up, faither,' Mary said.

'Dinnae talk to me like that. I'll gie you a good skelp when I get you hame.'

'I think you'll be sleepin it aff when you get hame,' said Sandy.

'Hey! Hey! Hey! Wha d'you think you are? Fuckin poacher is all you are. No good, like thon faither of yours. Got the sack fae Halley's, did he no?'

Sandy knew that his father had never worked for Halley's, far less been sacked by them, but he also knew the futility of

174

engaging a drunk in an argument.

'And your wee sister,' said Pat. 'Her that works in Salmond's? Wee goer, by all accounts.'

'Enough.'

'Cannae get enough of the laddies …'

'Enough.'

'Family of Dundee minks …'

Sandy grabbed his arm again and thrust his face into Pat's. Studied him. The decades of helplessness and misery in the bloodshot blankness of those eyes, that porous skin, nose expanding, grey pallor, dead expression.

'The morn,' he said, 'you'll no mind onythin aboot this. But she will.' He hitched his thumb towards Mary. 'And I will. I winnae forget. Noo, belt up and walk.'

Pat seemed to ponder for a moment, then shook himself free from Sandy's grip.

'Here, girl,' he said. 'Gie me my bike. I could eat a scabby donkey. I'm needin my tea.' He snatched the bike from Mary and tried to swing his leg over it, losing his balance and toppling over. He righted the bike and tried again.

'I dinnae think you should do that,' said Sandy.

'Are you a pheasant plucker, or a pheasant plucker's son?' He cackled as though he had told the funniest joke. 'Here, you're a Dundee mink, cannae speak the King's English. You try and say it. "I'm not a pheasant plucker, I'm a pheasant plucker's son." Come on. Try it. Fast as you can.'

He managed to sit astride the bicycle and hitched up his trousers and settled his foot on the pedal. 'Ah, fuck yous,' he said and pressed his weight on the pedal, causing the bicycle to career forwards. He tried to gain control of the handlebars and veered first left, then right. He sat heavily on the seat and turned the pedals once, twice, three times, heading straight towards the ditch at the side of the road.

'Faither!' shouted Mary, but it was too late and Pat and his bicycle crashed off the road into a ditch that was clearly much deeper than it looked, bearded as it was by summer growth. Pat lay three feet below them, staring up, entangled in the frame of the bicycle. He was half submerged in a pool of water, its surface glinting in the late sunlight.

'Help me,' he said, reaching out his hand.

Sandy shook his head. He reached into his pocket and pulled out a Capstan and lit it. He exhaled smoke in Pat's direction.

'Silly auld fool,' he said. 'You can bloody bide there.' He turned to Mary. 'Come on.'

'We cannae leave him …'

'It'll do him good. Sober him up. Come on.'

And Sandy marched forward. Mary faltered, looked at her faither, looked at Sandy's retreating back. She had no idea what to do next but she knew she didn't want to be left out here, alone with her faither. Finally, she hurried after Sandy, Pat the postie's roars reverberating in her ears.

*

Late evening, and Miško and Zoltán walked away from the Hungarian encampment. Zoltán was trying not to show fear. The overly friendly way Miško had invited him for a walk was disconcerting. Too nice. Too reasonable. Miško appeared a man without care. They walked uphill. The bustle of thousands of visitors had dissipated into the soggy calm of a Scottish evening. A crow flew overhead. Sparrows chirruped inside a hawthorn bush. Rabbits louped on the slope of a nearby hill. They sat together on the Loch Ness Monster and looked down over the campsite. The air was still humid and heavy but would clear soon. Miško spoke without looking at his companion.

'You follow me today,' he said.

'I was in camp all day …'

'Don't lie. I saw you. You are a worse horseman than I am.'

Zoltán wanted to argue, but that wouldn't have helped. He decided to admit his role. 'I followed you, yes, because I was curious. Riding all over the place. Middle of nowhere.'

'Am I not allowed to enjoy the countryside?'

'You weren't. You were looking for something.'

Miško turned and faced him. This was the crux of the discussion. 'What do you think?' he said. 'Did I find it?'

'I don't know.'

But there it was, that falter. A fraction of a second, no more, but enough. That momentary delay in replying told Miško what he needed to know. He looked around at the Perthshire skyline. The trouble with killing was that it never ended. It had taken him time to understand that. Too much time. Much too late.

'You saw?'

Zoltán's skin was prickling. Miško's tone was as affable as ever, apparently warm and friendly. And yet ... And yet, in that house, that body … Zoltán knew he was in danger. 'Yes,' he said, almost despite himself.

'Did you go inside the house?'

The inevitable question. And only one answer. 'No.'

The lie didn't work. Miško was satisfied. Zoltán knew. He had been there.

He would have to go.

Monday 24th July

A Day of Villainy

By eight o'clock, the first rush of Rovers wanting breakfast had dissipated. Bob wiped the back of his hand across his forehead and swept his hair into place. He handed Sandy Disdain a bacon roll and Sandy bit into it immediately, scoffing a quarter in one go.

'I wanted a word,' he said. 'Last night. Hellish thing. I was late gettin hame, on account of Pat the bloody postie …'

'What aboot Pat the postie?'

'I'll tell you later. There was polis oot the Laggan farm when I was goin hame. At the tap of the path that leads doon to Norrie Smith's hoose – you ken it?'

'Back end of Lady Mary's Walk?'

'Aye. Well, Maggie Caldwell was there. Biggest lugs in Crieff …'

'And that's sayin something …'

'She misses nothin. "Whit's goin on, Maggie?" I says to her. And she says, "Terrible shame, auld Norrie's gone and done himsel in …"'

'Plooman Norrie?'

'The same. Maggie had made some soup for her tea, she said, with the banes of yesterday's ham, and she decided to tak him some. On account of he doesnae look efter himsel. Found him deid on the flair. His auld pistol in his haund.'

Bob felt the world jolt, a tightness constrict his chest.

He grew instantly hot, his hearing turning fuzzy like he was underwater. Unbidden, the image of a kitchen came to him. A twelve-year-old-laddie keeking through the window, seeing his father dead on the floor, implement of death by his side.

'Sorry,' said Sandy, seeing Bob's reaction. 'I forgot about your faither …'

'It's fine.' Bob tried to close that compartment, step away from it, leave it for another time. The dead of night, awake in bed, Annie snoring by his side, that was his time for negotiating the past, communing with the dead, seeking an accommodation with a pain that never seemed to diminish.

'He hasnae been right in the heid since the war,' said Sandy. 'Bairn and grandbairn dyin one efter the other, then Frieda hingin hersel in front of the hoose. He even stopped openin the doonstairs curtains because every time he did he'd see the spot she killed hersel. Wid affect ony man, that. Even so, I never thocht he'd do this.'

'No, puir man was feart of his ain shadow. I'd never hae thocht he'd hae the courage.'

Sandy, knowing Bob's history, kept to himself his belief that suicide was a coward's solution and involved no bravery. He washed the last of his bacon roll down with a mouthful of tea.

'The queer thing, though – and this is why I came to see you – is that Maggie said earlier in the day she saw twa of the Rovers doon by the hoose. On cuddies. But no thegither. One was a couple of minutes ahint the other. And then, when I went hame, my mither said the exact same thing.'

'They were sure they were Rovers?'

'Aye, baith of them wearin shorts. On a cuddy.'

Bob nodded. 'That sounds like Rovers.'

'And the second ane had a stupit hat.'

'Grass?'

'Aye. So what d'you make of that?'

'Well.' Bob turned his mug in a three-hundred-and-sixty-degree revolution. 'We ken that Miško – thon Yugoslavian – hired a cuddy. He telt us that. So he could be the first ane. And the hat …'

'That's ane of the Hungarians.'

'And which Hungarian keeps poppin up aa ower the place?'

'Ivan.'

'István. Exactly.' Bob sat back and stared at the tent canopy above him. 'Right,' he said. 'We need to explore this. We ken Miško got his cuddy fae the Hydro stables. Let's go and see what we can find there.' He made to stand, but stopped. 'Pat the postie,' he said. 'What happened there?'

'Ach, nothin.' Sandy relayed the story of the previous evening, Pat's drunkenness, pitching himself and his bike into a ditch, Sandy walking off.

'You left him there?'

'Until I took Mary hame. Then I went back …'

'And?'

'He wasnae there.'

'What d'you mean, he wasnae there?'

'What I say. When I got back he was gone …'

'And you havenae done onythin aboot it?'

'He'll hae got oot by himsel. Gone hame. He's probably back at work already, hungover to buggery …'

'He isnae. Annie was in a wee while back. He missed the early morning delivery. Aabody's fair vexed wi him.'

'He'll turn up …'

'We hae to go and look for him.'

'How?'

Bob remembered the time some schoolchildren got lost in a blizzard. Confused and disorientated, they'd missed a turn they took every day on their way to and from school. Pat the postie could have emerged from the ditch, not known which direction he was facing and gone the wrong way.

'He could easy have gone in the ditch again. He could be

deid of the cauld.'

'In July?'

Bob stood and gathered their empty plates and mugs. 'Just come on,' he said.

*

Zoltán walked out of the Moot post office clutching the telegram from the Hungarian Rovers headquarters. He had no idea what he expected the response to be, but it was not this:

KEDALY OFFICIAL STOP DO NOT PURSUE STOP

"Official". What did official mean? An official? An official of what? Or simply officially accredited? Meant to be there? The answer was no answer at all. And then he realised that this was, indeed, what he had expected after all.

The world was growing more opaque.

*

'This is a waste of bloody time,' said Sandy as they marched downhill to Gilmerton. 'He's either hame or he's deid in a ditch. Either wey, there's nothin we can do aboot it.'

'Well, if he's the ane, that's grand. But if he's the ither we hae to find him. We cannae just leave him in a ditch, can we? Can you imagine the stink, for one thing?' He took Sandy's silence as assent. 'Annie and I were ahint you last nicht, and we turned aff onto the Hielanman Loan, so we'd hae seen him between there and Gilmerton. We need to search fae the Hielanman to the golf course.'

'Let's get on wi it, then.'

'You're a richt grumpy bugger.'

'Have you just noticed?'

'I've been mullin it over.'

The first of the Gilmerton bends, leading out of the village, was dark and cool, a guard of trees lining each side

181

of the road and coming together above them. The stillness was disturbed only by the chatter of sparrows. Gummie Gibbs, driving the Perth bus, waved as he passed them. He appeared to be indicating behind him as though alerting them to something.

'What's he sayin?' said Bob.

'I dinnae ken what Gummie Gibbs is sayin when he's standin richt in front of me, far less driving a bus at forty mile an hoor.'

'Aye, he could do wi some teeth.'

After a hundred yards the road took a sharp right, rising more steeply, as it now would all the way to the top of Crieff. Ahead, on their left, was the Highlandman Loan, long and straight downhill all the way to Duchlage, purportedly the route taken by Bonnie Prince Charlie's troops during the second Jacobite rebellion on their march south as far as Derby, before cowardice, avarice and incompetence impelled an ignominious and – finally – catastrophic retreat.

A sudden shriek drew their attention from their search of the gutters and, ahead of them, approaching a seventy-degree bend in the road far too fast for safety, was a bicycle, a bag of post perched in the front pannier. Riding it was a young woman.

'Is that no Mary?' said Bob.

She screamed as she careered into and out of the bend, almost running out of road on the left as she – just – negotiated the turn. Overcompensating, she steered too hard to the right and almost sheered off the road onto the Highlandman Loan. She oversteered again, screaming all the while. She lost control of the pedals and swung her legs up and outwards to avoid them as they whirred helplessly round and round. Bob and Sandy watched in astonishment as she streaked past them, still screaming, her hands gripping the handlebars, her terrified gaze fixed on the road in front of her.

Ahead, beyond her line of vision, was the bend Bob and

Sandy had just passed, a sharp left towards the village.

'She's goin too fast,' said Bob.

'You dinnae say.'

The bicycle continued to rush headlong towards the bend and Mary made no effort to steer into it, or to slow down. She let out one final yell as she continued her forward trajectory straight over the bend and through a hawthorn hedge and dropped five feet into the rough field beyond. Momentum took her another twenty yards before long grass brought her to a halt and the bicycle collapsed to the ground, taking Mary with it. Sundry letters and parcels fell loose from the postbag.

Bob and Sandy ran back to the bend and pushed their way through the hedge, cursing its sharp tines, before jumping down into the field.

'Are you okay?' Bob shouted. Sandy reached her first and extricated her from the battered bicycle. He helped her to her feet. Mary wiped grass and mud from her jacket, still dazed. She looked around as though she had no idea where she was or how she had come to be here.

'What were you doin?' said Sandy.

'Tryin to tak faither's delivery to the Moot,' she replied. She glared at him furiously. 'He got hame after one o'clock last night, no thanks to you ...'

'I tried to find him ...'

'And the state he was in this mornin, he could barely get oot of bed. I said I'd do the Moot run for him and he could do the rest of the round later.'

'Have you ever ridden a bicycle before?'

'No one as heavy as this.'

Sandy picked up the bike. Its handlebars had been driven almost sideways. He gripped the front wheel between his knees and, grunting, tried to pull them back into position. At first, they wouldn't budge, but finally they began to groan and shift. When he was satisfied they were true, he lifted

183

first the front and then the rear wheels and flicked them and tested the brakes. The front brake was all but useless but, he suspected, judging by what remained of the brake blocks, that had been the case before.

Mary was sobbing now, shock taking over from her anger at Sandy. Bob hugged her and rubbed her shoulder. 'Let's get you up to the site,' he said. 'James Meikle will mak you a hot cup of tea.'

As they trekked through the wet grass back to the road, Bob saw a McLagan's truck hurtling down the Gilmerton bends towards them. He leaped out of the field and hailed the van. Froggy Neilson drew to a halt alongside.

'Alright boys?' he said, leaning out of the window, cigarette ash falling to the asphalt.

'You goin to the Moot?' Bob asked.

'Aye, half a hunner weight of tatties. These laddies can eat.'

'Ony chance of a lift?'

'Nae bother, hop aboard.'

'Just Mary,' said Sandy. He opened the rear of the truck and threw Pat the postie's bike on board. He held out his hand for Mary.

'Whaur are we goin?' said Bob.

Sandy hitched his thumb in the direction of Crieff. 'Whaur we should hae gone first off,' he said. 'The Hydro.'

*

'Have you seen Bob today?' Zoltán Tóth smiled at James Meikle, his voluminous hat in his hand. James hadn't previously seen him hatless and he was surprised the older man had such lush hair. More Slavic than Hungarian, he thought.

'He was in first off. Went off with Sandy Disdain. Dunno where, but.'

'You know when he will be back?'

184

'Nae idea. Before tea time, though, I'd guess, knowin Bob.'

Zoltán laughed. 'Indeed,' he said. 'I come back later. If you see him, tell him I need to speak with him. Most important.'

*

Sandy lit a cigarette as he and Bob entered the Hydro stables. 'Nalda,' he shouted. Nalda Carter put down the pail of water she was carrying. She patted her hair and stood with her hands on her hips. 'How's your mither?' Sandy asked.

'At her wits' end. Granny Duncan's getting mair dottled by the day. We keep findin her doon the Earn, washin claes. Except there's nae claes. She's just dichtin her haunds in the watter.'

'Puir woman. She was aye prood, Patsy Duncan. She'd be black-affronted to think people kent she was daein that.'

'Aye, it's a blessin she hasnae a clue. What can I do for you?'

'You hired a cuddy to ane of thae Rovers the other day. Monday? Name Miško or somethin like that.'

'Aye. He's been in maist days.'

'Grand. Was he in yesterday? For a cuddy?'

'He was. Christ knows how he does it. In thae shorts.'

'Must hae thighs like cowhide.'

'Apart fae Miško,' said Bob, 'have you had any other Rover laddies hirin a cuddy?'

Bob and Sandy both saw Nalda freeze. She clearly had, and she was terrible at concealing the fact. Bob waited.

'No a laddie,' she said finally.

'But a Rover?'

'Stupit outfit, aye. Mad hat, ken? An auld man dressed in shorts like a bairn.'

'How auld?'

'I dinnae ken. All auld men look the same to me.' She

185

looked at Bob and Sandy, both no more than a handful of years older than her, as though this proved her point.

'D'ye ken his name?'

Again Nalda stopped, and again they waited until her mind whirred and an answer presented itself.

'It was some foreign name,' she said. 'I cannae mind.' What she did remember, though, was Mr Black coming out as she was looking to pocket the money and insisting the hire was logged in their register. 'It's in the book,' she said.

'Can we see?'

'How?'

'We're just interested.'

'I havenae done onythin wrang.'

'No, I ken.'

Nalda visibly relaxed. 'Come ben the office, then.'

Mr Black was seated by a bench that ran the length of the office, smoking a pipe and reading *The Courier*. He had clearly been watching the whole exchange but he greeted Sandy and Bob as though they were surprise visitors. Nalda opened the bookings register at the current entries and pointed to an entry in her own handwriting.

'That's it,' she said. 'Sultan Tosh. I couldnae swear to the spellin.'

'Zoltán Tóth,' said Bob, surprise registering in his voice. His was not the name he was expecting. 'Was there naebody else apart fae these two? Another Rover maybe, wi a fancy hat same as Zoltán's, but younger?'

'Nut,' she said. 'Just Mr Čurović and Tosh.'

Mr Black laid his pipe down on the bench. 'Nalda, awa and gie the cuddies a rub doon, hen. It's goin to be a hot efternoon.' Nalda made to object but Mr Black raised his palm. 'Awa,' he said.

Nalda turned petulantly and flounced out of the office towards the stables. Mr Black pointed at the register.

'There could easy hae been someone else yesterday,' he

said. 'That Nalda didnae log.'

'How?' said Bob.

'Nalda's been at it the past six months noo. No putting the hires in the book and takin the money. I havenae the heart to sack her. No wi her gran bein daft and her mother aff her heid with the worry.'

'Aye,' said Sandy, 'she's a good lass at heart. Feisty, mind. God help her husband if she ever gets merried.'

Bob exited into the stables again, sighing. 'So, oor horsemen are probably Miško and Zoltán but we cannae be sure. How can we no get cast-iron clues, like in the books?'

Sandy lit a Capstan from the remains of the previous one and threw that on the ground. 'Aye well,' he said, 'we'd best find Nalda and hire some cuddies oorsel.'

'Eh?'

'If you want mair clues, we need to get doon the Laggan. It'll tak an hoor fae here if we hoof it. Especially the speed you walk.'

'I cannae go a cuddy.'

'Thocht your faither worked the cuddies?'

'Aye, the heavy anes. You dinnae ride the buggers. Walk alangside them. Feed them. Pick up their shite.'

Sandy sighed. 'Whaur's your bike?'

'At the Moot.'

'Right. Get back there. Then get yourself to the Laggan. I'll meet you at Eppie Callum's tree in an hoor.'

*

Eppie Callum's Tree was a five-hundred-year-old oak named after a former owner of the Oakbank Inn, grown by her in a teapot on her windowsill and planted in the ground when it became too large. It was reputed once to have been the hiding place of Rob Roy McGregor after a disturbance at the Crieff Michaelmas Fair. Sandy Disdain was waiting on Jenny as Bob laboured up the hill past the recreation ground.

187

'You took your time.'

'I kent you were goin to say that.' Bob dismounted and leaned his bicycle on Eppie Callum's tree.

'Dinnae like to disappoint.'

'Since when did you gie a damn what onyone thocht?'

'I'm sure there was ae time.'

Bob patted the oak. 'So this is whaur my namesake hid after causin a ruckus at the fair.'

'Him and Bonnie Prince Charlie. He hid inside it.'

Bob stood back and appraised the tree. 'Must hae been a richt skinnymalink, then.'

'Italian fop.'

'It was named after the owner of the inn. She grew it fae an acorn in a teapot ...'

'Aye well, if she did, the acorn was already twa hunner year auld when she did. This thing's centuries aulder than she is.'

'A bit like your monkey puzzle tree.'

'Naethin's what you think it is.'

They turned onto the Laggan, high summer sun glinting on the leaves of beech and rowan trees, on holly bushes and whins. A kestrel hovered above the field to their right, poetry in its symmetry. A single cloud, too fluffy and unconvincing, like a child's drawing, sat overhead. After a mile, Sandy led his horse through a narrow gate at the entrance to an even narrower pathway, vegetation pressing in on both sides. Bob manoeuvred his bicycle through the gate and jumped aboard, following Sandy. The going was rough, exposed tree roots capillary-ing across the path. Sandy and Jenny progressed sedately, Jenny occasionally snuffling and shaking her head. About a mile further on, they emerged into a clearing, by the side of which stood a small, stone-built house.

'Talk aboot oot of the wey,' said Bob.

'Aye, Norrie wasnae a man for company.' The place seemed deserted. 'I thocht the polis would still be here.'

'Nah, once they've done a sweep of the hoose, unless they're suspicious, they'll no bother themsels ower much.'

'The voice of experience?'

'You could say.'

'And do you think there is onythin suspicious?'

'Dinnae ken yet.' Bob leaned his bike against a beech tree. 'But I'll tell you this: Crieff's a wee place. Twa unexplained deaths in just ower a week – if I was still in the polis that would cause me to think …'

He walked around the house, stopping at the back and studying the window. He edged close to the wall and viewed it sideways, screwing up his eyes.

'There,' he said. 'That's handprints. Someone's leaned up against the windae wi his haunds like this.' He demonstrated by pushing the first and second fingers of each hand together and pressing his thumbs on either side of his temple for support. 'To see inside.'

'So someone else has been here?'

'Well, when did you last keek in your ain windaes?' He tried the back door and was only mildly surprised to find it unlocked. 'Here's hopin they minded to tak the body awa, at least,' he said as he entered the kitchen. It seemed to be an old man's dwelling, dirty and dusty, nothing unusual. He went into the living room and immediately saw the blood stains on the wooden floor marking the spot where Norrie fell. Next to the armchair.

But not on it.

'Found on the flair, you say?'

'Aye. Shot himsel.'

Bob had replayed the circumstances of his father's death – or at least his version of them – a million times. Always, his father was seated on the kitchen chair. Support at the last. Comfort. He checked the armchair and there was blood spatter on one side, but Norrie had not been sitting in it when he pulled the trigger.

189

Or when the trigger was pulled.

He turned to the chest of drawers against the wall. It was long and the extent of it was untidy and dirty, but the right-hand side showed evidence of a gradual accumulation of junk, layer on layer, each one covered in dust. The left-hand side, though, was chaotic, as though someone had knocked everything from it and replaced it again any old how. He bent and picked a bottle top from the floor. Beside it was a clay vase, a fresh chip in the rim. The missing chip was nestled against the skirting board. Bob fixed it back in place to confirm the match and placed the vase on the chest of drawers. There was a circular mark, clean, everything around it encased in dust. Bob fixed the vase in the circular space. It fitted perfectly. Beside it was one half of a postcard. "*Sophienstraße*", it read.

'Whaur's that?' said Sandy.

'Germany, by the sound of it.'

'Funny picter for a postcard.'

'And why ripped in hauf?' He looked for the other half but found nothing. He turned the half around. There was no writing, no stamp, no postmark. 'Has Norrie ever been to Germany?'

'Dinnae be daft. Norrie's never been to Fife.'

Bob opened the cupboards beneath the chest of drawers. The one on the far left was empty. All the others were full. He stood in the centre of the room and looked around.

'Well?' said Sandy.

'What possible connection could Norrie Smith hae with the Rover lads?'

'You think there's something wrang here?'

'Is it no obvious?' He looked around again and stopped. He stared at the window, at the path leading to the front door, at the small wood beyond. Trees lining the road. 'What did you tell me? Aboot his curtains?'

'He ay kept them shut.'

Bob gestured to the dirty and fading curtains lining the window. 'Well, they're no shut noo.'

He went outside and walked around the house. His eye was drawn to a silver birch a few yards from the back door, which seemed to have something at its base. He could smell before he reached the tree that it was vomit, now dried and shrivelled.

'Could be Maggie?' he said.

'Nae wey. She was a nurse in the war, she'll hae seen worse than that.'

'One of the polis, then. If PC McAnuff was here, that would do for him, I'm sure.'

'Or someone else.'

Bob walked away. 'Maybe. Maggie says there were twa Rovers, but they werenae thegither. Maybe ane was following the other. Came across this efter ...' He caught a whiff of woodsmoke and followed the line of the trees towards the field beyond. By the fence, he found the remnants of a fire. He kicked through it.

'This'll be what was in thon empty cupboard,' he said. 'I'll bet Annie's granny on it.'

'What d'you think it was?'

'Nae idea. Papers, but I couldnae say what. Whaever did this, they made damned sure aathin was destroyed.'

'Wid have taken some time.'

'Especially yesterday. Wi all that rain, gettin a fire up as hot as this would need, that would hae taken some doin.' He pulled out his pipe and sucked on it. 'Somebody was gey determined to hide somethin,' he said.

'So wha was it?'

Bob sauntered back to his bicycle, kicking at the ground as he went. 'We're makin an assumption that the Rovers Maggie and your mither saw were Miško and Zoltán. Because we ken baith of them hired cuddies yesterday.'

'So they're in cahoots?'

Bob exhaled heavily. 'They werenae thegither, though. And ane of them's guffed his chaff by the tree. That doesnae suggest involvement.' He picked up his bike. 'But what really bothers me is that Crieff's wee, and twa unexplained deaths in a matter of a few days is highly unlikely. So much so, you'd hae to think they must be linked somehow. Aye?'

'Aye.'

'Neither ane of Miško or Zoltán were involved in Erling Hagen's death, as far as we ken.'

'No.'

'But István was. One wey or another.'

'Aye.'

'And we cannae say for certain, because of Nalda's wee scam, that István didnae hire a cuddy yesterday an aa.'

'No.'

'And while there's nae connection between Miško and Zoltán, there is between *István* and Zoltán.'

'Baith Hungarians.'

'Precisely.'

'But why would Zoltán tell us about István being a late arrival, then?' said Sandy. 'Why draw attention to him like that?'

'To deflect attention fae himsel? If he's the one in charge?'

'In charge of what?'

'I dinnae ken. But I'll tell you this, there's mair to all this than meets the eye.'

*

They left Loch More behind and were beginning to climb the lower slopes of the Knock. A large area of woodland had been felled, the timber laid in rows on the ground, ready should war be declared. The path grew steeper and they entered a wood, the air becoming fresher. An uprooted plane tree lay by the side of the path, roots stretching into the sky like branches in some inverted reality.

Zoltán Tóth knew he was going to die as he walked out of the campsite with Miško. He knew this at some atavistic level, in a way he could not understand. He knew, not because of anything Miško had said or done, but because his mind was consumed by memories of the past, by his family, by his life transfigured. Mária was walking beside him now, as she had done for twenty years, since they were teenagers navigating the poverty of the post-war years. Her presence was so strong he felt he could stretch out his hand and touch her. He could smell her scent. A pigeon took fright and lumbered out of an oak tree behind them and the sound morphed into the chug of a steam engine exiting the station, a family holiday, same destination every year, leaving Budapest for Esztergom, its basilica, the Danube bend, the Mária Valéria Bridge. Katalin and Margit, aged two and four, aged eight and ten, aged twelve and fourteen, Katalin and Margit through the years, inseparables squabbling and reconciling, plotting, dreaming. Katalin alone, aged fifteen, mourning a sister lost to a tram accident in Újpest, clingy that summer in a way she had never been before and never would be again. If he looked behind him she'd be trailing there, kicking her shoes in the dust, her head a labyrinth of poems and stories and riddles of love. *Night night, papa. Love you, my love. Safe journey. Be back soon. A present, bring me a present. Look after your mother. I love you. I love …*

'Why did you follow me?' Miško's voice was gentle, his demeanour as agreeable as always. And yet it chilled Zoltán. He thought for a moment. How to answer a murderer?

'I would like to know who you are,' he said.

'Why?' said Miško.

'And I would like to know how you're connected with István.'

'István?'

'You know each other. I saw it the other night, in the café. You pretended you didn't, but it was obvious.'

Miško sat in silence for some moments. 'Why do you think this?' he said.

'The way you looked at each other. Each checking the other out. István would speak and watch while you answered. Never take his eye off you. He was more interested in your face than your words, I think. He must have known the words would be lies. He look for truth in your expression. And you were doing the same to him.'

'You are imagining things.'

'Who is István? He was not on the list of Rovers from Hungary to attend the Moot, but arrived at the last minute. Paperwork perfect, not a single mistake. And I ask your Group Leader, Radoslav Ilić, about you. Funny, he say the same thing happen with you. Not part of the original party. This is strange, no?'

'Yugoslavia, we add four more names at the last minute. The Catholic Church, they pay for extra places. I gain one.'

'You're representing the Catholic Church?'

'I represent Yugoslavia. That is all.'

When they reached the top of the hill, the trees to their left thinned out and moorland below came into view, stretching into the distance before meeting a slope that would run towards the Turret Burn. Before them was a steep escarpment, some fifty or so feet deep. Part-way down was a stand of half a dozen trees, and the bottom was lined by a meandering hedge. A field of meadow grass pulsed in waves. In the middle of the field was a giant stone, pointing drunkenly to the sky, tilted to eleven o'clock.

'That is the Witches' Stone,' said Miško. 'And this, where we stand, is the Witch's Crag. A witch was burned to death here. Rolled down this slope. Very dangerous.'

'You've been here before?'

'Yes. There is death in the air here. You feel it, no? I can taste it, smell it. Some places bad things happen. Don't you think?'

'Like the cottage yesterday.'

'So you did go inside.'

'Of course.'

Miško studied him carefully. *The Hungarian was kind, probably honest. Not the sort to keep quiet, even if things turned against him. Pity, but there you go.*

'You plan to kill me, don't you? That's why we come here.'

'Don't take it personally.'

'I don't understand. Any of this.'

'Would it make any difference? If I explained?'

'I don't want to die for nothing.'

'You are going to die for nothing. That's just the way it is.'

'I would like to see my family again.'

'Close your eyes. You'll see them in your mind.'

'That's not the same.'

'That's all there is.'

Will you marry me? Come to bed, my love, hold me, hold me. For richer for poorer. Ashes to ashes. You're my special girl. My special girl. My girl. My love, my love, my love.

Daddy, daddy. Hold my hand. Taste my ice lolly. Push me, harder, higher, I can see for miles. I can see Budapest. I see our house, my room.

Zoltán Tóth no longer saw the Witches' Stone. He was not on the Witch's Crag. When he looked around he saw Mária, he saw Katalin, he saw Margit. His Mama and Papa. A toy boat he sailed on the pond in Pest. The air was warm. The afternoon smiled. It held him close. *Take you, take you.* When Zoltán felt a push in his back it was the push of a school chum in the queue for lunch. *Dumplings today. Hurry, Tóth, hurry, or the fifth formers will have the lot.* When he felt a push in his back it was Mária, encouraging him forward, suitor meeting father. When he felt a push in his back it was Katalin, wanting a donkey ride, it was Margit wanting to go

195

to the bakery for cakes for mama. When he felt a push in his back Zoltán Tóth lost his balance and toppled headlong down the Witch's Crag, tumbling in a confusion of flailing and shattering limbs, his head banging against the stony ground over and over until he crashed into the stand of trees forty feet below.

Miško watched for ten minutes but Zoltán did not move. His memories did not stir. The ghosts of the past evaporated in the afternoon stillness.

Miško lit a cigarette and returned to camp.

Rain began to fall once more.

Tuesday 25th July

A Day of Passing

Bob leaned on his broom and danced around the tables of the catering tent. He clasped it to his chest as though embracing his inamorata and swung through a circle, tackety boots gliding across the damp grass. The effect was at once delicate and humorous. He slid from side to side, raising his knees in turn and slapping them, and began to sing.

'Commence to dancing, commence to prancing.
Commence advancing, right and left a-glancing.
A-mooch, a-dancing, slide and glide entrancing.
You do the tango jiggle, to the Texas Tummy Wiggle.
Take your partner and you hold her, slightly enfold her,
A little bolder, just work your shoulder.
Snap your fingers one and all, in the hall, at the ball.
That's all, some ball.'
'I didn't know you were a dancer.'

Bob turned and flushed with embarrassment. Lord Kellett was holding open the entrance to the tent, homburg in his hand, a severe expression on his face at odds with the levity of his tone. He placed the homburg on a table and advanced, hand thrust forward. Bob wiped his hand on his apron and they exchanged a handshake.

'Laurel and Hardy,' Bob said. '*Way Out West*. They sing

197

that song. Do a soft shoe shuffle. It's Annie's favourite bit. That and *The Trail of the Lonesome Pine*.'

'I can't say I've seen it.'

'We've been three times.'

'Three times? To the same picture? Business must be doing well.'

'Well, it has been this week.'

'Yes, I was speaking to David earlier. The camp's been a great success.'

'It has, aye. Are you here about the body? I think we're stuck now. The Procurator Fiscal ...'

'No, I'm not here about that.' He unfolded one of the wooden folding chairs and beckoned to Bob to do likewise. 'I'm afraid I'm the bearer of bad news.'

Bob felt a burst of trepidation. Bad news had been his unsolicited companion most of his life. Bad news gnawed at his fragile defences, tested his endurance. The battle was prolonged and painful. He sat heavily.

'Victor,' said Lord Kellett, 'had another heart attack last night. Bad, this time.'

'Is he okay?'

Lord Kellett hung his head. He looked tired, grey. His mouth was tight, lips drawn inwards. 'I'm sorry. He was walking to the ARP headquarters at Fechney ... on his own ... by the time anyone found him ... gone ...'

He talked on but Bob had stopped listening. Victor Conoboy was dead. Bella was a widow.

Victor and Bella Conoboy had looked out for Bob since he was twelve. Victor had arranged his first job, with Perth City Police. Cloudland had been secured with money borrowed from the Conoboys, interest-free. Victor was the kindest man Bob had ever known, quiet and unassuming, clever, witty, a true gentleman. Tears fell down Bob's cheek. He did nothing to wipe them away.

'I'm very sorry,' said Lord Kellett.

'I'll mak some tea,' Bob said when he could no longer bear the prospect of sitting still. His hands shook as he filled two enamel mugs from the urn. He carried them to the table, losing half the contents on the way.

'The funeral's Saturday. Eleven-thirty. Congregational Church, then Wellshill Cemetery.'

'I'll be there.'

'Bella will appreciate that.' Silence engulfed them, awkward, painful. Both of them tried to think of something to say.

'I gather you're an ARP Warden yourself?' Lord Kellett said.

'Aye. Enrolled in March. Got my training earlier this month.'

'Good man. I'm Chairman of the Committee, ARP Headquarters. Victor's my Head Warden … Was.'

Bob closed his eyes. His hands were still shaking. His hearing seemed muffled, as though he was underwater. He knew already that today would be something to be endured, to suffer. Sleep would not release him from torment. Tomorrow would be the same. And tomorrow. And tomorrow.

'We're on call to distribute the gas masks,' he said. He had no idea why. Perhaps, one half of his brain trying to prevent the other half from suffering.

'We're still waiting for the government to send them to us,' Lord Kellett replied. 'Then we'll get them out to you chaps in the district, pronto. Doesn't instil confidence, I have to be honest, all these delays. I hope, when the war comes, they'll be quicker at handing out the weapons, or we'll be invaded before we know what's what. They haven't even decided whether Wardens will fit the masks door-to-door or ask people to come into centres to have them fitted.'

'Easier to get people to come in.'

'Except the ones who won't.'

'There's always some.'

'There are indeed.' He took a Camel cigarette from a silver case and lit it. 'We need good men at headquarters,' he said. 'We're in Fechney for now, but we're going to move into County Hall. Next to the Police station. The Police chaps are running the show. Inspector Harrison. You'll know him.'

'He was a sergeant in my time.'

'Done well for himself. It's all about logistics, you see. We've volunteers galore. More bodies than we need, frankly. What we need is intellect. Reason. Coordination.'

'I'm sure there's plenty good men around ...'

'Not so many. Chairman's an important role. I need someone I can trust. Right-hand man, you know? Victor was going to be that man.'

'I'm sorry.'

'The situation in Europe ...'

'Things have calmed down a bit.'

'Calm before the storm, I'm afraid. Hitler's not going to be satisfied. He wants his empire. There's going to be a war. And when there is ... Well, we need good men.' He flicked ash onto the grass. 'When it kicks off, you'll be called up. You're only young.'

'I imagine so.'

'The police are an exempt profession.'

'I'd have thought so, aye.'

'If you come and work for me, you'll be a police auxiliary. Exempt.'

'Me?'

'I told you, I need good men. Capable. Intelligent.'

Bob studied Lord Kellett's expression, trying to fathom it, wondered why this man was flattering him. 'I don't know,' he said.

'Think about it.' He stubbed out his cigarette and rose stiffly. 'We can talk again. On Saturday.'

'Aye.'

'I'll see myself out.'

*

Bob walked uphill to Meikle's Nook, where James and the boys were preparing to dismantle portions of the site that had remained unused, in preparation for Thursday's mass exodus.

'Any chance you could look efter my tent the day?' he said.

James was about to offer a sarcastic response when he saw Bob's haunted expression. He led him inside the nook and sat him down and Bob explained about Victor.

'He was like a dad to me,' he said, 'but kinder.'

James told him to go home and he would look after the catering tent. 'Will you be alright?'

'I'll be fine.'

Will I? Sometimes, Bob didn't know what "fine" meant. Alive? Sane? Was that enough to constitute "fine"? Or were different attributes needed? More dissembling? More delusion? Self-delusion? He felt as though he had to concentrate on breathing or he would forget and suffocate. He focused on breathing in and out, in and out, until he started to feel dizzy. His brow grew clammy. His fingers tingled. He felt the ground shift beneath him as though it was breaking open and he had to hold on to tufts of grass to stop himself from tilting into the void.

'Bob?' James was gripping his shoulder solicitously. He had been about to tell him that Zoltán was looking for him the day before, but he realised now was not the time. Bob needed away from this place. 'Go hame, aye?' he said. Bob nodded. 'D'ye want someone to go wi ye?'

'No, I'm grand, honest.' He stood up, his legs not feeling real. He thought he might fall but managed to stay upright. 'I've got my bike,' he said.

'Man, ye cannae take that. I've seen you try to ride that hing when there's nothin wrang wi ye. Ye'll end up in a ditch …'

201

But Bob waved his hand and walked away. Enough of this talk, he needed to be alone. He collected his bicycle and wheeled it down the cinder-strewn path to the lodge gate. He turned left onto the back road to Crieff through Glenturret. That way was longer but quieter, less chance of him falling beneath the wheels of an oncoming motor vehicle. Trees banked high to his right. Moorland, rough, pocked, ran to his left. Beyond that, laughter rang out from Loch More, the occasional splash of water as a Rover dived in. The road meandered, rising and falling, twisting in accord with the line of the hillside. Nearby ran the Falls of Shaggie and the Falls of Keltie and the sources of the Barvick and the grand Turret, all of them feeding the River Earn, the River Earn pulsing through the valley of Strathearn to Perth, to Kinnoull, in turn to feed the Tay, and the Tay running smooth and dark all the way to the sea. There is no such thing as time, only moments, fragments, one after the other, rupturing and breaking like existence itself. Victor Conoboy no longer breathed, walked, lived. Tomorrow will be, regardless of whether you are there to witness. Today is only a figment, a fantasy, a flight of fancy for good or ill. And yesterday is the root of all pain because it is the source of all experience.

Bob Kelty rode on, oblivious.

*

Sandy strode downhill to Meikle's Nook, dead rabbit in his hand. He spotted István idling beside some trees, waiting, watching, until he broke cover and approached as though this encounter were a complete accident.

'Sandy,' he said, extending his hand. Sandy shifted the rabbit from his right to his left hand, then offered a bloodied right hand. They shook.

'I was looking for Bob,' István said. 'I wanted to ask his advice.'

'He's no here.'

'You know where he is?'

'I'm no his keeper.'

Sandy Disdain rarely felt deeply enough about anyone to engender strong emotions but there was something about István that made his flesh crawl. The smile. The falseness. The creeping walk. The evidence from the Hydro suggested that Miško and Zoltán were the Rovers who were spotted near Norrie's house but that didn't mean István wasn't involved, too. Nalda could have pocketed a hiring fee from him and not recorded it in the book. That explanation made more sense to Sandy.

'Whaur were you last night?' he said.

'I was in Crieff. In the Green Restaurant.'

'You werenae oot the Laggan?'

'Where is that?'

'Outskirts of Crieff.'

'And why would I be out there?'

'You tell me. Maybe you were involved in the murder.'

István's smiling expression disappeared immediately. 'What murder?'

'Oot the Laggan. Auld fella, Norrie Smith. Plooman.'

'And why you think I would be involved in this?'

Sandy had spotted the change in István's demeanour but the expression that overtook his face was undoubtedly one of surprise. Whatever role István may have had in the death of Erling Hagen, he wasn't involved in Norrie Smith's.

'Nothin,' he said and walked away, the rabbit swinging in his hand.

István watched him go. He tried to understand what could have happened. Some old man was murdered. He thought perhaps he knew, but that was a scenario he did not like. Not at all. Elements were going rogue. Clearing up after a dead tinker had been easy. But this – the death of a local – this was going to be very, very difficult.

*

203

When Bob reflected on that day later, he could remember the details exactly but not how they came about. His memory was precise, but jagged. The only way he could describe it was that he was inside a Picasso painting, seeing reality from competing perspectives, a participant without agency, his actions the actions of a surrogate. He was there but he wasn't. A battle was raging and he was complicit in every moment, but whatever he did made no difference. For the second time in five days, he found himself in an interview room at Crieff Police Station, confronting Sergeant Rudd. As usual, the sergeant did not seem pleased to see him.

'I heard about Inspector Conoboy,' he said, his expression softening for a moment.

'Aye.'

'I didnae ken him that weel but I kent *of* him. Ane of the best.'

'He was. And, funnily enough, I spoke to him about this palaver on Saturday past …'

'Did you?' Sergeant Rudd sounded wary, a man expecting the conversation to turn in a direction that wasn't to his favour.

'He couldnae believe you werenae investigatin …'

'He wouldnae hae had all the details …'

'And that was afore the second murder …'

'What second murder?'

'Norrie Smith.'

'Norrie Smith? The man shot himsel.'

'Do you tak aathin you see at face value?'

'Do you see conspiracy at every turn?'

'No. Which is why I'm convinced there's somethin wrang wi this case.'

Rudd scratched his head. 'Listen son,' he said, 'maybe the Inspector's death is playin on your mind a bittie …'

'Sergeant, I ken what I'm sayin, and I'm tellin you that Norrie Smith didnae shoot himsel. You dinnae stand up in the middle of a room to shoot yoursel …'

'And you ken aboot this kind of thing, do you?'

'I do, aye. My faither shot himsel twelve year ago. And he wasnae standin up when he did it.'

'I'm sorry. I didnae ken that. But …'

'But that's no the thing that maks me certain …'

'Go on, then. Let's hear it.'

'First, twa Rovers were seen outside the hoose. No thegither. Separately. Ane followin the ither …'

'That's no a crime …'

'No, but it's odd, at the very least. Why on Earth would ae Rover, let alone twa, be all the wey oot the far end of the Laggan? Maist Crieff folk couldnae find Norrie's hoose.'

'Explorin. Got lost on Lady Mary's Walk. Easy happens …'

'Second, the fingerprints on the windae …'

'What fingerprints?'

'You see? You didnae spot them, did you? You havenae looked at that hoose as if it's a crime scene …'

'Because it isnae …'

'So wha's been keekin through the windae? And why?'

'Maggie Caldwell?'

'Why would she keek through the windae? She'd barge right in.'

'I'll gie you that.'

'Third, there's a cupboard in the chest of drawers that's been emptied …'

'How d'you ken that?'

'Because it's empty. And all the others are fu to the gunnels. Why would you leave ae cupboard empty and stuff the others fu?'

'Unusual, maybe. But how d'you get fae an empty cupboard to murder?'

'Did you see the bonfire?'

'What bonfire?'

'I'll tak that as a no. Oot the back, next to the fence, somethin's been burned, very, very carefully …'

'What?'

'I dinnae ken. Because it's been burned very, very carefully. Papers. No a trace left.' He pulled out his pipe. 'Probably what was in that cupboard.'

'That's just speculation …'

'That's what you do when you think somethin bad's happened and you dinnae ken what it was.'

'Aye, but thon's just fanciful.'

'Right. What aboot the curtains then? In the livin room?'

Rudd looked baffled but didn't want to confess to not knowing something else that Bob had spotted. 'What aboot them?' he said. 'There was nothin unusual aboot them …'

'Open or closed?'

'Open.'

'That's what's unusual.' Bob lit his pipe and waited until Rudd, although he didn't want to, asked him to explain. 'You ken aboot Norrie's wife?' he said.

'Hung hersel.'

'Aye. Where?'

'Near the hoose, was it no?'

'The woods. You could see it fae the livin room.'

'Aye?'

'Aye. Which is why Norrie never opened thae curtains. Couldnae bear to see it …'

'So?'

'So the killer, no kennin that, thocht it would look less suspicious if the curtains were open, it bein daytime. So he opened them.' Bob puffed on his pipe. A bloom of smoke rose from the bowl, the smell of Balkan Sobranie filling the room.

'And that's your evidence?' said Rudd.

'Nearly.'

'Nearly?'

'There's a pile of sick near the back door. I'm sure you spotted that?'

Rudd neither confirmed nor denied. 'Cannae see what that has to do wi onythin.'

'Could hae been the murderer. In a moment of shock at what he's done. But since it's his second murder in ten days, maybe no. And I said there were twa Rovers near the hoose, ane ahint the ither. So the second ane could hae come by efterwards, seen the crime, boaked ootside.'

As soon as Bob sat back, his explanation over, he remembered Victor. He sat forward again as though this hunched position could keep him in the moment, keep the feelings of grief at bay.

'You done noo?'

'Aye.'

Sergeant Rudd studied Bob and shook his head. 'You've brocht me lots of questions, son, I'll gie you that. But you've nae evidence of nothin. I was there. It looked like a straightforward case of suicide. Norrie was saft in the heid. Aabody kens that. You have to be honest, it's no a huge surprise, is it? It's only a wonder he didnae do it years ago. As for it bein ane of your Rovers, I can see you'd like to tie this into your ither fantasy of the deid tinker, but you've nae proof at aa that a Rover was involved in either ane of these deaths. So there were twa Rovers seen near Norrie's hoose – they've been aa ower town for the past week. You cannae go onywhere wi-oot runnin into someone wi shorts and a funny accent.

'And the biggest question of all – if it *was* a Rover, what for? What possible reason would they hae for killin Norrie Smith? It wasnae money. Norrie wouldnae hae tuppence-hapenny to his name and there's nae sign of robbery. There's just nae sense to what you're sayin.'

'But the fingerprints, the curtain, the bonfire, the boak …'

'Signify nothin.'
'You willnae look into it?'
'Son, there's naethin to look intae.'

*

Loch More shimmered in black and silver beneath the afternoon sun, ripples on the water from a light wind, a single, perfect circle radiating from the point where a trout had broken the surface. On the far bank, a handful of Rhodesian Rovers were lounging on the grass, smoking cigarettes and swapping stories. A turbaned Indian was perched on the jetty, preparing to slide into the water. He appeared apprehensive.

Miško watched all of this with detached indifference. He was lost to thought. Fear. Dread. These were emotions he knew he had to experience, in order to overcome them. The Norwegian boy's death had been unavoidable, a necessary act to prevent Erling Hagen, whom he'd tried to recruit to the *Abwehr* six months before, from blowing his cover. Bad luck, as much for Miško as for Hagen, despite the disparity in their respective outcomes. That could be explained. *Abwehr* HQ would accept he had to silence the boy or compromise his cover.

But Norman Smith?

When news reached the *Abwehr* of the death of the manager of one of their *post restante* addresses, Miško would be called to account. The old man had been harmless. He was safely embedded in his natural environment, his *Abwehr* connections unknown. There was no possibility such a man would voluntarily confess to his own authorities. All of this would be considered by the *Abwehr*. They would want to know why the old man had to be killed. In truth, Miško wanted to know, too. There was no sense to it. No sense, but there was a pattern, one Miško could recognise but not like.

Stupid people. Stupid people made him act this way,

208

made him angry, made him lose his temper. He confronted stupid people and saw losers. Failures. Miško came from a family of failures and he was not going to follow them. That meant he was entirely justified in ridding the world of the failure that was Norman Smith. Miško felt his tension ease. He could make his superiors understand. They always did.

He shifted listlessly. The Indian was now in the water, his turban bobbing above, the Rhodesians cheering him on. His thoughts turned to the Hungarian, Tóth. There was a possibility the *Abwehr* would never find out about him. Or, if they did, they would not or could not associate his death with Miško. Why should they? All the same, Zoltán Tóth troubled him. He was the Hungarian group leader, and someone with a particular interest in Miško's activities. It was likely, then, that he was an agent too but, if so, on which side, British or German? Was he supporting István or surveilling him? There were difficulties attached to either scenario, but they were different, and Miško wasn't sure how to proceed.

He resolved to say nothing. If asked, he would concoct a story. It had already occurred to him to pin the death of Smith on Zoltán. That could work. Anything, as long as Miško didn't get caught up in any repercussions.

'Control yourself,' he said aloud. 'It's done. It's done. It's done. Three times death. Each time it gets easier.' Each death felt less like it was he who had done it, more like an inevitability. 'Learn,' he said. 'Learn how to overcome this.' *Selbstüberwindung.*

*

When Bob returned to Cloudland after a day of aimless walking, Annie folded herself around him and rested his head on her shoulder. She looked out of the window at King Street. Night was falling, the fountain turning black, indistinct, the square grainy like a charcoal drawing.

'Come to bed,' she said and led him upstairs. Like an

automaton, Bob readied himself for bed and Annie smoothed back the bedsheets and let him climb in. He lay on his back and stared upwards. There would be no sleep tonight. He knew that, could sense already the long hours ahead, thoughts forging in his mind, memories and moments, emotions like an analeptic, anaesthetic. *Move me through the hours of silence, hold me in the act of day.* He raised his head and opened his eyes wide as though seeing the universe. The stars would be beginning their shape show, Sirius straight ahead, burning like a beacon from eternity.

*

The giant cross fashioned from a Douglas fir cast a shadow on the ground by the entrance to the Hungarian area. István detoured to avoid stepping on any part of the shadow, then made his way across the camp to the Yugoslav enclave. There were a couple of Rovers with their kit laid on the ground, ready to pack their rucksacks. István greeted them and enquired after Miško.

'He went off earlier, towards the lake,' one of them replied, a young man with a skinhead that made him look like an infant.

István thanked him and headed for the lake. It seemed a long shot that Miško would still be there but he had nothing better to work on. He had tried all week to avoid speaking to the Serbian buffoon, but now he had no option. A dead civilian. He needed to know what was going on in order to be able to rectify things.

He felt a surge of adrenaline when he saw Miško seated on the far side of the loch. From his reaction, it was clear that Miško had spotted him, too, but he made no attempt to escape as István traced the bank of the loch towards him.

'We need to talk,' István said.

'We shouldn't be seen together.'

'A bit late for that.'

'In what way?'

'Don't play the fool. You've killed a local man.'

'You keep up with the news. Impressive.'

'Why?'

'I had limited options.'

'Murder is always the last option. Especially in a foreign country.'

'Then I had no option.'

'Where's Zoltán?'

'I don't know.'

'He didn't come back to the camp last night.'

'Is that so?'

'I managed to cover up this morning. Said he went out early. But I can't keep that up for long. Where is he?'

'I don't know.'

'Have you killed him?'

Miško didn't answer. He pulled at a clump of grass and a handful of blades came away in his hand.

István hadn't genuinely believed Miško might have killed Zoltán but his silence was chilling. 'Fuck. You have.'

'I had to.'

'Why?'

'He knew.'

'Knew what?'

'About Smith being killed.'

'How could he?'

'He was there.'

István smashed his hand into the ground. '*Mi a fasz van veled*? I always knew you were a liability …'

'What side was he on?'

'He wasn't on anyone's side, you fool.' István stared across the water. 'I will have to report this …'

'You won't report it.'

'Don't try to threaten me.'

'I'm not threatening you. I'm only telling you that you

won't report it.'

'Why won't I?'

'Because if you do, I will blame you for killing Smith. You will naturally blame me. London, unable to know who is telling the truth, will blame us both. And that will be the end for us both. You know this is true. You know London don't like loose ends. Untidiness.' He opened his palm and let the blades of grass fall to the ground. The wind picked them up and blew them towards the lochside. 'We must work together on this. Back each other up. If I die, you die. If you die, I die.'

István stood up. The Rhodesians were now in the water, playing an improvised game of water polo. He envied their simplicity. He closed his eyes.

'Damn you,' he said.

Wednesday 26th July

A Day of Feasting

Annie was aware of how little Bob had slept the night before. She hadn't slept well herself, and when she woke four or five times she could sense Bob was awake, too. He was too rigid, unmoving, his breathing too shallow. She knew him of old, knew he would be thinking of Victor over and over, fixating on moments, words, events. He could easily lose himself in those thoughts, and the only hope was to try to focus his attention elsewhere before grief tore him to pieces.

'You think Norrie's death is linked to Erling's?' she said as they sat at the breakfast table.

Bob sat with his spoon buried in his porridge, making no attempt to eat. At first, Annie was uncertain whether he had even heard her but finally he shifted in his chair and faced her.

'Twa unexplained deaths in ten days. It's too much of a coincidence.'

'But why?'

'That's the trouble. I cannae see how they're *no* connected, but I cannae see how they *are* connected either. What connection could Norrie hae to a Norwegian laddie?'

'Or István.'

'Zoltán. I ken we've had István in mind fae the start, but it was Zoltán who hired the cuddy fae the Hydro. Him and Miško.'

213

'So, you think István's oot of it aathegither?'

'No. They're baith Hungarian. Could be them in cahoots.' Bob sighed. The question of Zoltán was troubling him. More and more, it seemed that he may be involved, yet that was at odds with Bob's impression of the man being entirely affable and friendly. Bob was always uncomfortable when facts and emotions collided.

'So what now?'

'I dinnae ken. I tried the polis. Rudd wasnae interested …'

'Lord Kellett?'

'The man's enough on his plate.'

'Geordie Macrae?'

'Or I could just go up to the square and try and reason wi one of the Diamond Jubilee lamp posts …'

'Wha would you get mair sense fae, Geordie Macrae or a lamp post?'

'Close-run thing …'

*

By the time Bob had finished the breakfast rush at nine-thirty, the entire Moot site was suffused with the most intoxicating smell of cooking meat and it was nothing to do with him. He collected Annie from the information tent and they went in search of the source, following their noses in the direction of the castle.

'Blimey,' shouted James, 'it's Bill and Maree, the Bisto Kids.'

'That smell's mair than just Bisto,' said Bob. 'What is it?'

'Bullocks.'

Bob recognised the set-up, provided the punchline. 'I only asked.'

'They brought in two bullocks yesterday. They're roastin them ower a spit all day, ready for the final ceremony the night. There'll be enough fur everybody.'

214

'Except the Hindu laddies,' said Annie.

'I'll huv their bit.'

'I may as well shut up shop noo,' said Bob. 'Naebody's goin to want my bacon rolls wi that smell goin roond.'

They watched from afar as the bullocks were roasted over huge fires on the castle grounds. James enquired after Annie, and they glossed over Bob's emotions, as befitted a Scots' Calvinist conversation. Bob outlined the theory he and Annie had developed that morning about István and Zoltán.

'But we cannae work oot why,' he concluded. 'Why kill the Norwegian? Why kill Norrie? And how are the twa connected?'

'That's the authorities' problem, but,' said James.

'I ken. But I went to the polis yesterday. They want nothin to do wi it.'

'No the polis. The authorities.'

'The Procurator Fiscal?'

'Aye.'

'I went to him last week. He wasnae interested either.'

'Aye, but that was when it was either a tink or a Norwegian who was deid. Whichever it was, why would he care? But now ye've a local man deid. That's different, surely?'

*

'Where is Zoltán?'

István had just arrived back in the camp from the railway station when Lörinc, one of the fresh-faced Hungarian Rovers, approached him. He sounded concerned, his brow creased, his mouth tight.

'I saw him yesterday,' István replied. 'He told me he was going to a party in Crieff, at Cloudland, that café we went to, remember? He said he might stay over if it got too late.'

István cursed himself. The first rule of lying was never to be unnecessarily specific. Why on earth had he mentioned

215

Cloudland? Lörinc knew Bob, knew he worked in the catering tent. He could easily go to him to verify what István had said. And then what?

'He hasn't been here since Monday,' Lörinc said.

'Yes, he was here yesterday. I saw him.' He lowered his voice and edged closer to Lörinc, feigning matiness. 'I think he is after that older woman who works in Cloudland. I think he fancies his chances, dirty old man …'

Throw in a joke, keep things light, deflect Lörinc from further enquiry. This was how to deal with conflict.

'I suppose. He will return soon, I hope. For the final practice for the parade.'

István breathed out. Crisis averted – for now. But this couldn't continue. He would need to fashion a new story.

*

'Mr Kelty.' Mr Harman's voice sounded tetchy. 'I hadn't expected to hear from you again. I won't pretend it's a pleasure.'

'It's not how I'd planned my Wednesday mornin, either. Have you heard about the death of Norrie Smith?'

'I have. Suicide.'

'It wasn't suicide.'

There was a lengthy silence, during which Bob listened to the hiss on the telephone line. He studied the staff quarters of the information tent, Brigadier Ross puffing on a cigarette as he read *The Scotsman*, Annie pretending to tidy as she listened to Bob's end of the conversation.

'Is this another of your fabulous stories?'

'You know I'm right about Erling Hagen. And I'm right about this, too. I need to …'

'Enough, Mr Kelty. I have no interest in what you have to say, now or any time.'

'But …'

'Good day, Mr Kelty.'

István hopped off the bus from Perth on the High Street and took the steep descent down King Street towards Crieff railway station. He waited until the Comrie train, standing at the Down platform, moved off on its trip westwards through the Meadows and then he entered the temporarily quiet station. He sought out the station master and struck up a conversation with him. He offered him a cigarette and the two decamped to the waiting room, where they could smoke in peace. István laughed loudly at some comment from the station master and a friendship was forged, business ready to be undertaken.

*

When James finally told Bob that Zoltán had been looking for him a couple of days before, Bob was curious. That was before the death of Norrie Smith. Was there a connection? He approached the Hungarian enclosure, busy with Rovers since there were no excursions arranged that morning.

'I'm looking for Zoltán,' he said to no one in particular.

Lőrinc looked at him quizzically. 'Is he not with you?' he replied, but before he could say more István emerged from a tent, still puffing after his return from the railway station, and hastened towards Bob, hand outstretched, radiating bonhomie.

'Bob,' he said. 'How are you? My black eye is healing nicely, as you can see. Come.' István wrapped his arm around Bob's shoulder and led him away from the Hungarian group. Bob noticed the strangeness of this procedure, but allowed himself to be steered towards the arena.

'Zoltán was looking for me a couple of days back,' he said. 'Juist dropped by to see if he was around, see how I can help.'

'Ah yes, he did mention to me he was wanting to speak

217

with you. I don't believe it was anything important.'

'D'you know where he is?'

'Alas, he has gone …'

'Gone?'

'First thing this morning. He get a telegram from Hungary. Important, I think, and he said he must return immediately. I said goodbye to him very early this morning, before seven I would say …'

'And did he say where he was goin?'

'The railway station. He needed to get a connection to Hull for a ferry to Europe.'

Bob stared at István. Was he lying? It was difficult to tell because his expression was generally so supercilious you could be sceptical if he tried to tell you your own name. But yes, almost certainly, he was lying.

'He didnae say anything aboot the day before? Sunday?'

'Not that I remember.'

'Didnae say anything aboot hiring a cuddy – a horse – fae the Hydro?'

'No.'

'And I don't suppose you hired a horse fae the Hydro on Sunday, either?'

'Me? On a horse? That would not be a good idea, I assure you.' He gave a laugh which was lamentably false. 'All this interest in horse riding, is it important?'

'No,' said Bob. 'In the scheme of things, I dinnae suppose it is.' He couldn't think what else to ask, how to probe this clearly insincere man. It was becoming increasingly likely that István and Zoltán were in this together, but what exactly was *this*? And, now that Zoltán was gone, how could he prove anything?

*

'That smell would mak a skeleton hungry,' said Annie.

Eight o'clock on the final evening of the Moot, and

218

Bob and Annie, James, Abdalla and Jozef were sitting on Annie's tartan picnic rug on light grass beneath the walls of Monzie Castle. Inside, the two bullocks had been roasting for eighteen hours and were close to cooked. Chefs from the castle, in chequered trousers, white jackets and toques oversaw the activity, while a couple of James's helpers from Meikle's Nook provided the brawn. All around the walls, Rovers were milling, looking for somewhere to sit, seeking new-found friends for one last evening's entertainment at the camp. A babel of chatter surrounded them, good-natured and contented. Music filtered through the air from the campsite above them, including the inevitable *Alouette*. Midges hung in clouds around the trees but smoke from the fires kept them at bay. The evening was still warm, slightly muggy, threatening rain. Sandy strode towards them from the direction of Culcrieff.

'Jessie Robertson's deid,' he said to Bob.

'Who's Jessie Robertson?'

'Tink. Workin at Duchlage. Heart attack on Monday. Keeled ower in a barley field.'

'Well,' said Bob, faltering, 'that's a damned shame.' He didn't want to ask "why are you telling me this?" for fear of sounding insensitive, but he had no idea who the woman was or why Sandy should have come all the way to the Moot camp to tell him.

'She's ane of the best-known tinks aroond,' Sandy said. 'Aabody looked up to her.'

'Right.' Bob still didn't follow.

'There'll be a richt send off for her.'

'I'm sure.'

Sandy shook his head as though frustrated at speaking to a dunderheided child. 'You dinnae see, do you? Tinks are big on funerals. They'll be comin from aa ower for this. See it as their duty. There'll be hunners here.'

'Aye.'

219

'In the name of God man, you really are dense, are you no? Eddie Williamson was a cousin of Jessie Robertson.' Sandy took out a Capstan and lit it. 'And that means we can be pretty sure we'll be seein Eddie back in toon the morn, efter all.'

Bob clapped his hands as realisation dawned. He'd all but given up hope of resolving Erling Hagen's murder but now, maybe, they had another chance. 'D'you hae a black tie?' he said.

'Aye,' said Sandy. 'My faither's. Only time I've ever used it was his funeral.'

Bob flinched as the discussion of death tilted his thoughts back, once more, to Victor Conoboy. Annie sensed it and took his hand.

'I'm sure you'll look grand in it,' she said to Sandy.

The Glasgow Rovers Pipe Band was assembling on the lawn before Monzie Castle, resplendent in red, their tam o'shanters fixed at jaunty angles. After a shout from the Drum Major they began the evening's entertainment with *The Rose of Kelvingrove*.

'I'll tell you something,' Bob said to Annie, 'our foreign friends'll never forget the sound of the bagpipes.'

'Probably no for want of tryin.'

'It is wonderful,' said Abdalla. 'Very … stirring.'

As the band played on, they debated the best word to describe pipe music. Martial. Raucous. Frightening. 'A right bloody din,' according to a Rover from Norwich sitting nearby, generating nods of agreement and shakes of the head in equal measure. When the band had finished to a ripple of applause extending up towards the arena, assorted clicks and whirring noises from the public address system alerted the group to microphones being switched on. Lord Somers stood on the castle ramparts.

'High-heid-yin alert,' said Sandy.

'Good evening, Rovers,' Lord Somers began, his

amplified voice carrying the length of the campsite. 'Today is our final day of the Rover Moot at Monzie Castle and I think you'll all agree it has been a magnificent experience. I only wish that all the nations of the world had been represented here. You are the future. You are the people who can make our world a better place, a kinder place, a safer place. I have watched you all this week, the way you have come together in peace and harmony, and I have no doubt whatsoever that, with you – the next generation – we will be in safe hands.'

Bob sat with his head bowed. *Peace and harmony, was it, Lord Somers? Only if you don't dig too deep. Only if you don't look too hard.*

'It is up to you, now, every one of you, to go out into the world and spread this doctrine of camaraderie and international cooperation. The future is yours.'

'I cannot believe this is the final day already,' said Abdalla.

'Despite everything, this has been the best week of my life,' said Jozef. 'I have learned so much. Made such good friends.'

'You must come to Egypt and visit me. All of you. I will show you the sights. We will go to the bazaar. Ride camels.'

'You'll no get me on the back of a camel,' said Bob.

'It very safe. I promise you.'

'Believe me,' said Annie, 'there's nothin been invented Bob couldnae hae an accident wi.'

Bob gave a pantomime nod of his head. 'She's right.'

'Crieff will be very quiet when we are gone,' Abdalla said to Bob. 'What will you do?'

'Oh, back to Cloudland. Tea and bannocks for the regulars. The odd fancy cake for the Misses Seaton, Beaton and Miller if there's naebody around to see them indulgin themsels. Some music lessons for the bairns efter school.'

'Sounds like a fine life.'

'I wouldnae hae it ony other wey. What aboot you?'

221

'I shall return to Alexandria. My father wants me to study law.'

'And is that what you want?'

Abdalla shrugged. 'Egypt is changing. The next few years …' He tried to turn his thoughts into English. 'The military and the courts, they will rule Egypt.'

'So studyin the law?'

'In Alexandria. I will be at the centre of events.'

'Is that good or bad?'

'My friend, I wish I knew. In ten years, I could be a government minister, or I could be dead. Who can say?' He turned to Jozef. 'What will you do next?'

Jozef was cross-legged on the grass and he picked a piece of clover and laid it on his bare knee. 'I return to Poland and join the army.'

'Really?'

'I have been thinking about this all week. What to do. Poland will be invaded soon. It is a matter of time. I must fight for my country.'

The intrusion of reality brought silence. Each of them thought about Jozef, and about war, and about camaraderie and honour. The last week had been unforgettable, the friendships they'd forged genuine. The idea of the world falling into perdition was unfathomable.

'I don't think war's inevitable,' said James. 'There's unrest all ower Europe, aye, but maist of that is internal. Like Yugoslavia. Folk talk aboot the Germans invadin there, but from whit I've read that's the least of their worries. They're goin to huv an uprisin sometime soon anyway. All that internal conflict. Bosnians and Serbians, hatin each other. Why would the Germans get involved? They'll reach an agreement wi them. Leave them alane. I'm sure of it.'

'That's what they said about Czechoslovakia,' said Jozef. 'And the Sudetenland.'

'Aye,' said Bob. 'Warm words swallowed by Mr

222

Chamberlain, with his "Peace in our time" nonsense. The truth is, Herr Hitler cannot be trusted.'

'I believe there will be war,' said Abdalla. 'Sorry. All this, this friendship, it is beautiful. I love it. And I love you all. But this is not the real world. Whatever that man said, we, the young people, we are not the leaders. What we think does not matter. War will come and we will be dragged into it, every one of us, whether we want to or not.'

Bob studied Abdalla's handsome face. Of all his new friends, Abdalla was the one he respected most. Although not the oldest among them – possibly not even twenty – he seemed the most mature, the wisest. Bob was disheartened by Abdalla's words because he knew they were probably true. Poland and Britain would fight together. Yugoslavia would remain neutral, as would Egypt. Hungary, homeland of István Kedály and Zoltán Tóth, would probably side with their old allies Austria and, by extension, Germany. István, a foe of sorts during the past week, would become an enemy for real.

Bob felt a blank fear. A future selling tea and bannocks and fancy cakes, teaching lassies the music scales? Really? A deep melancholy was settling on him, provoked by the loss of Victor and strengthened by the loss of innocence occasioned by these last twelve days. By the duplicity of István and Zoltán. Seeing the good in people was almost a compulsion for Bob and, whenever reality intervened to show him the credulousness of his approach, he found himself sliding into despondency. What had started so hopefully – this gathering of international youth in the shadow of international warfare – had been tarnished. These young men thought they could change the world. But what was becoming clear was that the world was already in them, for good or ill. They were players in the game of humanity, like everyone else, and the game did not play fair.

High on the ramparts, the Glasgow Rovers Pipe Band

had reassembled in single file, their pipes and bearskins silhouetted against the darkening sky, and they began to play *The Black Bear*. In the gloaming they were indistinct, like marionettes in a children's theatre, the darkness rendering them mere shapes. It added to the intensity of the music. They were joined a couple of minutes later by a pair of pipers cavorting near the eastern corner of the ramparts. There was something odd about them but with the fading light Bob couldn't make them out clearly enough. After a few moments they appeared to face up to one another. The band played on regardless as a punch was thrown and the two pipers seemed to scuffle with one another. The London contingent, down at the front nearest to the ramparts, let up a yell of approval. The pipers scuffled on until one appeared to grab the other and raise him high in the air. The Londoners roared their encouragement as the first piper hurled the second from the ramparts onto the ground below.

'What the ...' shouted Bob, rising to his feet.

'Sit doon,' said Sandy. 'It's no a real person.'

Laughter rang out from the group of Rovers in front of them. Four of them ran forward and picked up the victim of the violence on the ramparts, a straw man made up in highland garb. They raised it aloft and cheered. A noise behind Bob alerted him to activity and he turned and saw another group of the London lads processing towards the front with a coffin raised on their shoulders. "RIP Pipers" was written on the side. Mickey Peterfield was at their head. He waved at Bob.

'Told you we'd get the last laugh, Jock,' he shouted.

Bob clapped his hands and gave a dramatic bow as though in deference. 'Well done, lads,' he shouted to them. He turned back to the others.

'There's still the morn's morn, though,' he said. 'Extra early.'

'Five o'clock should do it,' said Sandy.

'My thochts exactly.'

*

Entertainment over, they took a final stroll round the campsite. They were quiet, last night blues creating a pall over them, the realisation that most of them would never see each other again. Without intending to, they found themselves at Loch More where thirty or so Rovers were taking a final dip in the cool, fresh water, while dozens more sat in small groups by the water's edge. Night had fallen and with it the air was cooling rapidly. The grass had grown moist, its smell filling the night air. Sandy lay back on the grass, seemingly unconcerned by the dampness. He smoked a Capstan as Annie laid out her tartan rug and the others congregated on it.

'Auld claes and porridge the morn,' he said.

'Cannae say I've seen you in your glad rags much this week,' said Bob.

'Never owned a glad rag in my life.'

'You and me baith. It's goin to feel strange wi-oot aabody.'

'Ach, you'll get back to normal soon enough. Nothin changes roond here. The powers that be see to that.'

'You're richt. We've got naewhere investigatin these murders. Cannae even get the polis to tak them seriously. And this is the last day. Zoltán's already done a bunk. Aabody else is decampin to Embra the morn. They'll be scattered aa ower Europe and the world. And there's naethin we can do aboot it.'

Sandy flicked his cigarette into the water. 'Maybe. Maybe no. We've still Eddie Williamson the morn …'

'If he turns up …'

'He'll be here. He wouldnae dare miss Jessie Robertson's funeral. He'd never hear the end of it.'

'If you say so.' He leaned back and felt for Annie's hand. 'But what can he tell us, onywey?'

225

'How come a deid laddie ended up in his tent.'

'I'm guessin he'll no be awfae keen to talk aboot that again. Seein as how he fled toon once to get awa fae it.'

'Chance to tell his side of the story. He's a tink. They dinnae usually get that.'

Without warning, Jozef punched Bob hard on the arm and Bob yowled and rubbed the skin. 'What was that for?' he said, but Jozef was pointing towards the far end of the loch, about a hundred yards distant, where it connected to rough moorland.

'István,' he shouted and Bob could see the outline of István, his distinctive gait, heading away from the camp. Jozef jumped up. Bob groaned.

'Leave it,' he said. 'There's nothin to ask him, nothin he's goin to tell us.'

But Jozef was tying up his boots and reaching for his jacket. 'I go,' he said. 'I don't care if you come, too.'

Bob reflected on Jozef's hot temper, knew there was no way he could leave him to confront István on his own. He rose to his feet and stretched his back and set off after Jozef who had streaked ahead.

'Bob!' shouted Annie.

'I'll be back. Chaperone work.' He sprinted away before Annie could argue. Jozef, meanwhile, marched on regardless. 'Jozef!' Bob shouted. 'Jozef, wait.'

Jozef turned to face him. 'If you don't like the way I do things, don't follow me.'

'It's because I dinnae like the wey you do things I hae to follow you. Just dinnae hit him this time, that's all I'm askin.'

Jozef walked on without reply, following the line of the loch more by sound than by sight now that they were moving away from the lighted area around the boathouse. Beyond a wooden hut was a path through a small area of woodland rising gently towards the back road to Crieff. Bob

226

knew there was nothing beyond that but moorland.

Moorland in which, Sandy had warned, an unsuspecting walker could easily sink and disappear. There was no reason why István – or anyone – would venture that way. And plenty reasons why they shouldn't.

'He cannae be here,' he said. 'There's nothin but moor and bog. He must have circled back …'

'We go on …'

'It's dangerous. Sandy says …'

'Sandy's not here. If you are a coward, go back. I not need you.'

Bob sighed in frustration and contemplated doing exactly that, but in that instant a shape crossed the moonlight, unmistakably human, unmistakably someone wearing an expansive, plumed hat. Closer up, they could tell that another person walked alongside.

'István!' Bob yelled. The bodies in the moonlight froze for an instant, then bolted out of view back into darkness. Jozef ran towards them and immediately sank ankle deep in a waterlogged sink. Bob stepped forward and did likewise.

'Damn,' he said. He extricated his foot and shifted sideways onto what he hoped was firmer group. It held. Jozef had pulled himself free and was running towards the spot where they had last seen István. Cursing, Bob followed.

Although he had tried to fix the point where they had seen István, the dark and the roughness of the terrain made it impossible to maintain his focus. He knew he was going in the right general direction but he had no comprehension of distance. Partly, he was not overly disappointed to be losing track of their man. Running about in almost complete darkness in a heather-covered peat bog was madness enough, without considering what might ensue if Jozef actually caught his man.

'There!' Jozef let out a cry and darted to his right, further away from the loch, where the darkness was even more pervasive. Bob stumbled on a high outcrop of heather as he tried to follow, falling forwards and landing knee-deep in a pool of ice-cold water. Jozef had made ten yards on István and Bob could only see the backs of his bare legs, pale in the meagre light. A second later, even that view was obliterated by darkness. He heard a yell and the sounds of scuffling and as he ran blindly forward he caught up with Jozef and saw him lunge and catch a trailing leg and both he and his quarry fell full-length. They tussled on the sodden heather, each trying to get on top of the other, and Bob could now see that the other man was indeed István. There was no sign of his companion.

Jozef swung a punch and caught István heavily on the jaw. István fell backwards but grabbed Jozef when he reared up, swinging his arms wildly. They wrestled for some moments with more vigour than skill before István took advantage of Jozef losing his footing and threw him into the darkness. Once more, Jozef fell flat but, this time as he tried to stand he found himself sinking into the peat. The more he tried to pull free, the deeper he sank.

Bob ran towards him. 'Jozef,' he shouted.

'Go after him. I'm okay.'

Bob faltered. He could just discern a flicker in the gloom which showed István fleeing back the way they had come.

'Go, go, go!' Jozef shouted. By now, he was stuck to his knees and Bob could feel the ground shifting beneath his own feet.

'I'll get help,' he shouted and ran blindly in the direction István had taken. He stumbled on, gradually sensing the ground was becoming flatter and firmer. In the distance, he could see lights and he realised they'd travelled in a loop and were heading back to the loch from the opposite end.

As the heather moor gave way to grassland István slowed, and Bob heard someone raise a shout. A shape appeared from the shadow of a beech tree, moving towards him. This

228

must be István's companion, no doubt, unaware that Bob was still in pursuit.

'István!' Bob shouted.

Immediately, the second person retreated once more into tree cover. István turned and slammed his palm against his forehead. 'Go away. Why you not leave me alone?'

'I dinnae mean you any harm. I just want to talk.'

'You must go.'

'Who is it you're here to meet? Come out, whoever you are.' He waited but no one emerged. 'Come back with me,' he said to István. 'The others are there. Annie, Abdalla, James, Sandy. We can talk about this calmly. You might have a perfectly good explanation for everythin that's been happenin this past twelve days, but I have to tell you at the moment I think you and Zoltán are mixed up in the killing of Erling Hagen and Norrie Smith.'

'You do not know what you're talking about.'

'So enlighten me.'

István seemed like he was about to argue but then he stopped and nodded wearily. 'We go back,' he said. He gestured towards the other side of the loch.

'What about your friend?' Bob looked back at the beech tree.

'You are mistaken. I have no friend.'

Bob wanted to insist on the other man showing himself, but his priority was getting István back where they could talk to him properly. The past few minutes had served only to increase his certainty that István was guilty of something. Moreover, he had to get back to Sandy to tell him to go and rescue Jozef, who was presumably still floundering in the bog. As they walked, Bob formulated questions in his mind, determined not to waste this last opportunity. He was deep in contemplation and didn't notice István falling a step behind him. He didn't hear a thick oak branch swinging towards him. He felt an instant agony, like his body had been plunged into ice, and then he had a sensation of drowning. He lost control of his limbs and he fell to the ground and Bob Kelty felt no more.

*

When, half an hour later, neither Jozef nor Bob had returned, Annie started to fret. She turned to Sandy. 'We need to find them.'

Sandy threw down his Capstan and got to his feet, cursing. Abdalla and James followed and they headed into the darkness, yelling Bob's name. Rovers by the waterside, thinking this a game, impersonated them and soon the whole of the Monzie estate was echoing to the sound of "Bob, Bob, Bob."

Bob Kelty lay beneath the oak tree and heard his name being called over and over, like a demented roll call of one. He listened to his name, baffled. What was happening? Was he dead? Was this some call from the netherworld, drawing him to the ranks of the exanimate? He shifted and groaned. His head felt like it had been cleaved in two. He looked up at a sky blanketed by clouds, starless, and the darkness in which he was engulfed was stupefying. Caliginous shadow washed over him, oblivion in spate, surging into his mouth, his gullet, his gut, spilling from his eyes, nose, the tips of his fingers, distending his frame, drenching, saturating his senses until its dead weight dragged him down, into the earth, into the beyond, into the territory of the damned and he looked up once more and thought he could see faces, the grimaces of the dead bearing down on him, their hands on his skin, their breath on his face and their shouts and cries, and their screaming and hollering.

Thursday 27ᵗʰ July

A Day of Discovery

He became conscious of a devilish din. Discordant, shrieking. Loud, growing louder. The noise was in his head, a part of him, his consciousness, rebounding and resounding. He had no knowledge of what it was, or *where* he was, or even, at that moment, *who* he was. There was pain in his head and this bedlam was its personification.

'Please go away.'

The noise began to resolve into something recognisable, as though the individual fragments were somehow coalescing. Music. A tune. What was that?

'Please. You'll wake the patients.' A woman's voice. Young.

There was something he needed to do. Urgent. But funny. Something. What was that noise? *The Black … The Black …*

'That's the point. We're trying to wake the patients …'

'They need to rest …'

Rest. Recuperation. Reviving. Coming back to life. Is that what was happening? How dramatic. Melodramatic. *The Black … The Black …* Music. There was music outside. Outside where?

The Black …

The Black Bear.

Bob opened his eyes and stared at a canvas roof. Surgical smell. Stuffy atmosphere. *The Black Bear*. And that's *The*

231

Green Hills of Tyrol. Bob's memory fluttered into activity once more and he remembered a five o'clock assignation with the Pipe Band. He tried to get out of bed but the movement made him dizzy.

'Are you awake?'

The voice was foreign. Friendly. Bob turned his head and in the bed next to his was Jozef, leaning on his elbow, grinning broadly. Like Bob, he was in pyjamas, but he was filthy.

'Evenin.'

'Morning, my friend. You've been out for hours.'

'What happened?'

'You got hit over the head. Need stitches.'

'What by?'

'Not what. Who.'

Bob felt his head. It was bandaged and the skin beneath was tender. Last night swam in and out of his memory, with István among the heather, chasing him, catching him, talking. And before that, Jozef in the bog …

'Are you alright?'

'Fine. Sandy, he come find me. Pull me out of the bog. They thought I might have … what is it when you are very, very cold, so it make you sick?'

'Hypothermia?'

'They thought I might have hypothermia. I tell them no.'

'And?'

'Not hypothermia. Just very, very cold, like I said.'

'And me?'

'You no remember?'

'Not much.'

'Abdalla find you. Somebody hit you over the head with a tree branch. István, of course. Now we know he is guilty.'

Bob tried to think through the fog of confusion. Last evening proved István had something to hide, certainly, but whether he was involved in the deaths of Erling Hagen or

Norrie Smith, of that there was still no proof. Outside, the noise from the Rover Pipe Band was fading as they made their way downhill for their final tormenting of the London boys. Bob lay back and stared at the canvas roof and tried to piece together the events of the previous evening. Half an hour later, the tent entrance was swept open and Sandy entered, Capstan fixed in his mouth. Abdalla and Annie followed.

'Attention seekin,' said Sandy.

'Our final band parade went very well,' said Abdalla. 'Half of the London boys cheered, the other half booed.'

'That's aboot the normal response, truth to tell.' Bob pulled himself upright and looked around. He shook his head but it felt normal – tender where the stitches had been applied but nothing worse than that. No dizziness. No headache. 'So whaur's István? Did you get to speak to him?'

'He has disappeared,' said Abdalla. 'I went to his tent last night but it was empty.'

'Could hae made the last train to Perth,' said Sandy. 'Could be onywhere by noo.'

'Him and Zoltán,' said Abdalla. 'Two bad men.'

'Aye,' said Bob, but something still troubled him. Something felt wrong. Zoltán Tóth. Bob was generally a good judge of character and Zoltán Tóth had seemed to him entirely kind, not at all the kind of person to become involved in such affairs. Niceness was Bob's Achilles' heel, he knew. He saw the best in everybody, but he was seldom wrong, and certainly not in such an apparently clear case. Zoltán Tóth was a gentleman. And a gentle man. Bob was sure of it.

'So what happens now?' he said to Abdalla. 'You're all decampin?'

'This morning, yes. Off to Edinburgh. One more night, a big parade tomorrow, and then it's all over. We go back home. We shall miss you.' He turned to Annie and Sandy.

'All of you.'

'Aye weel,' said Bob, pulling aside his bedclothes, 'I'm no missin your fareweel for onythin. I'll be at the station to wave you awa.' He swung his legs out of the bed and gripped the bed rail as he stood.

'You get back into bed,' said Annie.

'I'm richt as rain,' he said. 'It's juist a puckle stitches. I feel grand.' He shooed them away. 'Gie me peace to get my claes on.'

Annie tutted loudly but Bob knew that meant he'd won the argument. A rarity indeed, and he savoured the moment. 'Here then,' she said. 'Here's some fresh claes. Those things you had on last night are manky. I'll never get the stains oot …'

'Milk.'

'That's for blood, no peat.'

'Oh aye.'

*

Crieff Railway Station had never seen the like. The Up platform was submerged beneath a clamjamfrey of bodies, men in shorts and various styles of headgear, all carrying rucksacks, many bearing sundry souvenirs from the Moot, wooden markers pointing the way to the bank and post office and headquarters, signs from the encampments of the various countries or British regional groupings, flags, pennants, newspapers. A cacophony of languages commingled among the iron columns lining the platform and rose into the grey morning sky. The first of seven trains chartered to ferry the Rovers to Edinburgh stood on the platform. The Comrie train stood on the opposite platform and between them, on the middle line, a lengthy goods train was waiting until the way was clear. The Rovers' trains departed every quarter hour, each carrying some four hundred and fifty young men, and yet the platform seemed to grow no quieter. Abdalla, Jozef

234

and James waited with Bob and Annie as the first five trains departed, laughing and joking all the while. As the sixth train trundled into the station Abdalla took off his fez and bowed.

'I think, this time, we shall board the train,' he said.

'Are you in tents again the night?' said Annie.

'No, I believe we are being put up in local schools.'

'That doesnae sound awfae comfortable.'

'We have spent the last ten days sleeping on a Scottish hillside. After that, my poor back can cope with anything.'

The train ground to a halt and a guard blew his whistle. 'All aboard!' he shouted and made his way along the train, opening doors which had not already been opened by impatient Rovers.

'This is it,' said Abdalla, shaking first Bob's hand and then Annie's. 'Time to say goodbye.' Bob shook the hands of Jozef and James, and Annie did likewise. Jozef bent and kissed her cheek.

'Wish I'd thought to do that,' said James.

'Missed your chance, Glesga boy,' said Annie, but she raised her cheek towards him and he gave her the briefest peck. The five looked at one another and waited for someone to speak but there was nothing left to say. Abdalla waved his hand and lifted his rucksack onto his shoulder and stepped towards the train. James and Jozef followed, and Bob and Annie held hands as they watched them negotiate the steps and climb into the train. They tracked them as they walked down the passageway and, after a few moments, saw them enter an empty compartment. Abdalla lifted his rucksack onto the rack above the seats and then did the same with James's and Jozef's, and the three men sat down. A couple of Rhodesians joined them and Abdalla made some remark. Annie and Bob watched as all in the compartment burst simultaneously into laughter. The guard blew his whistle once more and began to shut the doors, each one slamming with the finality of a broken promise. When they were all closed he blew his whistle twice more, raising his hand, and the train began to chug the way it had come, back towards the Gleneagles junction and south.

'Dinnae suppose we'll ever see them again,' said Annie.

'I suppose no.'

'I'll miss them.'

They waved as the train began to move away. Abdalla opened the window and waved back and they watched until the train had rounded the bend on the way out of the station on its way to the Highlandman junction. Only when the train was out of sight did Bob and Annie stop waving.

'Aye weel,' said Bob.

'We'd best be getting back to Cloudland,' said Annie. 'We've been neglectin it this past fortnight.'

'I suppose so.' Annie turned to leave but Bob stayed where he was. 'On you go,' he said, 'I'll be back in a wee while. I juist hae a couple of things to do first.'

She looked at him solicitously. He looked so vulnerable with his bandaged head. He needed looking after.

'I'll be fine, honest. Dinnae worry. I'll be back for denner.' He kissed her and stroked her hair. She caressed his cheek and walked away.

'Dinnae be daein onythin daft,' she shouted without looking back.

'As if.'

The station was still filled with the last few hundred Rovers waiting for the final train. The goods train and the Comrie train had departed and the tracks were empty. Bob could see, on the opposite platform, the station master, Wullie Booth. He climbed the stairs and crossed the bridge and descended on the opposite platform.

'Wullie,' he shouted. Wullie Booth checked his pocket watch and decided he had enough time before the next train to indulge in passenger chit-chat.

'Morning Bob. Here to see the Rovers aff?'

'I was, aye. It's been grand haein them.'

'They've brought a bit of life to the toon.'

'But back to ordinar the morn.'

'Aye, the Misses Seaton, Beaton and Miller mumpin like buggery.'

'Mind, they didnae stop doin that last week, either. Talkin aboot the Rovers, you didnae happen to hae one of them in yesterday morn? Richt early, this would be.'

'First train oot, aye. Waitin at the gate when I opened up.'

'What did he look like?'

'Older. Too auld to be wearin laddies' breeks. Queerlike hat.'

'Carryin a rucksack?'

'Oh aye.'

'Thanks, Wullie.' Bob felt a tug of defeat. He had been half-hoping to disprove István's suggestion that Zoltán had skipped camp. Confirm his gut instinct. Endorse his view that people were essentially good. Over the way, another train was pulling into the platform, too short to be another of the Rovers' specials. 'Whaur's that goin?' he asked Wullie.

Wullie was already marching towards the bridge to take control of the new arrival. 'Perth,' he said.

On a whim, Bob decided to board it.

*

'I'm glad you came.'

'I wasn't sure if I should, ma'am.'

'Of course you should.' Bella Conoboy sat in her chair beside the fire and gestured to Bob to sit on the settee. A novel, *Goodbye to Berlin*, lay opened on the arm of her chair. She was staring at his bandaged head. 'What on earth happened?'

Bob cursed himself for not having thought of an excuse. He couldn't bother Mrs Conoboy with the truth, not at a time like this.

'Oh,' he said breezily, 'just an accident. Something landed on my head. In Cloudland.'

She smiled at him indulgently. 'Victor could never lie either.'

He smiled back, stared at the dun-coloured carpet, said nothing. Mina knocked and entered, carrying a tray of tea and cakes. She laid it on the table by the fire and exited.

'It's hard, at times like this,' Bella said, 'not to think about yourself. How you're feeling, what this means to you. Hard not to think about the loss you've sustained, how things can never, ever be the same again. And they won't be the same, ever again. They'll be different. But different doesn't mean bad. I had a wonderful life with Victor. I'd have liked longer, but this is what I got, and I'm grateful for every moment of it, even the times when we argued, even when we shouted at one another ...'

'I can't imagine there was much of that ...'

'What you see in public is only ever a fraction of the truth. A veneer. Disputable. We had our moments. Anyone who lives together forty years will. At times like this, the present is so oppressive it's hard to break away from it. Gain perspective. You get ravelled up in the minutiae of the minutes and you lose track of the hours. Dawn breaks, every morning. The world turns. There will be happiness again. There will be laughter. Victor will never share that, but we can share it with Victor. That's the difference. You see?'

'I think so.'

'He's left us, but he'll never be gone.'

Bob blinked, aware he was about to cry. 'Yes mu ... ma'am,' he said, correcting himself halfway through. He blinked again.

Bella picked up her teacup and placed it on the opposite chair arm to her novel. 'I would like you to say something at the funeral,' she said.

'I wouldn't know what ...'

'Whatever you like. Whatever you feel. It's important. Victor would have liked that.'

'Of course, ma'am.'

'And Robert …' She leaned over and stroked his arm. 'Everyone needs a mum, sometimes. Whenever you want to talk to her, I'm here.'

'Thank you.'

*

After the funeral of Jessie Robertson at St Andrew's Church on Ferntower Road, her plain wood coffin was laid on a cart pulled by a brown and white roan and Pete Stewart led it down Victoria Terrace and Coldwells Road onto the Roman line of Burrell Street. A hundred mourners followed, a quarter of a mile downhill to Crieff Cemetery on Ford Road.

There, another two hundred Travellers were formed in rows by the graveside, arranged in family groupings, all wearing mourning dress. Death was an important affair for the Scottish Traveller folk and many, women and men, wept openly while others stood in stoic silence. Jessie Robertson's grave had been dug by the Travellers themselves that morning, as was their custom. The coffin passed the gates of the cemetery and completed the final yards over rough stone paths to the graveside.

Sandy Disdain, deerstalker in his hand, unlit Capstan in his mouth, stood beneath a willow tree and pulled at the unwonted tie around his neck. He watched as the interment started. A quietude of solemnity. Proud, respectful, doleful. Sandy scanned the faces of the mourners until he saw the man he had come to find.

Eddie Williamson.

He watched until the body was lowered into the ground and the mourners began to disperse, then made his move.

'Eddie,' he said.

Eddie Williamson turned and eyed Sandy suspiciously.

A scaldy at a Traveller funeral was a rarity. And Eddie had cause to be nervous. He had not thought to return to Crieff for a long time, possibly ever, and Jessie's death had forced on him a quandary which only his sense of honour eventually resolved. All the same, he had intended to slip in and out of town unremarked.

'Wha wants to ken?' he said.

Sandy introduced himself. He mentioned travellers he'd worked with to establish his credentials. 'Jimmy McPhee, Alec Stewart.'

'Guid lads, baith. You'll be botherin me for a reason, though.'

Sandy offered him a Capstan but both waited until they had passed through the cemetery gates onto the path to Dallerie before lighting up. Sandy pulled off his tie and stuffed it in his jacket pocket. He couldn't tell, because of Eddie's cross-eyes, whether the man was looking at him or past him.

'I'm thinkin you were up Monzie,' he said. 'The other week.'

Sandy knew from the change in Eddie's expression that he'd found his man. 'You were tellin Habbie Goudie.'

'I didnae tell that moich so he could clype aboot it to aabody.'

'Aye well, you ken Habbie when he's got a drink in him. Likes to gab. I'm no efter you, though. I'm no causin trouble.'

'Is that right? In my experience, ony time you country hantle get involved in oor affairs, trouble's no far awa.'

'We fund your tent. On Monzie estate.' They studied each other warily, each trying to discern what the other knew. 'There was a deid body in it.'

'That was naethin to do wi me.'

'Aye, I ken that fine.' This seemed to reassure Eddie. He drew heavily on his cigarette as they walked along a narrow path overlooking a water meadow. In the distance, the Dallerie Laundry occupied the site of the old water mill, next to it the mill owner's house.

'You didnae even pitch thon tent, did ye?'

'Hell no. On Monzie land? Ye ken what the pooskie coull's like at Monzie.'

'I do, aye. The man's a bastard and no mistake. It was a richt amateur put thon tent up.'

'Every bow tent has its intricacies.'

'Especially if you've never pitched ane in your life.' Sandy threw his cigarette butt into a puddle on the path. 'So wha did pitch it?' Eddie was walking on as though he hadn't heard. 'I telt you, you'll get nae bother fae me. I juist want to ken what happened.'

Eddie asked for another cigarette and Sandy pulled out his packet. Four left. This had better be a short story.

'I was passin through Monzie,' Eddie said. 'Shortest wey fae the Sma Glen to Crieff, through Monzie, up to Ferntower.' Sandy nodded. 'This gadgie stopped me. Foreign …'

'What did he look like?'

'He was wearing a jaicket and broon shorts. Shorts. A grown man, like a bairn. Thinks I, I've seen it all, noo. And he said to me, "Can I buy your tent? And some claes?" I looked at him like he was crazy, ken, but he pulled oot ten pounds and held it oot to me. I says "twelve pounds", expectin that to be the end of it. "Yes," says he, and he draps another twa pounds into his femmels. He gied me it and I took it and I gied him the tent. "And some claes," says he, and I says "I've only got rags spare", but he wanted them just the same so I gave him an auld pair of brickets and a shirt that was mair hole than fabric. "And boots," says he. "Man," I says, "I've only the boots I'm standin in." He wasnae happy aboot that but what could I do?'

Sandy nodded. 'So you took the money?'

Eddie turned and stared up at Turleum Hill to the south.

241

'I took the money and scarpered. What else was I goin to do? But I wasnae happy, ken? It didnae mak sense. So I heard the pooskie coull shootin ower the top end of the estate, oot the Sma Glen wey, and I kent I was safe a while, so I went back …'

'He'd put your tent up?'

'Aye.'

'Wi the deid body inside it?'

'Aye. I didnae ken onythin aboot that until then.'

'The body was dressed in your claes?'

Eddie pondered. 'I'm thinking he was tryin to mak it look like it was me deid in the tent.' He'd come to this conclusion before but was happy to air it now and have it confirmed by someone else.

'Aye. My thocht an aa.'

'Man, he'd never get awa wi it.'

'But he has.' Eddie looked at him incredulously. 'Think aboot it. The polis find a tink deid in his tent. What are they goin to do?'

'Bugger all.'

'Exactly. And that's juist what they did.'

'So this gadgie – he moolied the man in the tent?'

'Aye. Killed him and tried to mak it look like an accident. Then set fire to the tent to mak absolutely sure.'

'Set fire to it?'

'Aye, it was three-quarters burnt when we fund it. The deid man an aa.'

'It wasnae when I left it.'

'Naw?'

They arrived at a small, twisting brae that led up to Sauchie. Eddie stopped. 'I'm goin this wey,' he said, pointing towards the railway line crossing the fields. 'My cuddy's tied up at the Laggan. I'm goin doon to Loch Fyne for the winter.'

Sandy was also intending to go to the Laggan, back home

for some dinner, but he recognised that Eddie had said all he wanted to say and would prefer his own company from now on. 'Aye well,' he said, 'thanks for the information.'

'What are you goin to do wi it?'

'Not a thing. The man wha did this slipped oot of camp last night. Probably on his wey back to Hungary as we speak.'

'It's a shan affair.'

'At least you got twelve quid oot of it.'

'Thon lour's tainted. And I spent half of it onywey, in Frank Thomson's buying cloth for a new bow tent and new brickets.'

'And a girdle.'

'Man, that was daft. I dinnae ken what I bocht it for. I kent, soon as I got back to Loch Fyne, my mither would be askin me aa aboot it. I'd never hear the end of it.'

'So you selt it?'

'To Chic Goudie. I ran into him aboot half an hoor afore I met Habbie.'

Sandy laughed. 'You were worried what your mither would say when she fund it. Exact same thing really happened to Chic. Run oot of toon by his auntie.'

'I kent it was bad luck.'

*

Annie watched as Mary Kemp hopped from foot to foot outside Cloudland, plucking up the courage to enter. She smiled encouragingly and gave a wave and finally Mary opened the door and crept inside.

'Hello,' she said. 'I was just passin.'

'So I see. Would you like some tea?'

'I wouldnae want to be a bother.'

'This is a tea shop. Makin tea's what we do.'

'I hear Bob had an accident. Is he alright?'

'Aye, fortunately they cracked him ower the heid, so

243

there's no damage done.'

'I'm glad.'

Annie could tell that, whatever Mary wanted to talk about, it wasn't Bob's injury. She waited, but no further conversation was forthcoming.

'Aye weel,' she said. 'I best start makin the morn's pies.'

The look of alarm that washed over Mary's face confirmed she had something else she wanted to say.

'Unless there was something you wanted to speak to me aboot?'

'The other day,' Mary said finally. 'Sandy arranged for me to go on ane of the Rovers' trips. Oot to Loch Rannoch power station.'

'Aye? That must hae been nice.'

'Pelly Duncan, he said we werenae allowed to tak any photies while we were there ...'

'In case of war, I suppose.'

Mary looked uncertain and Annie explained. 'Power station. Could be a target for bombs.'

'You think so?'

'Nae idea. But thon's as good an explanation as ony.' Mary bowed her head and Annie could sense a fierce debate raging in her head. 'How?' she said.

'When I was there, I took some photies ... of thon Rover fae Yugoslavia, Mitch or Misky ...'

'Miško?'

'Aye, him.'

'How?'

'He asked me to.'

'Just photies of him?'

'Aye.'

'That's alright. Just mementoes, to look at when he's back hame.'

'I suppose ...'

'But?'

'But … It's just the wey he wanted me to mak sure to get the power station in the shot …'

'To show whaur he was?'

'But if it really was … in case of war … if he was really …'

'A spy?'

'Aye. I mean … do you think I'll go to the jail?'

'For takin a laddie's photie?' Annie laughed but saw the concern on Mary's face. The trip to the Loch Rannoch power station had been nearly a week ago and Mary was still fretting. This lassie could worry for Scotland, Annie reflected. 'Honestly,' she said, 'I wouldnae get vexed aboot it. I mean, wha the hell would want to bomb Crieff onywey?' She stopped as a sudden thought overtook her.

'Miško, you say?'

'Aye.'

'Did he get you to tak ony mair picters?'

'The weir.'

'And did Pelly say no to tak picters of that an aa?'

'Aye.'

'All the while, was Miško askin you a lot questions?'

'Aye. Non-stop. What did I ken aboot this. Whaur was that. How far was Perth, Glesga. Fair wore me oot.'

Annie exhaled heavily. 'Damn it,' she said. 'Miško …'

*

Bob was standing by the King Street bridge overlooking the Meadows when Sandy walked along Union Terrace to the Station Bar. He was smoking his pipe and was oblivious of Sandy's approach.

'Awa wi the fairies,' said Sandy.

Bob pulled himself from his reverie and acknowledged Sandy with a shake of his head. 'Just aff the train,' he said. 'Gaitherin my thochts. I'm no ready to go hame yet. Annie – she'll be askin questions, how I'm feelin, is my heid sair, aa that. I'm no ready for questions yet.'

'Aye, I ken. The women ay want instant answers. Opinions plucked oot the air.' He lit a cigarette and threw the match into the cutting thirty feet below. 'You can come back to mines if you like. My mither'll hae the denner on.'

'Will she mind?'

'Why would she? I'll tell you aboot Eddie Williamson when we get there.'

The Disdain cottage was a half hour walk out of town, past MacRosty Park and Mary Kemp's workplace at Doctor McNeill's. They stopped and looked over the wall at the doctor's house below them, alongside the river. Rabbits louped lazily on the lawn, which Sandy seemed to take as a personal affront. He looked around, calculating whether there was any public land nearby where he could set some snares. There wasn't.

They climbed past the park and Eppie Callum's tree and turned onto the Laggan road. On the side of the Laggan Hill, in splendid isolation, overlooking the valley, was a small, whitewashed farmhand's cottage, home of the Disdains. Bob was hirpling by the time they reached it, his bandage swathed in sweat.

'Keeps you fit, bidin oot here.'

Sandy pointed towards the top of town and the peak of the Knock Hill. 'Especially if your work's maistly up yonder.'

Mrs Disdain was working in the kitchen garden when they entered the kitchen through the back door. She followed them, shooing Bob out of the way and depositing half a dozen carrots on the worktop beside the sink. Sandy introduced Bob as he filled the kettle with water. He hung it on a hook over an open hearth, above which was a funnel coming halfway down the wall. It opened out, forming a kind of chimney, covered inside and outside in soot.

'Quite a contraption, that,' said Bob.

'Hingin lum. There's probably no many of them still

aroond.'

Sandy filled a copper teapot when the water had boiled and while the tea was brewing they sat at the kitchen table. Mrs Disdain, her plump midriff wrapped in a black pinnie, began skinning and jointing a rabbit.

'So you met Eddie Williamson?' said Bob.

'He wasnae richt pleased to see me.'

'But he talked?'

'Telt me aa aboot it. He was takin a shortcut through the Monzie estate, came upon a Rover. "A grown man in shorts, like a bairn," he said.'

'He's no wrang,' said Mrs Disdain. 'They look bloody daft, dressed up like wee laddies. I saw ane of them on Sunday, on a cuddy oot back. Far too auld to be dressed like thon …'

'How auld?' Bob asked.

'Forties, maybe. Auld enough to ken better onyhow.'

Bob winced. He was still trying to absolve Zoltán from involvement but the evidence kept pointing to him. 'That must be Zoltán, then,' he conceded. 'Maybe just afore he killed Norrie.'

Mrs Disdain scoffed. 'Hark at you. You've been listenin to too many *Afternoon Dramas* on the wireless, son.'

Bob tried to laugh away his embarrassment. 'So what was he dressed like?'

'Broon shorts and jaicket and a daft hat on his heid.'

Bob tapped his mug with his finger. 'Prairie grass on it, aye?'

'A peewit could hae nested in there.'

Bob stared out of the window at the back lane Zoltán had ridden down. Why he was there was every bit as mysterious as why he would have killed Norrie Smith. As always, when Bob considered this case, nothing made sense. Then he gave a start.

Sandy spotted the change in his expression, stared at him

quizzically. 'What?' he said.

'Tell me again, what did Eddie say aboot the man wha bocht his tent?'

'He said he was wearing broon shorts, like a bairn.'

'Juist that? Wearin shorts like a bairn?'

'And a jaicket.'

Bob laid his hand flat on the table and regarded it for a moment. 'Damn, damn, damn,' he said.

'Dinnae blaspheme in this house, you wee bastard,' said Mrs Disdain.

Bob checked her expression to see if she was joking. Apparently, she wasn't. He apologised and exhaled heavily. 'How long ago did Eddie leave?'

Sandy shrugged. 'An hoor, maybe.'

'Damn – sorry – he'll be half wey to Comrie by noo. I dinnae suppose you hae a telephone?' The snorts from Disdains senior and junior provided the answer. 'Wha has?'

'The fairm. Doon the road.'

'Have they a car we could borrow?'

'I'm sure Malky's got a Jaguar 100 in the yard.'

'Maybe no that fancy …'

'He's got a tractor. His pride and joy.'

'Can you drive it?'

'Nae idea.'

'You'll pick it up. Come on.'

'How?'

'We're goin after Eddie.'

Bob sprinted out of the back door, leaving Sandy and his mother staring at one another.

'Is he ay like this?' said Mrs Disdain.

Sandy raised an eyebrow. 'You're no seein him at his best.'

Down on the farm, Bob pleaded with Mrs Bennett, the farmer's wife, to use their telephone and, after negotiating with first her and then the operator, he was finally connected to Annie.

'Whaur are you? You should hae been hame hoors ago.'

'I need you to get my bike and come and meet me at Dalvreck on the Comrie Road. Soon as you can …'

'How?'

'I'll explain when you get there. And can you bring the photie of the Rover lads in Cloudland fae the *Moot Pictorial*? It's in the drawer …'

'I ken whaur it is. What's goin on?'

'Soon as you can.' He hung up, largely to avoid having to debate the issue with her any longer and run the risk of her talking him out of this. When he thanked Mrs Bennett and went outside, Sandy was in the driver's seat of a green John Deere tractor, with Malky Bennett giving rudimentary instructions. Smoke from his cigarette curled into Sandy's left eye. He nodded continuously, staring at the fiendish-looking gear stick. Bob jumped onto the back and sat on the left mudguard.

'Are you sure you ken what you're doin?' shouted Farmer Bennett over the din of the engine. Sandy shrugged. Bob raised a thumb. He patted Sandy's shoulder and Sandy set off. The engine stalled. He inhaled heavily and blew smoke from the side of his mouth, turning the ignition once more. This time the tractor flew forward without incident and Bob was almost knocked off the back. He hung onto the rear of Sandy's chair as they bounced down the lane from the farm towards the Horseshoe Drive. Annie was already waiting by the side of the Comrie road when they reached Dalvreck, her bicycle by her side and her face framed with fury.

'You better have a good reason for this, Bob Kelty,' she said icily. 'I was in the middle of makin the morn's pies.'

Bob beckoned to her. 'Leave the bike,' he said. 'Jump on.'

'I'm no getting on that thing!'

'Well, bide here then.'

249

Her expression told Bob he could expect a frosty reception for the rest of the day, but he reached out his hand and she grabbed it and he pulled her onto the back of the tractor.

'You need to hold on,' he said.

'You dinnae say.'

'Have you got the photie?'

She glowered at him and gripped the side of Sandy's seat as though bracing herself to be hit by a typhoon. Bob tapped Sandy's shoulder and they set off in their John Deere tractor in pursuit of Eddie Williamson's horse and cart.

'Whaur hae you been all day?' Annie yelled over the roar of the engine.

'Seein Mrs Conoboy.'

Immediately, Annie softened. She reached with the hand that wasn't glued to Sandy's chair and stroked Bob's shoulder. She knew what an ordeal that must have been, how much it would have taken out of him. She didn't know why he'd felt the need to go and see Bella, but he had and that was enough. Bob, aware that Annie had been angry without fully understanding why, felt himself relax when he saw her accept his answer. Equilibrium. The state Bob Kelty sought for the conduct of his days.

They drove steadily for five or six miles, none of them able to appreciate, as they ordinarily would, the countryside through which they were travelling. Bob's hand was numb and he wasn't sure he would be able to prise it from the seat at journey's end. His eyes were streaming with the constant wind. In only shirt sleeves, he was feeling far colder than he should on a fine July evening.

A mile from Comrie they caught up with Eddie Williamson and Sandy passed him and flagged him down. Eddie, walking alongside the horse and cart, steadied the horse and they came to a halt.

'I've telt you aathin,' he growled at Sandy. He looked at Bob and Annie. 'I kent no good would come of speakin to a scaldy.'

'Mr Williamson,' Bob said, employing his police voice for the first time in years, 'we're sorry to bother you and we'll no keep you long. The Rover that bocht your tent, you said he wore broon shorts?'

'And jaicket, aye. You've followed me all this wey to ask me that?'

'Was there anythin else you noticed aboot him? What he was wearin?'

'No.'

'Nae hat, for example?'

'He micht hae been wearin a hat. I cannae mind. It's the shorts I mind. A grown man …'

'In shorts … I ken.' He opened the *Moot Pictorial* and pointed to the photograph of the Rovers taken in Cloudland by Andrew Wood. 'Is the man in this photie?'

Eddie took the paper, pulling it close to his face and squinting at it, cross-eyed. He appeared to study each man in turn, then pointed a gnarled and filthy finger at it.

'Him.'

'You're sure?'

'Some country hantle pays me twelve quid for my old bow tent and rotten claes, I'm no minded to forget him.' He pointed at the picture again. 'Him.'

'It's Miško, isn't it?' said Annie.

'Aye,' said Bob, showing her and Sandy the picture of Miško standing next to István and Zoltán in the back row. 'How did you ken?'

'Mary. She telt me aboot her trip to the power station. Miško was actin suspiciously.'

'I dinnae understand,' said Sandy. 'How's it Miško all of a sudden?'

'The dug that didnae bark,' said Bob.

'Eh?'

'The dug that didnae bark.'

251

'Is he right in the heid?' said Eddie, pointing to Bob's bandage.

'I'm beginnin to wonder,' said Sandy.

'*The Dug that Didnae Bark*,' said Annie.

'Christ,' said Eddie, 'she's at it, noo.'

'Sherlock Holmes,' said Annie.

'Exactly,' said Bob. 'Sandy, how did your mither describe the Rover she saw?'

'Shorts and stupit hat.'

'Right. And every single person who ever saw ane of the Hungarians' hats said the same thing: they were stupit. That's why I asked you to repeat what Eddie said to you ...' He nodded three or four times encouragingly. 'Because he didnae say it. The Rover he saw wasnae wearing a stupit hat. So he wasnae István or Zoltán.'

'And Miško was the other ane who hired a cuddy,' said Annie.

'Aye,' said Bob. 'We kind of overlooked him because we talked oorsels into there bein a connection between István and Zoltán.' He stroked the flank of Eddie's horse and she whinnied appreciatively. 'D'you no see?' he went on. 'All this time, we've been efter the wrang man. István kept tellin us, but we wouldnae listen. We were that damned sure of oorsels. And we were wrang. It wasnae István killed Erling Hagen, it was Miško. And I'm sure it was him who killed Norrie an aa. No Zoltán.'

'So what noo?' said Annie. 'It's too late. They've gone.'

'No they havenae. They're all in Embra. And Miško doesnae ken we're on to him. He'll be there the morn for the final parade.' He stared at Annie and Sandy.

'And?' said Annie.

'And when he joins it, we'll be there.'

Friday 28th July

A Day of Revelations

Bob woke up knowing he would go to Edinburgh alone. He'd lain awake most of the night pondering the case, trying to understand it, until eventually he realised there was nothing there which could be understood.

At least, not by him, or anyone like him.

There was something else at play here. That much was evident from the Procurator Fiscal's warning, his revelation that he had come under greater pressure to stifle this case than any other in his career. It was evident from Geordie Macrae – as decent a man as he was a terrible policeman – refusing to offer assistance. It was evident from the way even the Bailie and the Provost of the Town Council had been co-opted – perhaps even coerced – to try to stop him from pursuing his investigation. It was evident from the D-notice served on the *Strathearn Herald*. It was evident from the way everything remained at issue. Whatever was behind this was much, much bigger than Bob and he knew that, by confronting Miško in Edinburgh, he was provoking that *whatever* even more. He couldn't expose Annie to that risk. This was his decision, and the risk fell to him alone.

At five o'clock he slid out of bed noiselessly, got dressed, and spent an hour at the kitchen table, writing his eulogy to Victor Conoboy. His eyes were still filmy with tears as he waited outside Crieff station at seven for Wullie Booth to open the gates.

'You must be gettin used to people queuin up to get in,' he said.

'Eh?'

'The other mornin. That Rover mannie, waitin to get in first thing. You telt me aboot it yesterday.'

'Oh, aye. Aye.'

'You absolutely sure aboot that?'

'Aye.'

'It was an awfae good description you gied me of the man. Almost like you'd been telt it.'

'I dinnae ken what you mean.'

'Did someone pey you to say that?'

'I dinnae …'

'Was it another Rover. Wearin a stupit hat? Younger, though?'

Wullie blustered, noises and wheezes coming from his mouth but nothing as formed as speech.

'How much did he gie you?'

'Times are hard, son.'

'I ken, Wullie. And there's a war comin. Wha kens what's goin to happen next? How much did he pey you?'

'Ten shillin.'

'Ten shillin? I'm sure you could hae held oot for mair than that, man.'

'I didnae like it. But well, my laddie's got the polio, and this job, it doesnae pey …'

'It's grand, Wullie. Here's another ten bob.'

*

Edinburgh Castle looks best on a grey day, looming over the city like a glowering toad, sliding into indistinction in the mirk as though not wholly substantial, like some peculiarly Scottish wraith. Bob regarded it from his vantage point beside the statue of Allan Ramsey next to the Mound.

254

'Shite day for it.' A young man in a drab overcoat and fraying hat held out his hand as though to catch falling rain.

'It's been the same the hale ten days,' said Bob. 'Every time they hae a parade it rains.'

'You been with them all the way through?'

'Aye, I'm fae Crieff.'

'Poor bastard.'

Princes Street was closed off by voluminous lengths of rope, while a couple of police horses patrolled in between. Policemen in overcoats and capes stood opposite the dignitaries' dais, a wooden podium built in front of the Royal Scottish Academy where Lord Provost Steele was waiting to take the salute, being sheltered by an umbrella held by a functionary. A cheer from the Haymarket end of Princes Street alerted those around Bob to the Rovers' imminent arrival and all craned their necks to their left. Bob felt a strange weariness. He compared the moment to the excitement which had attended his first viewing of a Moot parade, twelve days before. Those intervening days had been long.

The forty-eight nations represented at the Moot began their procession in alphabetical order, two Rovers from Armenia holding between them a banner proclaiming the name of their country and a young man barely reached shaving age immediately behind bearing their national flag. The remaining Armenians followed in a ragtag group. Lord Provost Steele and the Moot officials saluted as they passed, completely out of step with one another, and they were followed by a much larger and more organised contingent from Austria.

'Is that all there is?' asked Bob's new friend. 'Laddies marchin by?'

'Aye. Three-and-a-half thoosand.'

'I'm awa to the pub.' The man looked behind him, saw the crowd nine or ten deep, and dipped under the rope onto

Princes Street, where a policeman, glad of something to do, grabbed him by the collar and escorted him away.

'Somethin you said, son?' an elderly woman said to Bob.

'I said I was fae Crieff.'

'Went there once. Hellish place. Blisters for a week. Who in the name of God would build a toon on the side of a mountain?'

Bob looked up at the castle, high on the hill, but said nothing.

A good ten minutes elapsed before the arrival of the Egyptian Rovers, raising their fezzes as they went and garnering huge cheers. Bob shouted to Abdalla, marching near the front, and Abdalla scanned the crowd to see where the shout had come from. He spotted Bob and became animated, stepping away from his colleagues and running towards him.

'Bob, I need to speak with you. At the end.' He gestured towards the east end of Princes Street where the parade would conclude. 'Very important,' he shouted before rejoining his group. He looked back and waved his fez as if to emphasise the point.

Bob looked around for a means of escape, but decided not to emulate the effort of his erstwhile friend and instead weaved his way back through the tightly-packed watchers. Umbrellas were an ever-present hazard but finally he escaped into Princes Street Gardens and made his way to Waverley Station, and back up to Princes Street. The procession had ended outside the Register Office and Bob looked around for the Egyptian contingent. They were easy to find in their fezzes, clustered round the statue of the Duke of Wellington. A couple of Abdalla's friends spotted him and shouted across, and Abdalla turned and saw him. He dashed across the street and shook Bob's hand expansively, clapping him on the back.

'I have seen István,' he said excitedly. 'I saw him go into

256

a hotel.'

'Where?' said Bob. This was most unexpected – they had all assumed that when István skipped camp he would be following whatever route Zoltán had taken out of the country. They had presumed never to see him again.

Abdalla pointed behind Bob. 'There.'

'The Balmoral Hotel? Blimey, that's a bit posh.'

'He came out of there, saw us coming from the railway station, and ran back inside again.'

'How long?'

'Ninety minutes.'

'Let's go and pay him a visit.'

'I cannot. We go directly to the final parade in Murrayfield Stadium now. Our bus is waiting.' He pointed to a row of buses parked outside the Register Office.

'I'll be fine on my ain, then.' Bob wasn't sure whether he was reassuring Abdalla or himself. 'I'll see you efter the final parade and tell you what happened.'

'Be careful, my friend.'

Have no fear, Bob thought. He entered the Balmoral and approached the reception and smiled at the concierge. 'You've a friend of mine stayin,' he said. 'István Kedály. Could you tell me his room number, please?' A look that Bob could only describe as revulsion overtook the concierge's face.

'A friend of Mr Kedály? I see. I'll have to remember that phrase in future, for describing people like you.'

'People like me?'

'Mr Kedály is in Room 128. First floor.' Without a further word, he turned away from Bob and pretended to flick through the register. Bob stared at his back in bemusement. In his experience Edinburgh folk were generally abrupt, but this was approaching a new height of discourtesy. He shrugged and went in search of a lift. The lobby was grand in a way Bob could scarcely comprehend, elegant marble throughout, thick-piled carpets, chandeliers hanging from the ceiling, and he wondered how István could possibly have afforded to stay in such a place.

Room 128 was three-quarters of the way down a narrow and dark corridor, made darker by a Royal Stuart tartan carpet that was heavily stained by years of outdoor footwear and the occasional burn marks of discarded cigarettes. He knocked on the door three times and waited. No answer. He knocked again and, on impulse, shouted 'Police! Open up!' He heard movement inside, voices, people scrambling, but no one heeded his shout. Just when he was about to conclude that István was not going to open up he heard the key turn in the lock and the door opened a fraction. István's head appeared in the gap. He saw Bob and visibly relaxed, and for the second time in a matter of minutes Bob was perplexed by the response he had elicited in others.

'You,' István said.

'Can I come in?'

'It's not convenient …'

Bob barged past, noticing that István was wearing only a hotel towel wrapped around his waist. He went into the room. Lying in the bed was the man he had seen István arrange the late-night rendezvous with the previous Sunday. Bob looked at István in confusion.

'Is this what your rendezvous at the loch was all about? Meetin him?'

'I told you, you didn't know what you were doing.'

'Well, why didn't you tell me?'

István pointed to the man in the bed. 'I believe what Pyotr and I do, this is illegal in your country as it is in mine?'

Bob made to speak but stopped. He turned to Pyotr in the bed. 'I'm awfae sorry,' he said. 'If I'd known I'd hae kept oot of it. Nane of my business.'

'When you said you were police, we thought we were going to be arrested.'

'I can see that. I'm sorry again.' He felt his bandage gingerly. 'I've been makin a richt hash of this.'

Pyotr pulled back the blankets and stepped out of the bed, naked. Bob looked away as he pulled on his underpants and buttoned his shirt, then crossed the room and kissed István.

'I go now,' he said. 'The mood has been lost. I think you and I together – we are very unlucky.' He finished dressing and fixed Bob with a reproving stare and walked past István and out of the room. Bob sat down in a chair beside the window. István gestured to Bob's bandage.

'I'm sorry I did that,' he said.

'Nae harm done.'

'Are you sure you want to be alone with me here?'

'I don't suppose I'm your type.'

'You're certainly not. But I was thinking more of the authorities coming in.'

Bob reflected on the concierge's reaction when he mentioned István's name. *People like you.* That made sense now.

'Did you ask for me at reception?' István asked.

'Aye.'

'Then we are not safe here. Go. I meet you in the lobby in five minutes.' István started to dress. Bob nodded and left, closing the door behind him. As he was approaching the stairs, two policemen entered the hallway. They nodded to Bob and he turned and watched them walk down the corridor until they reached István's door. As they knocked on it, Bob headed downstairs. What a strange country this was, where people could be murdered and nobody cared, but private activities behind closed doors could see the authorities mobilised in minutes.

He smoked his pipe as he waited on a settee by a window overlooking Princes Street. The Rovers had departed but the street still teemed with tourists and locals. Half an hour passed and he was beginning to think István had evaded

259

him yet again when he approached from the lift, smiling sardonically and raising his fedora to the concierge.

'Well,' he said to Bob, 'you may be a pain in the ass but you probably just saved me from being arrested. Pyotr would still have been with me when the police arrived if you hadn't disturbed us.'

'It was probably me who alerted them, askin for you at reception.'

'Possibly. Possibly not. I think the concierge, he was already suspicious.'

'He was, aye. "People like you", he said.'

'People like us? People like us who live our lives in fear of being arrested for the sin of enjoying ourselves?' He lit a cigarette and stared at Bob. 'You caused a lot of trouble,' he said.

'I often do.'

'You caused *me* a lot of trouble.'

'I know now it was Miško wha killed the Norwegian. We found the tinker who sold him the tent. He recognised him.'

'So you know I'm an innocent man. And you know now why some of my behaviour must have seemed suspicious, my meetings in secret. What I do may be illegal, but it is not immoral.'

'I agree. But there's still somethin no right. Your bloody clothin. How did that come aboot?'

'I cut myself.'

'Must have been a big cut. Where?'

'On my hand.'

'Show me.'

'I'm a quick healer.'

Bob had the sense István was enjoying himself. He had concluded he had the upper hand and was playing with Bob. That his lies were obvious didn't seem to matter to him.

'You know what's goin on, don't you?'

István gave a mocking lift of an eyebrow.

260

'You and Miško are involved somehow. Maybe Zoltán an aa.'

'You have a vivid imagination.'

'Crieff's a wee place. Nothin happens. We like it that wey. Anythin does happen, everybody knows aboot it. Since the Moot, we've had two sudden deaths. One murder made to look like an accident and another made to look like a suicide. In Crieff? Who are you tryin to kid?'

István lit a cigarette and blew smoke from his nose. 'When you put it like that,' he said, 'it does seem a bit of a mess.'

'A mess?'

'Unfortunate.'

Bob sighed heavily. 'There's a Norwegian laddie dead and cremated and his ashes spread God knows where, while his family are presumably at home, waitin for him to come back fae his grand adventure. You call that "unfortunate"? What happens to them? What do they do next week, next month, next year, when their wee laddie never comes home?'

'That will be dealt with.'

The banality of the way István spoke chilled Bob. For the first time in this man's company, he felt a pang of fear. 'How will it be dealt with?'

'Oh, I don't know. Some story will be concocted. Some explanation. Tragic. It is important not to leave traces.'

'Traces of what?'

István made as though he was considering his response. Bob knew it was an act. He waited.

'You should have kept out.'

'Kept out? When I came across a murdered laddie?'

István blew smoke across the room. 'Not then. I accept it was your duty to report this.'

'Not then? So there came a point where I should have left it alone, is that what you're sayin?'

'Yes. There must have been a point when the authorities

261

made it clear they did not want to investigate? Saw it as insignificant?'

Bob knew that to be true. But how did István know it to be true? What was his role in this?

'Well, as we just saw upstairs, not everythin the authorities does is right.'

'True. But you don't know what you're getting involved in.' He looked around the room, then edged closer to Bob. 'Matters of national security.'

'Erling Hagen was killed as a matter of national security? Norrie Smith? A crazy old plooman fae Crieff? Dinnae talk nonsense, man.'

'That is all I can tell you.'

'No, it isnae. You can tell me one thing I'm curious aboot.'

'Go on.'

'Zoltán.' István flinched and Bob knew then that his suspicions were probably correct. 'What's he got to do wi all this?'

'What do you know about Zoltán?'

Bob laughed. 'Tryin to see how much I know so you can work out how much you have to tell me?'

István clapped lazily. 'You are smarter than you look. You should be in my business.'

'Whatever your business is. Sorry, I'm probably too honest.'

'Yes, that would be a handicap.'

'Zoltán?'

'Zoltán was my group leader ...'

'"Was"?'

'The Moot is over.'

'No, it isnae. Not till tomorrow. You and Miško, the pair of you are fishy. But Zoltán ... The mair I think aboot Zoltán, the less sure I am he was involved in any of this ...'

'And yet he was ...'

262

'And yet he was. Quite. He was followin Miško, I know that much. He wanted to speak to me personally the day after Norrie Smith was killed. And he was seen near Norrie's hoose just before it must have happened. So what did he want to speak to me aboot? We'll never know, because the next morning he was oot of the camp. Apparently. Naebody saw him leave. Didnae say goodbye to onyone …'

'He said goodbye to me. He told me he was taking the train …'

'Aye, you fed me that line afore. Didnae believe it then, either. So I went and spoke to Wullie Booth, the station master. He told me, aye, Zoltán took the first train oot that mornin …'

'There you are, then.'

'Terrible liar, Wullie Booth. I spoke to him again this mornin, afore I came here. Ten bob you paid him. Cheap for an alibi.'

István's face was devoid of emotion. 'I do not know what you're talking about.'

'Of course you don't. Is Zoltán okay?'

'He is back in Hungary.'

'You're no that great at the lyin yoursel.'

'You think I'm not telling the truth?'

'I know you aren't.'

'But can you prove it?'

'No.'

'Then, despite what you think, I am a good liar. Come back to me when you can prove otherwise.'

'Have you hurt him?'

'Hand on heart, I have not.'

The blank expression momentarily gave way to a smirk. Smirk, then blank. It chilled Bob. 'Has Miško hurt him?'

'I cannot answer for Miško.'

A flash of the eyes to the right. That was the tell. That was when István was lying. 'Was he goin to tell me somethin?

263

When he wanted to speak to me? Did he see Miško kill Norrie?' A terrible notion formed in his mind. 'Did Miško kill Zoltán as well?'

Even as he spoke, he realised with baleful certainty that what he asked must be true. The man opposite him might not be a monster, but he operated within the ambit of monsters, oblivious of human decency. Bob felt a surge of pity for Zoltán Tóth, a kind and decent man. Then he felt an even stronger surge of anger.

'Who are you people?'

'Rovers. Here for the Moot.'

'Right.' He stood and fixed his bunnet on his head. 'I think it's time for me to go and hae a wee word wi Miško. See if he'll be a bit mair forthcomin.'

'I advise strongly against this. Seriously, my friend. I mean it when I say you don't know what you are getting into. You could get killed.' He saw the look of incredulity on Bob's face. 'Think what's happening in the world right now,' he went on. 'There will be war very soon. Everyone knows this. You agree?'

'Aye.'

'And what goes with war? Secrets and lies. Espionage.'

Bob laughed. 'You and Miško are spies?'

'I can't answer that.'

'Who for? Us or them?'

'I can't answer that.'

'I don't believe you.'

'You think the authorities, they refused to investigate a murder only because it was a gypsy who was killed? Really? You think that would be enough to make them cover something like that up? And now a local man has been killed. And guess what? Still they don't investigate. Tell me, who could be important enough to make that happen? To say that murder wasn't murder? Twice? Who?' He flashed a smile at Bob. 'You still don't believe me?'

'No,' said Bob. 'I believe in the law. And I believe if I mak a citizen's arrest of you and Miško they'll tak it seriously.'

'Look around this room.' He gestured towards the hotel waiting area. 'Do you notice anything odd?'

The foyer was possibly half-full. Two elderly couples sat at separate tables, sipping tea as though this was somehow a punishment. A man sat in a green armchair by the empty fire, fedora pulled down his head. Another man sat by the window, occasionally glancing onto Princes Street, and another man was seated near reception. A fourth man was reading *The Scotsman* on a settee beside a woman who was clearly not with him.

'Try to lay a finger on me and you'll quickly see.' István looked at each of the four men in turn, making sure Bob saw him.

'They're wi you?'

'I wouldn't say they are with me, exactly. But they all know who I am. And if anything happens to me, they will join in. Trust me on this.'

Each of the four men was now watching Bob. Bob had a strong sense of being out of his depth but he wasn't a stranger to fear. He had learned, over the years, how to manage it. How to live with it. He cocked his head at István.

'Enjoy your games,' he said. 'I'm off to Murrayfield to see our friend Miško.'

'Go anywhere near Miško and these gentlemen, or others like them, will be on you in moments. I promise you that.'

*

Bob spent the bus journey to Murrayfield Stadium reflecting on what István had said. Was it feasible he and Miško were spies? There were young men from all over the world at the Moot, all of them entering Britain for legitimate reasons. What better disguise for people on nefarious business than an international festival of brotherhood?

265

So there was some logic behind his claim. But, if so, why the deaths? Surely a prerequisite of successful espionage was to act unnoticed and unremarked? The facts of Erling Hagen's death looked like a crude attempt at a cover-up, making the dead body appear to be that of a tinker to conceal its true identity. Did that mean Erling was also a spy, or was he a victim of some international intrigue?

That all sounded fanciful, far-fetched even, yet Bob had to admit the lack of interest in the case from the authorities, their resolute refusal to investigate, gave some credence to István's claims.

And then there was the question of Norrie Smith. His death was wrapped up in this mystery for sure, but the idea that Norrie was a spy was absurd. The more Bob considered the facts, the more he seemed sure that Miško Čurović was the key. Throughout, he had appeared affable and outgoing, nothing like an archetypal spy. Surely, though, that was the best kind of spy – the one whom nobody suspected?

For two weeks, Bob and his friends had been pursuing István and, while István was surely involved, they had missed the principal participant, Miško. Not for the first time in his life, Bob took on himself the responsibility for a collective failure. Had he uncovered the truth earlier, not focused exclusively on pursuing István, perhaps Zoltán Tóth might still be alive.

Spies or not, the stakes were high.

He queued among several thousand Edinburgh citizens for entry to Murrayfield, clicking through the turnstile when his turn came and climbing the steps up to the terracing surrounding the stadium. Rain started to fall once more and he pulled his bunnet down on his head. The Duke of Gloucester, in the royal box, led the dignitaries for this final ceremony of the fortnight as Mickey Peterfield's London lads presented a vigorous gymnastic display which culminated in the Rovers stretching out on the grass to form a giant message proclaiming "Be Pals". It was impressive but Bob had wearied of the Rovers and their constant performances. What had, two weeks before, seemed charming and hopeful, was now tarnished by the knowledge of what had occurred on the periphery. He had thought the Moot to be an outpost of decency and fraternity in a dangerous world but now he realised that danger had been present all along, hidden in full view.

'They're awfae clever,' a woman next to him said.

'Even if they are English,' said her companion, a sad-eyed man of perhaps sixty with a nose that had exploded across his face.

'They're a grand bunch of lads,' Bob said as Mickey and his crew rose to their feet and gave the crowd a jaunty wave before exiting the park. They were replaced by the Rhodesians, reprising one final time their deafening "veldt yell". In the wide expanse of Murrayfield stadium it sounded considerably less effective.

Bob clapped dutifully as each country made its farewell, cheering the Egyptian and Polish contingents and waving at Abdalla and Jozef. But they, surrounded by thousands of visitors, did not spot him as they made their exits. Bob felt flat. Drained. He willed the spectacle to end.

When it finally did, he hurried down the terracing and jumped over the hoarding onto a cinder path circling the pitch. There were hundreds of Rovers milling about and the crowd appeared to be in no hurry to disperse. He headed for the Yugoslav Rovers who were chatting together near the centre spot. Miško gave a start when he saw him approach. Bob recognised a moment of fear in the man's expression before he fixed his usual genial smile in place and raised his hand in greeting.

'You cannot stay away from the Rovers?' he said.

'I wonder if we could have a wee word.'

'Of course.' Miško's tone suggested he would rather do

anything else, but he raised his hand towards Bob in a show of affability and they walked towards the touchline, Miško lighting a cigarette and Bob playing with his unlit pipe.

'I met a tinker yesterday,' Bob said. 'Had an interestin chat wi him.'

'I do not know this word, "tinker".'

'Traveller. Gypsy.'

'I see.'

'This traveller, two weeks ago he was up at the Moot site. And he told me that someone bought his tent aff him. And some clothes.'

'How remarkable.'

'Aye. And the most remarkable thing is we showed him this picter.' Bob unfolded his now tattered copy of the *Moot Pictorial* and pointed to the photograph of the gathering of Rovers in Cloudland. 'Guess who he identified as the person who bought the tent?'

'I couldn't say.'

'I think you probably could. Seein as it was you.'

Miško studied the photograph. 'It's not a good photograph,' he said. 'Very dark. Difficult to make out faces. Your gypsy, he must be mistaken.'

'Aye, maybe. What aboot this, then? Last Sunday, you hired a horse fae the Hydro.'

'I hired a horse on more than one occasion. Did I hire one on Sunday? I don't remember.'

'You know fine you did. And another Rover also hired a horse that day. Just after you. Zoltán.'

'Really?'

'And the pair of you were seen next to a house out in the woods. You watchin the house. Zoltán watchin you.'

'You are mistaken.'

'A man was shot dead in that house.'

Miško shook his head. 'Tragic.'

'So here's me, thinkin aboot you. You buy a tent off a

268

tinker and hoors later a man – someone else, no the tinker –
is found dead in it. And a few days efter that you're spotted
watchin a house where a man was found shot to death. And
the Rover that was watchin you, Zoltán, he disappears the
next day. Nobody's seen him since. How do you explain all
that?'

Miško looked amused. He threw his cigarette on the
cinder track and rested against the advertising hoarding. 'I
don't know,' he said. 'You seem to be the expert. How would
you explain it?'

Bob tried to stop himself taking the bait and losing his
temper. 'I havenae any way of explainin it. But the one thing
I do know, given how much I've uncovered, is that you seem
to be a pretty useless spy.'

Miško laughed. 'You think I'm a spy? Such melodrama,
Bob. You read too many books, I think.'

'No, I just piece aathin together and try to work out what
it all means.'

'And what do you think it means?'

'The Norwegian, Erling Hagen. I reckon he must have
recognised you. Was going to blow your cover. So you killed
him. Then tried to cover it up. Made it look like he was a
tinker. You set fire to the tent intendin there to be nothin to
identify, except it started to rain …'

'Set fire to the tent?'

Miško looked momentarily puzzled before regaining his
composure and trying to ride the moment but it was too late.
Bob tried to process what this meant. Miško didn't flinch
when Bob accused him of murder, but his reaction to the
news of the tent fire clearly seemed to suggest he knew
nothing about it.

Which meant he hadn't set the fire.

So who did?

It's important not to leave traces. That's what István
had said. Bob had the sense that István was not the killer of

269

either Erling Hagen or Norrie Smith. Yet he was implicated without doubt. Was he covering Miško's tracks for him? This new idea throbbed in Bob's head. The body had shown signs of being attacked twice. The Procurator Fiscal confirmed that. Two blows to the head, the second in the same place as though trying to conceal the fact. One blow by Miško. And then another by István? Bob shook his head.

'See when you hit Erling over the head wi a stone, did you actually make sure he was dead? Did you check he wasnae breathin?'

Miško didn't answer, as Bob knew he wouldn't, but he could tell the man was pondering the question all the same.

'Or did your knight in shining armour, István, ride in to save you? Found the Norwegian no dead after all, finished the job for you. Decided to burn doon the tent, which you hadnae thought of, although it seems pretty damned obvious to me. You really arenae very good, are you?'

'You don't know what you're talking about.'

'Aye, you're no the first that's said that to me the day. But believe me, I'm piecin it aa thegither just fine. István had to sort oot the mess you made wi Erling Hagen. And then, somehow, Zoltán was on to you. That's why he was followin you. What, did he see you kill Norrie? Is that why he's disappeared? Have you done him in as well?'

'You don't really expect me to answer any of these crazy questions, do you?'

Bob ignored him, too engrossed in his own thoughts. 'But why Norrie? That's the bit I cannae understand. He was harmless. A crazy auld man.' He frowned. 'You wouldnae have killed him just *because* he was Norrie. That wouldnae make sense. So what? Did he see somethin? What were you doin that he interrupted? What were you up to?'

'I've enjoyed your tales, my friend, but now I fear it is time I leave. I go back to Yugoslavia this evening. I must pack and head for the railway station.' He reached out his

270

hand. Bob batted it away.

'I'm makin a citizen's arrest,' he said.

'You're not.' Miško tilted his head slightly to both right and left and Bob turned to see, descending the terracing, four men, all wearing dark guard coats. Two of them had been in the lobby of the Balmoral Hotel, the others he didn't recognise. The man in the lead was the one who'd been looking out of the hotel window. Bob was conscious of an exchange of glances between him and Miško. Almost imperceptible. They surrounded Bob and the man drew his jacket aside to reveal a pistol in a holster tied round his waist.

'Come with me, please,' he said. 'You're under arrest.'

'What for?'

'We'll explain in due course.'

'Let me see your authorisation. Warrant card.'

He pulled back his jacket again and rested his left hand on the pistol butt. 'This is my authorisation,' he said. Two of the men positioned themselves directly behind Bob, pressing him forwards, forcing him to climb over the hoarding into the terrace. The fourth man indicated that he, too, was armed and with his phalanx of guards Bob was escorted from the terracing of Murrayfield Stadium. He stopped and turned.

Miško Čurović waved at him. His smile was undimmed.

*

There was no clock on the wall and his pocket watch had been removed along with the rest of his belongings when he was escorted to this tiny room and instructed to sit facing a wooden desk, an empty chair and a blank, grey-painted wall. The room was unfeasibly hot. There were no windows and a bare light bulb hung above him.

Bob was somewhere in the bowels of Murrayfield Stadium. He had no way of knowing how long he had been held there but he guessed a couple of hours. He had felt a surge of relief when the four goons who escorted him from

271

pitchside handed him over to a uniformed police officer, but the longer this solitary wait endured the more thoughts of danger and jeopardy returned.

The door opened behind him and with a triumph of willpower he resisted turning round. *Don't give them the satisfaction of seeing you're nervous.* He stared straight ahead as a balding, middle-aged man took the seat opposite, sliding a manila folder containing perhaps fifty or sixty foolscap pages onto the table. He glowered at Bob, tired-looking eyes hiding beneath bushy eyebrows. His skin was sallow, unhealthy. He pulled a cigarette from a silver case, slipped it into his mouth and lit it with a chunky silver lighter. He placed the lighter on the table beside the cigarette case. Ostentatious. Making a statement. Bob stared the man down, refused to be cowed.

'Mr Kelty.'

They knew his name. Whoever "they" were.

'Robert Kelty, Cloudland, James Square, Crieff. Odd name for a cafeteria. Is there some significance in that?'

Bob didn't reply.

'That is your name and address?'

'Why am I bein held?'

'Confirm your name and address.'

'I wish to consult a solicitor.'

'Are you a troublemaker, Mr Kelty, or does trouble follow you by chance?'

'I have done nothin wrong. I wish to be released.'

The man opened the folder and turned to a piece of typed foolscap, but Bob had the sense this was purely for show. There was no attempt to read from it. 'You were a principal witness in two trials at the High Court for capital misdemeanours within the space of a year. Most unusual.'

'You can't keep me like this.'

'We can do whatever we choose. You were once a police officer, I gather. Resigned your commission. I'm curious

272

about that. We can perhaps discuss that over the next few hours.'

'What do you mean, "next few hours"?'

'Ah, finally you engage me in conversation. Welcome, Mr Kelty. I've been looking forward to meeting you.'

'Who are you?'

'You can call me Quelch.'

'Who are you?'

'How do you know István Kedály?'

'I met him at the Moot.'

'How do you know Miško Čurović?'

'I met him at the Moot.'

'How do you know Erling Hagen?'

Bob looked up. This was the first time anyone had acknowledged the existence of Erling Hagen. 'I found his body. In a tent. At the Moot.'

Quelch acted as though he hadn't heard the answer. 'How do you know Günther von Kluge?'

'Who?'

'How do you know Zoltán Tóth?'

'I met him at the Moot.'

'Where is Mr Tóth?'

'I don't know.'

'Why did you go to the BBC and broadcast a scurrilous invention about a murder?'

'The BBC invited me to speak. They asked me a question. I telt them the answer.'

'You "telt" them, did you?' Quelch spoke mockingly. Bob, inured through long experience to such insults, ignored it.

'The very fact I'm here, bein interrogated by a man with a phony name, with no rights, no representation, pretty much suggests that what I said was certainly no a "scurrilous invention". Was I gettin too close to the truth for you?'

'At this moment, Mr Kelty, we're very much seeking to

discover what the truth is.'

*

'Geordie? It's Annie Kelty. Bob's gone missin. He should have been hame hoors ago.'

'He's a grown lad.' Geordie Macrae was conscious of his mother hovering, conscious of her dislike of him consorting with Bob Kelty.

'He went to the Moot event in Embra …'

'I telt him to keep oot …'

'I ken. But tellin Bob no to do a thing he's set his mind to is a waste of time, as you weel ken.'

Geordie sighed. 'Tell me what's happened.' He listened for ten minutes while Annie relayed the events of the day before, the testimony of Eddie Williamson, the exposure of Miško as the man who attacked Erling Hagen. The more he listened, the more worried Geordie became. This was outside his jurisdiction. Outside any police force's jurisdiction.

'Annie,' he said, 'I cannae help you, hen.'

'Please …'

The clock on the hallway wall read half past ten. Past his bedtime. 'I dinnae think there's onythin that I can dae,' he said. 'But I'll try.'

He told her to get some sleep and said goodnight. He listened to the exaggerated sounds of his mother clearing up in the kitchen, then picked up the telephone once more.

*

'Are you an anarchist, Mr Kelty?'

'No.'

'A communist?'

'The communists have some fine ideas. But they're no realistic. Dinnae tak into account human nature.'

'So you have some sympathy with the communist cause?'

'That's no what I said.'

274

'Yet you've chosen not to deny it.'

'I don't need to deny somethin I never said in the first place.'

'Even if it corrects the record?'

'What record?'

'Why did you leave the police force?'

'I didnae like the wey they did things.'

'In what respect?'

'How truth comes second to expedience. How justice gets diluted to suit.'

'That sounds distinctly communistic, to me.'

'I'm guessin you can mak anythin sound communist, if you try hard enough. That's kind of the point I was makin.'

'What was your business with Miško Čurović today?'

'I was goin to mak a citizen's arrest.'

'For what reason?'

'Attempted murder of Erling Hagen and murder of Norrie Smith.'

Quelch sat up. 'Attempted murder?'

Bob laughed. 'Is there nane of you guys ony good at what you do? Hell's bells, how to gie away what it is you dinnae ken without sayin so. Aye, Miško thocht he'd killed Erling but he didnae do much of a job of it. Someone else had to finish it for him.'

'And who was that?'

'Wha d'you think?'

'You?'

'Aye right. I kill a complete stranger and for the next two weeks I shout it fae the rooftops when naebody else believes onythin untoward has happened. You ken fine wha did it. I was speakin to him earlier the day in the Balmoral Hotel. You'll ken all aboot that, an aa.'

'I'd like to hear the name directly from you.'

'How? It's no as if you're goin to do anythin aboot it, are you?'

275

'That depends on what you mean by "anything".'

'Justice. Bein honourable.'

'And that depends on what you mean by "justice" or "honourable".'

'Truth. Integrity. Reparation.'

'None of those things, no.'

'So what is it you *are* goin to do? To mak him pay for what he's done?'

'That's not for me to say. There are facts yet to be uncovered. It could be anything from a medal to a noose.'

Bob looked away in exasperation. 'Who are you?'

'I am the state.'

'As if three hundred year of the enlightenment never happened?'

'If, by that, you mean that actions should be viewed in terms of their worth to society as a whole, rather than the powers that be, then yes, to an extent the enlightenment never did happen. *Plus ça change, plus c'est la même chose.* Do you speak French, Mr Kelty?'

'*L'état, c'est moi. Moi. Pas vous.*'

Quelch clapped his hands three times, slowly. 'Condemned from your own mouth. Communism as I live and breathe.' He took another cigarette and lit it.

'I'm tired,' said Bob. 'I'd like to go now.'

Quelch inhaled and exhaled heavily. He looked at this pocket watch. 'Ah,' he said, 'the witching hour, midnight. A new day begins. We've barely begun, Mr Kelty. I fear you have a rather long night ahead of you.'

'I've nothin to tell you.'

'On the contrary, I believe you have much to tell me. You can begin by telling me how you killed Zoltán Tóth.'

Saturday 29ᵗʰ July

A Night and Day of Interrogation

'I have the Procurator Fiscal for you.'

Annie sat heavily on the telephone seat in the hallway. It was after midnight and she had tried to sleep but realised that was pointless. Since then, she'd been pacing the flat, fretting, imagining, catastrophising. The shrill ring of the telephone had caused her to scream, the noise resounding through the darkness of the flat and in her head.

'Yes?'

The telephone exchange whirred and clicked. 'Mrs Kelty? Malcolm Harman here.' He continued without pausing for pleasantries. 'I had a call an hour ago from Lord Kellett, who was called by Sergeant Macrae, to do with your husband …'

'Is he okay?'

'I have no idea, Mrs Kelty.'

'Whaur is he?'

'He has been arrested by authorities in Edinburgh. That's all I know.'

'Arrested?'

'I've made enquiries and that is what I've been told. There is no suggestion of breach of the peace or anything happening in Edinburgh, and I can only assume this has to do with the dead body in the tent. If so, then I warned your husband against getting involved …'

'A laddie was killed …'

277

'I'm well aware of that. British intelligence is dealing with that matter, as I understand. Which is precisely why I told Mr Kelty not to get involved. I have one question to ask you, Mrs Kelty. I believe I know the answer, but I must ask anyway.'

'What?'

'Has your husband, during this whole affair, done anything nefarious? Illegal? Has he been in any way involved in the deaths, other than investigating them?'

'Of course not.'

'Thank you, Mrs Kelty. I didn't doubt that for a moment, but if I am to wake up the Minister in the middle of the night I want to be sure of my facts.'

'The Minister?'

'Secretary of State for Scotland. John Colville.'

*

Quelch continued his interrogation for the next two hours. At two am, he was replaced by a woman in her early thirties, hair tightly permed, wearing bright red lipstick.

'My name is Miss Bettany,' she said. 'How did you kill Zoltán Tóth?'

'Miško Čurović killed Zoltán Tóth.'

'Why would he do that?'

'I've nae idea. I've been through this with the other …'

'And now you're going through it with me.'

'What time is it?'

'Time is meaningless here.'

'I have a funeral in the morning.'

She smiled brightly. 'Have you? You should have said.'

'Can I go?'

'Of course. You can leave any time you wish. Just tell us how and why you killed Zoltán Tóth.'

Bob closed his eyes and hung his head. An image of Victor Conoboy appeared in his mind, so vivid it was as

278

though he were there. A rage of impotence overtook him. He opened his eyes again and stared at Miss Bettany.

'I had never met any of these people until the start of the Moot. I came across a deid body that was clearly the victim of a murder and, when the authorities refused to investigate, I started lookin into it mysel. There's been three deaths in the past two weeks and you people dinnae seem to care.'

'Three deaths? So you admit that Zoltán Tóth is dead?'

'That's what I was telt.'

'By whom?'

'I've already said. István Kedály.'

'Where is Zoltán Tóth's body?'

'When is a murder not a murder?'

'It's a little late for riddles, Mr Kelty.'

'When the authorities say so.'

Miss Bettany sat back and rested her arms on the table. 'That is the first sensible thing you've said all night. We might be getting somewhere.'

*

The hall clock said six o'clock when the telephone rang again. Annie had dozed lightly on top of the blankets for perhaps an hour and it made her feel worse. She had a headache and felt stiff all over.

'Mrs Kelty, I have spoken to the Minister.' Mr Harman sounded weary. 'You can imagine he was unappreciative of the lateness of the call but he made enquiries for me.'

'And?'

'Your husband is being interrogated by British intelligence.'

'What d'you mean?'

'What I say. He has been arrested under the powers of the Official Secrets Act and is being interrogated as a foreign spy.'

'Bob?'

279

'Ludicrous, I know. I have requested to be allowed to represent him but that has been refused.'

'He's on his ain?'

'As I understand. This is clearly nonsense, and I have no doubt that he'll be released in due course. Natural justice will prevail.'

Annie stared down the hallway at the front door. Nothing made sense. 'In due course?' she said. 'When will that be?'

'I couldn't say. Sometime today or tomorrow, I would imagine.'

'But that's no good! We need to get him oot. It's Inspector Conoboy's funeral this mornin.'

*

Miss Bettany's interrogation lasted three hours and when she was finished, after a thirty minute interlude she was replaced by a third person, a tall and ascetic-looking man calling himself Mr Chipping.

'I want to go to bed,' Bob said.

'I'm sure you do. A lovely warm bed, thick blankets, hot water bottle. Cup of cocoa. Wouldn't that be nice?'

An hour before, Bob had had difficulty keeping his eyes open. He was drifting into sleep and Miss Bettany's shrill voice kept dragging him back to his predicament. But now, oddly, he had worked his way through the fatigue and he felt clear-headed once more. He could barely remember Miss Bettany's cross-examination and he doubted whether he could even describe her adequately, but he appraised Mr Chipping and waited and listened. He felt strangely calm. The fact they kept asking him the same questions suggested they knew next to nothing.

'Why did you kill Zoltán Tóth?'

'Why are you so interested in Zoltán? Much more than you are Erling Hagen or Norrie Smith.'

'Why did you kill him?'

280

'Because you ken aboot those murders, don't you? Wha did it. And why.'

'What have you done with his body?'

'But you've nae idea aboot Zoltán's death. That must vex you, you bein intelligence an aa.'

'They tell me that beneath your gormless exterior you're quite intelligent, Mr Kelty.'

'Intelligent enough to ken you havenae a clue.'

'How did you gain employment at the Moot?'

'They put an advert in the *Herald* for anyone interested in gettin involved.'

'And why did you seek to get involved?'

'I thocht, five thousand laddies, I'd be able to do a rare trade.'

'How is business? Generally?'

'Fine.'

'A small café, I understand.'

'Aye, and I teach music an aa.'

'Enterprising. Still, with war coming, and the economic situation, things must be getting difficult. Do you struggle for money?'

'No really. We live quiet lives. Dinnae need much.'

'Did you know Norman Smith?'

'Norrie? No much. Saw him aboot toon, kent wha he was. Never really spoke to him. He wasnae someone wha would come into Cloudland.'

'And why is that?'

'Norrie was a loner.'

'Did you know that Norman Smith was a traitor?'

'Norrie?'

Mr Chipping's expression hadn't changed. He raised an eyebrow as though to confirm this was a genuine question. 'Did you know about his *post restante* activity?' he continued.

'His what?'

'Have you heard of Jessie Jordan?'

281

'The spy?'

'Did you know her?'

'No.'

'She also provided a *post restante* service for our enemies.'

'She took letters, did she no? And sent them to Germany?'

'That's what I've just said. So did Norman Smith.'

Bob blinked and stared at Mr Chipping, his blank face, dead eyes. Norrie Smith, a spy, a traitor? That was ridiculous. It couldn't be true. And yet … He'd known all along that something had to connect Norrie, a reclusive and sad old man who'd lived in Crieff his entire life, with Miško and Zoltán, with István and Erling. And here was a connection, however bizarre. He tried to remember the details of Norrie's house, extrapolate what might have happened there. The empty cupboard, the burned papers. Could that be? Could that be the connection? The reason behind all this? Miško had spent days riding round Crieff. All that time, was he looking for Norrie's house? It was far from civilisation, after all. In the end, had all this been about Norrie Smith?

'You look like you're cogitating, Mr Kelty.'

'Norrie's the link. Miško came here to kill him.'

Mr Chipping laughed. 'Beneath that gormless exterior you really are quite intelligent.'

*

Geordie Macrae, his uniform neatly pressed and buttons polished, strode into Cloudland at nine-thirty.

'Geordie,' said Annie, flustered, 'I havenae time, I need to get to the station for the train.'

'Nae need. That's why I'm here.' He gestured outside onto James Square, where he had parked his police Wolseley. 'Your chariot awaits.'

'You're a life-saver. I've been hingin on in case the telephone rings …'

'Nae word yet?'

'Other than they've mistaken him for Richard Hannay, nothin.' She snatched Bob's eulogy from the kitchen table and fixed her hat in place in front of the mirror, and she and Geordie descended to Cloudland, where Leslie was serving dry toast to the Misses Seaton, Beaton and Miller. The Misses sniffed in unison.

'Ay said she'd get arrested, that ane,' said Miss Beaton.

'She's fae Perth,' said Miss Miller. 'What can you expect?'

*

Miss Bettany returned and Bob regarded her balefully. 'What time is it?' he said.

'You asked me that before.'

'I have a funeral at eleven.'

'Yes, you mentioned that, too. In Perth, I understand?'

'Aye.'

'Well, it is now ten o'clock and, since we're in Edinburgh, there's no possibility of you making the funeral, so perhaps you could concentrate on the matter at hand?'

Bob felt a sickness deep in his stomach. The idea that he might miss Victor's funeral, that was too monstrous to comprehend. He blinked back a tear. 'Bastards,' he whispered.

'Do you know Doctor Rantzau?'

'No.'

'Kapitänleutnant Lothar Witzke?'

'I dinnae ken any of these people. I run a café in Crieff.'

'Do you know who the *Abwehr* are?'

'Are they a fitba team?'

'Do you know where Sophienstrasse is?'

Something registered in the back of Bob's mind but he couldn't bring it to the surface. He shook his head.

'Had you ever met István Kedály or Miško Čurović prior

to the Moot?'

'No.'

Miss Bettany leaned forward and stared directly at Bob. 'Did István and Miško know each other?'

Bob returned her gaze, curious. This was a new question, and the way she asked it was different. Her tone was more emollient. Emollient, yet probing. Bob got the immediate sense that she was interested in his response to this question in a way she hadn't been to any of his previous answers.

'Aye, but they tried to hide it.'

'What makes you think that?'

'The first time I saw them thegither, it was nae coincidence that Miško just turned up oot of the blue. He immediately latched himself onto István but baith of them made oot they were strangers.'

'How?'

'Awfae polite. Askin general questions.'

'But they knew each other?'

'I thocht it then. And István confirmed it efter.'

'What did he say about their relationship?'

Bob reflected on the conversation in the Balmoral Hotel. 'He didnae exactly admit they were baith spies, but he didnae deny it either.'

'Do you know who they were working for?'

'Should you no ken the answer to that?'

'I'm asking you.'

'Nae idea.'

'In the camp, did you see them speaking to anyone else? Any Norwegians, for example?'

'No.'

'Swedes? Danes?'

'No.'

Miss Bettany was noting down Bob's responses, something that none of his interrogators had done up to now. Bob watched her. He felt sure there was a pattern to their questioning. The early questions, implicating him in the crimes, accusing him of killing Zoltán, they were intended to cow him. Make him frightened. Open him up. More gentle questions followed, about his work, about the Moot, all designed to help him relax, perhaps even begin to trust his inquisitors. And now, it seemed, Miss Bettany was asking the questions they were really interested in, and they were nothing to do with him at all. Bob felt a surge of anger. Everything up to now, the last six hours of questioning, had been utterly pointless. They hadn't cared about any of his answers. The whole charade had been undertaken to soften him up for the real interrogation, which was starting now. And the line of questioning suggested to Bob that they had as little idea of what was going on as he did.

In that moment it became clear to him: if István and Miško were spies, nobody, not even the states who employed them, nor the trio of interrogators he had spent the night with, nobody seemed to know which side they were on. From the questions about them speaking to Rovers from Scandinavia, they were presumably at the Moot to recruit new spies. But who for?

'You havenae a clue, have you?' he said. 'You've men oot there runnin rogue and you dinnae ken what's goin on.'

'We'll leave it there for now.'

'The way I see it, István's ane of yours. And Miško turns up, and he's ane of yours, too. But then Erling Hagen gets killed. That's no right. No British spy should be killin a Norwegian. I suppose you spoke to Norwegian intelligence? What? Did you find somethin that links Erling to ane of your spies?'

Bob waited for a response but Miss Bettany's expression remained impassive. 'So now you're worried. Your spies might no be what you thocht they were. Miško's up to his neck in this. And István too. So the question you're askin yoursel – and the question you've been tryin to ask me for

285

the past six hoors, is: "whose side are they really on?"'

'We'll leave it there for now.'

'Are they spyin for the Germans an aa? That's what you're tryin to find oot, is it no?'

Miss Bettany rose from her chair, gathered her files and walked out of the room. Silence descended, and into that silence the presence of Victor Conoboy insinuated itself. Bob started to cry.

*

The Congregational Church was near to capacity by the time Annie and Geordie arrived. A police guard lined the walls on both sides. Lord Kellett and local dignitaries filled the right-hand benches. Bella Conoboy sat alone on the front row, staring ahead. She looked devastatingly alone. Suddenly, she turned and scanned the mourners until she found Annie. She gestured to her and Annie reluctantly stepped into the aisle and approached.

Bella patted the bench beside her. 'Mr Harman has explained to me about Robert,' she said. 'The boy will be broken-hearted. Sit with me, please, I don't want to be alone.'

Annie sat next to her and Bella took her hand and rested it on her lap. They stared forward in a silence that was somehow amplified by the church organist playing Mendelssohn's *Allegretto* from *Sonata No. 4*.

'No hymns,' whispered Bella. 'He insisted on that. The minister took some persuading.'

A sudden hush alerted them to the arrival of the coffin and the mourners stood as the body of Victor Conoboy was carried into the church by six uniformed police officers. Among them was Geordie Macrae. The pallbearers processed down the aisle and laid the coffin on a trestle below the pulpit and joined their fellow officers standing against the walls, heads bowed. Geordie gave the merest nod to Annie as he passed. Reverend Booker stepped into the circular pulpit.

286

'We are gathered today for the funeral of Victor Frederick Conoboy, a fine and gifted retired police inspector in the Perthshire Constabulary, a loving husband to Bella and father to the late Tom.'

Annie felt Bella's hand twitch and she heard her sob. She removed her hand from Bella's and wrapped her arm around her. Bella leaned into her and took her left hand. She smelled of peppermint and loss. Her hair brushed Annie's cheek. Her body pulsed with grief.

'The number of mourners today is testament to the respect in which Victor was held. An honest and honourable man, he served Perthshire with distinction for nearly forty years, rising from a callow constable in the time of Queen Victoria to the rank of Inspector, which he held until his retirement only three years ago. Being both liked and respected is not an easy combination to achieve but Victor did so with aplomb.

'Work was not his sole passion, however, and some of what I am about to say may be news to many of you. Victor's charitable acts, his secret donations, the hours of voluntary work he undertook, the support and advice he willingly and lovingly gave, they can be revealed now, with the permission of his wife, Bella. Victor, modest and unassuming, chose not to make his charitable work known in his lifetime. He sought no self-aggrandisement, only the knowledge that he was doing good work. And three charities in particular, Blesma, the Perth Night Shelter for Females on Watergate and the Duerden Home for Children, have especial reason to be grateful for Victor's largesse. I know that all three of those charities are represented here today and they will share the sense of loss that every one of us in this church feels.'

Reverend Booker asked the congregation to rise and they sang *Shallow Brown*, the words written on a card left on top of the Bibles in front of them. Annie had never heard anything quite like it.

'That song was especially requested by Bella, Victor's

287

wife, and beautiful it is. Now, also at Bella's request, I would like to call on Robert Kelty to say a few words.'

A shock of consternation flooded through Annie's body, an almost physical chill invading her bones and veins. Bob's eulogy was in her handbag. She opened the catch and pulled out the two sheets of paper. Automatically, she rose and made her way to the pulpit. Her head was buzzing, her chest throbbing. She gripped the pulpit and faced the mourners.

'Bob can't make it today. He's doin somethin that I know would have made Mr Conoboy proud. But he wrote this and I'd like to read it out.' She held the pages in front of her and they shook so much she feared she might not make out the words. She began to read.

'When I first came to Perth, it was over ten years ago, just after my dad died and I came to live with my gran. I was terrified. I was a wee boy from a wee village and Perth was that big and that noisy. I hated it. I used to cry myself to sleep at night. I wasn't good at making friends. All the children my own age thought I was old-fashioned, a teuchter from the country. The only place I felt safe was at home with Gran.

'And then, later, with the Conoboys.

'Gran cleaned for the Conoboys in the mornings. And that's the single, luckiest thing that's ever happened to me in my life. She'd take me during the school holidays and tell me I had to play in the garden and keep quiet and not be a bother to anybody. Mrs Conoboy was always there and she was lovely. When Gran was busy upstairs she'd sneak a biscuit out of the window for me. That was our wee secret.

'And sometimes Inspector Conoboy would be there, too. I knew he was important in the police and I was scared of him. Gran would say he'd lock me in the cells if I didn't behave but there was no point frightening me like that because I was too timid to misbehave anyway. And Inspector Conoboy – well, he was just the grandest man. He'd bring me into the house and sit me down and talk to me. I don't think anyone had ever really talked to me like that before. And he didn't just tell me what *he* thought or what *I* should believe, but he asked me questions. What did *I* think? What would *I* do? Mostly, I had no idea. I'd never thought that deeply about things before. Why would I? But Inspector Conoboy encouraged me. Argued with me. At first, I thought that meant I was being stupid and he was putting me right, but he said no, that wasn't it at all. This is how we learn, he said, talking to one another, understanding each other's points of view.

'"Since I'm a policeman I shouldn't say this," he said to me one time, "but there's really no such thing as truth." I've always remembered him saying that, but it's only in the last few days I've come to understand what he meant.

'He wasn't really a religious man.' Annie paused and looked around her. 'Sorry,' she said. She continued. 'He told me once, "I can't say there isn't a God. There's so much beauty in the world that something must have created it. And there must be some purpose to it. But there is evil, too, and I can't worship a God who stood by in Flanders during the war, who allows poverty and misery in the world, who lets the rich grow richer while the poor grow poorer." I remember those words as though it was yesterday, although actually it was three years ago. I know that because it was the day I buried my Gran. I'd asked him if he thought she was in heaven. He said he didn't know, but it didn't matter. Nothing like that mattered. All that matters is here, now, us, the world, and everybody in it.

'And that's what I learned from Inspector Conoboy, and from Bella. From their passion. Their goodness. Their kindness.' Annie took a deep breath when she saw the final line of Bob's eulogy. She looked up at Bella Conoboy before she spoke the words. Bella smiled.

'Victor Conoboy was a father to me. I love him. And I always will. And it makes me the proudest man in the world to call Bella Conoboy my mum.'

Annie folded the pages and closed her eyes. Tears started to stream down her cheek and Reverend Booker rushed forward to help her from the pulpit. She sat down next to Bella, still gripping Bob's eulogy. Bella kissed her cheek.

'Beautiful,' she said.

*

Quelch entered the interview room, bustled to his chair and sat down. He had no papers with him. He studied Bob with disdain. Bob returned the look.

'Worked oot whose side they're on yet?' he taunted.

Quelch blinked slowly. He looked tired. 'Honestly? Not fully. There's the matter of proof.'

'You're really not very good.'

'But we'll find out. Rest assured.' He lit a cigarette and placed his silver lighter on the table again. 'I understand people have been lobbying on your behalf through the night,' he said. 'High up. Ministers of state. Quite impressive. Not that it made any difference, but I thought you'd want to know.'

'Even a Minister of State can't control you people?'

'No. Reassuring, isn't it? I'm sure I don't need to advise you that nothing which has taken place over the past few hours really happened. Nothing that we've talked about will ever be talked of again …'

'Are you threatenin me?'

'Of course I am. We can do pretty much what we want already, but by Christmas it's likely the country will be at war. As soon as that happens, we will have total power.'

'"We"? The state?'

'The state.'

'I don't think I care for your state.'

'Be careful. That sort of sentiment is likely to see you locked up in the near future.'

'I doubt that. If it's to be war, you'll be needin me as cannon fodder. Me and millions like me, doin your dirty work.'

'If you believe defeating a tyrant and a monster is dirty work, I pity you.'

'If you believe settin the world at war wi itself again will fix anythin, in spite of all the evidence from the last time, I pity *you*.'

'Ah, the moral high ground. Such rarefied air you breathe, Mr Kelty. It must be wonderful to be so perfect.'

'I'm as far fae perfect as it's possible to be. But I ken what's right and I ken what's wrang.'

'Do you? Do you really? Six hours and more we've been interviewing you. And all that we've learned is that you know absolutely fuck all. You've been fiddling about in other people's business for two weeks and you haven't the faintest idea what any of that business actually is. Who anybody is. What they're doing. Don't you think that's rather sad?'

Bob looked at him contemptuously. 'Aye, I think it's sad. But probably no for the reason you do. I think it's sad because there's three people deid who didnae need to be. And it's sad because you dinnae gie a damn.'

'There are only so many damns in the world. If we wasted them on nobodies we'd get nowhere.'

'Nowhere's maybe no such a bad place.'

'Well, I'm pleased you think that. Because that's precisely where you're headed.' He stood up. 'Mr Kelty, it is my considered judgement that you are a complete nonentity and you are free to go.'

'Eh?'

'We thought you might be somebody. But we're satisfied, now, that you're not. Just an interfering fool with a Jesus complex.'

'Well, I may be a nonentity, and a fool. But there's somethin I've worked out that you havenae.'

291

'And what's that?'

'I ken that your twa spies are baith workin for Germany.'

'And how do you know that?'

'Did you ken there was a postcard fund in Norrie's hoose? Or half a postcard, to be precise?'

A look of panic overtook Quelch's face. He fumbled with the desk as though looking for the papers that weren't there and didn't reply.

'I'm guessin that's a no. I'm no surprised. Sergeant Rudd, he's a good man, but he's no the maist thorough of detectives. Wouldnae spot a clue if it bit his arse. Probably never thought to mention it to you. Did he?'

'Tell me about this postcard.'

'It was half a postcard. Of a street. In Germany. I cannae mind the name that was written on it but Miss Bettany mentioned it a while back. It's juist come back to me. A lang row of buildings, five or six storeys high.'

'Sophienstrasse?'

'That's the one. I thocht you'd probably ken. By any chance, is that whaur the German intelligence is based?'

Again, Quelch remained silent. He didn't look at Bob.

'I'll tak that as a yes. I was thinkin when I fund it, why would you rip a postcard in twa? Strange thing to do. That was before I kent all aboot this spyin lark. But maybe it's so that you can gie a half each to twa different folk, so when they meet up they'll ken wha they are. Wha's side they're on. So, if Norrie was a German spy, like you say, then the person wha had the other half is also a German spy ... Miško ...'

Quelch turned his gaze on Bob. His palms were rested on the desk. He was quite still.

'And whatever Miško was involved in, István was, too.' Bob stood up. 'In cahoots the hale time. You call me a fool? You've got folk runnin aboot, killin innocent people, and you cannae even work oot if they're on your side or theirs.

God help us when the war starts, if you idiots are in charge.'

'You're free to go, Mr Kelty. Remember what I said: nothing that took place here really happened.' He opened the door and Miss Bettany entered and deposited Bob's belongings on the table. Bob snatched at his pocket watch and studied it with dismay. Twelve o'clock. The funeral would be over. The interment would be happening. And he was sixty miles away.

'You didnae need to do this,' he said to Miss Bettany. 'Ony of it. Sheer cruelty, makin me miss the funeral of a man so fine you dinnae deserve to even speak his name …'

'Victor Conoboy.'

She smiled at him. Bob regarded her with impotent fury. She led him down a damp-smelling corridor until they reached an oddly narrow doorway. She opened it, revealing fresh air and an Edinburgh side street in late-morning gloom.

'I dinnae ken wha you people are …' Bob said.

'Correct.' She slammed the door in his face.

Saturday 29th July

An Evening of Endings

Bob got off the train and walked to Wellshill Cemetery. It was seven in the evening and the streets were quiet. In the cemetery, he spotted a recently-dug grave covered in flowers and walked towards it. Soil was still mounded above the grass surrounding it, not yet subsided to reflect the new reality. There was no marker yet denoting who lay beneath but Bob knew. *Don't think. Don't think about him down there. Don't think that.*

There was Bella's wreath, lilies intertwined, white and perfect. Beside it, Annie's and Bob's, irises and carnations. Bob stood with his head bowed and closed his eyes.

'He was a fine man.'

Malcolm Harman stood behind him, still in his funeral suit, arms behind his back. 'I was notified earlier that you'd been released,' he continued. 'I thought you'd come here.'

'They realised I was a nonentity.'

'You're very far from that, Mr Kelty.'

Bob shrugged. 'Today, it was convenient. I juist wish they'd fund out a bit quicker.'

'The funeral was a fine occasion. Mrs Kelty read your eulogy. Very moving. Not a dry eye, all that … You got to the heart of the man.'

'We need him now, mair than ever.'

'These are difficult times.'

294

'It's no the times that are difficult. This past fortnight, dealin wi the authorities. Actually, no, further back than that. Barossa Street. The Cuddies Strip. There's something happenin. D'you no feel it?'

'I'm not sure I understand.'

'All this truth, honesty, fairness, decency. All thae words about honour and justice. Do they apply to you lot?'

'My lot?'

'Authority. The polis. The politicians. The men in shadows. Seems to me there's a hale world goin on aroond us that we dinnae see and arenae part of, and they're leadin us a dance. Naethin that happened to me the day really happened, that's what they telt me. They juist changed history. Like they did wi Erling Hagen. Norrie Smith. Zoltán Tóth. Them … You ... The law, the folk in charge. The state. I dinnae mean it personally, but …'

'I've told you before, Mr Kelty, I admire you. Your youthful passion. Fervour, even. Your sense of right and wrong. That's far less common than you might imagine.'

'Certainly among the authorities. I'm learnin that.'

'But if you'll allow me to repeat a minor criticism I made the last time we met, you are very naïve. You tend, like many young people, to see the world in black and white. As you get older you'll find it's considerably more dubious than that.'

'Well, I've aged this past fortnight, richt enough. And it's opened my een. There's been some gey queer goins on and you lot in authority have been doin your damnedest to keep a lid on them. I hope you're proud …'

'I hope you'll acknowledge that not everyone in authority is possessed of the same outlook …'

'You're no all bad?'

'I hope you'll allow that?'

'I will. But I hope you'll allow me to think the opposite – that some in authority *are* bad?'

Mr Harman patted Bob's shoulder. 'Now you're learning.'

He turned and walked away and Bob watched until he passed through the gates of the cemetery.

*

It was late in the evening when Bob and Annie sat on the sofa, Bob comfortable with his wife's arms around him.

'So wha were they?' Annie said.

'They're naebody. Literally. They dinnae exist. Nothin that happened to me last night really happened. Erling Hagen wasnae murdered. Norrie wasnae a traitor and he wasnae murdered either. Zoltán Tóth hasnae disappeared. István Kedály and Miško Čurović, they arenae spies. These people, they're ootside anythin we ken, anythin wi rules or justice or law or decency.'

'How?'

'Wha kens. Probably, they've ay been there, skulkin. The world the wey it is, war comin, maybe it's just brocht them to the surface. Where we're goin – mair war, mair destruction – there's no goin to be any place for justice or law. It's goin to be kill or be killed. Right or wrong. Us or them.'

'So what can we do? Aboot Erling?'

'Nothin. There's nothin we can do against these folk. Erling's faimly have probably already been telt some tripe – he was involved in a terrible accident, body never recovered – and that's that. Same wi Zoltán, maybe. All in the name of national security.' He pulled his pipe from his pocket. 'You can do anythin you want if you say it's in the name of national security.'

'And we cannae do onythin?'

'No. But wait. Aathin comes around.' He took her hand. 'I'll see that lot again ae day, István and Miško, the men in shadows. We're no done yet.'

'Revenge is a dish best served cauld?'

'No revenge. Victor would've had no truck wi that sort of thing. "Bide your time," he'd hae said. "And do the right thing.'"

'You ay do, Bob Kelty.'

'I dinnae. But at least I try.'

They stopped talking and listened to Harold Walden's *Arcadian Follies* on the Scottish channel, a comforting combination of jokes and song, exactly what was needed to relieve the tension.

'Like haein a variety show in your ane livin room,' Bob said. Annie nestled her head against his chest as Flintoff Moore began to sing:

When I grow too old to dream
I'll have you to remember.
When I grow too old to dream
Your love will live in my heart,
So kiss me my sweet
And so let us part
And when I grow too old to dream
That kiss will live in my heart.

This was one of Annie's favourite songs but Bob hated it. Even the thought of parting left him bereft. He had endured so many partings already, and what remained was only a shadow of what could have been. A fatigue washed over him as he reflected on the past two weeks. All of us, every one, we have our truths. And who is to say that any one truth is less or more truthful than any other? As Victor said, there is no such thing as truth. Everything is contingent. Contestable. Unresolved.

Moot.

He switched off the radio and picked up his tin whistle and into the gloom he played *Nathaniel Gow's Lament for the Death of His Brother.* The fire crackled in the grate. He played *In and Out the Harbour*, slow and slower, and every descent through the octaves felt like an ordeal, every ascent like a promise amid the ruins of grief. A way through.

He began to cry and he couldn't have said what for, or who for. Victor, of course, and Erling, and even Norrie, Zoltán. Life and death in constant flux, in the seed of one the flower of the other. Lives played to an end. The terminus is a brutal place. But his tears were more than tears of loss. They were tears of wonder. This love he felt, the inhabitation of his psyche by the unwavering need to belong with the person by his side, this was something which grew more stupendous and more glorious and more frightening with every passing day.

There would be tomorrow.

And on. And on.

'I love you, Annie Kelty. I'll never be too old to dream, and I'll never let us part.'

Author's Notes

The Third World Rover Scout Moot in July 1939 was a major event, attended by 3500 young men from 48 countries worldwide. It had a very high profile, with extensive coverage in national newspapers and outside broadcasts live from the site by the BBC.

World Scout Moots still take place every four years and the next will be held in Portugal in 2025. Monzie 1939 remains the only time the Moot has been held in Scotland.

There were German agents in the UK before the outbreak of the Second World War, although they would have been largely based in London. It is entirely likely that German agents would have infiltrated the Moot, but they would probably have done this for intelligence-gathering rather than for recruitment of new agents. I would like to thank Dr Claire Hubbard-Hall of Bishop Grosseteste University for her advice on German spying tactics before the war.

Jessie Jordan was a Scottish hairdresser who lived in Perth and later Dundee and ran a *post restante* service for the German Abwehr. She was also a spy, sketching, photographing and writing about naval installations on the Scottish coast and sending the information to Germany. It is likely the Germans wanted this intelligence in order to identify targets for bombing in the event of war. Jessie Jordan was caught in 1938 and in 1939 was sentenced to four years imprisonment. After the war she was deported to Germany.

Rhodri Jeffreys-Jones, in his work Ring of Spies, calls Jessie Jordan a "minor spy with major consequences". Although her spying efforts were small-scale and amateurish, her apprehension led directly to the exposure of a major spying ring that had been operating in the USA.

I would like to thank Margaret Bennett for her wonderful work to preserve Perthshire's oral history and folklore, most recently in her outstanding collection of reminiscences, *Up the Glen and Doon the Village.* The preservation of our oral history and the continuation of our culture across generations – what Hamish Henderson called "the carrying stream" – is a vital endeavour.

As ever, I have had wonderful editorial support from Ringwood Publishing, in particular my two main editors, Rosie Hall and Hristo Karastoyanov, to whom I offer my sincere thanks for making this novel immeasurably better. Thanks also to Stewart Porter, Lily Tighe, Júlia Pujals Antolin and Rebecca McGuire for their excellent input.

Thanks to Skye Galloway for the cover design.

My sincere thanks as always to Isobel Freeman and Sandy Jamieson of Ringwood Publishing, whose tireless and selfless work greatly contributes to the ongoing strength of the Scottish literary scene.

Thanks to Paul Philippou and Ian Spring, directors of Tippermuir Books and Rymour Books respectively, for their support. Scotland's independent publishers are vibrant and wonderfully supportive.

And finally, but most importantly, thank you to all my readers, without whom all of this would simply be meaningless words on a page.

Novels only exist when somebody reads them.

About the Author

Rob McInroy was born in Crieff, Perthshire and his writing is all set in his home county, particularly Crieff, the Knock Hill and the River Earn. Moot is the third book in a twelve-part series which will take the central characters from the 1930s to the 2010s. A standalone short story, which introduced the character of Bob Kelty, was published in New Writing Scotland 39 in 2021.

In 2018 he was a winner of the Bradford Literature Festival Northern Noir Crime Novel competition with an early draft of Cuddies Strip and this first novel was subsequently longlisted for the CWA John Creasey First Blood Dagger Award.

He has an MA (with distinction) in Creative Writing and a PhD in American Literature, both from the University of Hull. He currently lives in Yorkshire.

www.facebook.com/muirtonenclosurepress

www.twitter.com/McInRob

www.robmcinroy.co.uk

By the same author:

Cuddies Strip

Two young sweethearts, Danny Kerrigan and Marjory Fenwick, walk home along the Cuddies Strip, a lover's lane on the outskirts of Perth. Suddenly, two shots ring out.

Eighteen-year-old Danny slumps to the ground. Seventeen-year-old Marjory flees, but is chased, caught, and brutally assaulted. What follows is an investigation which shook the quiet city of Perth.

Longlisted for the CWA Daggers first novel award, Winner of the Bradford Literature Festival Northern Noir crime novel award. Chosen by Val McDermid as one of three top picks for new crime fiction at Bloody Scotland 2021

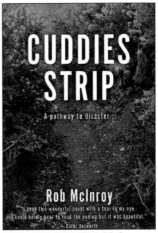

ISBN: 978-1-901514-88-9
£9.99

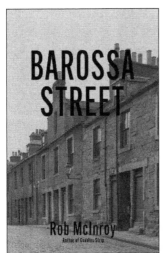

ISBN: 978-1-901514-41-4
£9.99

Barossa Street

Barossa Street follows Cuddies Strip protagonist, Bob Kelty, as he winds up in the throes of another gruesome murder case. He runs into an old friend with an urgent request and his desire to seek justice gets the better of him. Along with his girlfriend Annie, he takes on the task of tracking down the real killer, and clearing the name of his old friend.

Set in Perth, Barossa Street offers not only a look at the mishandling of justice in the face of 1930's prejudice, but also serves as a commentary of the British public's response to the government's shortcomings.

If you enjoyed Moot, you will most certainly like these other Ringwood books:

Raise Dragon
L.A. Kristiansen

In the year of 1306, Scotland is in turmoil. Robert the Bruce and the fighting Bishop Wishart's plans for rebellion put the Scottish kingdom at risk, whilst the hostile kingdom of England seems more invincible than ever. But Bishop Wishart has got a final card left to play: four brave Scottish knights set off in search of a mysterious ancient treasure that will bring Scotland to the centre of an international plot, changing the course of history forever.

ISBN: 978-1-901514-76-6
£9.99

ISBN: 978-1-901514-89-6
£9.99

Revenge of the Tyrants
L.A. Kristiansen

The fight for the nation's soul has begun, and nothing will ever be the same. While the King of Scots wages a desperate, bloody war for Scotland's independence, four intrepid Scottish knights embark on a treasure barge. What follows is a journey directly to the heart of the conflict, and a vivid depiction of the scheming, treachery and violence it entailed. Meanwhile, Kings Edward the first of England, Philip the fourth of France, and Haakon the fifth of Norway have their own reasons to thwart the Scots, and each will stop at nothing to gain their victory.

What You Call Free
Flora Johnston

Scotland, 1687. Pregnant and betrayed, eighteen-year-old Jonet escapes her public humiliations, and takes refuge among an outlawed group of religious dissidents.

Here, Widow Helen offers friendship and understanding, but her beliefs have seen her imprisoned before. This extraordinary tale of love and loss, struggle and sacrifice, autonomy and entrapment, urges us to consider what it means to be free and who can be free – if freedom exists at all.

ISBN: 978-1-901514-96-4
£9.99

ISBN: 9778-1-901514-83-4
£9.99

Bodysnatcher
Carol Margaret Davison

In the late 1820s, two Irish Immigrants, William Burke and William Hare, murdered 16 individuals and sold their corpses for use in anatomical dissections at the University of Edinburgh. Their killings ended when Hare turned King's Evidence, and Burke was hanged.

However, the question of whether their female accomplices, Nelly McDougal and Margaret Hare, were involved, has never been determined. Told by way of alternating confessions, Bodysnatcher is both a graphic depiction of one of Edinburgh's most notorious crimes, and a domestic story of a relationship unravelled by secrecy and violence.

The Hotel Hokusai
T. Y. Garner

It is 1893: When a young woman is found drowned in Yokohama Harbour under suspicious circumstances, downtrodden Korean eel salesboy Han compels the eccentric Glaswegian artist Archie Nith to help him investigate. Written from the perspectives of both Han and Nith, The Hotel Hokusai follows their journey as it snakes from Yokohama's harbour to its red-light district, stopping along the way to meet two of the famous Glasgow Boys and pay respects to the Dragon King.

ISBN: 978-1-901514-70-4
£9.99

The Bone on The Beach
Fiona Gillian Kerr

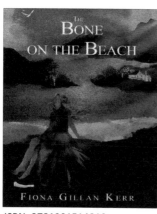

In 2002, in a tight-knit Highland village, a young woman named Deirdre mysteriously dies. Fifteen years later, Meghan, a lawyer, arrives in the village seeking a fresh start. But when a bone washes up on the beach, she is embroiled in the mystery. As the residents refuse to discuss the past, Meghan wonders what transpired in the village all those years ago. As she uncovers its storied history, she discovers that all is not as it seems in this village. Drawing on the ancient Celtic legend 'Deirdre of the Sorrows', and set in the otherworldly Highland landscape, this tale shows Deirdre as she has never been seen before.

ISBN: 9781901514919
£9.99